Austen Inspired

ALANA HIGHBURY

Shipsvold Press

Print ISBN: 979-8-9900284-5-6

E-book ISBN: 979-8-9900284-4-9

Chapter 1

It is a truth universally acknowledged that ~~girls~~ women ~~who want to find love~~ who are ~~seeking love~~ looking for love are

"The least likely to find it," I muttered just before face-planting on the wooden desk, just narrowly missing a collision with my poor laptop. "And the least likely to become best-selling novelists."

It shouldn't be this hard.

Writerly inspiration certainly wasn't lacking. With my father the successful novelist, my best friend the acclaimed writer, and of course, my beloved Jane Austen the timeless muse, everything was in my favor. The only thing lacking was, well, a happily ever after of my own to draw inspiration from, but Austen had managed without that. Surely I could too.

With a deep sigh, I dragged my eyes back up to my document and backspaced on the first line.

It is a truth universally acknowledged that _______.

Frustrated, I closed the laptop. Surely the words didn't simply flow out of every novelist easily at first, right? Scratching my head, I tried to remember the name of that movie where Nicolas Cage sat at his typewriter and couldn't manage to write, but then the itchiness reminded me I was overdue for a shower. Not bathing daily was one of the perks of living alone and working from home, even if the work that allowed this flexibility was about as thrilling as my beige walls and faded blue drapes. It was all temporary, right? Until I found something truly fulfilling ... like becoming a famous writer.

But what if I'm not good enough?

Then I'd settle for just being a writer, without the "famous" part. No one expected me to be great at anything anyway.

Lillian's the perfect daughter, not me.

And that was fine, really. It took the pressure off.

Still, I had to try. Even if it wasn't writing, there must be something. I was 31, and my life was comfortable. Fine. Nice. My old nemeses anxiety and self-doubt sometimes arose, but I could minimize them by arranging my life comfortably, at home or with my safe circle of friends. It was nice.

Nice?

Is that really enough?

The answer eluded me. I tried to ignore those questions arising in my mind with ever-increasing frequency. What if I did become a writer? I'd always wanted to, as a child looking up to my talented father. My parents had always been busy, leaving me abundant time to lose myself in books, as well as notebooks full of my own half-written stories.

A knock at my door startled me, and I leaped off the swiveling chair and made my way to the door while scratching my head again. Upon seeing my best friend's face through the peephole, I grinned and unlocked the door. Jack lived down the hall and had a key, but he always knocked anyway. Why couldn't all guys be as considerate and decent as him?

"Hey, Vivi," he said with a smile, his eyes crinkling slightly at the corners as they always did when he greeted me. His wavy, dark-brown hair was a little damp but neatly arranged off his forehead. Beneath his navy winter jacket was a crisp white button-down suggesting he had an in-person work engagement.

Ah, that's why he looked freshly showered. He tended to prioritize hygiene more than I did. Then again, most people did.

"How's your morning—"

"Jack!" I tugged on his jacket to pull him inside. "You know that crazy idea I had last night after, like, the third glass of wine?"

His mouth closed and then widened into a grin as he straightened his jacket sleeve. "Hmm. The one where you wanted us to move to England and start an Austen fan-fiction publisher based in Bath?"

My cheeks warmed. I'd forgotten about that. We'd just finished a movie, and I'd pleaded "just one more glass" before Jack went home.

I need to cut back on wine.

"Um, no. The, uh, the one where I write an Austen-inspired novel myself." I cringed, feeling my bravado waning. Jack was my best friend, one of my oldest friends, but it was still slightly—no, very—terrifying to try something new like this. I'd considered keeping the idea entirely to myself, but last night's chardonnay had ruined that plan.

"Of course, Vivi." Jack's smile widened. "One of your better ideas last night."

"You think?" I looked into his eyes, my brows crinkled.

"Oh, absolutely," he said before looking at his watch. "Hey, I would love to talk more about this, but I actually came to ask if you want a ride to Bolder today. I'm headed to a meeting in that part of town." He looked me up and down. "Or ... is your meeting canceled?"

"*Crap!*" I blurted, realizing it was Friday, when I had the weekly copyeditor meeting at Bolder Publishing. If I didn't leave in about two minutes, I'd be late and get an earful from my boss. I glanced down at my sweat-stained running clothes and felt my slick ponytail. "No, I lost track of time. Crap."

"Vivi, it's fine. You always look great."

I bit back a smile. "You do realize that means nothing when you say it all the time, right? It's like best friend obligatory flattery." Laughing, I started to run to my bedroom before calling out, "And such a blatant lie in this case."

When I looked back briefly, he was shaking his head with a tired smile. "Believe what you will, Vivi. Just maybe put on pants?"

Well, maybe showering infrequently wasn't always a perk.

Ready to duck out as soon as the meeting ended, I felt my heart sink when the editorial manager asked me to stay afterward.

"You too, Annie."

My friend groaned beside me. Annie, my former mentee from school, was now a fellow freelancer at Bolder.

I bit my lip, adjusting the hat I'd thrown over my hair. "Ellen, so sorry, but Jack's picking me up soon, so I can't stay long. If I'd known—"

"This shouldn't take long," my boss said, waving her manicured fingers lightly. Though Ellen took pains to look like the 20-something professional Black woman she'd been when we met, always current with the latest fashion and fitness fads, I knew she was, in fact, older. And so did the rest of the office, as she'd recently let it slip that her *younger* brother was 38. "What are you wearing? I can't—no, never mind. No time for that. They'll be here any minute."

"Who?" Annie asked, twirling her silky red hair with impatience. Unlike me, Annie didn't hate leaving her house, but she would rather be almost anywhere than stuck at the office.

Before Ellen could respond, the answer walked in the door. He was somewhat tall, with a blonde surfer guy haircut and a physique to match.

But he's no surfer dude. His polo shirt and pressed pants speak of money. Golf. Stock options. Whatever else rich people do. Far above the likes of me.

I glanced sideways, noticing that Annie's demeanor and posture changed instantly.

"Girls, this is Brandon Bolder, the legend."

At Ellen's introduction, he flashed an almost boyish smile at the three of us, his azure gaze lingering on Annie. "It's a pleasure to meet you ..."

"I'm Annie York," my friend said, stepping forward with a dazzling smile. After a pause, she added, "And this is Viviana Cantwell. We're editors here at, well, *your* publishing house." Then in a low voice that had even Ellen raising an eyebrow, she added, "It's great to finally meet you, sir."

The object of my attention let out a small cough and then a grin. "It's Brandon. No 'sir' or 'Mr. Bolder' or anything. And this guy," he said, stepping sideways to fully reveal the man behind him, "is my buddy, Gregory Fitzgerald. He's a hotshot in publishing in New York, and he came to the Twin Cities here on business with me. We go way back," he said with a sideways smile at his friend.

My breath caught in my throat as I took in the sight of the most attractive man I'd ever seen, at least in person. Gregory was tall and toned, his stance rigid as he looked me up and down with the darkest brown eyes and thick black lashes. Short, sleek black hair—or was it brown?—framed an angular face that I could only describe as beautiful, his brown skin somehow looking both smooth and masculine at the same time. My breath caught. He was the very definition of tall, dark, and handsome.

"It's nice to finally meet you, Brandon, and you too, Greg," I managed to say.

His mouth was set in a thin line as he replied in a deep voice, "My name is Gregory. But you can call me Dr. Fitzgerald." His eyes left me as he nodded to the others and walked out.

He just left.

He just—

He didn't even …

Who does that?

Astonished by his curt response and subsequent vanishing act, I stood there gaping for a moment. I'd been proud of myself for managing to speak at all.

Brandon winced. "I … truly sorry about that. We don't mean to offend. I'm just really happy to meet you," he said, flashing a wide smile suggesting that he was Gregory's polar opposite. Why on earth were they friends? "Oh, and there's an office party tonight, right? Where I can meet more of your people, Ellen?"

Before Ellen could answer though, I looked from Brandon to my boss with narrowed eyes. "Wait, what?"

"I sent a message about this last week, Viviana," Ellen said, her tone slightly chiding.

With my brow furrowed, I shook my head slowly. "I don't think—"

"Maybe you need to check your email more often, Viv," Ellen said breezily. "In any case, it's tonight, and I expect you all to be there. It's being catered by …" As Ellen droned on, I tuned her out, realizing it was pointless to argue that I had *not*, in fact, been informed about a mandatory work party. I made a face at Annie, who was staring at Brandon with obvious interest. She either hadn't heard Ellen or didn't care.

Looking at the clock, I stood up. "Sorry to interrupt, Ellen, but I really have to go. Jack's probably waiting outside for me."

Ellen opened her mouth to respond but slowly closed it and merely nodded instead, eyeing me oddly for a moment.

As I walked past them, I gave only a quick wave to Annie and Brandon, figuring I'd see them tonight anyway. I released a long sigh.

Hopefully he won't bring his moody friend.

I wasn't thrilled about having to return to the office today, but at least I'd had time to shower and make myself presentable. My outfit—a loose cotton dress with a blue and yellow flowery pattern over thick blue leggings—wasn't going to win me a "best dressed" award, but I had no one to impress anyway. I assumed this event was fairly casual since it was being held at the office, apparently at short notice, despite Ellen's awkward claims to the contrary.

As usual, though, Annie looked as if she'd stepped out of a fashion magazine.

"Annie! You look amazing in black, but aren't you freezing in that short skirt?" Nothing would compel me to do bare legs in February in Minnesota. But then I noticed the direction of Annie's gaze.

Brandon was chatting with some office staff on the other side of the large conference room that occasionally doubled as a party room. Tonight, someone had managed to transform the boring room into an almost elegant party space. The usual bland fluorescent lights were off; in their place were dozens of soft, subtly placed lights that cast the room, its occupants, and the tasteful decor in a warm glow. My mind reeled at the effort and money thrown at this last-minute event. I was probably underdressed, but how was I to know? The company never hosted events like this.

As if on cue, Brandon looked up just then. His eyes widened and locked with Annie's, and he flicked his head in invitation.

Before I could reflect on this presumptuous gesture from our boss, Annie grabbed my arm and steered me across the room.

"Oh, excuse me!" I said as I bumped into someone taller when we'd reached our destination. "Sorr—" My apology died on my lips. "Oh, it's you. Uh, sorry."

Gregory narrowed his dark eyes for a moment and then turned around to face Brandon.

"What—" I scoffed. "I believe it's customary to apologize when you bump into someone," I said loudly as I moved to stand next to him, hands coming up to my hips.

He probably would've ignored me, but Brandon and Annie cast amused eyes in my direction. Gregory exhaled, his lips pursed. Then he turned to me, his eyes full of disdain. "I was merely walking normally. In your carelessness, you collided with me."

His rudeness nearly stole my breath, and for a moment, no one spoke.

Finally, Brandon chuckled nervously. "Aww, Gregory, not feeling the chivalry tonight, eh?" Brandon said, patting his friend hard on the shoulder. When Gregory scowled at him, Brandon just laughed again. "Can't take him anywhere, you know."

"How ridiculous," Gregory replied curtly.

I watched as he glanced from Brandon to me. Was he calling Brandon's comment ridiculous or calling *me* ridiculous?

Maybe both. What a jerk. Why is he even here?

"My theory is that we all need a little ridiculous from time to time," Annie said, smiling as she moved to stand closer to Brandon.

"My thoughts exactly," Brandon said, his eyes lingering somewhere below my eye level.

Annie giggled. "I also think—"

"I can't listen to this," Gregory said, somewhat under his breath. Before I could respond with more outrage, he turned and walked away. My eyes flitted back to the flirting couple, but they didn't seem to have noticed. That was likely for the best.

Sighing, I scanned the room and reluctantly wandered over to a few people I barely knew. I disliked mingling, but I could fake it when necessary. At least I spotted a friendly face in the group, one of Jack's old friends.

"Hey, girl, I thought you'd drag Jack to this thing," said Jermaine, a graphic designer.

"If only," I said with a smile. "He's been so busy anyway lately though." When I had asked Ellen earlier if I could invite Jack, she'd hastily announced it was staff-only tonight. Apparently Gregory got a special pass though. I fought the urge to clench my teeth in resentment. Hoping dinner would be served soon, I glanced over at Ellen, who seemed to be arranging seating and talking to the caterers. Then Gregory approached Ellen. I quickly turned around, not wanting the man anywhere near my line of sight. I let out a frustrated breath, realizing it would be a long night even if I managed to avoid that snob for the rest of it.

"True, true," Jermaine was saying. "He couldn't even commit to the fantasy league for the upcoming season. You've got to talk some sense into him, Viviana."

I laughed but felt my brows lower slightly.

Wait, what? He didn't tell me. Jack is religious about fantasy base-ball. Is he really that busy?

I forced a smile. "You know I will. In fact—"

Suddenly Ellen was by my side, her long nails gripping my arm. "Viv, do me a favor, please. Can you go see if the florist is here yet? Maybe they're waiting outside."

I opened my mouth to ask if I was now her secretary, but then I clamped it shut before uttering any words. From the look in her eyes, Ellen didn't seem like she was in the mood for snark, so I merely nodded.

It was actually a good reason to escape the crowded space.

Before I could walk away, Ellen tugged on my arm again and whispered, "If they're not here yet, give them some time or a call, OK? You're a darling, Viv."

Before I could ask which florist I'd even be calling, Ellen disap-peared into the crowd. I shook my head and headed out into the hallway.

After a few minutes of searching the office suite and peering outside into the poorly lit parking lot, I didn't see anyone other than a couple of IT guys setting up a board game in a smaller conference room. My lips curved into a smile. I didn't know them very well, but surely hanging out with gamers would be far more fun than returning to that crowded party. Could I get away with it?

But as I walked tentatively toward the open door, I failed to notice a restroom door opening.

And too late, I saw the dark eyes.

No, no, no.

Not him.

This time, we didn't quite collide. His arm connected with my shoulder firmly, but not painfully.

Once we'd both righted ourselves, I stepped back quickly. "Um. Sorry, I guess."

"Likewise, I apologize," he said in that deep voice. My eyes widened. Who'd have thought he was capable of apologizing? "I didn't expect anyone to be roaming the halls."

I crossed my arms. "I'm not *roaming* the halls. I was just ... I mean, I *am* waiting for the florist."

For the first time, his frosty, conceited demeanor transformed into something else. Something like curiosity or amusement. "The florist?"

"Yes."

"In a darkened hallway?"

"Well ... maybe they'd gotten lost." It sounded weak even to my ears. I just winced, realizing I'd forgotten about the florist as I considered joining the random staffers' board game. Ellen would have been so angry.

So in a way, Gregory sort of saved the day?

No, no. Still a jerk.

"Ah."

"So, yeah." I didn't know what to say. He didn't move but only stood there staring at me with an impassive expression. I cleared my throat. "Have you seen a florist?"

His eyes swept over me at a leisurely pace. "No. But your dress ..."

My brows furrowed, and my voice rose an octave. "What about my dress?"

"It's floral," he said before tipping his chin down briefly and then strolling away.

I inhaled sharply. What ... was that? Was he making fun of my clothing? My heart rate rose. "That jerk! How could he ..." I muttered to myself.

Wait. Was it possible he was making a joke? Trying to lighten the mood?

Why is that man so maddening?

Chapter 2

Yawning, I walked into the Bolder office for the monthly free-lancers' luncheon. I'd woken up far too early for a run with Jack because he had to fly out to New York for a few days. Some writing thing. He hadn't been specific. Though we didn't do all of our training runs together, it was usually easier to get through the long miles with someone to talk to. But a 6:00 am run was brutal regardless of whether I had good company. Of course, today happened to be another mandatory day at the office, when I'd much rather be home working around my nap schedule.

Ellen ambushed me almost as soon as I stepped into the office suite. "Viviana, I was hoping I'd see you today. Thanks for coming to the party last Friday."

I eyed my manager warily. "As if I had a—"

"So I wanted to ask you, did you notice that Dr. Fitzgerald seemed ... well, *rude* and snobbish that night? He seemed particularly rude to *you*," Ellen said with a faux casual tone as she came to stand close in the narrow hallway. Although Ellen was my boss, I had considered her a friend for over a decade, since we'd met through an internship at the University of Wisconsin, when I was pursuing my bachelor's in English and Ellen was finishing her MBA. She was not a close friend, exactly, but a stable one at least, and we'd both ended up in the Twin Cities years later.

"Oh, don't even get me started on that, that ... that *jerk*," I said, heat rising in my face. Over the weekend, I'd given some thought to my interactions with him and concluded that his slightly less offensive behavior outside the restroom didn't excuse his outright rudeness in every other interaction. Plus, Monday mornings didn't exactly put me in a forgiving mood. "I saw him talking to you before dinner when you were arranging things with catering. He asked you to make sure he didn't have to sit by me, didn't he? What a—"

With a slightly mischievous glint in her eyes, Ellen interrupted, "I noticed he was being unfriendly to you. I wonder why."

"Maybe because he's a pompous jerk?" I clenched my teeth as I began pacing the short distance across the hallway. "You know, this is why I work from home. To avoid guys like that. And to avoid awkward social situations with colleagues in general. Didn't you promise me that the freelancer status would get me out of these things?" I stopped moving, narrowing my eyes as I turned back to Ellen.

"Girl, please. You've been contracting for us for four years, and this is the first office party I've made you attend. Maybe the second. You can suck it up like the rest of us from time to time." Ellen paused and glanced at her watch before her lips curved up slightly. "Back to *Dr. Fitz* though, do you think he's hot? No, a man like him ... handsome?"

"Ell, of course he's handsome," I said with a slightly bitter laugh, clenching and unclenching my fingers, a bad habit I'd only recently become aware of. "A supremely handsome, moody snob."

At the sound of heels clicking on the floor, I turned to see a young woman approaching with Ellen's coffee. "Ms. Swift, I—I hope this one is more to your liking." Ellen took the coffee from the girl's shaky hands and nodded dismissively before turning back to me.

"Who's that? Another new intern?"

"Oh yes, Shelly or Stacy or something."

"What happened to Bart?"

"Oh, he was terrible, Viv. Just terrible. This one's half decent so far."

"Bart was terrible? I liked him. He was so kind to everyone, and he had a lot of promise as an assistant editor. What did he do wrong?" I asked, my brow wrinkling.

But Ellen's mind was obviously elsewhere. "Maybe Gregory's just shy or socially awkward. A nice guy underneath all that pomposity."

"Pomposity? Is that even a word?" I attempted a light smile, aware of Ellen's piercing dark eyes scrutinizing me. After some silence, I sighed. "No, I don't think he's shy. I think he's just a rich, entitled jerk. Period."

"But, Viv, *what if* he's not? What if," Ellen said, pausing dramatically and waving her arms with intention as though painting a scene, "he's like Mr. Darcy, who *seems* like a jerk but is really just socially awkward ... well, and a little snobby at first. Unaware of how his privilege makes him seem to the rest of us, but when you get to know him ... What if?"

I started to laugh and then stopped, staring at my boss in disbelief. "You are joking, right? You have to be. Or you've lost your mind. You think Gregory is my Mr. Darcy? Sorry, I should say *Dr.* Fitzger—" I froze. "Oh my ... Fitz ... Fitzgerald, Fitzwilliam ... no, *no*, it's just a coincidence."

Ellen smirked. "Is it?"

Subtlety wasn't one of my boss's strengths. For unknown reasons, Ellen was obviously attempting to make me think it was my own idea. But as I departed from the office later that day, I was no longer certain. The damage was done: the seed had been planted.

A few days later, I had again replayed every interaction with Gregory in my head, too many times. And then the conversation with Ellen. The ridiculous conversation. It *was* ridiculous.

But is it?

Darcy had always been my ultimate, my one and only, and no nonfictional man had ever compared.

What if this is it? Finally, my Austen romance?

That's silly. No, ludicrous. Maybe even dangerous—

My pacing came to an abrupt stop when I cried out in pain. Landing on my hip, I rolled onto my butt on something hard and square shaped. "What the ..." I said aloud, scrambling to get up and away from whatever mess of clutter I'd stumbled into.

After standing up slowly, I started massaging my hip gently while surveying the floor beneath me.

"Speaking of dangerous," I said aloud, a bit in shock. When had I become such a slob? My brows furrowed, and then I burst into laughter. Determining what I'd tripped on was impossible, given the mess of random objects before me.

Shaking my head, I started to clean up the mess, bringing things to a hall closet where I occasionally stored random objects. OK, maybe not occasionally.

Apparently too often, as the closet turned out to be full.

Distracted for a moment, I noticed my old flute on a shelf and absently thought it might be a good idea to start taking lessons again. Shaking my head, I shoved the flute case farther back onto the shelf, remembering I had a writing career to build now.

No wonder my junk/hobby closet looked like this. Biting my lip, I eyed the sheer volume of abandoned project artifacts shoved into this small space. With new hobbies and interests, my enthusiasm-bordering-on-obsession more often than not led to a crash-and-burn scenario. An exception was my Austen obsession—my enduring passion, as I preferred to call it. Relationships, too, were somewhat of an exception, as I tended to become attached first and fall harder than the other person. Of course, my love life had been nonexistent for several years.

My former therapist had always told me to find creative, healthy outlets for what I suspected was an anxiety disorder or ADHD—my therapist didn't like labels, which itself made me anxious, but the idea of finding a different therapist caused even more anxiety.

Sometimes I vaguely wondered if I shouldn't have quit therapy a few years back, when I'd changed insurance plans. But I was doing fine. My life was good.

Everything's fine!

Having given up on the junk closet, I padded back into the living room and surveyed the area with a critical eye.

I sighed deeply.

Not fine.

I may be living alone, but my house doesn't have to be a disaster. And neither do I.

I can get this place into shape, and I can be a writer.

I can be better than fine!

After tidying up for a few hours, I got lost in my thoughts while sipping moderately priced wine, my only hope for inducing anything like creativity.

Suddenly, an idea sparked.

I could use *my* story to write my book.

My thoughts raced. Darcy, or Gregory, could be the inspiration for my book. Why not?

My long-awaited Austen book!

If the novel were based on real life, it would practically write itself, wouldn't it? I decided to find out.

Chapter 3

It is a truth universally acknowledged that _______.

*"Carl, did you hear that Mr. Bingley is coming to visit?
The higher-ups tell me that he'll actually rent a house
in the area while we go through this restructuring."*

I paused. Was calling the house Netherfield too much? Just one more read-through, and then I'd hit Send. My fingers hovered over the mouse as I hunched forward and skimmed over the email open on my laptop for the sixth time.

*"No, not a single word has been spoken about Mr. Bin-
gley throughout the office," said Carl, rolling his eyes.*

*"This is our big chance, Carl! He'll need an executive
assistant while he's here. And who knows, maybe something else too," Janice said with an exaggerated wink to
the managing editor. "We have to make sure our copy*

girls meet him right away, before he has a chance to consider anyone from the administrative department."

"Hold on. Let's not embarrass ourselves. You know Elizabeth is the only one even remotely qualified for the position. The rest would rather be writing articles for Teen Vogue or TikTok or whatever teenagers read nowadays," said Carl.

I looked away from the screen. "What do teenagers read? Is that sentence going to say more about my ignorance than Carl's?" I asked aloud to my audience of no one, chewing on my lip. Shaking my head, I zeroed in on the draft again.

Janice feigned shock before giving up, knowing that wouldn't work on Carl. His opinions of their staff were well known. She took a deep breath and tried to keep a level voice. "Carl, you know we have to try. Most of them will never get another opportunity like this. Can't you at least try to arrange a casual drop-by when everyone's in the office?"

Carl sighed. "I just don't see the point. If you're so hell-bent on having the girls meet him, email him yourself and ask him to come choose his assistant—or his bride—from our office."

Janice was too angry to see the laughter and delight in Carl's eyes. "Oh, why do you have to do this to me? Seriously. You have to be difficult. Always."

Carl laughed. "And that's why you love me, right?"

Janice decided she'd had enough and gave into her

rather frequent urge to dramatically storm out of his office. He may be the boss, but she didn't have to like it.

Unbeknownst to Janice and the department staff, Carl had already talked to Charles Bingley.

Back in the office, Janice was holding a meeting with the copywriters when Carl came in late. "So nice of you to join us," Janice said with disdain.

"Well, I wouldn't miss it. You know how I love your weekly meetings."

"Rather somber meeting, thanks to you," she grumbled. "I was just telling the ladies here that you're not interested in helping them succeed. They might as well resign themselves to working the copy desks forever."

"What's wrong with working the copy desks? I love my job," said Elizabeth.

Janice scowled. "Please. You can't be serious. Don't you want to move up in the world? Imagine the prestige and salary that you'd have if you were an assistant to—"

Carl interjected, "Have you all polished your resumes, girls? I'm sure Charles will be dying to see them."

"Oh, as if it matters, because you know as well as I do that none of us will ever get an introduction, thanks to you!" Janice said, her voice rising. "We won't be meeting with Charles Bingley after all, ladies. In fact, I am sick of talking about it. I'm sure he's a jerk anyway—or

worse, he probably has a girlfriend. I haven't even met him, and I already dislike him."

Carl stood up and walked toward the door. "Oh, that's too bad. I wish you'd told me earlier." When Janice didn't reply, he continued casually, "We've been emailing for days now, and he's going to come meet us as soon as he arrives. Well, it's too late now. We'll just have to grit our teeth and suffer through this visit until it's over—"

I stopped reading, sitting up straight. This was ridiculous. It was only a first draft. And it was only Jack.

Before losing my nerve, I clicked the Send button. Releasing a long breath, I quickly sent a text asking Jack to check his email.

Hands shaking slightly, I closed my laptop and rose from my swively desk chair, whose black seat had once been plush and comfortable but had worn thin since I'd spent most of my waking hours in it. After an awkward stretch to loosen up my stiff lower half, I started wandering aimlessly around the one-bedroom apartment, which admittedly had little space for wandering. I loved the open concept, except when I didn't: with my couch only a few steps from my work desk, it was difficult to observe any work/home life boundaries. I briefly considered folding the laundry gathering wrinkles in the basket near the couch or opening the stack of mail on the kitchen island that, along with the mismatched grey stools, doubled as a dining table—on the rare occasions I didn't eat on the couch.

An impossibly long minute later, I found myself sitting in my worn desk chair with my laptop open, absently checking my email and social media and tapping my heel on the floor. Perhaps I should have just walked down the hall to his apartment and knocked on the door.

When Jack's name flashed across the phone screen, I started, my heart racing as I swiped to answer the call. "Well?" I drew in a steadying breath after hearing his familiar, warm laugh.

"Well, hello to you too."

"Come on," I pleaded, "don't keep me waiting. How bad is it?"

"Well, I guess we're getting straight to it then, are we?" He chuckled.

"*Jack!*"

"Right, right. Well, I'm not sure where exactly to begin," he said carefully.

I began pacing around the room. Suddenly I was relieved I hadn't just walked down to his apartment. At least I could maintain a bit of dignity as I bit my lip to shreds.

"I mean, does it have potential? Absolutely, it does," Jack said slowly. "I do have a few pieces of, well, constructive criticism."

"Just say it."

"All right. What's up with the opening line?"

"Oh, you know, *Pride and Prejudice* spinoffs always start with something like that. It's like a hook for the crazed Austen fanatics."

"Oh, *those* fanatics," Jack said, coughing to suppress a laugh. "You say that as though you're not one of them."

"Ha-ha. Point taken. I mean, fans like me. But I'm not as obsessed as the rest." I could imagine his smirk in response, but being teased by Jack about my Jane Austen devotion didn't bother me. I'd been an Austen fan for almost all of the fifteen years we'd been friends. "So, what else?"

"Well, where's the distinguished *Mr. Dah-cy*?" Jack asked, his voice deepening intentionally as he spoke the sacred name of my fictional true love.

"He hasn't been introduced yet." I sighed, slumping once again into my desk chair. "I'm not sure what to call him. I'm trying to keep the names faithful to the original, but Fitzwilliam? Most contemporary authors tend to change it to William or Will or Fitz—or even something totally different, like Mark in *Bridget Jones' Diary*."

"What's wrong with Fitzwilliam?"

"Are you serious? You like it?"

"Are *you* serious?" Jack nearly choked over the words, unable to conceal his amusement. At my silence, he continued, "Well, no. I'm not a fan of the name. It makes him sound like—I don't know—a weirdo, or worse."

"*A weirdo?* So eloquent, coming from Jack Normandy, the esteemed writer," I said with a teasing tone. "But I kind of like it. I mean, he is *Mr. Darcy* after all. I feel like I should be authentic and respect his first name at least."

"Sure, if that's important to you," Jack conceded. I imagined him shrugging with a friendly tilt of the head, as he usually did when we disagreed about anything, big or small. "Other than that, I think the dialogue needs some work. A bit contrived, a little flat. You need a great deal more setting and scene details, that sort of thing. I didn't really get any sense for the space they're in, and there's a risk of seeming like talking heads. The characters seem a little overdone to me, the syntax a bit, uh, simplistic."

I groaned while slumping further in my chair. I ran my fingers through my wavy hair, its oily feel reminding me I'd forgotten, once again, to wash it after yesterday's run. I shook my head briefly and inhaled deeply. "Jack, you're my best friend, so please be honest when you answer this: Is there anything you *did* like about it?"

"Everything else. I liked everything else," Jack said, his tone soothing now. "Seriously, Vivi, writing the first chapter is always the hardest part. Good for you."

But two weeks later, I had written very little, already feeling stalled in my own novel because of the stalled progress in my real-life ~~love~~ story. I'd encountered Gregory only once since the office party, and his stiff nod to me (or maybe to the man walking behind me) in the Bolder office hallway hadn't inspired me to write a sentence, much less a chapter. I needed chapters.

Inspiration arose one morning in the form of a dinner party invitation. Another work party? I initially groaned while dressing for my morning run. Normally I would immediately start devising excuses not to attend. But I wasn't about to miss *this* party. Although the invitation was emailed by Brandon himself, Ellen had to be involved, given her rather obvious matchmaking agenda.

Lost in thought, I started when I heard a brief knock just before Jack opened the door and walked in. "Are you ready?"

"Almost." I turned to the kitchen to retrieve my water bottle. When I pivoted back toward him, my intended greeting died on my lips upon noticing the dark circles under his normally bright blue eyes as he tried to yawn discreetly. His usually neatly parted brown hair was disheveled. His running pants and shirt hung on his lean frame, rumpled as though he'd slept in them. I tilted my head with concern. "Are you OK, Jack?"

He sighed deeply, studying a spot on the ceiling before turning tired eyes toward me. "Do I look that awful?"

"You could never look awful, just … you look a little tired," I said, fastening my Garmin to my wrist and then holding it up to the window until the GPS signal finally appeared. "Up late on deadline on a *Sunday* night?"

"Yes," he said.

I waited for him to explain, but he simply glanced down at his own watch and then back at the door.

If I didn't know better, I'd say he was agitated, but that was incredibly unlike him. He must be working on a very important article. Despite his relatively short career thus far, Jack was a highly respected writer for *Randall's*, that magazine of literary and cultural content rivaled only by *The Atlantic*. Most of the time, he was working on a highly relevant, extensively researched feature piece, and sometimes he was also writing a book simultaneously. But he was one of those rare individuals who maintained a good work/life balance with little effort. Well, most of the time. Apparently not today.

Today's run, part of our current half-marathon training plan, was merely a four-miler, and the weather conditions were nearly ideal for running. Like every other season in Minneapolis, spring was rather unpredictable. It could be 80 degrees, or it could be well below zero with several feet of snow—the latter scenario being much more common, of course. But today, the first day of March, was only slightly cool, and most of the snow had melted the previous week, at least on the partially wooded bike trail where we often ran, just two blocks from our apartment building in the city.

About two miles in, Jack was still rather quiet and seemed distracted. Though awkward silences sometimes made me anxious, my easy friendship with him usually made for rather comfortable silences, ones I cherished, actually. Still, during a run, I much preferred chatting to avoid thinking about how many miles or minutes or even hours were remaining.

Hesitating a bit, I considered how to capture his attention. After a few more minutes of silent running, I broached the subject of the upcoming dinner party, to which Jack had also been invited.

"You actually don't sound like you're dreading it, Vivi," he said, giving me a sideways glance and a brief half-smile as he unscrewed his water bottle cap, spilling some on his pants.

"Well ..." I paused. "I guess I'm not."

"Hmm."

That's it? I observed him as he closed his water bottle, seeming unaware of how much had splattered on his clothes. Being absent-minded was so unlike him. I expected more of a reaction than *Hmm*, but he only offered me a quick glance before staring at the ground again. He looked almost ... forlorn. Something must truly be bothering him. Or I was hallucinating.

After nearly tripping over a large tree root across the path—shocking, as he was never clumsy—he suddenly lengthened his stride, pumping his arms considerably faster. "Let's aim for a negative split today, Vivi."

He knew how much I hated those, but I wasn't about to protest now. "Oh, OK," I said as talking became more difficult. Either he was attempting to avoid conversation by running at a faster pace, or he simply wanted to return home sooner for some unknown reason. Either possibility was disturbing.

It wasn't in Jack's nature, at least around me, to be distant or withdrawn or sullen. He was usually an open book—well, except when it came to his love life, where he was always very discreet. Once upon a time, I'd been annoyed by his unwillingness to share absolutely *everything* with me, even about his love life, as I did with him. However, I had eventually, grudgingly begun to accept that there was usually nothing to talk about anyway—he was too busy for a love life and had rarely, if ever, shown serious interest in someone. The latter was understandable, as his own mother had married for the third time when Jack was only six years old. Had that relationship actually lasted, perhaps he could have finally seen what a stable, loving relationship could look like, but like all the others, Toni's third marriage had lasted only a matter of years. He rarely talked about it; I learned bits of their history from his sister, but naturally, his experience must have affected his own outlook on long-term relationships. Still, his reluctance to share that side of himself had irked me for many years. Eventually, I began to see his discretion as honorable and even wise—something to admire, especially since I could never quite manage that sort of discretion myself. Jack was nothing if not honorable.

And that's why I knew he was dealing with something, or some-*one*, but wasn't likely to confide in me easily.

I gazed at the evening sun descending toward the horizon beyond my laptop screen. Living in a small apartment in a major city, I could find many things to complain about, but my view wasn't one of them. Only recently I'd decided to move my desk in front of the window so I could actually enjoy the view. The window was small, and the drapes were a dull shade of light blue that, like the walls, I would never have chosen myself, but I had never given any serious thought to redecorating. Or even buying a comfortable new chair. It wasn't that I couldn't afford to put a little time or money into making my apartment more to my own tastes or even that I wouldn't enjoy it—no, it was the sense that this place was only temporary. I wouldn't live in a small apartment forever. I wouldn't live alone forever. Right? So this was just a short-term thing. Except that it had been nearly five years and counting, and I was now in my 30s. I gazed up at the faded, dusty curtains and wondered to myself whether they were even blue originally. Surely they'd once had some luster.

My screen went dark, since I'd been zoning out for a while. Looking down at my screen, I scrolled around in the document and decided that this page was as good a stopping point as I was likely to find in this long slog of an edit.

Closing my laptop, I gazed again at the scene outdoors, a small, square park that was perfect for watching the sunset in the spring and even more perfect for admiring the blooming flowers in summer. And admire them I did; there was little I liked better than a floral scene, as long as I was not the one doing the painstaking work of gardening, of course. Jack was into gardening, but I had a brown thumb. Not for the first time, I fantasized about owning a large garden, a formal garden on a large estate perhaps, where I could take leisurely strolls among the neatly trimmed hedgerows with the scent of flowers, walking arm in arm with some faceless but surely handsome, well-dressed gentleman. Jeremy Northam, maybe. Gwyneth Paltrow's *Emma* had much to criticize, but Northam was still my favorite Knightley.

Wrong Austen story.

I smiled, deciding it would be an Austen kind of night. I could text Jack and plead with him to watch *Pride and Prejudice* with me for the hundredth time, but something held me back. Given that he'd been uncharacteristically moody, he might not even want to come over.

But I might have just imagined it, and Austen can cheer anyone up, right? It was worth a try.

I was unsure how to react to this unusually curt response. Of course, his reply might not be seen as curt by most people, but it was unusual for Jack. Perhaps I was reading too much into two simple words though.

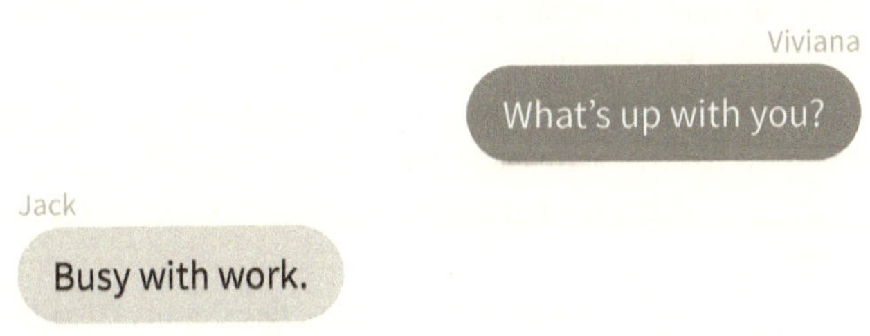

He was definitely being curt. Jack wasn't exactly in the habit of writing long explanatory texts, but this was abrupt even for him. My mind rifled through our recent interactions. I frowned, realizing I'd never asked him how the recent New York trip went. He hadn't told me what the trip was for, which had seemed odd weeks ago when he'd casually mentioned it the day before—he always told me about his work trips. Biting the edge of my lip, I beelined to the kitchen for some caramel cheesecake ice cream to enjoy with the movie.

I groaned loudly. Of course, I was out of my favorite ice cream, and none of the other flavors would do. I wasn't even sure why I had other flavors in my freezer. Jack had probably left them there. Maybe I should call him or walk over to his place. Maybe—

When my phone buzzed, I quickly forgot about Jack's aloofness.

I rolled my eyes. Annie, an old friend, had a tendency to pursue the most commitment-phobic jerks, to put it mildly. After numerous unsuccessful attempts to save Annie from these jerks, I had finally given up and decided to let my younger friend make her own mistakes. My interfering didn't seem to help anyway, and the last thing I wanted was for man troubles to interfere with our friendship. Annie was no longer a naïve undergrad under my wing at the University of Minnesota, where I'd done my master's. It was time I stepped back and respected my friend's choices, cringe-worthy as they might be.

I had slight suspicions about Brandon, despite his friendly demeanor. I mean, how could any decent person choose to associate with a standoffish jerk like Gregory? And as for Brandon himself, being *that* flirtatious and rich and—let's face it—unfairly attractive was never a good thing, was it?

Nevertheless, Brandon was easy to like. He, unlike Gregory, was friendly to everyone, not just to attractive women. He went out of his way to invite me, Annie, and other contract editors to participate in conversations, and I'd met enough jerks to see that Brandon's almost-but-not-quite boy-next-door smile was genuine, even friendly. *So* unlike his friend. At the first party, Brandon had apologized to nearly everyone for his friend's unfriendly behavior. That was certainly a good sign. Still, I wasn't sure whether to approve when I began to suspect he was singling out Annie in his attention.

I promised not to meddle anymore. Even having an opinion is risky.

After pouring a generous glass of wine, I returned to the living room and turned on the movie while settling into the couch with a favorite Etsy purchase, a soft, well-used blanket embroidered with hundreds of book covers.

Despite countless prior viewings of *Pride & Prejudice*, especially the 1995 version, this time was different. My heart lurched as I felt acutely attuned to Lizzie's situation, particularly her initially intense dislike for Mr. Darcy. Lizzie and I were kindred spirits, the difference being that Austen's character didn't recognize Darcy as her true love. Of course, I wasn't ready to call Gregory my true love or to consider him in the same league with Colin Firth. Who could be? That would be ridiculous. I grimaced, realizing I was far more invested in our relationship—which didn't yet exist—than I probably should be.

As I watched Jane dance with Bingley at the Netherfield ball, my thoughts strayed to Annie. I sat up straighter as an idea struck me.

Could Annie and Brandon be playing the real-life roles of Jane and Bingley? Or was I just being ridiculous or, perhaps worse, meddlesome? I paused the movie to consider the possibilities anew, but my musing was cut short by a buzz from my phone.

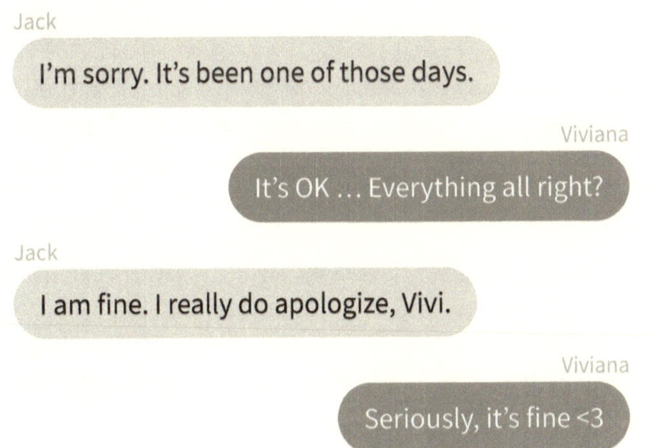

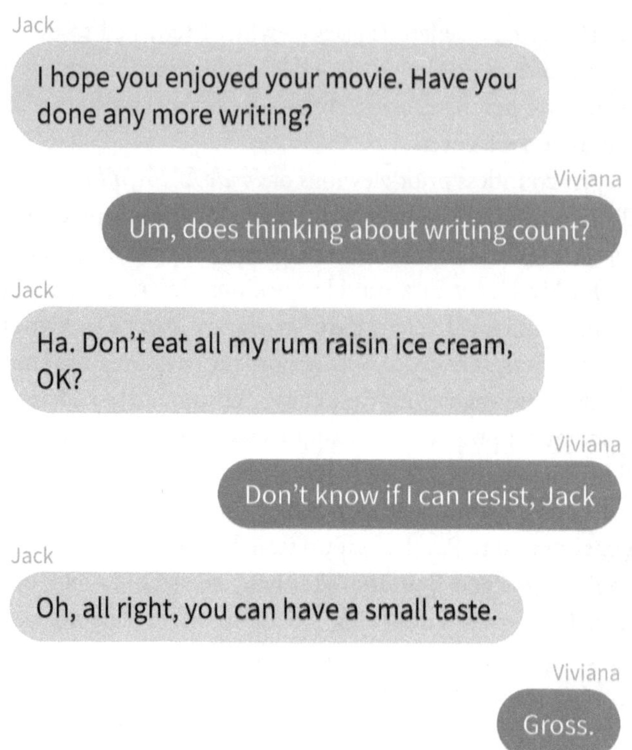

Giggling, I set my phone back on the coffee table and resumed watching the movie, while my thoughts returned to Annie.

Is it really meddling if I'm helping someone find their true love?

No.

Well, maybe.

But I'd be steering her toward the *right* guy rather than my usual tactic of trying to drag her away from the wrong one.

In fact, all evidence suggested that Annie would not even need any steering. Surely my Jane was already falling for my Bingley without any meddling necessary.

Chapter 4

A few days after hearing of Carl's newly formed friendship with Charles Bingley, Elizabeth was at Jane's house getting ready for a ball.

I bit my lip and stretched out my fingers. A ball? No, my characters were just regular people. This was the 21st century, where regular people go to parties, not balls.

A few days after hearing of Carl's newly formed friendship with Charles Bingley, Elizabeth was at Jane's house getting ready for a party. Apparently Charles had rented a house with his friend Fitzwilliam in the area for the duration of his visit, and despite his friend's protests, Charles had insisted on throwing a housewarming party.

"Who throws a housewarming party for a house they're renting for a business trip?" Elizabeth remarked, sit-

ting on a stool in the bathroom as Jane curled her hair.

"It is a bit unusual, I suppose," Jane conceded.

"Just a bit," Elizabeth said with a half-smile. "So, what's he like?"

"Who?" Jane asked as she turned to set down the curling iron.

"You know. Charles." Elizabeth added, "You seemed a great deal more excited about this party after you bumped into him at the office this morning. Admit it, Jane."

Jane quickly turned to retrieve her lipstick, but not before Elizabeth caught a glimpse of her blushing. "Well, he seemed nice."

"Nice?" Elizabeth gave her a look. "Nice is what you call someone when there's literally nothing else to say about someone ... or when you're hiding something. Come on, spill it."

My brow creased as I realized the story needed some physical details about Jane, who was doing her hair and makeup while Elizabeth was, by contrast, just sitting and watching. Jane was, after all, supposed to be the pretty one. Did my writing suggest that Jane was superficial and Elizabeth didn't care about her appearance? That wasn't exactly my intent, at least not in those stereotyped extremes. I sighed and wondered for the hundredth time whether I could be any good at this novel writing thing. Shaking my head, I resolved to forge ahead to avoid losing momentum. That's what revisions were for ... and maybe writing classes, let's be honest.

Before I could decide whether to keep writing or pour some wine, or both, my phone buzzed.

Annie

> **At the hotel bar … you should stop by!**

Viviana

> **Which hotel?**

Annie

> **Four Seasons of course, where Brandon and Greg are staying**

I rolled my eyes. Though I liked the idea of being financially comfortable as much as the next person, I was decidedly unimpressed by luxury hotels and ostentatious displays of wealth, even by good-looking men—*especially* by good-looking men. Looking at the oversized clock near the couch, I yawned and told Annie I needed to sleep if I wanted to have any chance of finishing my work tomorrow morning.

After strolling to the kitchen to obtain an oversized glass of wine, I padded to my bedroom to find my pajamas. Once in bed, I retrieved my latest Austen spinoff novel from the nightstand and sipped my wine—well, Jack always said that "sip" wasn't the right word for an action that resulted in my downing half the glass, but I didn't have to keep it classy in my own house, let alone my bedroom (whatever classy meant anyway). The wine nearly spilled when my phone buzzed again.

Annie

> **You really should reconsider! I think Greg wants to talk…**

With my brow wrinkled, I tried to digest this new information. His occasional breaks from rudeness to me never included any attempts to converse like a normal person. I sat up slowly, considering the dilemma. Getting into my pajamas and cozily reading an Austenesque novel at home—wasn't that the very definition of happiness for a homebody with a bit of an Austen obsession?

I smoothed down my soft covers with care as I reviewed my options. Luxury wasn't something I could usually afford, but I liked to splurge on bed covers and sheets, as I found the softness soothing. And maybe ...

Maybe it helped me forget I was always sleeping alone.

A small bit of luxury then. Not like Four Seasons luxury.

Yet I pushed back the covers with a loud sigh. I had zero chance of finding my real-life Austen hero if I always stayed home.

Is this whole Gregory-as-Darcy idea just crazy, or is there something there?

I decided to find out. Perhaps this would be worth getting out of pajamas for.

As soon as I stepped into the elevator at the Four Seasons, I started doubting my decision to visit the hotel of two rich, handsome men late at night. I considered texting Jack to let him know my location, for safety reasons, of course.

Then again, most women would be thrilled at such an opportunity. I shook my head at this silliness. Soon I would see Gregory and find out where my own Austen adventure would take me. But how should I act, playing the role of Lizzie yet *knowing* I was playing that role? *Living* that role. Frowning, I puzzled over this thought—*Lizzie didn't know that Darcy was the one*—and the question of how this particular piece of the story would fit with the others.

I knocked on the door and waited for several minutes, growing ever more impatient and starting to question again why on earth I'd decided to come.

"Viv!" Annie said as she flung open the door and immediately lunged for a hug. Her champagne sloshed around in the elegant flute she was holding, and I patted the dampened skin on her back gingerly before stepping back and noticing her red bikini—quite a flattering one. There was little, if anything, that didn't look amazing on Annie, whose looks had probably carried her through much of life, at least until I decided *I* would be the one to draw out more from her. My mentee was smart and incredibly kind, it turned out, even though most people just noticed her lush red hair, green eyes that seemed to almost sparkle, and slim yet gently curved figure. People were annoyingly predictable, I'd realized, yet they were right: Annie was gorgeous. Not only that, but she was outgoing and often even bubbly, and people just gravitated toward her.

I'd be lying if I claimed to feel zero envy—I am human, after all.

"Viviana, come join us," Brandon shouted from beyond the door to the large suite's balcony. The lighting was dim, but I could still see him and Gregory in a Jacuzzi.

"Hi, guys," I said, chewing on my lip. "I'm afraid I didn't bring my—"

"Oh, there's tons of swimsuits in the closet—just go grab one," Annie said, smiling and sashaying back to the balcony.

I raised my eyebrows and stepped tentatively toward the walk-in closet, which, though large, was only a small part of this spacious hotel suite—the largest I'd ever seen. My shoulders felt a little tight with low-level anxiety when I thought about putting on a swimsuit practically the moment I arrived. It didn't help that I was probably the only sober one here tonight, my poor oversized wine glass at home abandoned after a few sips. Still, I strode toward the closet as Annie joined the men on the balcony. The closet displayed a dizzying array of one- and two-piece suits—and some with more than two pieces. Why would a couple of single men have a large collection of women's bathing suits in their hotel room? Did they seduce hundreds of women everywhere they went? I shook my head at this fanciful thought—this was real life, not a romance novel. Was it typical for fancy hotels to supply swimwear for rooms with Jacuzzis? I didn't know, as my experience with fancy hotels was limited to, well, this one.

Hearing Annie's impatient shout from the other room, I reluctantly pulled a rather plain, modest one-piece and a wrap off their hangers and then headed to the adjacent restroom to change.

Minutes later, Annie and Brandon greeted me with drunken enthusiasm as I stepped onto the balcony. As I removed my wrap, Annie laughed. "Of course, you chose the most conservative bathing suit you could find. But the color suits you … really complements your eyes. You look hot, lady."

Grinning good-naturedly, Brandon chimed in, "No disagreements here." Elbowing Gregory, he asked, "She looks hot, man, am I right?"

Gregory looked up with a bored expression that morphed into a slow yawn when his eyes landed on me. This certainly was not the reaction I'd hoped for, but I sighed and reminded myself that Elizabeth Bennet hadn't won over Mr. Darcy over with a swimsuit competition. I sank into the steaming water quickly, wincing as the sudden heat enveloped my skin.

"This man obviously needs another drink," Brandon looked at Gregory, shaking his head in dismay.

Annie squealed, "Drinking game!" Obviously of a like mind, Brandon sprung out of the hot tub and went to retrieve the shot glasses as I observed his dripping wet, chiseled form. The weight bench he'd brought into his office this week came to mind. Did he spend more time working out than actually working? I chided myself for the uncharitable thought.

Not all men are jerks like Gregory.

Gregory sat up straighter and began to protest that he was—indeed, we all were—too old for drinking games. Before he could finish, Brandon handed him a shot and grinned. "Afraid of a little alcohol, old man? Let's all take one shot to start."

Gregory clenched his jaw and accepted the glass. "I will drink it, but no game. Play your juvenile games later when I've retired to my room."

I raised an eyebrow while Annie and Brandon looked at each other with barely suppressed laughter.

Gregory then proceeded to give all his attention to his phone.

He must have some important work emails, right? Why else would he give his phone so much attention while in the presence of alcohol and women in bathing suits?

I was on the verge of saying exactly that when he proceeded to make an actual phone call, while still in the hot tub.

I inched closer in the water and whispered to my friend. "Has he been like this all evening, Annie?"

Annie giggled as she passed me a shot. "Have you met Gregory before?"

"Point taken," I said, feeling peevish as my eyes narrowed at Gregory and then darted away. I could also play the ignoring game.

As the evening wore on and more shots were passed around, Gregory started to speak more, though he mostly ignored me even when I had, in my view, offered some reasonably intelligent contributions to the conversation. He had seemed momentarily surprised when Annie and I actually participated in a conversation about corporate social responsibility. He'd likely expected or hoped that the conversation would exclude us, but he'd forgotten that we both edited boring business tomes for his friend's company for a living and were well versed in business jargon. His look of surprise was fleeting though, the subject abandoned almost as quickly.

When we belatedly realized our fingers were very wrinkled, having been in the Jacuzzi far too long, I was the first to step out. I'd become increasingly tired of being here, especially Gregory's blatant disregard.

As I waited for Annie to rise, I snuck a glance at Gregory, whose eyes were not on his phone. They were ... on me. My pulse jumped. He was *staring* at me.

But this look was something beyond staring, his eyes aflame with something I couldn't quite name, eyelids heavy, his full lips slightly parted.

My breath becoming shallow, I recognized his look. It was want. Need. Longing. Sizzling. No, something else, something more. I was shocked at the directness, the rawness, the intensity, in his gaze. Feeling the heat, I was powerless to do anything except to stare back.

Finally, I fumbled for my towel sitting on a table outside the spa on my left side. And just like that, Gregory's eyes snapped back to his phone, his lips pressed together in a thin line, and the moment passed. I turned around quickly, heart pounding, not trusting myself to avoid staring at *him* when he rose from the tub.

The rest of the evening passed in much the same way except that we sat around the bar in the suite: I snuck nervous glances at Gregory, but he continued to ignore me. The liquor made him even more arrogant and moody, if that was possible. He was particularly insufferable when we began to play cards. Stung by his hot/cold treatment and more than a little lightheaded from the alcohol and the late hour, I couldn't wait to go home.

Chapter 5

No amount of coffee could help me concentrate on work the next day, or the day after that, as my mind constantly wandered to *that look* from Gregory. I repeatedly reminded myself of all the times he'd been rude and condescending, of how he had ignored me and others, and of how he had grown increasingly moody and difficult to tolerate as the evening wore on.

It was just a look.

He was drunk, I was drunk, and even if it were the sexiest thing I've ever seen, it wouldn't mean that this relationship had any remote chance of happening.

"I don't need Gregory to write my story or to be happy. I will *not* be the kind of woman who waits around for some jerk to notice her," I declared aloud, just before leaving my apartment on Friday evening to meet Annie at her car downstairs.

When we arrived at the party, we were ushered to a semiprivate area at Merlot, a Minneapolis restaurant/bar that was normally quite a bit beyond Ellen's department budget, but Brandon was paying. I scanned the upscale space, impressed at the understated yet elegant decor. So many restaurants boasted an industrial look these days, a trend I wasn't a fan of. Then again, Merlot had more $ signs on its Yelp page than I was used to seeing.

We immediately sought out Ellen, who was looking bored in a conversation with several of the in-house editors and designers. Bolder relied heavily on a contractor model for its publications, but a few of its senior editors were employed full time. I gave a friendly smile as I passed Jermaine and another friend of Jack's.

"Ladies, look at you!" Ellen gushed, with a look of relief in her dark eyes. "You both look amazing. I hope this means we've got good news on the male front."

I winced at the double entendre from my boss. My knee-length dress was a rich burgundy with black and silver trim. Elegant but simple. At least I hoped so.

Annie put her hands on her hips dramatically, which only called more attention to her backless black dress and how stunning she looked in it, especially with her sleek red hair newly cut just over her slim shoulders. "This old thing? I'd forgotten I even owned it!"

Ellen and I laughed, knowing that Annie always made sure to look her best. Despite her contractor pay, she was rarely seen wearing the same outfit twice.

"Haha, laugh it up, ladies." Annie pretended to pout. "OK, so I only went to six shops before I found this gem. That's almost a record for me. Six is nothing. But anyway, look at Viviana—fabulous dress, and your hair! I thought you said you weren't going to put in the effort."

I shrugged while self-consciously rearranging my artificially smooth hair. I usually didn't bother with the straightening iron, but today I'd dug it out of my bathroom closet. "Yeah, I wasn't. But it doesn't hurt to look good once in a while. Maybe I'll meet someone new."

"Someone new, eh? Given up on Darcy already?" Ellen said, nudging me with her elbow.

Not understanding Ellen's meaning, Annie shook her head, tossed her sleek red hair over her shoulder, and proceeded to drag me toward the bar. "Colin Firth is lovely, but we need to find you a living, breathing man this time," she said with a grin, "and for that, we need booze."

As we waited for our drinks, my breath caught as Gregory entered the room with Brandon. His expression as he looked around the room was hard to read, unlike his face last night. I had been tipsy, for sure, but I hadn't imagined that gaze—such a look could hardly be imagined! The intensity in his gaze was unlike anything I had ever seen or felt. Oh, I had read about it in books and seen it in movies (obviously, Colin Firth), but no one had ever looked at me like that in real life. It spoke of heat, passion, desire ... all the things that you'd find in Mr. Darcy and *none* of the things I was used to seeing from Gregory. I lowered my eyes, hoping Annie hadn't noticed the direction and intensity of my gaze.

Fortunately or not, the men headed over to greet Ron first, and I sighed with relief. The overly chatty editor-in-chief would keep them occupied for a while. I turned to Annie and asked, with a tone as casual as I could muster, "How are things going with Brandon? He seems really into you, and it's pretty obvious you're already into him."

Annie's mouth curved downward at the corners. "I'll pretend I don't hear the forced 'I'm-not-judging' tone in your voice."

I grimaced. "Annie, I'm sorry. I'm really trying to step back and stop mothering."

"It's OK. I know it's not easy for you." Annie turned to smile at me before returning her gaze to Brandon across the room. "I was just teasing you. Mostly. Anyway, it's going great with Brandon. He's unbelievably hot, as you and anyone else can see." She hesitated a bit before continuing, "I think he is interested, but it's always hard to tell with guys like that. We're going to hang out tomorrow—he's got a friend who's into snowboarding, and I've always wanted to try it!"

"That sounds fun, actually. I'm not exactly the thrill-seeking type, as you know, but something about snowboarding strangely appeals to me," I confessed as the bartender handed me a drink.

"You should totally come then! It would be—"

"Oh, no, that's not what I meant. I didn't mean to invite myself."

"It's *me*, one of your best friends. You can invite yourself whenever you want."

I gave her a grateful smile but shook my head. "No, I am actually looking forward to having the weekend to myself, so I'll pass."

"Having the weekend to yourself?" Annie, the confirmed extrovert, wrinkled her nose. "But you always have the weekend to yourself... and the weekdays and weeknights and everything else. We work from home, silly."

"I know, I just want to do some writing. And I might try to get ahead on next week's editing."

Annie's eyes widened. "There's a guy! I knew it. You have a date this weekend, don't you? Who is it?"

I shook my head. "No, definitely not. I just want to hang out alone."

"Please don't tell me Jack needs your input on his latest snoozefest article."

My eyes went wide. "Jack is a fantastic writer! But no, he doesn't need me. He's been so busy I haven't even seen much of him," I said, my brow slightly furrowed. "I just want some *me* time, alone."

Annie narrowed my eyes. "Are you sure it's not a guy? Because I have to know, if it is."

I laughed. "It's not a guy." *Not a real guy, anyway*, I mused, thinking of my novel.

"Hey, that reminds me, did you see that look that Gregory gave you last night? For a moment, I thought maybe he was *into* you, but then he just became regular Gregory again just like that." Annie paused. "It's not him, is it? Are you having a secret sexy thing with him?"

I sighed. "No, Annie, I'm serious. There's no guy. And it sure as heck wouldn't be him. He's a certified snob. Clearly even you can see that."

"Even me?" Annie raised her eyebrows.

"Yes, even you. You always like to give people the benefit of the doubt," I said. She *was* very Jane Bennet–like. "But back to you and Brandon, do you think he—" I stopped talking then as he began to approach us, sans Gregory. "Oh, hi, Brandon," I said, though he was clearly focusing all his attention on Annie, looking her up and down as he offered an appreciative smile.

I grimaced. He might be a blond specimen of male perfection, but he might also be a sexist pig for ogling her.

Then again, Annie does look amazing and loves the attention. Who wouldn't want to drink it all in?

"Annie, Viviana, thanks for coming! Sorry I kept you all up so late last night, on a weeknight. I hope you're ready for the weekend." He winked at Annie.

He actually winked? Who does that? My grandpa, I think. Or maybe a flirt the likes of which I'd never encountered before. I needed to keep an eye on him. Should I go snowboarding with them so I could monitor things? But this wasn't a regency romance: Annie didn't need a chaperone. Besides, being a third wheel with a newly infatuated couple was usually about as fun as a root canal—or so I imagined, as I'd never had one.

As Annie and Brandon quickly began to disappear into their own little world, talking and gazing at one another, I scanned the room. Gregory was now looking at me as he talked to Ellen at the other end of the bar. It wasn't *the look* though; it was a spark of mild interest—faint interest, really, perhaps even intellectual, but coming from Gregory, any interest seemed worth noting. Then the moment passed, and his full attention returned to Ellen.

I turned in time to see Jack arriving with his sister and waved to them. Belinda lived in Eau Claire, a smallish city in Wisconsin just over an hour east of St. Paul, but she and her husband, Choua, visited her older brother quite often, ostensibly to make sure he was taking care of himself and not becoming a recluse. But it was not hard to see her true motivation: she was a foodie, and the Twin Cities had some excellent local cuisine.

"Vivi, it's been forever! Your hair is getting so long, and you look fantastic in that dress," Belinda gushed as she hugged me. She was the only person other than Jack who called me Vivi. Our friendship went back as far as middle school, though with distance and life changes, we hadn't been quite as close in recent years.

"Thanks, Belinda, though I think you visited just last month, or was it this month even? Only a few weeks ago you came to the opening of that new Hmong restaurant in St. Paul, right?" I asked as Jack stifled a laugh, nudging his sister affectionately. The two of them had always been close, bonding with each other at a young age by necessity as their mother cycled rapidly through marriages, jobs, and homes.

"You got me, Vivi," Belinda confessed. "And it was worth the trip, if you remember. Sorry that Choua couldn't come tonight. We're here for an architect conference, and he made some dinner plans with some other architects."

"Other architects? You mean there's more than one?" I teased. "I still remember when we first met Choua, and we couldn't believe he was an actual architect. Who knew that job actually existed outside of movies and New York?" Choua had met Belinda in France while they were both in a University of Minnesota study abroad group for one semester. She dropped out of college to become a baker, while he became an architect. They married and moved to Eau Claire, Choua's hometown. When she decided to open her own bakery there, he went to night school to get an MBA. Now they co-owned Bel's Bakery, and he also worked as an architect and consultant at a local organization for Hmong American housing assistance. Unlike some of my other friends, Belinda and Choua cherished their childless freedom and had no intention of becoming parents. I didn't necessarily feel the same, yet I envied the couple—at least they knew what they wanted and didn't want.

"I know, right?" Belinda giggled, tossing her auburn hair back. "Or Seattle. Tom Hanks."

Jack cleared his throat then, an amused smile on his face as he looked at his sister and me.

"Oh, I've been rude, so sorry! Let me introduce you and Jack to Brandon," I said, turning slightly. "This is Brandon Bolder, president of Bolder Publishing House. So, he's basically our boss's boss's boss's boss, or something like that. Brandon, this is Jack Normandy and his sister, Belinda Vue. Two of my oldest friends."

The two men shook hands, and Brandon gave a friendly smile to Belinda. I continued, "Jack doesn't work for Bolder, but he's an esteemed writer for *Randall's*, so—"

"And I know half the staff here, so I get roped into attending publisher parties all the time," Jack interrupted with a slightly embarrassed smile before I could continue gushing about him. "Or at least that's what they tell me."

Gregory suddenly appeared, standing near Brandon and me, and introduced himself to Jack as the high-powered publishing executive that he was.

Jack didn't seem overly impressed but instead gave him a curious look. Before he could speak in return, Gregory turned away abruptly to speak to Brandon, who probably didn't appreciate being interrupted in his little bubble with Annie.

"Brandon, tell me again why we're here," Gregory said in a low voice that was still loud enough for me to hear, just a foot away. "I assumed this would be a more exclusive party. How is it useful for the president of Bolder to dine with ... these people? Clearly some of the lower rungs on the company ladder."

I gasped, my mouth not working for several seconds.

Did he really just say that?

Glaring at him, I stomped off, not waiting to hear Brandon's answer. While I didn't think Brandon capable of such snobbery, I could not understand why he would associate with, much less befriend, someone like Gregory.

Jack and Belinda followed me to the spacious private dining room Brandon had reserved, where multiple waiters—or maybe they were hosts—came to seat them and take their orders. Unfortunately, the spot next to me remained empty, and Gregory sat there. I glanced over at Ellen in misery, but to my surprise, her eyes twinkled. My eyes widened in recognition. She arranged this! My surprise turned to amusement and then dread, remembering his rude comment minutes ago. We had a long night ahead.

"So, are you from the Twin Cities area?"

I paused in chewing my salmon, quite possibly the best I'd ever tasted, and turned slowly toward Gregory, assuming I must have misheard. Was he talking to me? I shot a questioning look to Jack and Belinda on my other side, but their attention was elsewhere.

"Vivian?"

I turned back to Gregory, realizing he was addressing me after all. "Uh, it's Viviana, not Vivian. I grew up here, yes, and returned for grad school."

"I see," he said.

And then ... nothing. He looked down and began to cut his steak.

I watched him and debated whether or not I should attempt to continue the conversation. Because, of course, I was curious about his sudden interest, not because I was interested in *him*.

"How about you, Gregory? I mean Dr. Fitzgerald. Where are you from?"

Without looking up, he replied, "I was born in India but grew up in New York City."

"Oh, how did you and Brandon meet? He's from Minnesota, isn't he?" I asked.

He sighed and put his utensils down, as if answering my questions was tedious. "We met at a conference," he said with an air of finality, as if there was nothing more to say about that.

Sensing his desire to end the conversation, I said only, "Oh."

But apparently he was not finished. "Does your family live here still?"

I hesitated, biting my lip. I was generally an open person, but my father was a well-known but also somewhat reclusive author who preferred to keep his private life, including family life, entirely private. With his work being highly acclaimed on its own merits, he'd managed to avoid most of the book signings and other self-promotion that authors typically do. Finally, I answered, "No."

"They moved away then?"

"They live north of the Cities," I said reluctantly as a waiter came to refill my wine glass. The best course of action was to change the subject. All men liked talking about themselves, surely. "What about your family? Are they still in New York?"

Instead of answering though, he proceeded to pepper me with several more pointed questions about my family that wouldn't have seemed so intrusive coming from anyone but him. Jack tried to join the conversation at one point, mentioning his own recent trip to New York, but Gregory continued the questioning as though Jack hadn't spoken at all.

The sudden interest was odd, his questions somewhat jarring. What was his intent, and was he really this socially awkward (or rude)? If so, how on earth did he achieve such a prestigious position in the fairly inaccessible world of publishing? When I'd stalked him online after meeting him, I discovered he was a senior acquisition editor at Elliot, a major New York publisher. Some people have all the luck ... or connections.

I certainly had some impressive connections of my own, particularly my father and the few people with whom he openly had contact in the literary world. But I'd never felt like I could take advantage of these connections, since my father valued our privacy so much. And my mother's writing experience was limited to scientific publications essential to her professorship at the University of Minnesota—not exactly an opening into the more interesting world of novel publishing that I secretly wished to inhabit. As I frequently told myself, I should be content with copyediting for a respectable, if small, publishing company. After all, I was just five years out of grad school, even if my skills were sometimes wasted on fixing hyphen and comma errors in books and articles that were unlikely to thrill anyone or change the world. Granted, my job seemed likely to eventually be replaced by AI—but I tried not to dwell on that.

I forced myself to pay attention to Gregory's questions, which were now transitioning from my mother's work at the university to my father's vocation.

Is he trying to get information about Dad? Does he know who Dad is?

I shook my head, dismissing the idea as silly. Surely Gregory Fitzgerald would have extensive connections allowing him access to *any* writer still living, so he needn't use a lowly contract editor to pry into my father's life. Most likely he would never have guessed that I had an important connection anyway; I didn't exactly boast about my father or his success. Very few people even knew of our connection at all, especially since my father had insisted my sister and I take our mother's last name.

I eyed Gregory, unsure whether to feel intrigued by his awkward attempts at conversation or to be annoyed by his unpredictable nature. Even his attempts at being friendly didn't feel very friendly. Or natural.

But even while I wondered about his intent, his attention was not entirely unwelcome. He was ridiculously handsome, after all. His dark brown eyes were penetrating, framed by his flawless dark skin, beautiful jawline, and nearly black hair. And good looks aside, there was something about his intensity in contrast to his aloofness that drew me to him.

As I scrambled to think of another subject to bring up, any subject but my family, Jack cleared his throat and leaned over, brushing shoulders with me. "Vivi, if you're not terribly busy answering 20 questions, I need you to settle this debate with Belinda."

I smiled at Jack's attempt to rescue me. The trouble was—I hadn't yet decided whether I needed rescuing.

Chapter 6

The next morning, I awoke with a start from an Austen-inspired nightmare, disoriented and drenched in sweat. Flashes of Mr. Darcy being brutally crushed beneath a carriage coursed through my mind as I sat up in panic, clutching my damp sheets as I clawed my sleep mask off my face. Still shaken ten minutes later, I seriously considered cancelling my next morning run with Jack.

But bailing on Jack wasn't an option. Today's half-marathon training plan required 12 miles, which would be difficult to get through alone. *Maybe Jack can help me get this dream out of my mind*, I thought briefly while knocking on his door at 7:30 a.m. *Or maybe he'll just think I'm insane.*

"Hey, come on in," he said while opening his door. He lived in one of the building's nicer apartments, with two guest rooms, much more spacious than my modest one-bedroom place. I often wondered why he hadn't moved to a nicer place or perhaps bought a house or condo by now, given how financially well off he must be. Jack was nothing if not sensible, including with money. But I was loath to ask him. After all, I didn't want him to move; having my best friend down the hallway was more than just a convenience—it was a lifeline, at times. Best not to even risk putting that idea in his head by asking about it.

I walked in and quickly sank into the nearest chair, yawning. Too late, I realized I'd sat on a book. It must be Belinda's, as Jack was too tidy to ever leave a book lying on a chair. Belinda was the exact opposite. The two of them had had a warm brother–sister relationship for as long as I'd known them, though I preferred to think that Jack considered *me* his closest friend anyway. "Bel's still sleeping, I assume?"

"Of course, as most normal people do if they aren't waking up early to run double-digit miles." He chuckled as he eyed me. "Choua says hello, by the way. He was hoping to treat us all to lunch today, but apparently his brother asked him to fill in for him in the early morning shift. I didn't even know their store was open so early."

"Yeah," I said, distracted.

After a few moments of silence as he finished putting his shoes and running gear on, he turned to me. "You're quiet. Are you all right?"

I nodded and looked at my watch, trying to stifle another yawn. "I'm super."

"If you say so," he said, giving me a sideways glance as we left his apartment.

After just one mile of running, the early morning sun promising a beautiful spring day, I felt sluggish and more winded than usual. And more than a little grouchy. Reluctantly, I told Jack I needed a walk break.

He slowed his pace and then looked at me with renewed concern as he touched my arm gently. "Already? Are you not feeling well today? Or just not feeling the run?"

"Maybe it's just not my day," I admitted. "But only a mile in, it's hard to tell."

"Yeah, but I know you. Something's up."

"I don't know."

"You don't know if something's up? Or you don't know if you want to talk about it?"

I resumed our running pace while avoiding the stray branches and twigs and random patches of ice that hadn't yet melted on the paved trail. "Lots of branches on the ground this morning. I didn't realize that weird spring storm last week was so bad."

I felt his eyes on me, but he said nothing.

"At least it's not snow," I added.

"True."

"That wouldn't be unusual this time of year."

"Right."

After several more attempts at bland conversation, I groaned. It was hopeless to keep anything from my best friend. Besides, we still had two long hours of running to survive this morning. I took a few measured breaths. "OK, if you must know ..." When his eyes swung over to me, I continued, "I just had a bad dream last night."

He didn't speak at first, obviously uncertain how to respond to such a declaration. "A bad dream?"

"Yes, I sound like I'm in kindergarten," I said, my brows scrunched together. "But I had a bad dream, and it's really staying with me for some reason. That's it. Big mystery solved."

After a moment, he asked softly, "Care to talk about it?"

I was silent as we ran up a steep hill. When I recovered my breath, I mumbled, "I don't know ... I'm sure you'll laugh."

"Me, laugh at you? Why, I never," he said in his friendly Jack way. "I'll be on my best behavior, Vivi. Shoot."

I eyed him briefly, trying not to betray my misery. This was Jack. Kind, supportive, wonderful Jack. "OK, I had a dream about *Pride & Prejudice*, but in this version, Mr. Darcy ... he died."

When he didn't immediately respond, my defenses rose. "Laugh it up. I realize how silly this sounds."

"It's not silly, Vivi, it's—whoa, careful!" He lunged to grasp my upper arm as I tripped and started to fall over a thick branch that I'd been too distracted to notice. His other hand held my waist as I tried to regain my footing.

I rose, abruptly putting distance between us, and kicked the offending branch off the path. "Thanks, but you don't have to try to save me. I'm not incapable of taking care of myself," I snapped as I started running again.

Jack gasped. But even knowing my anger was irrational, I couldn't stop the torrent of feelings as I tried to avoid eye contact.

"I didn't say that you couldn't take care of ... *what* is going on, Vivi?" He tried unsuccessfully to grasp my hand and then slowed again to a walk.

Bristling, I considered continuing to run on without him. But no, it would be tough to get through all those miles alone, especially in this mood. And this situation wasn't his fault. I knew this, yet ...

"Sorry," I muttered, slowing to a walking pace. "It's not important."

"Vivi, dear Vivi." This time, when he reached for my hand, I reluctantly gave it to him. "I'm here to listen. We're out here running for two and a half hours, so I've got nothing but time," he said with a gentle laugh, obviously trying to lighten the mood. "But I'll respect your decision if you'd rather not."

I shook my head in frustration, letting my hand drop to my side. I had no idea what I wanted, in this conversation or in anything else. Confiding in Jack usually came so naturally, but this time was different, for a reason I couldn't identify.

You can't tell Jack what you don't even know how to tell yourself.

Silently chiding my internal critic for being so melodramatic, I drew in a centering breath. "The dream just really affected me. Logically, it's silly. I know it's just a dream. I'm not a child. But I can't let go of the feeling, and there's something—"

"It's not silly, Vivi. Quit saying that." He sounded almost angry, for some reason. "Austen's characters mean a lot to you."

"Right, but they're just characters in a book, and I'm—"

"They're not just characters in a book though. Austen's work speaks to you, and you've loved her for as long as I've known you," Jack said, his eyes scanning my face. "There's nothing wrong with that."

"Yes, yes, but it's not just about Austen. You don't understand. I haven't told you everything ... it's about *me* and my life now," I said in a small voice. I couldn't hide how embarrassed and reluctant I felt to admit aloud that Austen's writing was spilling over into real life.

"Right, you're writing a book. I know how intense writing can be, how it can transport you to another time, how you become engrossed in that world." He looked at me intently. He was likely talking more about his own feelings about writing than about mine. "It's why I am a writer—"

It was my turn to interrupt. "No, you don't understand. It's more than that."

"OK. Tell me." He turned to me as we walked and waited patiently while I mustered the courage to explain.

"I ... I think I'm ... sort of ... living the story, as in real life," I stammered, wanting the ground to swallow me whole.

"Come again?" He continued to study me, his brow wrinkling slightly. "What do you mean?"

I took a deep breath and spoke quickly before I could lose my nerve. "I think I'm Elizabeth, and I might have found my Darcy. Maybe my Jane and Bingley too."

Regret washed over me as I registered his silence and unreadable expression as we continued walking. "Look, I know it sounds crazy. Believe me, I wouldn't be saying this to anyone but my best friend. But I think I've found a guy who could be *my* Darcy, and I can't decide how to feel about it. I thought I didn't care and the whole thing was silly, but the dream," I said, my voice shaky, "the dream—it scared me. I keep thinking that this could be my chance. My chance to find love. The gloom and doom of the dream, portending a bleak future if I don't give Mr. Darcy a chance." All the while the words were leaving my mouth, I *knew* it sounded ridiculous. Why was I saying this aloud? These were fanciful thoughts even for me, and they sounded so much more insane when I expressed them out loud.

I waited, as Jack was clearly pondering this revelation and probably considering carefully how to respond. "Let's run again. This walk break has been far too long, and we've still got many miles ahead of us," I said, speeding up.

He resumed running with me and said slowly, "Thanks for trusting me enough to share this, Vivi."

"Oh, Jack, stop it. You're my best friend, so I share everything with you. It was only a matter of *when*, not *if*, I confided in you about this," I said with a nervous laugh. "I just feel silly, vulnerable, I guess. You've probably figured out who Mr. Darcy is, and you probably think I'm crazy for even thinking of giving Gregory a chance—for even thinking that he might *want* a chance."

He didn't answer at first, giving me a strange look before gazing out at the frosty lake not far from the trail. He must be carefully deciding how to phrase his response to avoid hurting my feelings. "I don't think it's crazy. Why wouldn't he want a chance with you? Look at you. You're ... you. I don't really know the guy," he admitted. After a moment, he turned, the strange look fully replaced by a reassuring smile. "Hey, cheer up. If it's meant to be, it'll happen. If not, then ... you'll get through this. I'm here for you."

"Thanks," I said dryly, "and I know, there's more fish in the sea. Such wisdom."

His grin widened. "Anytime. Sorry, point taken. I'll have to work on my pep talks in the future." Then he paused. "I'm not quite sure what to think, since I don't know very much about him or the situation. So, you do have feelings for him?"

I bit my lip as he patiently waited for my answer. We had to stop at a busy intersection of road, trail, and lake, and I waited until we'd finished crossing. "I don't know. I might? I feel *something*, but I can't put my finger on it. I don't know if it's worth pursuing or, well, getting my hopes up."

He was silent for a minute, probably trying to improve his best friend advice act over his previously poor attempt. Or maybe he was merely concentrating on his breathing or his running form. When he finally spoke, his voice sounded strained. "I think ... if being with Gregory has a chance of making you happy, then maybe it's worth getting your hopes up. I don't want you to get hurt, but you're a strong, capable, beautiful woman able to make your own decisions about when to put your heart on the line."

My cheeks reddened at the compliments, which he didn't often bestow so generously. I didn't necessarily agree with him, but my mouth curved into a grin. "At least I'm no longer the awkward 14-year-old kid sister type tagging along and annoying you and your friends."

"Thank goodness for that!" he said, his eyes twinkling. "I thought I would never get rid of you."

"Eh, you had your chance, Jack Normandy. You went off to college, and you could've been rid of me forever, yet you chose to follow me in grad school."

"Follow you?" He laughed. "I think it was the other way around. You hadn't even given a thought to grad school until after I was already working on my PhD there."

"True," I admitted. "OK, so I guess we both tagged along with the other. I'd say it worked out in your favor though. Now you have a best-friend-slash-bratty-little-sister type just down the hall to annoy you any time she wishes." With that, I quickened my stride and started running ahead of him. "Catch me if you can."

He didn't miss a beat, immediately speeding up to keep pace. "You can't outrun me, little brat," he said in a teasing voice as he tried to tug on my ponytail. "But you can certainly try." I squealed and whipped my hair around before he could grasp it.

"That sounds like a challenge, which you know I can't pass up."

"Liz, there he is! That's Charles, with his friend Fitz I told you about," Jane said in hushed tones as they entered the house.

Elizabeth eyed the two men, one of them dragging the other toward her. She guessed the blonde, eager-looking one was Charles, and his reluctant companion must be Fitz.

"Jane, you came!" Charles said, not even trying to hide his wide smile. After a long moment, he turned to Elizabeth. "You must be Liz. And this is my buddy Fitz."

Fitz stiffened. "Hello. I am Fitzwilliam."

"He's a bit stuffy, but you get used to him," Charles said in a theatrical whisper, elbowing Fitz good-naturedly.

Fitz's stance became even more rigid, his lips pressed in a line.

"Glad to meet you, Fitz," Jane said warmly. "Are you enjoying your visit to ______ [fill in later]?"

Elizabeth took the opportunity to stare at him. He would be really attractive if he smiled, she thought. Gosh, he's hot even when he doesn't smile.

Finally, he spoke. "It is fine."

"Only fine?" Elizabeth said lightly. "Such praise."

His piercing eyes turned to her. "I was attempting to be polite. While I'm sure this place … has its charms, I can hardly say I enjoy this place or its people."

Elizabeth reared back as if struck. Did he really just say that? She looked at Charles and Jane for confirmation, and both were cringing. Before they could start to make excuses for him, she spun on her heel and left.

I removed my hands from the keyboard and shook them out. I considered getting up to stretch or get a drink, but I leaned forward instead, rereading the scene. Fitz needed some physical description, probably. I wasn't a natural at writing descriptive details, but describing Darcy seemed kind of important. I closed my eyes, trying to imagine the character. He couldn't just look exactly like Gregory. Or Colin Firth or Matthew Macfadyen. Sighing, I inserted a placeholder comment so I could move on in the story. After what felt like an eternity of writers' block, I finally felt like writing again, so I had to take advantage of it, not get hung up on small details.

After almost two more hours of writing and scarcely glancing up from my laptop screen, my stomach growled, quite loudly, and my body felt stiff from sitting for so long. My calzone was sitting right next to me on the desk, still in its takeout box, cold and untouched. Wow. Who knew I was capable of thinking about *anything but a calzone* while in such close proximity to a calzone? Indeed, I doubted anyone was capable of that.

This must be that elusive feeling of "flow" that writers and artists always talk about—well, those who are lucky enough to experience it. Standing up to stretch, I felt invigorated and tired simultaneously, which puzzled me exceedingly until I recalled the long run this morning. So immersed was I in writing—in *my* Elizabeth and Darcy's world—that this morning felt like days ago.

I'd forgotten this morning to ask how Jack's week had gone, especially since he'd been uncharacteristically moody earlier in the week. What was even bothering him? Perhaps I had imagined his strange moods of late. But I didn't think so. I knew Jack.

After puzzling for a moment, I shrugged it off, as I had more pressing things on my mind tonight. Elizabeth and Darcy. What would be the next step in their story? My musing was cut short though as my stomach growled again, reminding me of my shocking calzone neglect.

While strolling to the kitchen to warm up my dinner, I considered sending my freshly written chapters to Jack.

But something held me back, putting a knot in my stomach. I didn't want to share my story with him. My writing felt more personal now, bringing a sense of vulnerability that I hadn't felt when originally sharing my work with him, despite being nervous that first time.

This wasn't like sending him a draft of a research paper—though I was sometimes sensitive about that too—I was much more emotionally invested in this. This was, in a way, a personal journey. My life. Maybe ... my heart.

Jolted by the sound of the microwave beeping, I shook my head. I shouldn't be uncomfortable sharing anything with Jack. We'd known each other since high school, and he'd helped me save face after an embarrassing breakup. Grimacing, I remembered my intended prom date, Matt. He'd been my boyfriend of six months, my longest relationship by far, and being a clueless teenager, I'd been ready to jump into bed with him. The day before prom, he dumped me in a Facebook message. He gave no reason, but I later found out he'd been dating a senior, Holly Halter.

After patiently consoling me during a long, harrowing cry session, Belinda had insisted I still go to prom. "You have to show the Matt Freaking Penders of the world that you will always rise up, that you're better off," she'd said, already a passionate feminist at 16. She called up Jack, her older brother who was a freshman at the University of Chicago but was home for spring break, and convinced him to take me to the prom.

Despite my initial embarrassment about what was surely a pity date, I felt instantly at ease with him. That summer when he was home from college, we hung out together often. One night at a party where he was driving me home, I stupidly became intoxicated and confessed to having a slight crush on him. He'd let me down gently, calling me "kiddo"; I was embarrassed but pretended not to care. Self-preservation was everything to me. Things were soon normal between us again, and he became my best friend. He knew me better than anyone, better than my girl friends. I cried on his shoulder; I went to him for advice. I had long since ceased thinking of him in a romantic way. He was like my right arm. Not romantic, but essential to my happiness nonetheless.

After all this time, I could handle Jack gently critiquing or even laughing about almost anything I decided to do or say. But today's problems were different. This time, I might be writing about my own life, and therefore, it felt sacred somehow.

I didn't want to feel vulnerable.

At least not yet.

Jack would never intentionally hurt me, but my feelings about the Gregory situation were so new and uncertain, and I didn't trust myself to handle even the slightest, most good-intentioned criticism. Could I even handle a more technical critique? Maybe not. I didn't even know how to feel, much less how to talk to him about it or how to process any kind of feedback I might get. I squeezed my eyes closed, trying to shut out the swirling thoughts and feelings.

I opened my calzone container and plated it before taking a bite of deliciousness. I *could* share my writing with Annie, but it was probably best to keep this close to home. I wasn't quite ready to reveal my thoughts and feelings about Gregory to Annie, and I *definitely* was not ready to reveal my matchmaking scheme for Annie and Brandon—though I'd probably take credit for it openly once my success was certain. Annie was, in any case, probably busy with Brandon at this very moment.

After deciding to keep my novel to myself for now, I sighed in relief. Settling onto the couch with my dinner, I picked up my latest read, a modern-day adaptation of *Persuasion*. It was an Austen kind of night, but not just *any* kind of Austen. I needed to take a breather from Darcy, real or imagined, and a good dose of Captain Wentworth would be just the ticket.

Chapter 7

Elizabeth didn't sound wistful though. She sounded harsh. "Well, that burst of writing energy was short-lived. Thanks, Wentworth." I grimaced and rose to stretch my glutes, which were stiff after sitting at my laptop for two hours straight while barely writing a word.

Before I could admit to myself that Austen's captain didn't bear the blame for my writer's block, my phone buzzed with a text from Jennifer Weston, one of my best friends and close confidants. Our friendship, including Belinda, dated back to the cringeworthy teenage years, and I loved that we were all still close. Well, when they had time for me.

Jenn

Hey, so sorry, but I have to cancel on our lunch plans for today. Family stuff, so sorry!

Viviana

That's OK. Can you chat on the phone for a bit? I'm having man troubles.

A half hour later, the phone rang. "Hi, good to hear from you! I wanted—"

"Shh, you need to be quiet, Tyler. Sofia has a headache!" Jenn hissed. Her 2-year-old protested in outrage as she said, "Hi, Viv, I'm sorry, it's been a crazy weekend."

"I can see that! I don't know how you do it," I admitted.

"It?"

"The whole mom thing."

"Oh." Jenn laughed. "Yeah, me neither." After issuing another stern warning to her son, she resumed, "Sorry about the lunch. Sofia has this piano thing later, and Kieran was going to take her, but he's apparently got this work thing that he failed to mention. I won't bore you with the details."

"Oh, it's fine. I never get bored hearing about your perfect and beautiful little family," I said with only a smidge of sarcasm.

"Yeah, right." Jenn cackled. "I haven't completely forgotten what it's like to be single and childless and free and decidedly *not* interested in hearing about people's children. I've become my old self's worst nightmare. So, what's this about man troubles? I hope it's an exciting new romance because you know I have to experience great romantic moments vicariously through you, since I don't even have time for rom-coms these days."

"I wish I could say I really feel for you, Jenn, but you don't have it so bad. You snagged the perfect husband!" I reminded her. "So it's this guy I know through work—"

"Oh, an office romance! I love a good Jim and Pam story."

"Not really anything like *The Office*. He works at a major publishing house in New York, and he's way, way above me. I know him through Brandon Bolder, who's apparently his close friend."

"Oh, like a Mr. Darcy situation!"

"Exactly!" I was relieved to hear that my oldest friend was still as perceptive as ever when it came to my love life, despite having long since retired from dating life herself. In fact, it was thanks to my intervention that Jenn and Kieran found each other, an unlikely love match if there ever was one. Kieran was the ultimate jock in college, and Jenn hated breaking a sweat. In addition to excelling at sports, he was also smart and even bookish; she, on the other hand, hated school. She'd managed to finish a child psychology degree shortly before jumping headlong into the marriage-and-kids life. The only thing they had in common, at least outwardly, was their ridiculously good looks. She was tall, lean, and gorgeous, with long, flowy, ash-blonde hair that looked like she just stepped out of a haircare product ad. He had an athlete's body while also sporting the adorably nerdy look at the same time. They were night and day, but somehow perfect for each other. Introducing them had been one of my greatest accomplishments. "I knew you'd understand, Jenn."

"So, what's the problem?" Jenn said, once again pausing to admonish her toddler, though I doubted he could hear his mother over his own antics.

"Well, he's a jerk."

"A jerk as in the Darcy type, who *seems* like a jerk but is actually an amazing guy, or a jerk as in, like, he's just a jerk. Like Mr. Big?"

I gasped. "But we loved Mr. Big!"

"Yeah, we loved Big, and so did Carrie, but did he love us back? Let's face it, even in the end, he was still a self-absorbed jerk. A hot one, but still a jerk."

"I guess," I mumbled, unwilling to admit that the *Sex and the City* character, who I sometimes saw as a modern-day Darcy, was simply a jerk. I was even less willing to admit that, perhaps, that type of man might have been appealing to me then and even now.

"So which is he?" Jenn probed. "He's not Big, is he?"

I sighed. I still had no inkling of an answer to that question. "I am still trying to figure that out, so I need your help."

"What does Jack think?"

"He ... well, he isn't a fan. But he doesn't know Gregory that well."

"Jack doesn't approve? Interesting. I think I need to hear more."

"Well, I wouldn't say—"

Jenn raised her voice, clearly having lost her patience with her son. "OK, no more TV. I asked you to be quieter." Once I heard Tyler start crying—well, more like wailing—I knew the phone conversation was essentially over.

"Sorry, Viv, it's not a great time. Can we talk later? Lunch or something next Sunday?"

"Sure, I'll talk to you later," I mumbled, unable to conceal my disappointment. Of course, Jenn couldn't help it, but still. Losing friends to parenthood was hard.

Especially when my own life is so, so far from being ready to settle down in a cozy little family phase.

Before I could process my dismay about the brush-off from my oldest friend, my phone buzzed. It was Annie asking me out to lunch with "the guys," and I didn't even have to think about my answer this time.

Viviana

No, I'm tired. Need me time. Going to nap.

Annie

Me time again? Must be serious.

Viviana

I'm really just tired.

But Annie wouldn't give up easily. So I switched my phone on silent and headed to my bedroom, succumbing to the strong urge to escape all my confusing feelings in a blissful afternoon nap.

"Lillian sends regrets, as usual," my mother said, passing around cloth napkins.

"And wonders why we can't host family dinners at family-friendly times," my dad added, uncorking an aged wine and placing it on the table.

I sighed. It was on the tip of my tongue to remind them that my sister and her perfect little family took up plenty of their time already with research conferences and children's recitals and parties and who knows what else.

Why couldn't I have just this? A once-a-month adult dinner with my family? As my father returned to the kitchen, my eyes lazily swept the room and landed on Jack seated nearby. Well, Jack too. He might as well be family, as often as he joined us for dinner.

The door to the dining room swung open, and my father brought out the steaming pan of lasagna, placing it on the table near Jack, who smiled with anticipation. "I'll never tired of your homemade pasta dishes, Mark. And Janet, your desserts—"

"Jack's easy to please." I smirked. "But he's right that Dad's pasta is the best, and everyone knows it. Including Dad." After my father performed an elaborate bow that garnered chuckles around the table, he pulled out his chair and sat down.

We had scarcely taken a bite before my mother spoke up. "We have an announcement to make."

I dropped my fork, vaguely noting the red sauce splattering on my white sleeve as my eyes flew up to my parents' faces.

Please don't let it be cancer. Or divorce. Or financial ruin. Or—

"Janet," my dad said, "I can see by her face that she's conjuring up all sorts of awful predictions, so let's just come out with it."

My mother nodded. "Viviana, dearest, it's nothing like that. Your father and I have decided to spend next year abroad, renting a home in Italy."

At my blank expression, she added, "Your father is set to publish his tenth book next year, which is of course a major accomplishment in literary fiction. And I'm turning 60 soon. I ... I have considered retirement, but I'm not ready. Instead, I've gotten approval for an extended sabbatical. You and your sister are welcome to come vacation there and stay with us anytime, if you'd like. Maybe we could all plan a summer month together?"

"We've always wanted to do a long trip abroad," my father chimed in. "I mean, we went on some trips when you kids were younger, but we couldn't afford to go abroad for more than a weekend for business or research."

My eyes slowly swung back and forth between my parents. This was ... news. My brain was slow to catch up, so I said the first thing that came to mind. "Does Lil already know?" I sighed heavily. "Of course she does. Silly question."

"Lillian is putting in long hours on a tough grant proposal, and I thought it might be a while before we could get the whole family together to discuss. So, yes, I mentioned it to her at lunch yesterday," my mother said. Both my mom and sister were academics at the

University of Minnesota, so naturally, they saw each other often. I tried not to be jealous; I *tried* to tell myself I wasn't even the jealous type. But I could admit this: it bothered me that unlike Lillian, who'd successfully followed our mother's path, I not only had *not* followed in anyone's footsteps but also had failed to do anything else exciting career-wise. Still, I liked my life. Mostly. Freelance editing from home was a dream, right? Of course, once upon a time, my dream was to be like my father. To be an author. Write books. But that was forever ago. Dad was a unicorn; I wasn't.

Jack—sensing I felt a bit lost at sea because, well, he knew me better than anyone—chose that moment to chime in. "Janet, Mark, how exciting for the two of you. Vivi, you look a little shell-shocked, but this is wonderful news, isn't it? Maybe you could join them for a summer trip next year. You've always wanted to go to Italy."

As I slowly turned to look at Jack, the brain fog began to clear. My mouth curved upward slightly at the corners as I nodded. "You're right. Mom, Dad, we'll miss you, but ... this is great news. You'll have to send me all the info about where you'll be staying. I need photos!"

"Let's eat, and then we'll show you some photos online," my mother suggested, picking up her utensils again.

I let out a long breath. I was excited. It *was* exciting. But something was ... off. Something making me anxious. But what? Frowning, I noticed the reddish-orange stain on my sleeve but resumed eating.

An hour later, I'd eaten my fill and drunk probably more than my share. Everyone was excitedly browsing through online photos of the vacation home, which I had to admit boasted an amazing view.

Then it hit me.

If Lillian and I decided to accompany them for part of this dream vacation, I'd be going solo. The only one.

My parents had each other.

Lillian had her husband, her three children.

I had no partner, no children. Not even a pet. Just myself. Not even an important career that I could use as an excuse not to go. Or an excuse to be single.

"Vivi, what's wrong?"

Of course, Jack would notice right away.

He put his hand on my forearm gently, but I moved away slightly. "Ah, nothing, just, I don't know, maybe I ate too much."

"Honey, we know you better than that," my mother said. "That's not your I-ate-too-much-lasagna face."

Despite my inner turmoil, I almost laughed. When everyone seemed to be waiting for more of a response, I sighed. "Fine. I'm only saying this because I'm a little tipsy, probably, but I was just thinking about how I'd probably have to take this big family trip *solo*. You have Dad, Lil has her family, and I have no one, and that's not likely to change in a year, let's be realistic." When my eyes rose from my lap, the three of them were staring at me. "I know, stupid. I shouldn't have said anything. Ugh, how much wine did I have?"

My father chuckled. "Honey, you can always share anything with us, you know that. Wine or not. Feelings aren't stupid. And whether to go or not is your choice. Lillian hasn't committed one way or another yet either. But you know, or you should, that you aren't any more or less valuable to us whether or not you are flying solo."

"I mean, in theory, but ..." I shrugged, trying to keep my expression neutral.

"Well, maybe if he's not too booked at work, Jack could come as your plus one. I mean, Jack, you're almost family anyway," my mother said warmly, smiling at him.

Jack glanced at me with a slight smile. "Of course I would, if that would make Viviana happy."

I glared at him and snapped, "Jack, be serious."

His face shuttered, but before he could speak, my father started, "Viv, I don't think—"

I stood up, raising a hand to silence him and anyone else who might speak more. "I'm sorry. I'm just not feeling well, and I really need to go home. Jack, can you drive? You are still sober, right?"

He nodded, with his brow furrowed as he stood and walked me out in silence.

Chapter 8

Somewhere between the editing, the writing, and the running, I survived the week with surprisingly little rumination about my parents' big trip and shockingly few obsessive thoughts about Gregory. I was so pleased with my writing progress that I would have whistled, if I were the whistling type. Alas, I settled for smiling while strolling into the Bolder office on Friday morning for the weekly copyeditors' meeting. Sometimes Ellen held the meeting virtually, but she believed it was beneficial for us to meet in person at least occasionally. I didn't know why, but today, I didn't care because I'd resolved to have a great day.

The meeting was longer than it needed to be because Ellen just liked to talk and, even better, for others to hear her talk. A few possible changes to the in-house style guide were discussed, prompting a brief but passionate grammar discussion. It was the sort of conversation I lived for, but I tapped my foot impatiently but lightly under the table. I was full of nervous energy but unsure why. As soon as I stepped out of the conference room, Ellen pulled me into her office next door. "Viv, you look radiant today! Do spill."

I laughed nervously, averting my eyes. "I've just had a good week of writing—I mean editing." I wasn't ready to tell Ellen about my novel. In fact, Ellen would very likely be the last to hear about it. I liked my boss, usually, but she couldn't be discreet to save her life.

Ellen sat in a comfortable purple chair instead of behind her desk. Somehow she'd secured the largest office in the suite, even though she certainly wasn't in the highest-ranking position. She'd taken advantage of the space and spent a great deal of time and money on decorating. Her office served dual roles—depending on Ellen's goals at the moment, she could either laugh and relax (or even flirt) with someone on the comfortable but expensive furniture or sit behind her executive-style desk in a high-backed chair that somehow made her look intimidating.

Ellen waved me over to the empty turquoise chair beside her. "Have you been smiling like a fool because you got a lot of editing done? Was it a book on erotica?"

"Haha, you know very well I was editing Mastersen's book." I couldn't help but smile. "What can I tell you? It's 360 dull pages on, well, banking. And law. It isn't exactly thrilling, but sometimes the feeling of accomplishing that much is just so ... so ..." I faltered, searching for a convincing word. "Invigorating." Regret poured in. It was probably the least convincing word I could've chosen. Invigorating? Not even a banking lawyer would say that.

"I'm not buying it," Ellen started, before her eyes darted to her office doorway. I turned to look as Gregory and Brandon passed in the hallway. Ellen was of course immediately on her feet, calling to them and ushering them inside.

I stood up, biting my lip as I smoothed my hair. I hadn't expected to see Gregory here today. Perhaps a tiny part of me had wished for it, though. The sight of him was certainly not one I'd regret. He was dressed for business, but instead of looking dull in a suit, he was as handsome as ever, perhaps even more so, despite the lack of any smile gracing his face.

"Brandon, Gregory, nice of you to brighten our office this Friday morning. Can I help you find something?" Ellen said, a bright smile adorning her dark features. I looked over and saw her eyes twitching.

Is she nervous? Oh. No. Her eyelashes are fluttering. She's—is she flirting?

Brandon looked around, flashing a friendly smile at Ellen. "We were actually stopping in just to steal Annie for lunch—"

"You were, Brandon," Gregory interrupted, looking bored. "*I* came to meet with Ron. We just happened to meet outside."

"Yes, but of course you'll join us for lunch, right? Surely it'll be a short meeting," said Brandon dismissively, as though his lunch plans were of far greater consequence than a meeting with Bolder's editor in chief.

"I certainly hope so," Gregory said sharply. "The meeting, that is. I will not be joining anyone for lunch. I have an appointment with my trainer immediately after this."

Brandon gave him a sideways glance, shaking his head. He turned fully toward Ellen and me with an apologetic smile. "He's training for a triathlon, so his trainer is basically his love life."

Looking even more annoyed than usual, Gregory started to turn to leave, just as Ellen took a step toward him and briefly touched his arm to stop his retreat. "A triathlon! You must be a runner then, just like Viviana here. She's training for her *third* half marathon."

Gregory sighed, undoubtedly realizing he was not going to escape the conversation so quickly. "Yes, I run. It is, in fact, one of the three activities constituting a triathlon."

Either missing or choosing to ignore his blatant condescension, Ellen continued, "You two could train together! Viviana's always telling me how she could use a new running partner."

I widened my eyes at the audacity of Ellen's lie. "Ell, you know I always run with Jack. I'm sure Greg—I mean, Dr. Fitzgerald has better things to do than run with us."

"Indeed." He nodded, either not realizing how rude he sounded or not caring.

I blinked rapidly and then narrowed my eyes. "Well, then," I snapped. "You'd better get on with your important meetings and training then. Don't let us keep you."

He nodded again and left the room as they all stood gaping and silent.

Brandon was the first to speak, a pained look of apology in his eyes. "I'm sorry. He doesn't mean to be rude. He's just, he's just …"

"It's all right, Brandon. You don't have to defend him. Jack and I already have a great running partnership anyway, being matched in pace and being really old friends who can put up with all of each other's annoying running habits," I said, forcing a laugh. "Trust me, it's for the best. And you're not responsible for your friend's actions in any case." Why did I feel the need to soothe Brandon's feelings? Maybe because he seemed like a genuinely nice and pleasant man who was just unfortunate enough to have found an awful friend. Perhaps his only flaw was being overly generous in giving people the benefit of the doubt and looking beyond *their* flaws. Like Jane Bennet and Charles Bingley …

"I can see why Annie speaks so highly of you, Viviana. Gosh, everyone here is just so great!" he exclaimed, smiling at Ellen.

Could he be *any more like Charles Bingley?*, I marveled as he began making excuses to go find Annie.

Once Ellen and I were safely alone, I closed the door and sank into the turquoise chair. "Ell, I can't imagine how we ever thought Gregory was anything like Mr. Darcy. I really don't think he has a heart of gold beneath all that arrogance. Or a heart of anything."

Ellen sighed, striding over to sit behind her desk. "He does sometimes test my patience … and my theory about you two." She paused, looking thoughtful for a few moments. "But I'm not often wrong about people, so I'm not giving up yet. Maybe he'll surprise us. Have you seen a softer side at all? I know from Annie that you've spent some time together."

"Not really, I don't know what to make of him. But 'softer side' definitely isn't what comes to mind. Not even a glimmer of kindness or laughter. He's—"

Just then, the door opened after a brief knock. Gregory re-entered, stopping near my chair as I looked up in confusion. "Vivian,

I have had a change of heart. Would you like to join me for a run tomorrow morning?" His voice sounded a bit pained.

I narrowed my eyes. "It's *Viviana*."

He nodded briefly. "I'm sorry. Viviana."

I took a deep breath and glanced at Ellen quickly before returning my attention to him. Astoundingly, he looked somewhat contrite. "You can tag along with Jack and me, if you'd like. We usually start on the Midtown Greenway around 8 a.m. every Saturday."

"Is Jack the fellow you brought to Ellen's dinner engagement?"

"Yes, Jack Normandy. That is, I—I didn't *bring* him to the party, but he was there," I stammered. "We're—we're old friends. And running partners. He's like a brother, that's all." As soon as the words left my mouth, I wondered why I'd felt the need to explain my friendship with Jack. Why would Gregory care? And even if he did care, did he deserve an explanation?

He tilted his head and wore a puzzled expression, probably just as surprised as I was about my odd explanation. He cleared his throat. "Good. I shall see you tomorrow morning then. At which part of the trail should we meet?"

"Uh, Hamlet Avenue," I replied, still in disbelief. "Harriet Avenue, I mean. Not Hamlet. I don't know why I said that. Then again, I think I dreamt about Shakespeare recently. But it's not Hamlet; it's Harriet. Harriet Avenue. In South Minneapolis. Harriet is—"

"I will look it up. See you then," he said briskly, making his exit as abrupt as his entrance.

The moment he closed the door, Ellen exclaimed, "*See*? He must be into you. He sought you out, *and* he apologized. He doesn't strike me as the kind of man who apologizes, ever."

I chuckled, refusing to acknowledge the flutter of nerves rising up. "Probably because he got my name wrong the first five times he said it. Even *he* realized that was more than a little rude." With Ellen looking at me expectantly, I sighed and allowed a small grin. "Maybe you're right. Maybe there's a small glimmer of hope that he isn't a *complete* jerk. It's still pretty small though. Minuscule." I gazed out the window and shrugged. I didn't want Ellen to think I cared—that I was actually invested in this unlikely love story.

"Would it be incredibly cliché for someone who works in publishing to say 'Methinks the lady doth protest too much'?" Ellen didn't even try to hide her sly smile.

"Cliché, maybe. But tragically incorrect, for sure. Hamlet's mother said 'The lady—'"

"You can take off your editor hat, Viv. I know what she said. I'm just trying to bait you, which is very easy to do today." Ellen raised a thin eyebrow. "It must be love that has you so easily riled up. What else could it be? Surely not banking law."

I laughed despite myself. "Definitely not that. But I'm not *riled up*. You're imagining things, Ell. He's just a confusing person, that's all. And I'm hungry."

Ellen was silent for a moment, eyeing me knowingly. "And Shakespeare? What was that?"

I buried my face in my hands. "I am mortified, Ell. How idiotic did I sound?"

"Idiotic isn't the word I'd use. It was … ." Ellen gestured, looking for the right word. "It was … charming. I've only ever seen you ramble like that once before, with that Anthony guy years ago."

I groaned at the mention of my former relationship disaster. Anthony Rivera was the business development manager at Bolder when I started contracting there over four years ago, and we'd started dating almost immediately after meeting at a networking event. Despite being a few years younger than me, Anthony had seemed more mature and emotionally available than the commitment-phobic guys I'd dated in college. He was responsible and ambitious, with a good job. He had a nice apartment, nice clothes, a nice Puerto Rican family, and no posters on his wall. But after a year of dating, he found a better-paying position elsewhere (to my shock, as I hadn't been aware he was job hunting), and he dumped me. Ghosted me, actually. I figured he was too good-looking, maybe a little arrogant and self-centered, and although I stayed at his place often, he never asked me to move in. I thought I was in love, but for reasons I couldn't pinpoint, I hadn't even felt comfortable bringing a toothbrush to his place. I'd either failed to notice his flaws or convinced myself they were no big deal. I'd been cautious and even a bit bitter about men ever since. And wasn't I still? But I was opening up to at least the *possibility* of something developing with Gregory—that is, if I could keep my cool and not ramble like an idiot next time.

"I can't believe I have to face Gregory after that. Maybe I'll tell him I forgot to eat this morning, which is actually half true. Or maybe I should just cancel—this running date is a disaster waiting to happen."

Ellen shook her head as she pulled her chair closer to her desk and flipped open her laptop, usually the sign that a conversation was becoming tedious and she was moving on. "No, you won't do that. Go eat. And text me tomorrow after the run."

Taking my cue to leave, I rose. "No, I mean, I don't know if—"

Ignoring my protest, Ellen added, "I need to hear how this goes, OK? He's as much of a mystery to me as he is to you." She gazed at me thoughtfully, as if considering whether to say more. "Did you know he was in a car accident with his younger sister when they were both very young? She didn't survive."

I gasped. "No, I ... I had no idea. That's terrible."

Ellen nodded. "I don't know all the details, but I managed to pry it out of Brandon. I can't help thinking it's really affected him." She paused, staring at some distant spot on the wall for a long moment and then finally refocusing her gaze on me. "I do love me some romance heroes with a tortured history. Hell, if I were 10 years younger, I'd no doubt be pursuing Gregory myself." I laughed but also winced. Sometimes Ellen's words were startling if not cringe-worthy coming from a married woman. And so soon after divulging the tragic information about Gregory. I was still trying to digest the information when Ellen added, "I'll just have to settle for hearing about your love life."

My eyes widened.

Ellen put on her work glasses and narrowed her eyes. "So you'd better make it good."

Chapter 9

I awoke with a start, assuming I'd overslept. But seeing 6:35 on the clock, I breathed a sigh of relief. After checking to make sure my alarm was still set for 7:30, I buried myself under the soft covers again. But as I started thinking about the morning ahead, I felt increasingly awake and decided to rise early.

Minutes later, I was standing in my kitchen buttering a bagel, my favorite pre-run breakfast. When my phone buzzed with a text from my sister, I nearly jumped out of my skin. I cleared the notification, telling myself I would read it later. Texts from Lillian were never urgent. I turned off the coffeemaker and decided that some soothing green tea might be more appropriate this morning.

Why am I so jumpy? I asked myself while filling my favorite Austen mug. It had been a gift from Jack last year, fittingly saying, "It's rudely early," a quote from Sidney Parker in Austen's unfinished work *Sanditon*.

Instead of dwelling on that question, I decided to take a quick shower. *It's usually pointless to shower before a workout, but this would be a good way to wake up.*

Not that I needed to look good or anything.

Freshly showered, I stood in front of my mirror, debating whether to wear makeup. *Foundation and lipstick have sunscreen in them, so it's probably a good idea.*

Not that I needed to look good or anything.

Gathering my running clothes, I remembered the new sports bra I hadn't broken in yet. A massively popular purchase in the women's running community recently, this bra was supposed to be less unflattering than a typical sports bra. *It would at least provide better breast support, and maybe less chafing, by virtue of being new instead of worn out,* I assured myself as I pulled on the pink bra and admired my form in the mirror.

Not that I needed to look good or anything.

At the sudden knock on the door, I quickly pulled on my running tee. The weather was supposed to be warmer this weekend, but given the early hour of the day, I opted for capri leggings. After opening the door, I said hello and waved Jack in.

"Morning, Vivi," he said cheerfully, always the morning person. His eyes widened a little as they skimmed over me. "Well, you look quite nice for a sweaty long run. What's the occasion?"

Jack didn't yet know about the addition to their running group, as I feared he'd be tempted to cancel and leave me alone with Gregory. I was not ready to be alone with him yet, especially since I still hadn't figured out his motives. Or whether I even liked him.

I looked away from Jack, blushing and waving my hand as if he were exaggerating. "Nothing, I, uh, I mean, I just woke up earlier than usual, so I figured I might as well shower and put in a little bit of effort." Seeing Jack's amused expression, I added, "No big deal, really."

Jack's easy laugh usually made me feel at ease, but this time, my nerves only increased. My anxiety would be super obvious to him as soon as he saw Gregory ... or as soon as I told him.

"Sure, Vivi. Ready to go?"

"I am."

When we left the building and headed out the door toward the trail, only a few blocks away, we both noticed simultaneously that I was walking very fast.

"Are you in a hurry today, Vivi? Are we running late for an important event?" He looked at me curiously.

"Oh, did I not mention?" Now was the time to tell him, before I could lose my nerve. "Dr. Fitzgerald is meeting us to run this morning. It's not a big thing."

His eyes widened in surprise and then something else, maybe dismay or even hurt.

But that's silly. Why would he be hurt?

"He is? Why?"

"It's Ellen's fault. He's training for a triathlon, and suggested we all run together. Her idea," I explained, looking at the sidewalk, the trees, anywhere but Jack.

"Ah, Ellen," he said softly, nodding as if that explained everything.

"*I* didn't invite him!"

"OK, I got it." He paused for a moment. Then, in a voice that sounded somehow different than my best friend's, he said, "But it would be all right if you did invite him."

I didn't know what to say to that. "But I didn't. I don't even think I like him."

"I see," he said, his eyes shuttered. My lips curved into a frown, realizing he disapproved of Gregory.

But of course he does. Gregory's only good quality is being insanely hot, and Jack is a straight guy. Well, Greg is also rich. Also not something that should matter much to Jack. Or me.

After a few moments of silence, I forced a casual tone. "It'll be interesting, if nothing else. He's not a great conversationalist, from what I've seen."

"That's rather obvious to anyone, I would think. But we can give him another chance," he said with an easy laugh, the strange tension, or disapproval, or whatever it was having faded as quickly as it came on. Though Jack's approval wasn't required, I always felt better having it.

But why did it matter what Jack thought? When I looked inward, only one reason surfaced.

It matters because I want this to be real.

If Jack believed, maybe I too could believe this crazy theory that Gregory was my real-life Darcy. Maybe I could let my guard down and even fall in love—it had been a long while since I had allowed myself to do that. Maybe Darcy, er, Gregory would fall for me. Maybe by next year, I could even whisk him away to Italy to meet my parents. Was it too much to hope for?

Interrupting my internal dialogue as we reached Harriet Avenue, Jack nudged me. "Well, there he is. He gets points for being punctual."

Gregory was standing near the running trail at the designated meeting place, stretching his calves. Since he hadn't seen us yet, my eyes swept over him. He looked gorgeous even while standing there doing stretches. The man took "tall, dark, and handsome" to another level, one that apparently rendered his lack of social graces unimportant. There was something about him in a natural setting too, as though the surrounding trees, birdsong, and morning sky made him seem a little more human.

"Hello, Greg—Dr. Fitzgerald." I strode toward him while Jack trailed a bit behind. But when Gregory's eyes met mine, disaster struck.

I promptly tripped on a tree branch, landing hard on the ground.

"Are you OK, Vivi?" Jack stepped forward quickly, concern etched on his face. He offered a hand to help me up, while Gregory moved into a hamstring stretch without a word.

I closed my eyes, steeling myself against the mortification. Why was I always embarrassing myself around him? "I'm fine, just a bit of grass stain," I said with a shaky laugh. "Dr. Fitzgerald, I'm pleased to see you this morning. Have you been waiting long?"

Jack gave me an odd look as his eyes shifted between us, having never heard such formalities when greeting a running partner. Gregory must be rubbing off on me. It wasn't possible that I was trying to speak formally like him to impress him. No, that couldn't be it.

After a full minute of silence, except the birds high in the sky, Gregory finished stretching and stood tall, looking at me directly. "Good morning, yes, I have been here a while. I have been cycling on this loop for the past hour."

"Is that your bike?" I asked, pointing to a cycle not two feet away from him. I groaned inwardly. What an idiotic question.

"It is."

"Right, yep, triathlon training." My head bobbed up and down. "Is this your first one?"

"Yes, it is," Gregory said before looking at his watch. "I'm on a tight schedule. Are you ready to begin running?"

Early in the run, Jack tried to make small talk, but Gregory barely responded. Jack gave me a meaningful glance, which I ignored, determined to give Gregory a chance this morning. Besides, I was becoming used to his disdain for small talk. Perhaps he *was* just socially awkward. Like the real Mr. Darcy.

Well, technically, Mr. Darcy isn't real.

I shook my head to clear my mind. "Dr. Fitzgerald, where did you get your PhD, and what did you study?" I found myself thinking about Ellen's divulgence that young Gregory had tragically lost a sister. How did his family experience the loss? But I couldn't very well come right out and ask him about something so delicate ... at least not yet. Instead, I attempted to draw him into a conversation that he might actually want to partake in.

He took the bait. "I studied at Yale and then Oxford before coming to Columbia for my PhD. It seemed somewhat pedestrian to return to New York after my time abroad, but my father wanted to begin grooming me for the publishing world. My PhD was in literature, of course, and then I returned for an MBA."

Pedestrian to attend Columbia University? OK, he was definitely a snob, but we couldn't blame him for his upbringing. "That's interesting, both a literature PhD and an MBA."

"Is it interesting?" Gregory asked.

"I guess the sort of people I've known with literature degrees have just been very different from the business sort. I've never known anyone with interest in both," I admitted. "Then again, I don't have such high connections in the publishing world."

"Indeed," Gregory said.

I sucked in a breath.

Did he, with his impaired social skills, mistakenly believe that using the word "indeed" somehow made it acceptable to be rude? He'd said it twice now in response to my self-deprecating remarks. Could one hold a prestigious role in the publishing industry while lacking such basic social graces? I made a mental note to ask my father, who surely knew of many publishing types, though likely from a distance.

Jack cut in, eager to defend me. "Well, that's not entirely true. You have me as a connection, Vivi."

"And your father," Gregory added. "Certainly your father must have such connections."

I nearly choked on the water I'd been drinking. How much did he know about Dad? I'd said very little when he'd awkwardly questioned me before. Did Gregory know him? Surely not. My father had been somewhat more open about his identity at the very beginning of his career, before he'd realized he could withdraw from the public aspect. But back then, Gregory would have been, well, a toddler. "Perhaps he does, but he prefers a quiet life, so he has fewer connections than one might expect."

"Of course, one hardly needs connections when one is as talented as he," said Jack good-naturedly, apparently ascertaining that Gregory did know something of my father. "He doesn't need to play the game."

"I must agree," Gregory said. "Though it is probable that his prospects and wealth could increase considerably if he did make an effort to, as you say, play the game."

I said nothing. My view was sometimes similar, but I respected my father's desire to live quietly and not seek fame or recognition. My parents didn't consider themselves rich, but they lived quite comfortably. That hadn't always been so, however. Although Mom came from wealth, Dad's background was middle class. Because he was stubborn and a bit prideful, they'd spent years devoting their earnings to paying off his large student loans from grad school, which took quite some time for a not-yet-established writer and an associate professor working long hours while trying to provide for their two daughters. Fortunately, I was introverted myself, so I hadn't actively resented any lack of attention from their time-consuming careers, and Lillian had always been self-sufficient. We weren't deprived as young children and certainly not as teenagers. Unlike our parents, we weren't saddled with a mass of student debt—only a modest amount. Lillian had married a banker soon after obtaining her biology PhD, and I assumed from my sister's wealthy neighborhood that they were set financially. In my much less lucrative career as an editor, I was not wealthy by any means and had some debt still to pay off, but I was as comfortable as I needed to be. Or so I often told myself. In my early 30s, I still had plenty of time to get rich or snag a rich husband like Gregory, right?

I bit my lip.

What a ridiculous thought. As if Gregory would marry someone like me. Why am I even thinking about marriage anyway? My life isn't a Regency novel.

In any case, my goal in life had never been wealth; I only wanted to be happy. If only I knew what that even meant. Of their own accord, my eyes drifted over to Jack, who was eyeing me thoughtfully.

Our running pace had become uncomfortably fast for me, so I slowed a bit, refocusing on my surroundings.

After catching my breath, I attempted to return the subject to his lofty education, which was a safer subject than my father's career. "So, Gregory, what was your dissertation on?"

"Yeah, I'm curious as to how your literature PhD informs your work on the business side of literature, as you might say," Jack added. I smiled at his attempt to be friendly despite disliking my new love interest.

To this, Gregory spoke for several minutes about his dissertation, ignoring Jack and his question altogether. He spoke quite freely and naturally about his doctoral work, and I wondered if being in the business world felt stifling to him. Perhaps academia was his true calling, and he was stuck in an elite publishing job against his will.

I groaned inwardly, realizing that was taking my assumptions too far.

Let's not start feeling bad for the smart, handsome guy with more wealth and privilege than I could imagine.

After a break in the conversation—or rather, the monologue—Gregory asked, "Do you always run so slowly, or is this a recovery run for you?"

Clearly startled by Gregory's bluntness, Jack coughed. "Do you always blurt—"

"Well, Jack and me," I cut in, before Jack could say something probably very un-Jack-like, "we could be a lot faster, but I'm pretty stoked that we're no longer in the back of the pack at races. What's your normal pace, Gregory? I mean, Dr. Fitzgerald? Sorry again."

Seeming not to hear my question, Gregory said nothing and, a moment later, returned to inquiring about my family, this time peppering me with questions about my mother's work. I told him that Mom was a scientist, omitting any details. Although she wasn't secretive about her work and had no reason to be, Dad often worried that fans (or critics) would find him through me, so I usually tried to steer any conversation away from both of my parents.

Yet Gregory could hardly be a threat, given his own high connections. It was probably safe to speak more openly about my mother's work as a tenured professor. He appeared to listen intently, until Jack cut in.

"Janet is a very interesting woman. They make an interesting pair, the two of them. She's very much his opposite in nearly every way, yet I've never met a happier couple. Vivi, you're very lucky to have such a happy model of what marriage can be like."

"Yes, I am lucky. But maybe, well … maybe they set the bar too high," I said with a laugh.

"How so?" Gregory said.

"Oh, I just mean, I—since I'm still, uh," I stammered, "well, never mind. They're lovely people, really. I am very lucky—"

"How often do you see them? Do you visit them, or do they visit you?" Gregory resumed his questioning.

I sighed before answering him. His social skills would need some work if we were ever going to get serious.

Get serious? Wow, that's taking a big leap. We're just running together. With a chaperone. Let's not book the wedding venue just yet.

All the same, my mind began conjuring up visions of wedding dresses. And Italian beach scenes.

I glanced at Jack, who wore a slight grimace. He was probably frustrated, or perhaps the miles were wearing on him. The air was growing warm and a bit humid by now, and I would normally be feeling quite hot and tired at this point, yet the conversation with Gregory—awkward though it sometimes was—was invigorating to me.

When Jack finally made eye contact with me again, I smiled apologetically, knowing this run was likely far from invigorating for him. Even for me, I wouldn't have suffered through this conversation for anyone else. That had to mean something. *Gregory* had to mean something.

Chapter 10

Enjoying the familiar feeling of being tired but content after a long run, I nearly fell asleep on the couch late in the afternoon while relaxing with a new book. I looked toward the window, seeing that it was still sunny, blindingly so. My thoughts strayed to a certain gorgeous, toned triathlete and lingered there until my eyes lazily shifted to the dusty, dull greyish blue curtains framing the window.

This would not do. Frowning, I grabbed my phone. I'd never liked these curtains, and they'd only grown more worn and shabbier since I'd moved in. I didn't even like grey, or even blue, that much. My tastes ran more toward green ... maybe purple? Not blue, and definitely not grey.

But when I opened the shopping app, the deals of the day appeared, and I promptly forgot about the curtains.

Yawning as I scrolled through pages and pages of cute running shorts in varying colors and styles, I could no longer remember why I was using the shopping app. I forced myself to stand up and stretch my stiff legs. My stomach growled loudly, yet the idea of cooking or doing anything productive made me grimace, so I decided to visit my favorite local café.

After locking my apartment door, I walked down the hall to knock on Jack's door out of habit, but he didn't answer. I shrugged and made my way to the café, just a block away from our apartment building.

Upon entering the Krumkake Café, I smiled slightly while inhaling the scents of their many sweet and savory offerings. While scanning the familiar but enchanting European-style café décor with Scandinavian accents, my eyes landed with surprise on Jack, his back turned, probably waiting for a takeout order.

I tapped him on the shoulder. "Jack?"

He turned with some surprise, briefly saying my name before turning back to the cashier handing him his order. After a moment, he turned to face me fully.

"You came here without me?" Though I tried to keep my expression neutral, I was probably failing miserably. "It's our thing—we always go together *or* get takeout for each other."

"Sorry, I was in a hurry, and I figured you were busy."

"Busy? Why would I be busy?"

I studied his face, which was unreadable. Exhaling softly, I decided to be cheerful and ignore the slight. "It's just another Saturday night staying in with Austen, and I have to make the all-important decision: book or movie. Care to join me?" I forced a smile to hide the lingering feeling of disappointment. Or tension. Or something I couldn't name.

"Sorry, I have a late work call and want to work on a new piece after that." His eyes shifted away for a moment. "How's your writing going, by the way?

Ignoring his question, I narrowed my eyes. "A work call on a Saturday night? That seems a little odd."

"Yeah, but it's with the boss," he said, rubbing his temples lightly as though he had a headache. But Jack never had headaches. "So I can't just cancel. Irene is a bit demanding these days."

"Oh, how so? I mean, other than Saturday night work calls," I said, making a face. Irene Pruett was the highly successful managing editor at *Randall's*, and her excessive demands on Jack and, presumably, on her other writers were well known. She made my own boss look like a kindergarten teacher. I'd heard about Irene frequently in the last three years since she had become a rising star at the well-known literary magazine.

He averted his gaze, shuffling his feet. Jack was not a shuffler. "I'd rather not get into it. Sorry, Vivi. I wish I could stay and chat, but I need to get back soon."

"I see. Sorry, I didn't mean to *take up your time.*" My voice sounded irritable and probably childish, but I couldn't help it.

"You know that's not what I meant," he said, throwing one arm around me for a half-hearted hug.

I jerked away as though scalded. Why was I so on edge? I shrugged nonchalantly to conceal my weird reaction. Avoiding his eyes, I turned to scan the bakery display in front of us. "I guess you'd better go then," I said, adopting a neutral expression while pretending to examine the scone selection. "You probably don't have enough time to wait so we can walk back together," I added a bit wistfully.

After a long pause, he finally said, "Right then. I hope you have a good night staying in with Austen, Vivi. I'll see you Monday for our next run." His hand rose, in the friendly habit of hugging or patting me on the shoulder when we parted, but he apparently thought better of it and let his hand drop to his side.

"You too. Bye, Jack," I said, trying to sound as normal as possible as he walked toward the exit.

The cashier walked over then and offered a sympathetic smile, her dark brows scrunched together. "I tried not to overhear," said Melanie, "but are you all right, dear? I was surprised when the two of you showed up separately. Trouble in lovers' paradise?"

I rolled my eyes. "Oh, Ms. Martinez, you know it's not like that."

"I know nothing of the sort," said the older woman with a grin. "And for goodness sake, call me Mel, or I'll charge you extra."

I managed to smile. "You win, Mel."

"Ready to order, dear?"

Before I could speak, three children came running into the café toward the counter, while a man who must be their father tried valiantly to keep up. "Abuela! Abuela! Happy birthday!"

As Melanie greeted them, the father turned and smiled apologetically at me. "So sorry, they're a little excited to see Grandma today." He was tall and handsome, with warm brown eyes, an open smile, and short yet thick brown hair without a trace of silver. He was probably in his mid-30s.

"Jordan, this is Viviana, one of our favorite customers," Melanie said, gesturing quickly toward me before handing the children some muffins. "Viviana, this is my son. I've often thought you two should meet. He's been single since Christmas, and you've been single since, well, I can't remember, it's been so long. He is—"

"Mama, stop," Jordan said, looking embarrassed. "I'm sure Viviana came here for food, not a date."

I smiled broadly, extending my hand. "It's nice to meet you, Jordan. Have no fear. You're probably the fiftieth person she's tried to set me up with. It would've been quite strange if she *didn't* try. At least this time it's not a setup with another customer."

Jordan turned to pick up his youngest son, who was reaching up toward his grandmother. "Good to know. I think." He laughed again. "It was nice to meet you, but please don't let us keep you."

"I'm sure you have plenty of catching up to do, Mel. I'll wait over there." I pointed to a nearby seating area. "And happy birthday!"

"She's fifteen. I mean fifty. Can you believe she's *fifty*?" The oldest child whispered loudly in my direction.

I nodded and smiled at the boy.

As I sat down to wait in one of the café's large, cushioned armchairs near the wall, my thoughts turned to Jack again. What was going on with him? He was generally so *normal*, so predictable—in a nice, comfortable, reliable way that I really needed in my life—but he was acting a little peculiar lately. I was fairly certain Irene's "demands" weren't limited to Saturday night work calls; in fact, I often suspected something *else* going on between them. I knew Jack would never admit it, having always been very discreet, even with me. It used to bother me that Jack never confided in me about his love life, but I'd long ago learned to accept it—well, mostly.

More importantly, why hadn't Jack stopped over to my apartment first to ask if I wanted anything from the café? Melanie was right that *something* was off with us. But what? Was he trying to avoid me? Was he annoyed that he had to deal with Gregory during our run this morning? Was he somehow jealous?

I nearly laughed out loud as I shook my head.

This is Jack. He is almost certainly none of those things, and I'm almost certainly imagining some dramatic explanation that has no basis in reality.

This silly romantic imagination of mine was the reason I must write. Dreaming up crazy stories was what a good writer did, right?

Interrupting my reverie, Jordan appeared in front of me, holding out his hand with my takeout bag. "I thought I'd bring this over, as my mother's rather busy with the three hellions at the moment."

I took the steaming bag from him while rising to stand. "Thank you. Mel looks busy, but please tell her I said thanks. And I hope she has a great day and gets off work early!"

Jordan smiled and ran his hand through his dark hair. "I will pass it along; that's kind of you. By the way, I—it was nice to meet you." He opened his mouth to say more but then closed it.

"You too," I said, flashing a quick but friendly smile and turning to leave.

As I strolled home, forgetting quickly all about the café drama, I wondered what Gregory was doing. Probably working, which was what I should be doing. Shaking my head slightly, I vowed to spend some time writing tonight before popping in an Austen movie.

On second thought, maybe I'd watch something else, maybe a recent rom-com.

I'm not obsessed with Austen. Or Darcy.

Perhaps if I repeated that enough times, it would become true.

Chapter 11

"We're making good time," I said to Jack as we neared the end of our first mile on Monday, the bright sun providing a small bit of warmth on a frosty spring morning. "How was your weekend? I hope you didn't work through all of it?"

He looked down at his running watch, squinting to read past the glare. "Yes, quite fast this morning." He paused, nodding politely to another runner on the trail. "Jermaine and his brother came over to watch the Twins game yesterday. But other than that, unfortunately, work did take up most of my weekend. And you?"

"Let's just say I wasn't very productive." Yesterday, I'd caught myself reading the same sentences three or four times, fixing comma errors but not comprehending anything I read. Even with extra coffee, my brain wouldn't focus on words, whether editing or writing. Sadly, I was fresh out of material for my Darcy story, and I hadn't even written a sentence. Things had progressed with Gregory somewhat, but I needed more material and I needed clarity. When would I see him again? *Would* I see him again? I knew very little about what he was doing in the city with Brandon and what business he had with Bolder, if any. I'd considered consulting Jack for writing motivation tips but elected not to, for reasons unknown.

"And another cancellation from Jenn, a typical Sunday. I did write a bit though."

"Oh no, she canceled again? Jenn's always so busy now."

"Yes, well, this time they were sick, which I can definitely believe, with two toddlers in the house. At least she mentioned hosting a board game night to make it up to me."

"I feel for her," he said sympathetically. He turned toward me briefly. "But also for you, Vivi. It must be hard to have your friend be less available now."

"Yes, in more ways than one," I mumbled, thinking of Jack's elusiveness in the past week.

"What's that?"

"Nothing."

For the next half a mile, which was mostly uphill, we were both quiet. Despite the early spring chill, there were signs of life all around. Among the patches of green, some brave plants were emerging, and quite a few squirrels, birds, and rabbits could be seen foraging in the wooded area to the left of the trail. I inhaled the invigorating cool air.

"Walk break? Run feels good, but those hills are brutal today."

"Sure," he said, slowing to a walk. "That's probably because we were running two miles per hour faster than usual, Vivi."

"That fast?" I asked between heavy breaths. "Well, that explains it. I didn't realize ... It's just such a beautiful morning, isn't it?"

He nodded, a look of contentment on his face. "I know just what you mean."

"You always do," I said, my eyes bright.

Our eyes met, and we both smiled before returning to gaze at our peaceful surroundings.

After nearly two minutes of walking, we resumed running, and I decided to venture into riskier conversation territory, if nothing else to amuse myself for the next few miles. "So Jack, did Irene go easy on you Saturday night, or did your 'work call' take up most of the night?" I kept my tone light and glanced over, expecting to see him stiffen, but his expression was still open and friendly.

As Jack opened his mouth to reply, a deep, cultured voice called out behind us.

"Hello, Viviana. Jack," said Gregory as he ran up alongside us and then slowed to match our pace. He wasn't even out of breath, though he must have run quite a bit faster to have caught us from out of nowhere.

When I stole a glance at Jack, he was grimacing. Whether it was Gregory's appearance or the mention of Irene, I wasn't sure, but it could be both.

"Dr. Fitzgerald! We didn't expect to see you out here this morning." I offered a hesitant smile in his direction.

"I have found this trail surprisingly suitable for both the running and biking arms of my training, so I will likely be frequenting it more often," Gregory replied.

Who uses words like "frequenting" in everyday speech?

"Ah. It's nice to see another soul outside this early on a Monday morning." When Gregory didn't reply, I added, "We're here earlier than usual, since Jack has a work engagement later this morning."

Jack, who had been looking off in the other direction, chose this moment to chime in, "Yes, I do have that lunch meeting. In fact, I ... if you don't mind, I'll just leave you two to finish the miles, as I actually need to go prep for that meeting."

I turned toward Jack in surprise, my eyes narrowing. "I didn't realize you were in a hurry."

"Yes, unfortunately. I'll catch up with you later," Jack said with a smile that didn't reach his eyes. He nodded to Gregory and turned to follow a narrow offshoot of the trail that I knew from experience would return him home more quickly.

Gregory didn't speak at first, so I was left alone with my thoughts as we ran. What had gotten into Jack? The casual comment about Irene was probably unwise. Something was obviously going on there, and for whatever reason, he was uncomfortable and edgy about it. His odd behavior was all the more noticeable because Jack was never uncomfortable and edgy; he was the most even-tempered person I knew. I supposed an office romance (or whatever it was) would start to become extra complicated when one person was the boss. In fact, he and Irene had been merely colleagues of a similar rank until a few months ago, when she had assumed the managing editor role and he became one of her direct reports. I was uncertain whether their relationship (or whatever it was) had begun before or after that, since Jack had rarely spoken of her. When we met, Irene had always narrowed her piercing eyes at me in ways that made me feel vaguely uncomfortable or at least inferior, for reasons I couldn't understand. His boss was certainly an unusual woman, much more demanding and self-assured than most women even higher up the ladder, and I was never quite sure whether to admire her or despise her.

Or perhaps something less dramatic, I thought with a chuckle.

Maybe I'd grant Jack some space with his Irene problem (or whatever it was). If the problem were important enough, surely he would share it with me. Or so I told myself.

As we rounded a curve, I squinted as the sun shone on my eyes and realized that we'd been running together for several minutes without speaking. Why on earth was I thinking about Jack when I had my very own Mr. Darcy right next to me? "Sorry, I was lost in my thoughts for a bit there." I offered an apologetic smile, though he was looking straight ahead.

"You need not apologize. I prefer running in silence."

"Oh ... OK."

How could I respond to that? Why did he want to run with me then? Jack and I talked a great deal during our training runs; it was the benefit of having a running partner to endure through the long miles. Though I could also be comfortably silent with Jack. At least until recently. I frowned, trying to recall when or why this slight tension had arisen between us. It was useless to deny that something was off lately.

I shook my head to clear my thoughts and looked at Gregory, unsure what to say.

"We can converse, if you prefer that," Gregory said, his tone stiff, his eyes still on the ground directly a few paces ahead of him.

He was so oddly formal sometimes, but maybe that wasn't a bad thing. It was definitely more Darcy-like.

After a moment, I responded, "I'm pretty flexible. But I would like to hear more about what you're doing in town with Brandon. Actually, I know very little about your history together."

"Our history?" He glanced at me finally, his brow furrowed as though I'd asked a difficult question.

"You know, as friends. How did you become friends?"

"We met at a conference in San Francisco." Gregory paused for a moment, which was unusual for him. He was usually so confident in speaking that he seemingly had no reason to think before he spoke. "I cannot recall why we became friends, though we had mutual business acquaintances. He lived in New York for quite some time, which is where we forged a closer connection."

"You mean a closer friendship, right? You guys are friends, not just business acquaintances, right?" I gazed at him, pondering his mysterious words.

"Yes, I consider him both a friend and a business associate in a manner that has been mutually beneficial, though I suspect he benefits more from the connection," he said, as though it were a business transaction and he the superior partner.

How could I follow that bizarre comment? "So, what do you guys like to do in your free time, when you're not working?"

"I spend a considerable amount of time training, especially lately, with the triathlon date approaching."

"And what else? When you're not working or working out?"

"There is not a great deal of time outside of those pursuits."

"What about travel, parties, *fun*? There must be some fabulous parties in publishing, in *New York* and all the many inspiring places you travel to," I said, growing animated. He did not strike me as an avid partygoer—nor was I—but I hoped my questions would lend more insight into who this mysterious man was when he *wasn't* Dr. Fitzgerald in publishing.

"Yes, such things occur," he said, again with a mysterious pause. He glanced at me for a moment, his face unreadable. "I suppose I enjoy them as much as any man in my position."

I raised my eyebrows, as it was hard to imagine Gregory truly enjoying anything. Even in a jacuzzi, he'd been attached to his cell phone and barely interested in socializing at all. He might see himself as far above the likes of me and Annie, but surely even he could not be completely immune to the appeal of alcohol and women.

Unless—oh no! Is he gay? Why didn't I consider that? It would be just my luck.

I frowned. How could I find out? Or would that be considered rude? I remained quiet for a few moments, trying to determine how to subtly confirm or disconfirm this new possibility. Ultimately, I decided to just be direct(ish). Running long miles with someone often had a way of breaking down the usual barriers.

"Are you seeing anyone?" I hastily added, "I just wondered because it must be difficult when you travel and work so much."

"I am not. It is indeed difficult," he admitted.

"Not impossible though?"

"No, certainly not. I do not require a serious relationship at the moment. I have many years still to produce an heir."

I burst out laughing before managing to contain my mirth, not wanting to offend him. "Has anyone ever told you that you sometimes sound like you came out of the pages of a nineteenth-century novel?"

He seemed at a loss for how to respond. His voice sounded strained when he finally said, "No, you are the first."

"Oh, I mean no offense. I'm a great fan of Regency and Victorian novels myself," I reassured him. "I just haven't heard anyone speak of *producing an heir* for a long time, or maybe ever, outside the pages of a book."

"Well, I do read widely, so perhaps I have acquired some of the affectations of the works of literature I have read."

"That makes sense, actually." I was dying to ask if he was a reader and/or lover of Austen or perhaps Bronte, but I was also afraid of his answer. If he said no, it would likely break my heart, though it wouldn't be surprising. And if he said yes ... I wasn't ready to think about what that could mean. Instead, I continued my previous line of questioning. "So, no women waiting for you back home?" I asked. "Or perhaps men?"

"No women that I know of and certainly no men," he said, still no trace of emotion in his words.

So, he was indeed interested in women—though no one in particular.

"How about your family, back in New York, I imagine?" I hoped my innocent-sounding question would lead him to confide about his sister's death. I didn't want to pry, but I *had* to. I needed to learn more, to know *why* he was the way he was. To understand Mr. Darcy.

"Yes, they have a residence in New York, among other places."

Multiple homes ... how rich is his family?

"Uh, what are your parents like? Any—" I stopped before saying "siblings," watching the muscles in his jaw tighten.

He finally replied in a tone that was curiously dispassionate, given the subject. "Typical Asian parents with high expectations and obsession with reputation, I suppose."

I wondered how those expectations might have influenced his life, his personality, his disdain for most people and things. He interrupted my thoughts, however, reminding me that we were almost finished with our loop. "I will be heading to the pool after this. Perhaps we can run together in the future." His intonation suggested this was more of a statement than a question, but he did look at me as though awaiting an answer.

I scrambled to respond. "Uh. Sure! It was fun getting to know you a bit, Gregory," I said with as much enthusiasm as I could muster. "Er, Dr. Fitzgerald. Do you really prefer such a formal name?"

He didn't reply initially but slowed his pace to a fast walk. Had he heard me? Finally, he looked at me directly, frowned, and said, "I see nothing wrong with using formal names." He paused as his brows furrowed in concentration. "If it is simply too difficult for you to address me formally, you may call me Gregory, but never Greg."

"Right, you ... you don't seem like the nickname sort."

He said nothing as we reached a small parking area. I stopped and began to stretch my calves, assuming he would halt as well. Instead, he stepped off the trail and started toward what I assumed was a rental car, sleek black and parked at a distance from the few other cars in the area.

"Have fun swimming," I called out, hating the desperate edge in my voice.

Really? That was the best I could think of?

As he walked away, I couldn't stop staring at his muscled, dark legs while I stretched my quads.

He paused abruptly and turned. "Thank you." I diverted my glance quickly from his lower half to his expressionless face before he continued on his way.

I sighed. Could one reasonably expect any more from him? He *had* opened up a fair amount today, and just the fact that he showed up had to mean something, didn't it? Gregory Fitzgerald wouldn't condescend to spend his time with just anyone. He must have taken *some* liking to me—whether on a friendly or romantic level, I couldn't tell. His arrogance, at least, seemed to be fading a bit as he spoke to me more like a person than someone *or something* far beneath him. Didn't Mr. Darcy undergo the same transformation? I smiled, shivering with excitement—or perhaps from the cool wind, as I was no longer running but standing still in a triceps stretch.

I gazed up at the sky, where the sun journeyed ever higher amidst only a few small clouds. Smiling at the slight warmth of the sun on my face, I felt the butterflies in my stomach and realized I was truly excited about this would-be love story. Giddy even. Especially when I allowed myself to dream, to imagine *what if?* and to let my heart feel what it would feel.

Upon finishing my usual stretches, I retrieved my empty water bottle from the ground and immediately tripped over an exposed tree root, twisting to land on my bottom on the cold, damp ground.

Instead of cursing and rising from the ground though, I arranged my legs more comfortably on the ground and took a deep breath of the still frosty air, admiring the budding spring scene around me. I rarely stopped thinking and planning and doing to simply enjoy a beautiful day.

That changes today.

Chapter 12

Upon returning home a while later, shivering from the cold, I encountered Jack in the small lobby of our building. I flashed him a smile, still feeling invigorated yet content from my morning interlude.

"Hi, Vivi, I'm just heading out for the meeting."

"You left so abruptly," I observed, my brow wrinkled in concern. "Is everything all right?"

"Of course, everything's fine." He looked away for a moment and then back to me. "I just had a lot to do and ... well, yes, I needed to prep for the meeting. Vivi, come away from the door. You look frozen!"

I put my hands on my hips, ignoring his concern. "Is that all? You hadn't said a word about needing to leave early until Gregory showed up."

"Didn't I? Well, I probably should have, but I know you prefer not to run alone. Dr. Fitz solved that problem," he said, giving me a half-smile.

I met his eyes steadily, waiting for what I knew was to come.

"And honestly ..." He paused, with a slightly pained expression on his face. "I just don't like the guy. Sorry, Vivi. I know you *do* like him, but I'd rather not ... spend my time in his presence." Trust Jack to lay it out for me simply and factually, but never hurtfully. At least not intentionally.

I sighed, leaning back against the door frame. Unsurprised, I couldn't really blame Jack. Gregory was ... well, I didn't know what he was. "That's not really surprising. But I wondered if I said something wrong—if there was anything else bothering you."

"No."

I gazed into his blue-grey eyes intently. "Seriously, you can tell me if I overstepped with the comment about Irene. I was just teasing." It was risky to bring up her name again, but I simply had to clear the air.

To my relief, he chuckled. "We've known each other for how many years now? This is me, Vivi. You can say whatever you want to me." He sighed, looking at the checkered tile design on the floor before raising his eyes to mine. "I just don't want to talk about Irene because, well, I spend enough time dealing with Irene issues that I'd rather not *also* spend time talking about them. Does that make sense?"

It *did* make sense on some level, though it's certainly not how *I* would handle "issues" I was having with a person. For that matter, I still had no idea what the issues with Irene were. I had my guesses, of course.

Before I could probe further, Jack gently placed a warm hand on my chilled arm. "Vivi, I have to head out. We can talk later if you'd like. Go upstairs and warm up, will you?"

As he left me standing in the lobby, I stared after him. What were these issues he alluded to, and why was he so reluctant to talk about them? Still, I knew ... I'd do what I always did, allowing him to have his secrets and just being available to talk if he wished. A dull ache lodged in my chest. His confession that he didn't like Gregory was more than a little unsettling, even though I couldn't blame him at all. That, I knew, made no sense.

I shook my head slightly to clear my thoughts as I turned to head upstairs, my calf muscle aching slightly as I walked. My thoughts abruptly turned to *Gregory's* athletic calves.

Now there's something more fun to think about, now that we're actually talking and his Darcy layers are unraveling. Can layers unravel? Unlayer?

I winced before succumbing to self-deprecating laughter. And I was supposedly becoming a writer? Yet I couldn't wait to further unlayer my leading man.

Early that evening, I encountered Jack again while returning home. "Vivi, it's you again. Just getting back?" he asked with a smile.

"Yeah. I'm just getting back and probably going to make dinner." I pointed to the shopping bag I was holding.

"Want some company?" he asked in his usual even tone. "Would you believe I finally have a free evening—"

"Oh, no thanks. I need 'me time.' You enjoy your night though." I gave him a perfunctory smile while starting to walk past him.

"Vivi, are you OK?"

I turned back quickly with what I hoped was a reassuring smile, avoiding his discerning eyes. "I'm fine! Enjoy your night, Jack."

"Ah—OK," he said, frowning slightly. "I'll see you around then."

While walking upstairs, I felt a twinge of guilt but quickened my steps. Although hurt by Jack's recent behavior, objectively speaking, I had no right to be upset with him, so it would be useless to try to explain why I was. *If* I was. And I wasn't lying—I did need some time to myself, though not at home. Despite being a certified homebody, I occasionally felt a strong need to get out, alone, to go outside or to some public place where I could be anonymous. One of my favorite outings was to visit Bookshop, one of the few remaining local bookstores on my side of the city. Bookshop was a book lover's dream, full of not only books but cozy nooks in which to read and escape.

After the outing, I lugged my bag of new books that was far too heavy and far too expensive over to my couch, where I planned to happily sift through my new treasures as soon as I found something to satisfy my growling stomach. As I strolled to the kitchen, my phone vibrated in my pocket.

Annie

Viv, please tell me you're not going to be a homebody all this week

Viviana

Depends on what my choices are :)

Annie

You, me, two rich hotties, and the hottest new restaurant in St. Paul!

Viviana

That or my boring apartment? Hmm …

Annie

It shouldn't be a hard choice

Viviana

I'll think about it and let you know

Annie

Srsly??

Viviana

No. I'll be there. ;) Friday night?

Absently putting the phone down next to me, I grinned sheepishly. I hadn't even hesitated about saying yes to Annie. After all, things with Gregory were becoming more promising. I could even *call* him Gregory, he had conceded, albeit reluctantly.

Feeling a surge of inspiration, I decided to write.

Janice walked her out, complaining all the way about her latest row with Carl. As they neared the exit, the doors opened, and in walked Fitz and Charles. Janice instantly perked up.

"Fitz, Charlie, we were just talking about you!"

Liz looked at her with narrowed eyes but decided not to question the lie.

"All good, I hope. Good morning, ladies," Charles said with a smile, nudging Fitz.

"Good morning."

As Janice made chitchat with them, well, with Charles, Liz looked down at her watch, seeing Fitz doing the same.

"I need to head out for a run before it becomes too sweltering out there," Liz said, fanning her face. Like an idiot. Everyone in this conversation knew what it meant to be hot outside, right? She shook her head.

Janice turned to Fitz and opened her mouth, but before she could speak, he said, "Elizabeth, right?"

Pursing her lips, she nodded. As if he didn't know her name by now!

"Elizabeth, would you like to run with me? I am eager to start today's training run too, as it happens."

She hardly knew what to say, so shocked she was. She simply nodded, and he followed her outside as Janice shouted after her to text her later.

They agreed to meet by the trail in 20 minutes. She was already in her running clothes, but he needed to change at his hotel, which was just a block away from the office. As she waited, she decided to do a light warmup lap, not wanting to get too sweaty but also not wanting to start the run feeling achy and stiff.

When he joined her, the pace was a bit faster than was typically comfortable for her, but she managed to keep up. She started making conversation, first chatting inanely about the weather and then asking him about his plans for the upcoming holiday.

"Elizabeth, I am British. I do not celebrate July 4th."

She died a little inside. "Of course, how silly of me."

"Do you talk by rule, then, while you are running?"

She looked at him then, feeling a shiver for a reason she couldn't name. "I, uh ..." She shook her head to clear the feeling. "I suppose I do. One must speak a little, you know."

As I reclined against the nearly flat desk chair cushion, I reflected on the Austen quotes I snuck in. How satisfying to combine my old love of Austen with my new love of writing—and even running. Today, the words were just flowing out of me, and it was glorious. But before I could return to my writing, my phone buzzed.

Jack

Hey, I hope you're OK. Sorry for ditching you on the run.

Viviana

It's fine, really. I get it.

Jack

Lunch tomorrow? Make it up to you?

I mean, on Wednesday? Big deadline tomorrow.

My stomach growled. *What? How did I forget to eat?*

Viviana

You don't have to make up anything, but sure. Your treat? :)

Jack

Of course. See you around noon Wed.?

Viviana

Sure.

Most likely, I was being overly sensitive, and Jack was just being Jack, right? But I didn't feel like analyzing it further. I had a story to write (and to live!), and a minor disagreement with a friend did not fit into that story. Or did it? Perhaps Jack was Charlotte Lucas. Oh, that was a little unflattering. I cringed and then chuckled.

But where the bonnet fits, right?

Chapter 13

At the Krumkake Café with Jack, I felt at ease once again. We were chatting amiably and getting along famously, as we always did, without a hint of the tension from the past few days. That is, until Irene herself entered the café. A short, thin woman with unassuming short brown hair, she somehow commanded attention wherever she went. When Irene's steel-grey eyes landed on us, she proceeded to stare while waiting in line to order. I forced a polite smile, and Jack waved and smiled—also forced, or so I preferred to think.

After placing her order, Irene walked briskly over to our table, her very high heels clicking on the tiled floor. She nodded curtly to me before addressing Jack. "Jack. You didn't reply to my email this morning."

"The email you just sent a half hour ago? I've been having lunch with a friend, Irene, as you can see," Jack said, lightly gesturing toward me.

Glancing at me, she was about to speak but then apparently thought better of it, setting her lips in a firm line as she turned her steely eyes to Jack again. "I see."

"I'll get back to you this afternoon, Irene. I know it's an important project," he said calmly, with an easy smile.

"I'm glad you recognize that. I look forward to your reply when you've finished your *lunch with a friend*," Irene said, putting a strange emphasis on the words. She abruptly pivoted and returned to the front counter to await her takeout order.

I let out a slow breath. After Irene was out of hearing distance, I hissed, "Oh my, she is tightly wound! And more than a little demanding. Is she always like that, or is it the stress of the big project?"

Jack sighed, running his hand through his neatly styled brown hair, a gesture I rarely saw from him, only when he was particularly stressed or frustrated. "A little of both, I'd say."

"How do you cope with it? I can't imagine having such a demanding boss." I shook my head and bit into my sandwich. Unlike Irene, my demanding boss was usually also supportive and not socially inept.

Jack appeared to be carefully considering his next words while gathering the last bits of salad onto his fork. "It's complicated."

For some reason, I pressed on. "How so?"

"It's hard to explain. She has a lot on her plate," he said slowly. "She means well, mostly. And she's been through a great deal in her career. It hasn't been easy for her."

I sighed, knowing it was pointless to ask for more details, as Jack wouldn't betray a friend, or boss, or whatever she was.

Or lover. Ugh, hopefully not.

"Well, I hope you're all right. I hope she's not stressing you out too much."

"I'm fine. I can certainly handle Irene," he said, putting his fork down and sipping his ice water. "Do you want to get scones, or shall we pass on dessert today?"

I opened my mouth in mock horror. "Skip the scones? Are you crazy?"

His head rolled back with laughter. "Right, that's why you love this place. Well then, I have my answer."

My mouth curved into a wide grin. My Jack was back. His easy smile, his laugh, his steadying force in my life—I didn't realize how much I depended on those things until they were in short supply. I wondered vaguely what Irene was attracted to. Jack was surely attractive in a number of ways, but Irene was an unusual woman; it was hard to imagine that she could really appreciate all of Jack's great qualities as a friend, as a writer. It was even harder to imagine that their relationship could be primarily a physical attraction. Though he was an objectively attractive man, that would hardly be enough for a woman like Irene. Or perhaps she was just the sort to take advantage of her position with a younger direct report.

I shook my head slightly. This was none of my business, unless he chose to confide in me, and I only wanted him to be happy after all. Being happy with someone as inherently *unhappy* as Irene seemed like an oxymoron at best, an impossibility at worst. Still, I could and would be a supportive friend. Jack had certainly done the same for me many times, and even though he disliked Gregory, he would support me. Heck, Jack would probably even find something to *like* about Gregory if it meant that much to me.

At the counter, we chatted with Melanie and debated which types of scones to buy and how many. In the end, we purchased too many and proceeded to devour one together on the short walk home. "I'm glad we did this today, Jack. It was nice. It *is* nice, and even the weather is agreeing with us today," I said warmly, leaning over and biting from the scone at the same time he did, our faces very nearly colliding. My breath caught as we both backed up a bit.

Enough of this unnecessary awkwardness. Maybe we could … embrace it.

I giggled and snagged the first bite. "Mmmm. I'm sorry if I've been weird lately or put you in weird situations or whatever."

He paused in his stride and turned toward me, his arms pulling me into a quick embrace. He backed up and then stopped and held me at arm's length while looking into my eyes searchingly. "No need to apologize. It's me, Jack. I've been dealing with your weirdness for more years than I can remember."

I crossed my arms with a look of mock outrage.

The corners of his mouth twitched while his eyes twinkled. "All right, I suppose you've been dealing with mine too."

"That's more like it," I said, nudging him with my elbow as we resumed walking. "Well, I hope the rest of your day is better, and hopefully that urgent email isn't as earth-shattering as Irene made it sound."

His smile wavered for just a second, and then he laughed. "So do I, Vivi. So do I."

Chapter 14

The days passed quickly, and Friday morning was soon upon me. When Ellen canceled the weekly copyeditors' meeting because half the staff was ill, I was ecstatic at first. I would be free to spend much of the day getting ready for tonight's dinner! But my smile slipped as I realized that waiting *all day* for this double date to start—and for the pre-date nerves to dissipate—was likely to drive my nerves sky high in the meantime.

I needed someone to talk to or distract me. Jack wouldn't understand.

From the comfort of my couch, I first tried calling Annie but reached voicemail. I texted Jenn, not expecting a response but receiving one almost immediately. Apparently the children were napping, and this was Jenn's chance for "mom time"—usually time for cleaning, but Jenn was determined to make an exception today to hear all the delicious details of my life.

After thoroughly filling Jenn in on my situation, I waited for the verdict, biting a nail on my free hand before stopping myself. Another bad habit I did not need.

"Viv, this is *perfect*. I don't even need to pick up a novel. I can just follow your life! Oh, I can't tell you how happy this makes me."

I laughed nervously. "Thanks, I think?"

"No, thank *you*."

I paused, trying to decide how to probe further. "Am I being an idiot? I mean, how bad is this?"

Jenn burst out laughing. "Oh darn, I really need to be quieter; I don't want anyone waking up and denying me this absolute *joy*."

"Jenn ..."

"Sorry, Viv. It's just, well, I needed this today. Let's leave it at that." She paused. "Are you being an idiot? Well, maybe."

"What? You—"

"But *who cares*!" Jenn caught herself again and lowered her voice. "Aren't we all idiots in love? I mean, sometimes it doesn't work out and then we're left with sorrow and still being an idiot. But sometimes we end up really, really happy."

I laughed. "Look at you, right?"

"Viv, sorry to cut this short, because I am loving this. But I need a few quiet minutes to sink my teeth into some heavenly mini-cheese-cake bites before the kiddos wake. Swear you'll keep me posted?"

After ending the call, I grabbed my laptop and sank into the couch, deciding to write in comfort for once. I had some secondary characters to bring to life.

Fitz watched through heavy-lidded eyes as Liz walked away past the bar.

"I can imagine what you're thinking. This place is so tiresome," said Caroline Bingley, interrupting his reverie as she sauntered up to him and placed well-manicured fingers on his forearm. "Let's get out of here."

He pried her fingers from his arm, frowning. "No, I wasn't thinking of leaving yet. In fact, I was admiring a woman's beautiful form, her fine eyes in particular."

Caroline's eyes widened in a practiced look. "Fitz, you've never spoken quite so—"

"Her name is Elizabeth."

"Liz Bennet? You—you are interested in her?" she sputtered. "How long has this been going on? I suppose I should offer best wishes."

"It's a bit premature for that," he said dryly, finally looking at her for a moment. "But what do you know about her connection with that Wickham man?"

Caroline's lips curved up slightly, and she looped her arm through his. "Fitz, love, let's go out to the patio. I need some air." She smiled flirtatiously at him. "And I'll tell you what I know about her and Wickham."

I awoke with a start. My cortisol rising sharply, I glanced at the clock. Why hadn't my alarm gone off? After a three-hour nap, I was left with only one hour before I had to leave for the restaurant, and despite being a bit rusty in the dating department, I remembered that my pre–first date routine usually took a full two hours.

Frantic, I skipped my usual post-nap rituals, such as getting coffee or checking my phone and email, and instead headed to the shower. Fortunately, I'd laid out two possible date outfits earlier in the day, so that would help shave time off my normal getting-ready routine. Speaking of shaving, I'd better do that too if I didn't want him to immediately be horrified and leave. Personal grooming was easily neglected when one worked from home, or so I always rationalized to myself.

Only an hour later, I left my apartment in a rush, dashing down to the parking garage and nearly tripping in my heels, which were still stiff from lack of use. Maybe running late was a good thing. I didn't have time to get nervous. I started my car and sighed.

Who was I kidding? I was obviously nervous, but imagine being late for the *real* Mr. Darcy—surely I could handle *this*.

At any other time, I might have cringed, but in my current excitement, I smiled. I was allowing myself to think unabashedly romantic thoughts, even referring to Gregory as Mr. Darcy. Throwing caution to the wind was something I rarely did, especially in my love life but also, I had to admit, in many other areas.

Arriving at the new restaurant, Shipsvold, I smiled, some of my nerves having been eased by my romantic fantasies on the way there. From the parking lot, the place looked small but cozy, with lights strung around the eaves. I'd heard this place started as a pop-up restaurant by some chef who'd been inspired by an actual small town in southern Minnesota, but I wasn't sure if the rumors were true.

Before I could open one of the fashionably tinted doors to enter, two smartly dressed hosts opened them for me. Forgetting to thank them, I marveled at the atmosphere of the restaurant assailing my senses. The decor was a combination of rich, dark blues and varying shades of grey, white, and black amid a lighting scheme and ambience that seemed somehow both formal and romantic simultaneously. I might have to rethink my aversion to blue and grey decor. Instead of food, I smelled the expensive perfume of some expensively dressed guests nearby, whose melodic foreign words I could not understand, as they surely weren't in English.

Eyeing the hostess behind a desk, I quickly looked down at my own outfit, an emerald green dress that was certainly not expensive but did look amazing on me. Confidence wasn't exactly my strong suit, typically, but I held my head up and walked toward the hostess to announce my presence. The hostess, looking bored, gave me a once-over and then led me to a secluded table, where Gregory was waiting.

As he looked down at his phone, I fully indulged in staring at him for a few moments, drinking in every delicious detail. He was a stunningly gorgeous man, his smooth dark skin showing no sign of aging though he was probably at least mid-30s. His glossy hair was the darkest brown, not quite black, and I could easily imagine running my hands through it. He wasn't even looking at me, yet the dim blue and grey lighting made him somehow even more impossibly handsome, even elegant.

I cleared my throat before greeting him with a bright smile and sliding into the round booth, partially secluded from the other diners by a curtain half drawn.

Gregory said hello with just the briefest of glances as he continued to type on his phone. My smile faltered as I waited for him to fully acknowledge me.

Please don't ruin this, please don't ruin this.

I wasn't sure whether the plea should be directed toward him or toward myself.

When he finally looked up, I was treated to a brief look of surprise in his dark eyes as they swept over me. It wasn't the look of unguarded lust that I remembered from the hotel, but I was fairly confident he liked what he saw. I bit my lip to suppress a triumphant smile.

"Hello, uh, Viviana," he said, pausing to clear his throat. "I was not certain whether you would be arriving. You did not reply to my message."

"What message?" I asked, tilting my head in confusion. "Oh, actually I haven't checked my phone in a while. Things were a little hectic at home—" I pressed my lips together, fearing I could be admitting too much. I'd obviously had time to make myself look amazing, yet not enough time to check my phone? I shook my head with a slight smile.

"I merely asked if we should postpone," he said, sounding a bit irritable.

"Oh ..." My smile faded as my eyes scanned the area. "Why? Where are Annie and Brandon?"

He sighed. "You truly haven't checked your messages. Evidently, they are delayed and would meet us later at the hotel. They said they would inform you hours ago, but because she had not heard from you, Annie suggested I show up and make sure you would not arrive and find yourself alone."

Stunned, I opened my mouth to speak, but no words came. I *never* missed checking my phone. But I'd been so rushed. Getting ready for the date was far more important than checking my phone, which rarely held any urgent message. Honestly, I'd been terrible about not checking and replying to messages lately.

Darn, I still needed to read and reply to Lillian's texts. I made a mental note to call my sister this weekend. I wasn't ready to talk about the cursed Italy thing yet, but I was experienced at shutting down certain topics with my sister.

His jaw muscles tense, he said, "We needn't stay. We can indeed cancel and go home. I actually have a great deal to—"

"No, let's stay," I interrupted. "Ah, I mean, if you want to. That is, well, I ... we ... we could eat."

He was silent at first, as if thinking carefully about his answer. "Are you certain? Do you not have work to do?"

"It's Friday night; I can take the night off. Or at least a couple hours, or you know, however long this takes. That is, if you want to," I added nervously, searching his face for signs of interest.

His eyes veered toward his phone briefly and then rose to my anxious face. "Fine, we shall stay for dinner," he said evenly. "Let me just conclude this email briefly."

I placed my purse on the seat next to me and waited patiently, figuring it was only courteous to do so, given that I'd interrupted his email writing when I arrived at the table. My fingers itched to unlock my own phone and frantically text Annie, demanding an explanation, but I assumed my friend wouldn't answer. This was obviously a setup. Annie was encased in luxury at the Four Seasons, having a good laugh at my expense and probably some wild sex in a Jacuzzi or whatever one does with a lover in a ritzy hotel.

After several minutes, the server, an older but impeccably dressed man, approached the table. With a mild look of annoyance toward Gregory, who was still on his phone, I turned to greet the waiter and ordered chardonnay. The infuriating man chose that moment to finally glance up from his phone, only to order a mineral water.

What an odd choice. Mineral water is gross at any time, but it's certainly unusual for a date.

The waiter placed one small menu carefully on the table, nodded briefly, and walked away. I took a deep breath and forced a smile as Gregory began studying the menu. "Apparently we have to share the menu," I offered. When he didn't reply or even acknowledge me with eye contact, I asked, a bit louder, "So, Gregory, how was your day?"

"My day?" As his eyes landed on me, he tilted his head slightly as if confused. "It was perfectly fine. I accomplished many things, and indeed, the day is not finished. Why do you ask?"

I flinched and sat straighter, my defenses rising. "Well, I don't know. Call me crazy, but I believe it's a social nicety to ask about someone's day. Is it not?"

"I wouldn't know."

"What do you mean you wouldn't know? You don't observe social niceties?"

"I have better things to spend my time and my thoughts on, Viviana," he said, not without condescension. At my silence, he sighed and added, "I suppose I do on some level. Don't we all? But it's not something I actively think about. If I want to know about someone's day, I ask, but typically I don't find that particular information enlightening. The most common reply is merely 'good,' and when it is not, well, the answer still has little relevance to me. In either case, I would regret having asked. Of course, a strategic client meeting might necessitate greater attention to such niceties, as you call them."

I stared at Gregory as the elderly waiter placed our drinks on the table, and then I burst into laughter.

"Something amusing?"

"Yes, I find you ..." I trailed off. "You're different. I'm not sure bluntness is always a good thing, but it can certainly be refreshing at times. Or amusing, I suppose."

"How so?"

"Like that." I took a sip of wine. "Your response there was merely intended to be polite, a common courtesy if you will. You're not that interested in my answer, yet you still made an effort, albeit a minimal one, to pretend to be."

"Indeed." His phone forgotten for the moment, he met my gaze with a sort of reluctant curiosity, clearly unused to discussing his social skills or being assessed so frankly.

"I confess I'm not enamored with small talk either, so I suppose that's why I find your view refreshing, if occasionally a bit too blunt for my taste." I laughed, relaxing against the back of the booth. "How's that for bluntness? See, you're rubbing off on me."

He eyed me silently for a moment, his expression giving away none of his feelings, before glancing at the waiter returning to our table. "I am surprised, as you seem to have a particular fondness for 'small talk,' as you call it."

As I opened my mouth to reply, the waiter cleared his throat impatiently and asked if we were ready to order. Gregory turned to ask a question about the menu, so I used the opportunity to stare at him. Somehow I was actually enjoying the conversation and beginning to relax a bit. As he placed his order, I smiled, eagerly awaiting more conversation.

The server looked at me with barely veiled impatience. "Oh, sorry. I haven't actually looked at the menu yet." I saw that Gregory had set the single menu back in the middle of the table instead of handing it to me. He wasn't very gallant, I confirmed.

"What will you have, ma'am?" The server was definitely irritated now, his lips a thin line and his eyes the same steely grey as his hair.

"I will have ..." I scanned quickly. I didn't recognize the names of many menu items, so I merely pointed at one in the middle. "That. I'll have that."

Without a word, the server clasped the menu and spun on his heel, apparently having given up all pretense of courtesy.

"Can you believe that man?" My brow furrowed as I turned to Gregory.

He looked up slowly from his phone. "Sorry, what?"

I glared at him. "Never mind."

And just like that, he returned his attention to his phone. For. A. Long. Time.

My newfound optimism faded quickly. I couldn't keep up with his changing nature and at times blatant rudeness.

When our dinner arrived, the intimidating server was nowhere in sight. I breathed a sigh of relief. Gregory simply set his phone on the table near his plate and arranged his napkin carefully in his lap.

Finally breaking the tense silence, I tried to ask about his culinary tastes, fully knowing that this sort of small talk would not endear me to him. But what else could I do? He essentially ignored my feeble attempts, instead dividing his attention between his food and his phone. A cursory glance or a one-word answer here and there was apparently all I would get from him tonight.

But I couldn't help staring. He was so ... masculine. Both intellectual and sexy. And beyond frustrating. I didn't know how to feel. His rudeness was so infuriating, even shocking, that I couldn't even enjoy my new surroundings or the delicious food. But still—

Gregory abruptly set his utensils down and made eye contact—the first time he'd done so for more than a split second all night. My hopes began to rise until he initiated another round of questioning about my family life.

At this point in the evening though, the hot and cold, the abrupt changes, barely phased me. Fortunately, the second glass of chardonnay had begun to take the edge off, and I stopped caring after a while. I just wanted this miserable experience to be over.

Thank you, wine.

I glumly picked at my food and mumbled short replies to his questions about my parents and my sister. As soon as I mentioned that Mom and Lillian were scientists, he changed the subject again.

Does my leading man have a problem with women scientists? Is he a raging sexist?

No, surely not.

The haughty server returned once we'd finished our dinner, and he spoke only to Gregory, who promptly declined dessert on behalf of us both and requested the checks. Two checks. I shouldn't have been surprised at that point, but it still stung. Embarrassed, I avoided eye contact with the server. And declining dessert without even asking me! Jack would *never* make that mistake.

I furrowed my brows at the thought. How was that relevant? Jack was a friend, not a dating prospect.

Moments later, when we'd paid both bills, I stood up to leave abruptly, not trusting myself to remain calm in this intolerable atmosphere any longer. But then he looked at me—actually *looked* at me. His dark, heavy-lidded eyes swept up and down until resting on my face, with a look conveying something like ... *feeling*. And before I knew it, he was standing up too and placing his phone in his pocket to help me put my coat on, his fingertips lingering at my shoulders.

And just like that, he quickly removed his hands, as well as his eyes and his attention. "I will walk you to your car," he said simply as he turned and headed briskly for the exit.

When we reached the exit door, I parted my lips to speak, but he spoke first.

"I hope you agree it was a pleasant meal. Goodnight, Viviana," he said formally—or stiffly, with no hint of the living, breathing man I'd briefly caught a glimpse of inside.

"Wait, Gregory—could you—I mean, would you give me a lift to the hotel?" I asked, wincing. "I'm just a tiny bit tipsy."

"To the hotel?" His eyes widened. "Why?"

I stared at him, realizing he must have misunderstood. "Not ... I mean, because Annie wanted us all to hang out after dinner, right?"

"I see." He exhaled slowly and nodded, presumably in the direction of his car, and then turned.

"Thanks," I mumbled and nearly stumbled in my heels while trying to keep up with his long strides.

A silent car ride and an hour later, I could scarcely enjoy the posh hotel bar and its mostly attractive (or at least rich) clientele. The decor was somehow both lavish and understated, and I felt out of place in such luxury. Mostly though, I was stewing with frustration, coupled with mild jealousy at how happy and carefree Annie and Brandon seemed to be. We scooted into their dimly lit booth in the corner of the bar. The plush ebony seat felt like sitting on a cloud, and I wanted to lean back against the cushy back. But relaxing around Gregory was proving difficult. He had hardly spoken to me, which of course was nothing new, but it still stung. Frowning, I had started to lose patience—and hope. Not for the first time, I asked myself why on earth I put myself through this. How was it even worth it?

Sensing the tension, Annie pulled me aside. "Are you OK? You don't seem to be having a lot of fun."

Fuming, I glowered at her. "I'm not. *He* has hardly said two words to me all night, and the restaurant wasn't much better. It's like he went on a date with his phone. And you guys are off in your own little bubble. Don't get me wrong—I'm really happy for you, but it leaves me stuck talking to this guy who, well, doesn't talk. I don't even know why I'm here ... I'm going to call for a ride."

"Viv, no, not yet!" Annie grabbed my shoulders and pleaded. "Please, give it one more chance. I promise I'll find a way to liven things up. Or to thaw him out."

I sighed, ready to go home but unable to resist her pleas. "Fine. Just for a bit."

As we returned to the men, Annie threw her arms up and loudly declared, "Drinking game!"

Both Gregory and I groaned, while Brandon grinned.

"This again? A drinking game? This isn't a solution," I hissed. "There's a reason we're not teenagers anymore, you know."

Annie smiled widely. "This one isn't for teenagers."

I narrowed my eyes. "Somehow that doesn't ease my mind."

"Relax, let's give it a try. But let's go up to your hotel suite, guys."

Looking doubtful, Gregory opened his mouth to protest but then simply sighed as he rose to his feet. He probably agreed to go upstairs to their rooms for the same reason I did: at least in their suite, we wouldn't make a fool out of ourselves in public.

An hour later, we were all at least slightly tipsy, if not intoxicated, lounging on the deck of the guys' spacious suite. Annie's drinking game seemed remarkably similar to Truth or Dare, but she claimed it was for adults. The twist was that drinking a shot was always an option to avoid the truth or dare; one way or another, everyone would be acting foolish by the end, I assumed. At first, I dodged any invasive questions and dares by taking shots, but as I gained liquid courage, I started to loosen up and choose questions or dares. Gregory seemed to be on a similar, if slower, trajectory.

I even deigned to answer Brandon's pointed question about what my ideal man looked like. Playing it safe, I described Firth's Darcy rather than making a fool of myself by describing Gregory. At least I hoped that's what I'd done—things were getting a bit hazy by that point.

Fortunately or not, the game didn't last much longer. Annie was announcing the start of a new round when Gregory suddenly pushed back his chair on the deck. "I really don't have time for this. I'm going to go inside and answer some emails."

Annie merely stuck out her lower lip and turned to Brandon with a giggle.

As Gregory started to walk away, I stared at him in disbelief and then muttered, "You're unbelievable."

He halted and turned around slowly, seemingly a bit disoriented. "I beg your pardon?"

"I think you heard me," I said, my lips set in a thin line.

"Indeed," he said, looking genuinely confused, "though I do not understand the statement."

I crossed my arms, despite knowing the gesture was immature. "Of course you don't."

Wide-eyed as she looked from me to Gregory and back, Annie rose from her seat and grasped Brandon's hand. "Come on, Brandon. I think we should go inside and let them have it out ... whatever this is."

Brandon grinned as he rose from the deck chair. "Yeah, let's. I'm sure we can find *something* to do by ourselves." Snickering, they went inside hand in hand.

After the sliding door was closed, Gregory spoke again, this time with a touch of impatience, crossing his muscled arms over his firm chest. "Explain. I don't have all night."

"Exactly this," I spit out, standing up to glare at him at eye level. "Mr. Self-Important, no, *Dr.* Self-Important, who doesn't have time for anyone, who is attached to his work emails day and night, who can't be bothered to be, um, *decent* to anyone, who thinks he is so far—"

"Enough." He put his hand up to silence me. "I see. I did not realize I was so intolerable to you."

"You didn't?" I glowered, resisting the urge to point a finger in his face. "Because I thought maybe you did. Your behavior towards me and, well, most people is so unbelievably rude that it almost has to be intentional. It's not like you don't *know* how to be polite, decent, *not an asshole* ... or else you wouldn't be as successful as you are. You just ... you just ... choose to be that way. Why, I can't understand. Your conceit, sir, knows no bounds."

As I scowled, he remained silent and stoic for a long moment. Suddenly his expression changed, becoming simultaneously more unreadable and more familiar. This was a Gregory I hadn't seen before.

Or maybe I have seen it … that night, the night of the look, the one that—

As my head spun, he suddenly clutched my shoulders tightly and brought his lips to mine. Intuitively, I swayed into him, and he responded by gripping my arms more tightly, almost painfully. The kiss was hard, fiery, *demanding*, and my response was yielding. The intensity was beyond expectations even in my most far-fetched Gregory fantasies.

This man knows how to kiss.

My fingers found their way into his dark, silky hair as he deepened the kiss. Was the room spinning because this was an amazing kiss or because I'd consumed too much alcohol? I didn't know or care. All I knew is that I *had* him. Gregory wanted me.

He wanted *me*.

This was a game-changer.

Abruptly, he tore his scorching lips from mine, his hands lingering on my shoulders for a split second before he let go and stepped back.

We stared at each other.

"I'm sorry," he said.

Still feeling a bit off balance, I gripped the back of a nearby deck chair to steady myself. My lips curved upward into a grin. "No need to apologize. For the kiss, that is. You can certainly apologize for everything before that though."

His eyes pierced mine before his face again became a mask, devoid of expression. "I will not apologize for what I am."

Brows furrowed, I looked at him and struggled for words. Interesting that he referred to himself as *what* rather than *who*. I took a deep breath, trying to sort out my thoughts. I was simultaneously giddy about the kiss *and* still irritated about his behavior both before and after the kiss.

Apparently assuming I had no more to say, he nodded to me—*nodded to me!*—and then turned to leave without a word. He didn't even look back as he slid the door shut.

Stunned, I stumbled back into the closest chair and stared at the closed door for several long moments. What just happened? I didn't know how to feel or what to think or ... anything.

Did this even happen? Maybe I was more drunk than I'd realized.

But my lips felt ... kissed. Explored. Sensitive, even. My hair was mussed. I hadn't imagined this. He had kissed me, inexplicably. But why? And then his disdain afterwards, what was that about? I couldn't even remember what I'd said to him.

When I finally decided to venture inside, I breathed a sigh of relief when it appeared that everyone had gone to their rooms. Realizing I couldn't drive home yet, I scanned the suite, spotting a deep red or maroon sofa on the far side of the main room. Sinking into its luxurious depths, I pondered my situation. The last thing I wanted to do was wake up tomorrow and face *him* or, worse yet, face the whole group. Yet calling a taxi seemed like a great deal of effort. As I looked around the lavishly furnished room, my eyes landed on a blanket near the sofa, and my decision was made. I'd snooze on the couch but set my alarm very early to avoid any awkward encounters in the morning. Given my muddled thoughts and feelings, they wouldn't want to see me like this—and the idea of seeing any of them, especially Gregory, was more than I could bear.

Chapter 15

I woke slowly, my eyelids heavy with grogginess and a dull pain in my head. I stretched my limbs, feeling stiff and sore everywhere. Oh, right: I'd slept on a couch for a few hours before coming home and collapsing into my own bed. I reached for my phone, a bad habit first thing in the morning, but ... it was better than thinking. I couldn't handle thinking right now.

The first thing I read was a text from Gregory, early this morning. The message wasn't shocking: He was canceling on our run this morning, with only a vague excuse that he was busy.

I wasn't an idiot. Anyone who knew him would know, without a doubt, that regardless of how busy Gregory was, he would still make time for training. But I felt only relief, as I wasn't ready to see him again. Besides, it was late morning by now, and he'd likely already finished his run.

Alone, like he belongs, the ridiculously confusing man.

I was better off running with Jack. It was our thing, especially for Saturday long runs. Anyone who didn't put me through a confusing jumble of anger and hope and hopelessness and, well, *desire* the way that Gregory constantly did *had* to be a better person to run with. I threw off the silky covers and reluctantly rose from the bed.

Rummaging around in the mess of laundry I'd chosen to ignore yesterday, I found my running clothes, wincing at the headache that worsened with each movement. I sent Jack a quick text saying I'd be ready soon, apologizing for the late hour. I needed coffee, and I needed it fast.

When Jack arrived, it took him mere seconds to spot something wrong. "Are you feeling OK, Vivi? You don't look the best."

I forced a smile. "Of course, why wouldn't I be? And thanks for the compliment."

He ignored the sarcasm and spoke slowly. "I don't *know* why you wouldn't be feeling OK, which is why I asked you. But you definitely look tired and maybe ... in pain?"

My eyebrows furrowed, and my eyes darted away before returning to his concerned face. "So glad I can always count on the brutal honesty of my closest friend."

He looked at me in that no-nonsense way that only a best friend can get away with. "Physical pain or another kind?"

I said nothing as I finished lacing my shoes and grabbed my running gear from a nearby chair. "Just a headache. Let's go," I said in a clipped tone as I walked out into the hallway.

"Vivi, hold up," he said, walking after me and reaching out to touch my shoulder. When I reluctantly stopped a few feet outside my door, he said, "What's going on?"

"Jack," I replied with a pained sigh, "I don't know if I feel like talking. Can we just run? We're only two weeks out from race day."

"I'm worried about you, Vivi—"

"All right, I'm not feeling my best. But that's really all I want to say." I stopped short of admitting that I didn't even want to talk. Or run. Or do anything requiring effort. Not when I'd much rather drown my sorrows or sleep them off. Not sorrows exactly. Frustration. Confusion. I didn't know what to feel anymore, but last night had changed the game, and I hadn't processed it yet. Where could I even start?

Canceling on Jack wouldn't be fair to him though, especially since he'd spent most of the morning waiting while I slept off my stupid decisions. "Sorry, Jack."

He was silent for a moment, his clear eyes searching my bleary ones until I looked away. "OK, Vivi. You know I'm here to talk, but I won't push. Let's go knock out some miles," Jack said, giving me a light pat on the shoulder. Then, a bit tentatively, he added, "I trust it'll be just the two of us this morning?"

I debated not responding, as I *really* wasn't in the mood right now to hear Jack's take on Gregory. Instead, I said, "That's right."

We started our run in silence for the first mile along the sunny trail. I gritted my teeth. I'd had enough of the awkward silence. After last night, the very last thing I wanted was to spend *more* time in awkward silences with a man. Even if that man was just Jack. *Especially* if that man was just Jack. Awkward silences weren't our thing. Companionable silences, sure. Occasional angry silences, sometimes. But never awkward ones.

"Um, Jack? I don't want to talk about my issues, but not talking at all is probably just making things unnecessarily weird, and I don't need that either. Let's talk about ... anything but me. Distract me from this pain that you perceive me to be feeling," I said. The corners of my mouth curved upward slightly as I glanced at him.

He looked back at me with a pleasant smile. "Sure thing. Let me just sort through my massive closet of best friend hats and find the Distractor Hat."

I chuckled. Chatting with Jack might be just the thing. To forget, to think about anything but my life, even to laugh. "Tell me about your work projects, Bel's latest culinary creations, the start of the baseball season, your mom's latest boyfriend, your rooftop garden, anything." I wanted to kick myself after mentioning his mother's love life; though my own dating stories were sometimes amusing, Toni's poor track record with long-term commitments was at times a sore spot for him (though he'd never admit it).

Jack's eyes widened, and his lips twitched. "Wow, you really *don't* want to talk about yourself. You hate hearing about my garden."

Relieved he was reacting with levity, I laughed openly. "I don't—OK, I wouldn't say hate, but you know that rooftop gardening is one of those things I absolutely love the *idea* of but can't muster any interest or enthusiasm for the details or actual work of it. Especially when it's just ... vegetables."

"I'll try to think of something a little more scintillating," he said, giving me a good-natured nudge in the arm as we ran. "Hmmm, my current work project is not very fascinating, but I can tell you about what I hope is my next piece."

"Oh, I'd love to hear it. Are you almost ready to wrap up the current one?" I was relieved to talk about something that had absolutely nothing to do with me, especially my love life.

"That's ... somewhat undetermined at the moment," he said, his voice wavering slightly, "but this next one is something I've been wanting to work on for at least a year or more."

He became increasingly animated as he began to describe his next work project, a piece on environmental justice that was obviously very important to him. I noticed he'd dodged yet another question related to his current work with Irene. But I could let it go for now; I'd have plenty of time to pepper him with questions later on.

As it happened, an opportunity to ask about his boss came from Irene herself, on a brief walk break when Jack checked his phone. As if it were the most natural thing in the world, I stole a glance over his shoulder. "Irene has called no less than four times! What could be so urgent on a Saturday morning?"

Jack put his phone back in his waist pack and shook his head. "I don't know. It could be anything. Everything is urgent to her."

I nodded, beginning to understand. "So she's one of those people who always believe their priority should be everyone else's urgent priority. It all makes sense now."

He was silent while gazing in the other direction, where we could see nothing but trees. Spring hadn't truly sprung yet, so there wasn't much to look at.

"Well, am I wrong?"

"No—yes—it's complicated." His voice sounded a bit frustrated and oddly devoid of its usual easygoing nature.

"We have another four miles, Jack," I pointed out after checking my running watch. "We've got time. What's so complicated?" I knew I was pushing it—but if not now, when?

"No," he said sharply.

"No?"

"We're not doing this."

"This?"

"I'm not doing this with you now."

"What is *this*?"

Struggling to find the right words, Jack was quiet for a moment before he said, "*This*, this thing you do. You want to know everything and then—" he stopped.

"And then what?" I asked, worried that I wouldn't like his answer.

He closed his eyes briefly and sighed. "Nothing, Vivi. Nothing. Let's just do what we came out here to do. Let's run."

He abruptly upped the pace, leaving me struggling to catch up and more than a little frustrated with his continually elusive ways. It was very unlike Jack to snap at me though; his version of being moody was just smiling a little less than usual.

After some silent brooding, I stole a glance at him and confirmed I wasn't the only one breathing hard from this faster pace.

Fine, I'd give him what he wanted. I was tired of trying to pry frustrating men out of their shells, tired of being treated as though I wasn't worthy of their conversation, at least about anything important—tired of, just, well, tired of it all. I decided right then and there I was going to stay home the rest of the weekend, running and men and friends be damned.

When we finished our last mile and walked the last few minutes home, I glanced at Jack, who was looking at me hesitantly. "Not one of the most enjoyable runs we've had together, eh?"

I nodded, shifting my eyes to the ground.

"Vivi—" he began while tugging on my arm.

I stopped suddenly and faced him, pulling my arm away. "Don't, Jack. It's fine. You don't have to tell me anything about your life that you don't want to. It's true now, and it's always been true. But ... it doesn't mean I always have to like it."

He met my eyes and then rubbed his jaw thoughtfully. For a moment, he'd seemed thoughtful in a different way than I'd seen before, in a way I couldn't put my finger on, and only for a moment. "You're right. You don't. But thank you all the same. I know I'm not always easy to understand or tolerate—"

I turned to keep walking while still looking at him. "But that's just it! You *are* easy to understand and tolerate and just ... easy everything. Almost always. I treasure our friendship in part because it *is* so easy, always has been, and I never have to worry about things getting complicated or ... difficult, I suppose, would be the opposite of easy."

His face was hard to read now, almost stoic but something else too.

I continued, "I mean that in the best possible way. You're always easy, *we're* always easy. Except when we're not. Which is rare. You know?"

His deep blue eyes remained focused on me. He was quiet but attentive, as if waiting for me to say more.

"I'm not explaining myself very well," I muttered. "It's just, just, it's just *because* things are always so easy that it makes it extra hard for me to cope during those rare occasions when it's *not* easy. When you're not ... easy to figure out."

He was still silent but began to nod slowly.

"I'm just spoiled, Jack," I said with a slight laugh, suddenly ready to lighten the mood. I wanted to reach out and hug him, but the timing felt strange.

He finally broke eye contact for a moment as we entered our building, and then he eyed me again. "Maybe I am too, a little."

"What do you mean?"

"I'm used to you being an open book. I'm used to easy too, Vivi. Maybe not the same kind of easy, but it's easy and comfortable and familiar, and you know I'm the kind of guy who likes comfortable. And predictable."

"But I don't ... What are you saying?" I stopped as we reached the door to my apartment.

"You've been more guarded lately," he said, with not a little hesitation. "That I can handle and can respect. But ..." He looked at me, his lips moving soundlessly as he searched for the right words.

"But? You have always been the kind of guy friend who doesn't need to hear all the details," I observed, "but doesn't mind listening when I want to spill them. It's one of your best qualities."

"I'm just a bit worried, that's all. The Vivi I know is open and honest with me." His eyes held mine as he placed a hand lightly on my shoulder. "And ... with herself."

I reared back. "I see."

He frowned, looking concerned as he took a tentative step toward me. "Do you see? I'm not sure you do—"

"Oh, I do. Crystal clear, Jack Normandy. Thanks for spelling it out for me, since I can't do it for myself." My jaw was tight and my eyes started to dampen as I fumbled in my pack for my key.

"Vivi, wait, I don't think you see. I didn't mean ... that," he said, running his hand through his dark hair and looking pained. "You ... we ... I just care—"

"Got it, Jack. Thanks," I said briskly while opening the door to my apartment. "I have to go."

Avoiding eye contact, I stepped inside and shut the door as quickly as I could. Of course, that was probably unkind and, well, immature. But at any moment, I'd no longer be able to hide behind anger.

I was definitely staying in this weekend. Nothing could stop me. As the tears began to fall, I sniffed.

No more damn men or meddling friends. Not even Mr. Darcy.

Chapter 16

"You came!" Jenn said as she opened the door, immediately leaning in for a hug as soon as I stepped into the foyer of the townhouse.

"Of course," I said, taking off my coat. "I wouldn't miss it."

"I know, I know, I'm the flake, not you," Jenn said as she picked up a stray toy from the floor.

"So where are the kiddos tonight?" I looked around at the relatively tidy home that was usually wall-to-wall toys and other kid items.

"Not here!" Jenn said with a bright smile. "They're at Grandpa's house. *I'm free.* It's party time! Look, I even did my hair."

"You look gorgeous. For board game night—you're such a hard partier, Jenn," I smirked.

"Well, I do have to cater to my guests," Jenn retorted.

"No arguments here," I said. "A board game night is as wild as this old lady gets." I tried not to think about last night, which I'd spent much of today trying to forget through naps and Netflix.

"Hey, until you've had kids, you don't get to feel like an old lady. And yes, I said kids plural. It's the second one that really ruins your figure. Exhibit A: pancakes, formerly known as breasts." Jenn pointed to her chest and grimaced.

"Oh please, you look amazing as always. Even more gorgeous than usual, somehow. And for tonight, you're free!" I followed Jenn to the kitchen. "I know you, though. By 7 o'clock, you'll be missing the kiddos like crazy."

"Oh, for sure," Jenn said with a laugh. "So you'd better enjoy this carefree version of me while it lasts."

"Hi, Kieran," I said as we entered the kitchen and encountered Jenn's husband. I nearly tripped over my own feet when I saw who Kieran was talking to. "Jack! I ... I didn't know you were coming."

"Hello to you too," he said with an easy laugh. "Do I ever miss a board game night?"

"Why wouldn't he be here?" Jenn asked, raising an eyebrow.

I was silent for a long moment, avoiding everyone's eyes. "No, but lately you're so busy ..."

Just then, Jenn paused in the pouring of drinks, her eyebrows raised as she looked at Jack and me. "Is something going on? You two seem weird. What's happening? You must tell. I need my gossip." When we didn't respond right away, she turned pleading eyes to us. "Kieran will tell you. I need adult talk. *Please.*"

Jack chuckled as Kieran nodded knowingly. "We'll do our best to meet your dire need, Jenn. Won't we, Vivi?"

I fought to conceal the tension I felt when facing Jack again after the uncomfortable ending to our run yesterday. Something about the incident still felt unresolved or awkward, a feeling I was not accustomed to experiencing around my best friend. Still, this wasn't the time or the place to air our problems—if indeed there was any such place, as I didn't feel like examining my lingering feelings of discontent in *any* setting. I took a breath and forced a smile. "You have a wild imagination, Jenn. So, what's on the snack menu tonight? Tell me you made my favorite garlic rolls."

Jenn narrowed her eyes slightly, knowing me well enough to discern I was hiding something. She dropped the subject while strolling to the oven to check on the snack fare. "How could I not? The garlic rolls guarantee that you'll stay at least two hours."

"If you have enough of them," I teased. "And beer. Don't forget beer."

Kieran nodded as he raised his mug. "Never forget beer. We may all be well beyond our partying days, but what's a board game night without beer?"

"I'll take this over poker games with whiskey any day," Jenn said, and we all groaned.

"You had to remind us, didn't you?" I said with an exaggerated shudder. "I can't believe I used to drink that stuff. More like guzzle. How did we not all become raging alcoholics?"

"Because you had me," Jack said, nudging me gently with his arm.

Stiffening, I looked away and remained silent, but Jenn couldn't let his claim go unanswered. "Oh, Jack, you'd like us all to forget that we *did* convince you to take a shot once in a while. Or shots, plural."

Kieran grinned and raised his glass. "Need I remind you—"

Jack held up his hands with a sheepish smile. "No, no reminder necessary. I suppose I might have succumbed once or twice." His smile faded when he looked at me.

I was frowning and looking at my watch. "Well, what are we playing tonight? I brought Island of Plague," I said quickly, eager to avoid further awkward chitchat. The sooner we started playing, the sooner it would end and the sooner I could go home. As much as I *loved* games, I loved self-preservation in the comfort of my own home even more.

"Oh, did you finally buy the Legacy version?" Kieran asked, his eyes wide. For a university athletic director who'd played every sport in high school and college, Jenn's husband was also surprisingly fond of intense strategy or roleplay games, better known as nerd games.

"No." I looked pointedly at Kieran and Jenn. "That would require regular, frequent play, and I don't see you busy parents often enough for that." Legacy games were my favorite, but such long-running, episodic, continuous games took commitment and time, both of which were hard to come by among my friends these days.

Jenn frowned, but then her face lit up. "Let's play another kind of game tonight. Let's pretend we're not old and busy and overworked. Pretend we're …"

"Board game geeks in our early twenties? The glory days?" her husband asked with a twinkle in his eye.

"Sounds like a perfect night to me," Jack said, looking sideways at me. "Let's go set up, Vivi?"

An hour later, I was notably more relaxed. It might have been the beer or the pure enjoyment of playing a game with my closest friends, always one of my favorite pastimes. I even started to warm up to Jack again, feeling like my old self, and he was his normal easygoing self.

Winning the first game certainly helped my mood. Since the nature of the game was to work together rather than against other players, the good vibes were contagious, especially when the much-anticipated garlic rolls were brought in on an oversized tray.

As we set up our next game, an old favorite, Jenn turned to me. "So, anything new with, uh, Gary?"

Ah, crap.

I bit my lip, chiding myself silently for not being better prepared for this. "Mmm, I don't know," I said as casually as I could.

Jack coughed and said quietly, "I think she means Gregory."

Jenn's lips curved into a wide smile. "Gregory, right! So I need the juicy details. Spill." When I said nothing and pretended to be too focused on game setup, Jenn resorted to pleading. "Oh, come on. You know I need my romance fix, Viv—an old married lady with two kids can use some of that, even if it's someone else's romance."

I looked at Kieran and then back to Jenn. "Old? Need I remind you, we're the same age. And you guys are … well, you two are still as in love as anyone I've ever seen. Marriage and children haven't changed that a bit."

Jenn fought a grin, her baby blue eyes twinkling as they landed on Kieran. "OK, maybe you're a little bit right. I'm still enamored with the jock, and somehow he's still into me—whatever the opposite of a jock is. But don't change the subject. We need you to spill already, Viv."

I looked around the room. How could I shut down this conversation without arousing suspicion?

Before I could respond, Jack spoke up, his tone light. "I think she doesn't want to talk about it."

I turned to him, feeling oddly annoyed at his well-intentioned intervention.

He's clearly trying to help, and I should be grateful, but...

Jenn eyed the two of us with suspicion. "But it's *us*. You always want to spill. What's going on?"

This time Jack didn't speak on my behalf, and I wasn't sure whether to be relieved or irritated. I settled on irritated. "Jack's right," I said in a clipped tone. "I just don't feel like oversharing, for once."

After an awkward silence, a rare thing among us, Jenn rose from her seat and declared that everyone needed more beer. Kieran tried unsuccessfully to fill the silence, and when Jenn returned, she tapped me on the shoulder.

When I looked up, Jenn said, "Let's switch chairs. It's easier to play Lost Villa when we're sitting next to our partners."

I suppressed a groan. Usually when we played partner games with just the four of us, Jack and I paired up against Jenn and Kieran. But I couldn't demand a different partner and thus make another scene that would only invite unwanted questioning. I clenched my teeth and rose from my chair, moving to Jenn's vacant seat next to Jack and wishing I could go home instead.

When I glanced at Jack, he was eyeing me expectantly. I forced a smile and picked up our game pieces and cards.

He leaned close to me, his breath warm on my cheek as he whispered, "Come on, Vivi, relax. This is one of your favorite games. I won't bite."

How was I supposed to respond to that? I offered what I hoped passed for a cheerful smile and tried to put a little space between us in a non-obvious way.

As the game progressed, it became harder to enjoy myself, since I had to converse frequently with Jack. Whenever I glanced at him, he looked completely at ease, his usual self, of course. That should have been calming to me—his steadiness usually was—but tonight it just irked me.

It irked me even more that I couldn't explain why.

And it irked me that it irked me.

Apparently I was not doing a very good job concealing my unease. Halfway through the game, Jenn lured me into the kitchen to help with the dessert tray.

After silently walking to the kitchen, I didn't mince words as Jenn turned to open the refrigerator. "That is the most cliche excuse ever, you know, not to mention incredibly obvious."

"What?"

"Pretending to need help in the kitchen."

Jenn set the tray down on the kitchen counter and put her hands on her hips. "OK, Viv, what gives? I get that you're cranky, probably love life problems, and I can understand that. Your Greg sounds like an enigma, to put it mildly. But you seem especially cranky toward *Jack*—hostile, even—while he seems mostly normal. I can't figure it out."

I stared at the floor and sighed, realizing Jenn wasn't going to let me escape this time.

"Are you guys ... in some kind of best friend fight?" Jenn asked, her tone softening.

"Oh gosh, at our age, that sounds so silly." When Jenn merely eyed me patiently, I said, "I guess, something like that. I think ... I think we both just want space."

"Space?" Jenn raised an eyebrow. "From each other? Why?"

"It's hard to explain. It's just ... I don't know what his deal is because he won't tell me anything. He's always been like that. Something is going on with him, but I don't know what. It's fine though, really."

Jenn narrowed her eyes. "It doesn't seem fine. I know you. *You* aren't fine." When I didn't respond, Jenn added, "But he seems pretty normal to me, and if you weren't being weird, I wouldn't have even guessed that anything was wrong on his end."

I crossed my arms. "Of course he acts normal. He's Jack." After a long sigh, my hands flew up. "I don't know. Maybe it's nothing. To be honest, I'm dealing with my own stuff, and I just haven't felt like talking about it. Not to him, not to anyone. It's not about Jack at all."

Studying me intently, Jenn was silent for a long moment before she raised her palms in surrender. "OK. You can have your space. For now. You still need to tell me what happened with the date—don't think I've forgotten." She leaned in and pulled me into a hug. "But if you want to talk, just you and me, just say the word. I know, I know, I'm busy with the family and I cancel all the time. But I will seriously move mountains to make time if you really need me. You know that, right?"

And this was why she was my oldest friend. Also the most wonderful. I nodded and thanked her quietly as we turned to head back to the game room.

When we returned, the men looked up with friendly smiles, each with a beer in hand. "Did you have to make the dessert from scratch, honey?" Kieran teased, throwing his arm around Jenn as she sat close to him.

"You know I'm allergic to *honey*, honey," she replied, giggling as she turned to kiss him.

Jack cleared his throat. "Is this apple crisp? Smells delicious."

After Jenn explained that they were actually caramel apple crumble bars, Kieran added, "Once you try these, you'll never want boring old apple pie or apple crisp again. These are amazing. Thanks, internet cookbook."

Biting into the sweet, warm, and crumbly treat, I had to agree. After savoring my first few bites, throwing back another beer, and quietly observing the conversation around me, I decided to stop moping and feeling resentful toward Jack.

Gregory kissed me! If that isn't a reason to stop moping and to be deliriously happy, then what is?

Forcing myself to think about the man who'd made me feel wanted, if only for a minute, instead of the man here whom I couldn't confide in—couldn't *reach*—I decided to throw my energy into one of my favorite games, even giving Jack a hesitant smile as I picked up the cards.

After another round, he scooted closer to me on the couch. "I don't know how Jenn worked her magic this time, but whatever she did, I'm glad. You seem like you're enjoying yourself now."

I looked into his warm blue eyes and grinned. "Maybe I am."

Jack didn't need to know that I was thinking about Mr. Darcy. I shivered, wondering why I've spent this whole day moping instead of daydreaming about Gregory. Sure, he acted weird afterward, but he was probably embarrassed about losing control, which is obviously a very precious thing to him. The fact that I made him lose control, well, that had to mean something.

I covered my mouth to hide a laugh, reflecting that my sudden mood change probably had my friends thinking I was crazy. I stole a glance at Jack and then at the others.

Let them think I'm crazy. Maybe I am. But it's Mr. Darcy! What living, breathing, straight woman wouldn't lose her sense over him?

Chapter 17

"I so wish I could go, but I have a nightmare headache. I'm afraid I'm just going to stay here and lie in the dark," said Liz.

"Are you sure?" Charlotte said, looking concerned. "I feel terrible—"

"You certainly must be very ill to want to stay home and miss dinner with the de Bourghs," Collin interrupted. "You poor thing. We will send her your warmest regards, of course."

Liz groaned inwardly. She had nothing like warm regards for the old snob and her equally snooty daughter, and she wasn't above faking a headache to get out of a miserable evening with them. She tried to smile as she thanked Collin and Charlotte. "You go enjoy yourselves," she said, waving them away.

Not a half hour later, the doorbell rang. She nearly jumped out of her seat, not having expected any visitors. Before she knew it, she was opening the door to a very agitated-looking Fitz.

"Uh, hi, I didn't expect—"

"Elizabeth."

He stared at her for what seemed an eternity. Then he strode into the sitting room to a chair, and then almost immediately rose to his feet. She stood looking on with wariness, crossing her arms over her chest.

"In vain I have struggled," he said. He seemed about to say more, but in seconds he was before her, clasping her shoulders as his lips crushed hers. Shocked, she tried to pull back and speak, but his arms tightened around her as he deepened the kiss.

And then just as she began to respond, he abruptly pulled back. "My ... my apologies."

She stared at him, touching her fingers to her parted lips.

Before she could think of anything to say, he nodded to her (nodded!) and said firmly, "I must go."

With mixed feelings, I closed my laptop to answer the ringing doorbell. I was reluctant to step away from my story, which had seen a great deal of progress and inspiration today, yet I was also excited to see Annie and prep for tonight's event. When Ellen had texted me with an invite to yet another dinner party—who throws a party on a *Tuesday* with only a day's notice?—I hadn't even needed to be coerced into attending.

As Annie scoured my closet, her topic of conversation was the new love of her life, of course.

"I'm having a really hard time finding anything wrong with this one, Viviana," Annie said, pausing to cough quietly. "He's, he's ..."

"Your soulmate?" I asked with a teasing smile. I was lounging on the bed with my favorite kind of scone while Annie did all the hard work, the all-important (or so she said) task of finding the perfect outfit. I couldn't bring myself to feel guilty at all for lazing about, as I'd eventually be the one to clean up the growing heap of clothes discarded by Annie on the floor. And the scone crumbs. "After all these years, you've found the one?"

Annie rolled her eyes. "That's so cheesy, Viv, and it's not like I'm *so* old. But I find that—" she paused, suddenly looking wistful in a way that I hadn't often seen in my younger friend. The moment was gone in a flash though when she started to cough again. "I find him so—" she started again hoarsely.

"So perfect?" I cut in with a smile. I'd heard this speech from Annie more than once before, but because I was in a good mood, I wouldn't remind her of that. "I'm actually finding it hard to spot anything wrong with him too, I'll admit," I confessed. I stopped short of telling Annie about their likeness to Jane and Bingley. Annie didn't know very much about my novel yet, and I wanted to keep it that way. For now.

When she sneezed, I looked at her with friendly concern. "Hey, don't cough all over my clothes now. Are you feeling OK?"

Annie waved her hand dismissively. "Oh, I'm fine. Don't start your worrying thing. Just a tiny cough, probably just a touch of hay fever."

I frowned, as Annie had never mentioned seasonal allergies in the years I'd known her. Besides, wasn't hay fever a late summer or fall allergy? Not a spring one. Still, Annie was a grown woman who could take care of herself. I shook my head, mentally chiding myself for ruminating. I had enough to think about already. Like how should I act around Gregory after that insane kiss? My breath caught for a moment. Was he even attending tonight?

"Annie, is Gregory coming?"

My friend blew her nose, which sounded like more than a touch of allergies. After throwing her tissue away, she looked at me and grinned. "As if Brandon would go anywhere without him. Maybe I shouldn't be telling you this, but he's just as keen on setting up you and Greg as I am. Brandon speaks well of you to Greg."

"Oh, I didn't realize ... well, then." I stared at a spot on the wall for a moment and then laughed nervously. "Annie, I hope we live up to your expectations."

"We? You're speaking in 'we' now? That has got to be a good sign," Annie said with a sly grin as she sauntered over to the bed and sat down. "Tell me everything! I promise I won't cough on you."

I wasn't ready to confide in anyone about the kiss yet, though I wasn't exactly sure why. "There isn't much to tell. It's—" I stopped as Annie coughed again, this one sounding worse than the others. "Annie, are you sure you're well enough to go out tonight? I'm sure Ellen would be fine with you sitting this one out."

She scowled at me, her reddened nostrils flaring. "You're changing the subject. You know, you're not as good at that as you think you are."

I had to laugh. "Well, maybe, but you really do seem ill. I *am* starting to worry about you."

"I'll be fine," Annie said in a nasally voice as she walked back over to the closet, gracefully dodging the piles of clothes. "I would press you for more deets, but I need to focus on finding the right dress for you. I wish we had time to go shopping. You just don't give me much to work with here, Viv. And I still have to do my hair, but we *will* continue this conversation later," she warned.

Despite successfully dodging that conversation with Annie again, a nagging sense of worry lingered. Early in the evening, when we hadn't yet eaten, she seemed to feel even worse, and even Brandon urged her to go home.

"Oh, I couldn't possibly just abandon you," Annie exclaimed, or at least as much as anyone in her condition was capable of exclaiming. "I'm fine."

"You're not, love," Brandon said as he massaged her shoulders. "Go home—I'll bring you some chicken soup tonight after we're done here." His wink followed by a whisper in Annie's ear seemed to change her mind.

"Oh, if you insist," Annie said. She sighed and looked at me. "Be sure to keep Brandon company. Maybe if you're sober, you can give him a ride to my place afterward?"

Suddenly, Gregory was standing next to Brandon, apparently having overheard. Since I arrived, he'd been talking with Ellen's husband on the other side of the room. I had assumed he hadn't noticed our arrival. "I will take care of it. Brandon will be fine without you. Go home before you infect the rest of us."

I glared at him, ready with a retort, but when I looked over at Annie, she didn't seem to care. She was too busy giving Brandon regretful looks and whispering in his ear.

Sighing, I mumbled, "Probably too late for that."

An hour later, we were enjoying a decadent chocolate lasagna for dessert, and I found even more to like about Brandon, who insisted on sitting next to me at dinner. Interestingly, Gregory stayed pretty close all evening too, even though he didn't offer more than a few polite statements about the weather. But any attempt at pleasantries coming from Gregory was progress, right?

As we all decided to head out to Ellen's spacious, heated back patio, Brandon grabbed an extra glass of wine for each of us, ushering me outside ahead of the others. "We have to get the best seats," he explained, a twinkle in his eye.

I had visited Ellen's house many times and still had no idea what he'd meant by the "best seats," but I nodded pleasantly.

As it turned out, the best seats were in a dimly lit corner, some-what distant from the others. Nerves fluttered through my chest until I realized that Gregory meant to sit on the other side of me. For some reason, that eased the nerves.

How often do I get to sit between two gorgeous men outdoors on a starlit night?

I watched Brandon arrange his chair closer to mine. Did he want to discuss something important or delicate? Perhaps he wanted to talk about getting serious with Annie, maybe even to propose, with my blessing. Or he wanted to give *his* blessing for me and Gregory to date. I almost laughed out loud at the fanciful thoughts, no doubt prompted by all the wine I'd consumed. This wasn't an Austen novel—not really.

When Brandon offered to pour more wine, I smiled at him en-couragingly, even when he fumbled with the glass and accidentally brushed my hand. "So, Brandon, how is your visit so far? Have you found much to like about the Twin Cities?"

He grinned and leaned in. "Oh, you know I have. I can't imagine a more ... delightful place."

I wanted to scream: *Could you be any more like Charles Bingley?* Instead, I said, "I'm glad to hear it. Your visit has certainly made some people very ... delighted."

He gazed at me for a long time, as if trying to decide whether to say more. I smiled again to reassure him that he could confide in me.

Before Brandon could reply though, Gregory spoke up while staring out at the night sky, "Delightful is one word for it. Tedious is another."

I gasped, looking over at him. "You do know that I live here, right? And that I can hear you blatantly insulting where I live?"

He studied me for a long moment. "I do not naturally assume that people enjoy the places where they live. Where I live has rarely, if ever, been dictated by whether I liked the place."

"Business, right." I shook my head. "Well, whatever works for you."

"Indeed," he responded and then returned to his customary silence.

From there, the evening began to take a different turn.

Brandon's tone began to change in ways that were subtle at first and hard to pin down. Was he nervous about talking to his lover's best friend and perhaps uncertain about whether he should talk about Annie?

But he never brought up her name.

Even worse, he began to sound openly flirtatious. And not just in a general "I'm so friendly that I come across as a flirt to all women" kind of way, a la Charles Bingley. No, if I didn't know better, I'd think ... he was coming on to me.

I must be misinterpreting the situation. Surely he meant well. Right?

Everyone knew he was a flirt, but in a harmless way.

But when he asked me—whispering, for my ears alone—if I wanted to join him for a walk on a nearby path along the darkened lake below, I began to feel distinctly uncomfortable. The alarm bells went off in my head as my body stiffened.

Maybe he just wants some privacy to talk about Annie, I tried to reason with myself while attempting to dismiss the growing knot in my stomach.

But I knew flirting when I saw it; I knew lust. Brandon was propositioning me. Brandon!

So much for finding a Bingley for our Jane.

Shaking my head in disgust, I wished I'd asked Jack to come along. Surely Ellen had invited him, but he must have declined on account of his workload. I frowned.

Or on account of me.

I politely declined Brandon's offer, but his heavy-lidded eyes shone with determination. He leaned in and put his arm around my shaky shoulders, his breath hot on my cheeks. Flustered, I rose abruptly before he could whisper something I didn't want to hear.

Gregory rose as well. "Are you leaving, Viviana?"

Dismayed, I studied him and then Brandon, whose brows were furrowed. Had Gregory heard everything? He didn't seem upset, yet how else would he know I wanted to leave? "I ... I think I am, yes."

"I'll escort you out," Gregory said. Was he being gallant for once?

I searched his face, but it was unreadable as usual. Apparently he, unlike the rest of the party, had been unaffected by the copious amounts of wine. "No, you stay. You are bringing Brandon home." My eyes darted to Brandon, whose face showed a sneer I'd never seen before. I shivered, eager to escape.

"Yes, I am. But I will walk you outside," Gregory said.

I bit my lower lip as I nodded and then gave Brandon one last look, intending a curt goodbye. Until I saw what he was doing. The man had picked up his phone and started swiping through photos of women. Was he on Tinder? My jaw dropped.

First hitting on me and then, as soon as that falls flat, looking for a new hookup before the last attempt has even left the room. Who the hell is this guy?

I shook my head, full of confusion and tipsiness as I let Gregory lead me back through the house and out the front door. Fortunately, I didn't encounter Ellen, who would have tried to persuade me to stay. Once outside, I rummaged in my purse for my phone and arranged an Uber.

"My ride should be here soon," I said, shivering. Emboldened by drink and by darkness, I placed my hand on his arm. "Gregory, thank you."

His eyes slowly traveled down to where my gloved hand rested on his forearm, and I felt his warm muscles tense even through his expensive, well-lined jacket. He remained still, not moving away but also not coming closer. "For what am I owed thanks?"

"I think you know." I looked at him pointedly before letting my arm drop to my side. "Things were becoming rather uncomfortable in there. And it's cold. You didn't have to do that."

"Well, I ..." His brows lowered, appearing to think carefully about his next words. "I am pleased that I could be of service."

I smiled at him tentatively.

"I actually wanted a moment of privacy to ask you a question," he said, clearing his throat and sounding almost nervous. Or perhaps just awkward. "I know this is short notice, but if you are available this weekend, I wondered if you might like to attend the literary convention in Duluth as my guest."

I stilled, certain I'd misheard. I was aware of this convention, of course, as my father attended every year, as did the Bolder management team, including Ellen in some years. But I myself hadn't ever attended or been invited to attend. "You—you want *me* to go with you?"

"Yes." He gazed into my eyes with an expression that could only be called ... serious. Not lustful, not dismissing. Serious. I had no idea how to interpret that, except to conclude that he wasn't joking. As if he ever did.

"I, um ..." Realizing I was nodding vigorously, I felt my cheeks redden as I dropped my phone in my purse.

"I am aware that it is probably outside of your normal weekend pursuits, but I would be pleased if you would attend as my guest."

I stiffened. Was he being condescending again? Maybe. But this was just Gregory's way. It was Darcy's way too. I paused to think it over.

But what is there to think over? This insanely attractive and successful man is inviting me to spend a weekend with him. Does it matter where or why?

I was grateful he couldn't read my thoughts at that moment.

"Yes, that sounds lovely," I heard myself saying.

"Good. Thank you." His eyes shifted to a car passing through the night and then returned to me. "Viviana."

"Yes?" I gazed up at him, my eyes shining.

"May I kiss you?" he asked. "I confess I find myself attracted to you, though my tastes usually run toward more sophisticated women."

My face fell as I returned his stare. This, more than his other comments recently, couldn't be interpreted as anything but a slight. Yet ... I couldn't bring myself to truly feel anger as I remembered the famous speech of Darcy's, in which he proposed to Lizzie while thoroughly insulting her and my family. That terrible speech certainly led to a happily ever after ... eventually. Besides, kissing Gregory seemed like the best antidote for any hurt feelings. "You may," I said, as calmly as I could.

He stepped forward and placed one hand behind my head, drawing me closer and kissing me gently but firmly.

When he pulled away after just a few seconds, I lightly touched my lips with my gloved fingertips. "Well, it wasn't quite like our first kiss."

I winced. Why on earth had I spoken those words aloud?

"Indeed, no. This was a more proper kiss. I apologize for the previous one," he said, still looking into my eyes as he stepped back to arm's length.

"Well, I ... I quite liked the first one. It was passionate, intense, spontaneous—" I clamped my mouth shut, again wondering why I was speaking any of this aloud. Perhaps I'd drunk more than I realized.

"Spontaneous? You prefer spontaneous?" he asked, furrowing his brow.

"Well, not always. A well-planned romantic scene, and the effort that goes into it, does not go amiss," I explained. "But don't we all need some spontaneity in our lives sometimes?"

My next move was one that, when reflected upon later, I could scarcely believe I'd made. Punctuating my explanation about spontaneity with a spontaneous kiss of my own, I leaned forward to place my lips on his while grasping his shoulders to steady myself.

The kiss was, well, lovely, and I was relieved when he returned my bold move with some enthusiasm. But he broke it off shortly as headlights came into sight, a car slowing in front of us.

"I see what you mean," he said, with a rare lightness in his eyes. "I will concede that was more enjoyable than the prior one."

I had to laugh at his formal tone, *still*, after an evening spent together and not one but *two* kisses. There was no cause for doubt now: my Mr. Darcy was warming to me. Indeed, most of the evening, he'd appeared to be enjoying himself—or at least he hadn't been obviously miserable or bored, as in the past gatherings we'd both attended.

He handed me into the waiting car, and I wanted to swoon. "Goodnight, Viviana. We will meet Friday at the convention, as agreed. I shall have my assistant send you the details. Thank you for a pleasant evening."

"Thank *you*, Gregory," I all but gushed, smiling from ear to ear, though I couldn't feel my ears in the biting cold. "Truly, this was ... really nice. I look forward to this weekend!"

Really nice? That's all you could come up with?

I was still smiling like a fool as the car drove away.

Chapter 18

Still floating on a cloud, I woke up just before dawn. Stretching my arms and legs under my soft sheets and still basking in the afterglow of last night with Gregory, I decided to be ambitious and rise for an early morning run. When I wasn't running with Jack, I usually procrastinated and delayed training runs until the afternoon, but after temperatures hovering around zero for the past few days, the afternoon was predicted to become unseasonably warm and, since this was Minnesota, overly humid.

On my way out, I stopped at Jack's door.

"Good morning! Am I too late to go running with my best friend this morning?" I asked cheerfully.

"Really, what gave it away?" he said with a laugh, looking down at his running clothes and wiping his brow. "Sorry, it's another busy work week, so I'll likely be running around 5 a.m. most days. Probably too early for you?"

"*Five*? You know me. Five is definitely too early. Here I was feeling proud of myself for getting up at 6:30 to run on a weekday," I said, still smiling.

He looked at me thoughtfully, his eyes sweeping over my face, which was devoid of makeup except perhaps some black smudges around the eyes from yesterday. "So what's a beautiful smile doing on your face at this hour on a Wednesday?"

I flushed and lowered my lashes. I was unused to hearing the word "beautiful" to describe me, other than by my parents, although having Gregory admit to an attraction to me had considerably boosted my confidence in recent days. "Oh, I don't know. Probably just a fluke. You know me."

"Hey, whatever it is, I'll take it." He chuckled. "It's just nice to see you happy, Vivi."

I impulsively leaned forward and stretched my arms around to his back. But before he could raise his arms to hug me back, I jumped back just as quickly.

Awkwardness brewed within me, inexplicably, and I offered the first explanation that entered my mind. "Oh, sorry, I'd forgotten what it's like to smell runner sweat on someone else when I'm not soaked in it myself." I winced, hoping that didn't sound as rude to him as it did to me.

His mouth twisted into a wry smile as he crossed his glistening arms over his chest. "Always appreciate your honesty, Vivi."

"Anyway, I ..." I took a deep breath and closed my eyes briefly. "Jack, I'm just glad that whatever that weirdness was in the past few weeks—I'm glad it seems to be gone. I want my best friend back. It's OK that you're super busy. I'll wait, and then we'll need to have a ridiculously long catch-up session. Or several." I paused and then grinned. "After all, I'm sure you miss being forced to watch Austen movies with me at least once a week."

"How'd you know?" He laughed and nudged my elbow with his. "All right, off with you then. I need to wash up and get some work done, and you need to get your miles in. Less than two weeks until race day! Thanks for stopping over, Vivi."

As I turned and walked down the short hallway, I thought about the few words exchanged but also the importance they signified. Our friendship was fine, and we didn't need to have a long, drawn-out conversation to figure that out.

It's easy, we're Jack and Vivi.

I smiled, taking a few steps outside into the already warm, sticky air. Upon seeing my elderly neighbor approaching, I walked back to the door to hold it open for him.

"Why thank you, Vivian," said the short, pale, white-haired man as he walked slowly to the door. "It pains me that I can't open doors for *you* though, girl. It's what a man is meant to do."

"You're most welcome, Mr.—"

"Oh, I always say, you can call me Samuel. None of that Mister nonsense." Thank goodness he interrupted me, as I was never certain I would remember his name correctly, even though he usually got mine wrong.

My smile was bright as I nodded. "Samuel, I hope you are feeling well today? It seems quite hot for March."

"Heavens, yes, it's miserable. But I had to come out here because I saw from my window that Elouise's cat had escaped again. That darn thing will be the death of me. If something else doesn't get me quicker." He laughed then, as though the idea of his death was hilarious. "But you know I couldn't let it go. Elouise would be so heartbroken."

I nodded sympathetically. Elouise was a quirky older woman who lived down the hall from him—and from Jack and me—for as long as I could remember, and likely far longer. I imagined they must be madly in love, but I had yet to see any concrete evidence of a romantic relationship, and they obviously lived apart. Still, they always looked out for one another, and when I'd seen them together, their eyes shone with a simple joy and peace that I'd never seen between any two adults, apart from maybe my parents. They were probably just discreet; Samuel was rather traditional, while Elouise was anything but. Or perhaps Samuel was allergic to her cats.

"I'm still confused about how the cat escapes though," I admitted. "He must climb out the window and down from there, somehow. I doubt he's figured out how to open doors or travel by elevator."

"Indeed, indeed." Samuel nodded. "I won't keep you, Vivian. I'm sure you have more important things to do than talk to an old man."

My smile widened. "What could be more important than that?"

He patted my arm and chuckled. "Ah, well, you've a lovely smile, made this old man very happy this morning. Now run along and have a nice day."

I said farewell and began to walk toward the trail. For a few moments I breathed in the fresh, albeit humid air and exhaled contentedly as I observed the signs and sounds of spring in the city. Spring was my favorite season; it was a time of rebirth. Being in love at Samuel's age was a bit like the spring. After a long winter of loneliness that seemed to never end, with his wife having died decades ago, he'd found someone to make him happy again, or so it appeared. Samuel and his capacity for love and joy were reborn, even in his late stage of life. I only hoped I'd one day find happiness too. And love.

Perhaps I was well on my way.

Grinning, I began running once I reached the trail. I realized I was grateful to be running by myself this morning; I would have uninterrupted time to think about Gregory, to replay last night's kisses in my mind repeatedly and, of course, to imagine all the kisses to come. Among other important things.

My perma-smile faltered when some unwelcome thoughts came to mind: Brandon's odious behavior—and whether I should tell Annie. I'd sent a text asking if Annie was feeling better earlier today but hadn't heard back from her.

Should I tell her? Should I confront him?

Not now.

No, I wasn't going to worry about it yet. I wouldn't allow it to ruin my morning.

As I reached the halfway point and turned to run back toward home, I wiped my damp brow and started thinking ahead to the literary convention. I should probably call my father and arrange to see him there. He would probably prefer a private meeting, as he liked to avoid crowds. Dad, otherwise known as Mark Jamison, attended such events mostly anonymously, even wearing a silly disguise and using the name Dr. Carroll, which was neither his real name nor his pen name. I didn't entirely understand why my father went to such great lengths to stay under the radar, though it stemmed partly from his aunt's difficulty navigating the writer life as one of the few introverts in the family. Occasionally, someone would recognize him, but he'd largely been successful in avoiding widespread attention at most industry events in the past. Or so I'd heard, as I hadn't attended them myself.

When I returned home, I took a moment to freshen up but decided to postpone showering so I could call my father right away. After soaking a hand towel in ice water, I ambled over to the couch and sat down, placing the towel on my neck as I gulped down a sports drink. Once I no longer felt like I'd spent the day in a sauna, I pressed my dad's profile photo on my phone to call him.

"This is an honor, sweetie," my father said, a subtle question in his voice.

"Hi, Dad. I'm sorry it's been a while since I called. Life has been a bit crazy lately," I confessed.

"Oh, you know I don't mind, sweetie," my father assured me. And I believed him, since he was even more introverted than I was. Phone calls, even from close family, weren't at the top of his list of things to do.

"So, I have some big news, Dad! I'll be attending the convention in Duluth this coming weekend. I know you never miss those, so I figured it'd be a great chance to see each other."

After a moment of silence, he responded, "Ah, I'm happy to hear it, sweetie. To what do we owe this honor? Is it a work thing?"

"Sort of ... not exactly," I admitted. "I'm attending with someone I know through work, kind of, but our relationship is not a professional one. It's, um ..."

"A new friend? Boyfriend?"

"Neither," I said nervously. "But we're sort of seeing each other ... I think."

"You think?" He paused. "Well, I'm sure your mother and I would be honored to meet him, but if you think it's too soon, that's also fine. I can observe surreptitiously from afar, you know."

I laughed. "Sure, whatever you'd like. Maybe let's see how things go, and I'll let you know if I'm feeling up to a meeting. Meeting the parents is, you know, not something to take lightly."

Especially not when one of those parents is a famous person, albeit one who is well hidden from the public eye.

"Have you booked your travel and room, then? If not, you could drive up there with us," he said, his tone hopeful.

"I haven't, actually. Gregory said he'd send me the hotel details, so I hadn't given much thought to it yet. But ... I'd be happy to ride along with you, Dad, if you don't mind going a little out of your way to pick me up. Or maybe I could just drive to your house the night before," I added, not wanting to inconvenience him.

"Sure, sweetie. Whatever you'd like." He paused briefly. "Listen, I'd love to catch up with you more, but if we'll be seeing you later this week, we can save it until then."

He'd never pass up a chance to avoid a lengthy phone call. "Sure, Dad. Tell Mom I said 'hi'!"

Upon hanging up, I put up my feet and arranged an old throw pillow behind my back. As I stretched out my tired, aching muscles, I realized the travel arrangements had barely entered my mind. Gregory hadn't planned on driving me there. He probably had a first-class airline ticket booked already, or maybe he had a private jet. I probably also needed to book my own room; he likely hadn't planned on sharing a room with me, or he'd have told me already.

Don't get ahead of yourself, I told myself silently. *Must keep cool to avoid scaring him—he doesn't need to know that you've projected onto him more than a decade of hopes and dreams for finding your own Mr. Darcy!*

Chapter 19

After a mid-afternoon shower, I was lounging on my couch in my favorite pink silk robe and lavender slippers, with an oversized mug of my favorite mint green tea warming my hands. I'd chosen to treat myself to a cozy afternoon on the couch doing nothing. Well, nothing but basking in the thought that Gregory wanted to spend a weekend with me—not just a date, a weekend!

But instead of relaxing, my mind kept circling back to Brandon's flirtation and deliberating about how to deal with it. I needed to do something. Surely Annie deserved to know, but was it my place to tell her? Should I text Brandon myself? Perhaps in the light of day, with both of us sober, I could convince him to confess to Annie so I wouldn't have to.

As the dinner hour approached, I still hadn't come up with any satisfying course of action, so I decided to satisfy my growling stomach and an oddly specific craving for Italian pasta salad. I quickly dressed, grabbed my coat, and put my hair in a loose ponytail before leaving in search of said salad at a neighborhood shop.

As I was leaving the building, walking fast and deep in thought about my predicament, I suddenly slammed into something very hard and warm. "Oh!" I exclaimed, stepping back unsteadily as I righted my footing and looked up. "Jack! I didn't see you coming."

"Nor did I, obviously," he said, the corners of his mouth turning up slightly. "Sorry about the smell. And the sweat. And, well, bumping into you."

"Oh, it's ... probably my fault. I was distracted. You've just come back from another run?" My heart was still beating unusually fast, and I stammered, "I mean, of course you have. You're wearing running clothes and sweaty. I mean, not that you're sweaty, I mean you probably are, maybe you are, but not—"

He crossed his arms over his broad chest, clearly amused. "Vivi?"

"I'm just going to stop talking."

"By all means, continue."

"Jack—"

He laughed, patting me on the arm. "Relax, Vivi. I don't run twice in one day. I was just lifting a bit at the gym. I know you're not a fan of strength training, but I try to fit in a few sets here and there. You should see your face right now. I can see I was correct in assuming you wouldn't want to renew our old gym memberships," he said, laughter in his eyes.

I just smirked, willing my pulse to settle down.

He looked thoughtful for a moment. "I also figured you must have been too busy as well—too busy to work out, that is."

I sighed, releasing some of the tension. "Guilty as charged. That is, work is just the usual, but I've been trying to be more efficient so I have time for my novel. I've only gotten in, like, two runs this week. Or was it one? I can't remember."

"Oh, how's the writing going?" he said, pulling his leg back for a quad stretch. My eyes were drawn to his quad muscles lengthening, but I averted my eyes when I realized I was staring.

What on earth?

"What?"

"Your book, Vivi. How's it going, writing your book?" He looked at me with slightly narrowed eyes.

I flushed. What was wrong with me? I wasn't attracted to Jack, of all people!

I must be ... projecting my excitement for this weekend onto the nearest male form. Yes, that's it. Act normal, dammit.

"Oh, it's going well, very well actually," I said, as even toned as I could. "In fact, I'll have fresh material to write about soon because, um, Gregory invited me to go to Duluth with him this weekend." When Jack didn't reply, seeming intensely focused on stretching his hamstrings, I added, "And how about you, Jack, how are things?"

"Oh, you know me. Always staying afloat. Always fine." He punctuated this statement with a laugh that sounded anything but fine. It sounded a little hollow.

I knew better than to probe deeper though, so I glanced down at my watch.

"On your way to somewhere important?" he asked lightly as he began to stretch his arms, which I vowed I wouldn't look at.

Food. Talk about food. That always makes things better.

"Well, if you count putting my stomach out of its growling misery as important, then yes." I chuckled to prove I was being normal. "I should go, before the growling starts embarrassing us both."

Jack laughed, this time a richer, deeper sound. "Oh, Vivi, your growling stomach and I have been dear friends all these years, don't you know?"

My mouth twitched at the corners. Surely he had no idea how similar that statement was to a comment from one Mr. Bennet in my favorite book: *You mistake me, my dear. I have the utmost respect for your nerves. They've been my constant companion these twenty years.*

"Oh Jack, you're right, of course. You tolerate it better than I do."

"Go on then. I've got a pile of work to get back to anyway. Long run tomorrow morning, since you'll be gone Saturday?" he asked tentatively. "Or ... do you have other plans?"

I shook my head slowly. "No plans. I'll see you at 7?"

"On the nose," he said, popping me on the nose and turning to leave with a tired smile. "Have a nice evening, Vivi. And Vivi's stomach."

What just happened? I breathed a sigh of relief that the tension of recent weeks had lessened, though there was some lingering, or even new, awkwardness—likely all on my side. Misplaced lust? I shook my head with a chuckle and recalled the weekend ahead, ripe with romantic opportunities with Gregory.

Jack and I would fully return to our usual, comfortable relationship, just the way I liked it.

My stomach sank as I remembered my Annie/Brandon dilemma.

Darn it, I should've asked Jack for advice. He can always figure out the sensible thing to do.

That evening, I stood at Annie's apartment door, my hand raised in a position to knock. I hesitated, biting my lip. I still hadn't fully determined how to handle the situation, but I knew I should at least visit to see how Annie was doing. After pulling into the parking lot, I'd driven around to make sure Brandon's rental car wasn't there. The last thing I wanted was to see him again.

I forced myself to take a deep breath because, I rationalized, that's what one does in this situation, right? Never mind the fact that taking deep breaths had oftentimes worsened the feeling of anxiety for me, rather than alleviating it. Why couldn't I just be normal and calmly count breaths or something? I shook my head, trying to clear the distracting thoughts and focus on my mission.

When I finally knocked, no response came from within. But after several more knocks, the door finally swung open. Sporting a messy ponytail, worn-out slippers, and cough syrup-stained pajamas, Annie uttered a muffled-sounding greeting as she turned and headed back to the couch, where she had spent the last 24 hours, from the looks of it.

"That bad, huh?" I asked, clearing off space on a nearby chair and gathering up crumpled tissues nearby.

"Yuh—" Annie started to say, though it came out more as a growl. After a few long coughs, her voice cleared a bit, and she moaned, "Yeah, I guess so. I'm so embarrassed. This is so not me. I never get sick. Never."

I nodded sympathetically. "That's true. Your immune system is legendary."

My friend scowled, taking a sip from a microwaveable soup container.

"I'm glad to see I wasn't the first to bring you soup. Have Rafael and Rainn been taking good care of you?"

"Well, they're men, so not particularly. But they try, or at least they did before they had to go to the gym," Annie replied, rolling her eyes.

I chuckled. "They mean well." And they did. Annie's roommates were awesome; they almost made me I wish I had roommates. Almost but not quite.

Annie buried her face in her hands. "It had to be this week, didn't it?"

Hiding a smile, I continued tidying up.

"Brandon came by with some sick-person supplies," Annie explained after a sneezing fit. "You just missed him—he came by just 10 minutes ago, maybe 15, I don't know. Did you know that time is all warped when one feels like this?" She rubbed a tissue on her already red nose and tossed it on the floor.

"You're lucky to have not experienced sick brain much in your life," I said as a frown formed. "Brandon was just here a bit ago? And he didn't stay and take care of you?"

Annie yawned and shook her head. "Oh, no, I wouldn't let him. I didn't even want him to come over at all—he doesn't need to get sick from me, and he doesn't need to see me like this. When have I ever looked worse? Besides, he had an important work thing come up last night after the party. Work has been occupying all his time apparently." She reached for the tissue box yet again and then turned to fully look at me. "Did he mention the work thing to you last night? Oh, and how did last night go with Gregory?"

"He didn't mention ... that." He'd likely found a date on Tinder rather than some important work to do. So, he was not only a flirt and a cheater but also a liar.

"Oh, well, how was the party anyway?" Annie said, sitting up to show interest as best she could with what little energy she had. As much as she loved going to parties, gossiping about them was almost as good, in Annie's eyes.

"It was fine," I said hastily. I opened my mouth to speak and then closed it. Should I say more? How? I pretended to study my nails, which sorely needed a fresh coat of polish, I realized absently.

"Viv? I may be sick, but I'm not blind. Did something happen with you and Gregory?"

I bit my lip, remaining silent for a long moment before finally meeting her eyes. "Annie, I don't know how to say this."

Her brows furrowed as she tilted her head. "To say what? What happened? You can tell me anything."

"I know, it's just ... I'm not sure it's my place," I said miserably. "And you're already feeling so crappy. I would hate to make you—"

"What the—this is about *me*?" Annie asked, eyes widening. After another coughing fit, she managed to fully sit up and looked steadily at me. "What's going on, Viv?"

"It's just ..." I trailed off, unsure how to say it. "He was, Brandon was, well, kind of—"

"Kind of what?"

"Flirty," I blurted out.

Annie stared at me for a moment and then abruptly laughed. When I grimaced instead of laughing with her, she rolled her eyes. "Oh, you're serious? Come on, this is Brandon. He's naturally very friendly to women, to everyone. Haven't you noticed that about him before? It's part of his charm."

I chewed on my upper lip. "I suppose. But—"

"He comes across as flirty, but I don't think he means it that way. In fact, I know he doesn't. It doesn't mean anything. Trust me, I know the difference. I've *felt* the difference," she said with a slight laugh, or maybe more of a cough.

Steeling myself, I waited until my friend finished blowing her nose again. "Annie, I … I know the difference too. It was—it was more than that. He was coming onto me, er, directly." *There, I said it,* I thought, feeling relieved for just a brief moment.

Annie's jaw dropped. "You have got to be kidding. Please tell me you're kidding. You don't seriously think *he* would be interested in …"

I clenched my jaw. "In me? Well, I wouldn't have thought so, but I know what I saw. I didn't imagine this. Gregory saw it too."

We sat in stony silence for a while, and then Annie spoke quietly, "Ah, that's it. This is about Gregory, and things are not going the way you'd like. I can't believe I'm saying this, but I think *you* … you are jealous."

Eyes wide, I stared at her. "I can't believe I'm *hearing* this. You—you think I would dream this up just because I'm hurt about what's going on with Gregory? Which I'm not, by the way. Things are going great. My love life is fine."

Annie stood abruptly, looking a little dizzy but determined as she headed to the kitchen. "We're done here, Viv. I don't know what's gotten into you, but I don't have the energy for it right now."

Standing up slowly, I stared at my friend with my mouth agape. Annie had never spoken to me this way before, or to anyone, as far as I knew. "I can't even … You don't believe me? Why would I lie? Why would—" I stopped as my disbelief abruptly turned to outrage. "You know what, it doesn't matter. Forget I said anything. I was trying to be a good friend. I'm always trying to be a good friend to you." When Annie didn't turn around, I added bitterly, "And it's a thankless job."

A bit unsteady still, Annie whirled around, her green eyes flashing as she pointed to the door. "Just go. I think I need a break from this 'good friend' that you think you are." With that last parting shot, she picked up her tissue box and strode to her bedroom.

Fuming, I headed to the door to leave and then turned back, the words "How dare you" on the tip of my tongue. But I forced myself to take a deep breath. "Not worth it," I muttered. Things would only escalate. Instead, I slammed the door shut on my way out.

Real mature, I told myself, but I didn't care. I'd had enough adulting for today.

Chapter 20

At the crack of dawn, I spent half an hour under the covers trying to devise an acceptable excuse to skip the planned long run with Jack. Nothing came to mind, at least nothing he'd believe. I definitely wasn't ready to talk to him about the disaster that was last night. Reluctantly, I dragged myself out of bed, reminding myself of the old runners' wisdom: the worst run is always the one you skipped. Or something like that.

The run was uneventful. With both of us wrapped up in our own thoughts, we didn't speak much. Definitely not about Gregory or Irene or Annie or anything potentially contentious—none of the torturous thoughts and feelings disrupting my world the past few days.

But when we did talk, it was light and friendly. Nothing unusual. Normal and dependable, just as I liked it.

Still, I was glad to return to my apartment by myself.

Jenn called as I was unlocking my apartment door, and I answered reluctantly.

"Viv! I've been calling you all morning. The kids are at their grandpa's house, and I'm dying for some adult talk. I'm so glad you picked up! Where were you so early on a Saturday?"

"Saturday long run. Jack and I had ten miles on the schedule for today," I said as I wiped the sweat off my face.

"Oh." Jenn paused. "How'd that go? You and Jack are good now?"

I exhaled loudly. "I think so. I don't know. We didn't get much chance to talk."

"You spent two hours running with him, and you didn't have a chance to talk? Explain."

"Honestly, it was just too hot. Have you been outside yet this morning? It's so bizarre for late March. Last weekend it was freezing, and today is hot—no, stifling. Hard to breathe. One of those kinds of runs, you know."

Jenn didn't really know, as she'd never been a runner, vastly preferring team sports if she had to do sports at all. She pressed on. "Oh, I see. How's he doing then?"

"OK, I think?" I locked my door after putting my running gear on a nearby end table. "Honestly, my mind was elsewhere. I may have forgotten to ask how he was doing. But, you know, he's Jack. He's always doing fine, except when he's not, and then he doesn't really want to talk about it."

Again, Jenn didn't really know, as she wasn't as close to Jack. Focusing on the other part of my reply, Jenn said, "Your mind was elsewhere, eh? Do tell!"

I took a long drink of ice-cold water as I contemplated my answer. The cold reminded me of the ice bath I should probably take soon. Like most humans, I loathed sitting in ice water, but I knew my sore legs would thank me later.

Jenn interrupted my thoughts. "*Viv!* I'm not taking 'no' for an answer this time."

I laughed. "I wasn't saying 'no.' I was drinking some water. Running on a hot day like this—ah, you don't care about that," I said, sighing.

"You're right, I couldn't care less," Jenn conceded. "Not when you've got juicy stories for me. I know you do! You and Dr. Gregory?"

"I don't know about juicy, but ..." I said, pausing to take a deep breath. "You know, I think I *do* need to talk. I've been weird about this with everyone, and I don't even know why."

Grabbing a pseudo-healthy granola bar from my tiny pantry, I headed to the couch. "Writing is my only confidante lately, but it doesn't talk back. It doesn't give me a hug, even a virtual one. Jack and I have been distant to each other, you are always busy, and now Annie and I are not even on speaking terms—" I stopped, realizing my voice was wobbly and my eyelashes damp.

"Oh no, are you crying? Oh, Viv, poor Viv, it sounds like I called at the right time. What's going on with you and Annie? Never mind, let's start from where we left off last time. I have all morning for you."

I sniffed, feeling relieved but also self-conscious. After a moment, I wiped my eyes and began, "Thanks, Jenn. Well, as you know, it all started with these two ridiculously hot, successful men who came into town and disrupted our lives."

"Now that is the kind of story opener I love," Jenn said eagerly, unable to suppress a laugh. "Oh fine, I'll be quiet now. Spill."

Nearly an hour later, I said hoarsely, "And that's all of it. I think you're caught up." I took a long drink of water and felt a substantial weight slip off my shoulders.

"Wow. So much excitement. I'm dying of envy over here," Jenn said longingly.

"Well, it certainly hasn't felt enviable, most of it anyway."

"Right, but it's been *exciting* even when it sucked. Am I right?"

"I suppose. Less exciting though when you can't share it with anyone."

"So, *tomorrow night* is the night. I'm so excited for you! I can't believe you didn't *lead* with that. Do you know what you're wearing? Where you're staying? What he's—"

"Jenn, it's a professional conference, not a fashion show." I laughed. "But no, I don't know what I'm wearing yet. I may text you later for fashion advice. I ... You know what? I *am* excited. I deserve this. Most of the time, I have no idea what to make of him or whether this Darcy stuff is just me being completely delusional, at best—"

"Not impossible," Jenn conceded. "But still, you said he's gorgeous, and oh, the *passion*. I miss that." She let out a long-suffering sigh.

"Oh, please. I've seen the way you and Kieran look at each other, still. You can't tell me there's no passion left."

"Well, I didn't say that, exactly ..." Jenn trailed off, and she chuckled lightly. "OK, you're right. But it's a different kind of passion. A damn good one, plenty of steam still, but not the new-love kind that you're experiencing. Sure, I wouldn't want to go through all the absolute crap that goes along with a new love all over again, but that's the best part of experiencing it through you, Viv."

"I'm glad I could entertain you," I said wryly, swinging my legs from the couch onto the floor, noticing how heavy they felt and reminding myself I needed ice packs. "But seriously, thank you for listening. I'm already feeling a million times better. I was afraid this stuff with Annie was going to ruin my weekend with Gregory."

Jenn was quick to respond. "Don't worry about her, Viv. She may be young and beautiful and carefree, but she's also young and *naive* and, well, stupid. No offense to her. But we're all stupid when we're that age. Annie will get over it, and she'll realize you were just being a good friend. Until then, try not to let it get to you. It's not worth it."

"Thanks, you're right. We probably both just need time," I admitted as I tried to stretch my sore legs. "But speaking of time, aren't you going to spend part of your kidless morning with Kieran?"

"Yikes, yes, thanks for reminding me. We've got a lunch date, and after hearing your exciting tale, there's no way I'm going to just sit on the couch with my husband and eat PB&J sandwiches. We're going out!"

"Good for you," I said, and I meant it. "Well, I've put this off long enough; I need to at least shower and do some ice treatment. Have a great lunch, and thanks again, so much. You're truly the best."

"I know." Jenn chuckled. "All right, go take a shower and a nap and, most importantly, have an amazing sexy time this weekend. And whatever you do, don't forget to tell me about it afterward!"

Chapter 21

High hopes were difficult to stifle, and that was definitely true when my love interest asked to spend a weekend with me. Granted, it wasn't a weekend alone, but there would still be plenty of opportunities for alone time. Any man who invites a woman he's dating on a weekend away must have at least considered, and maybe even counted on, the possibility of romance or intimacy. *Maybe both*.

It was with those hopeful thoughts that my parents and I arrived in Duluth on Friday morning. After driving to their suburban home in North Oaks on Thursday night, I'd gone to bed early so we could be on the road by 6 o'clock.

As the harbor came into view, I was struck, as always, by its beauty. Somehow even the dusty industrial scene created by the shipyards and rails could scarcely mar the allure of the pristine lake, the seagulls circling near, the historic lighthouse, and even a glimpse of a ship or two far off in the distance. Duluth had always held a special place in my heart, and despite many prior visits, each time I felt as though I was witnessing the beauty of the lake for the first time. Earlier in my life, I'd considered moving there, but it was too risky because my beloved Duluth might lose its magic if I saw it every day—if I did such dull things as work and shop for groceries there. No, I'd decided, Duluth would remain my favorite getaway; I couldn't and wouldn't give that up.

At the hotel, just a block from the great thawing Lake Superior, we checked into our rooms and received a packet of materials for the convention. Not the Four Seasons, but it was more than comfortable and tastefully decorated. After unpacking a few essentials in my room, I sat on the bed and opened the brochure containing the schedule. Glancing at the clock on the wall, I realized the first session was starting soon. I'd arranged to meet my parents at their suite to walk down to the conference rooms together. Scanning over the brochure listing the sessions available this morning, I circled a few possibly interesting ones before standing and gathering my bag and a water bottle.

As I found a seat in the main convention room, I was vaguely aware of my parents conversing with a nearby couple. Looking around, I smiled, feeling very grown up and, well, professional. As much as I loved my work-from-home job and the rarity of required social events, there was something about being surrounded by people in the literary community and publishing industry. These people had *made it.* Maybe I could too. I was, after all, well on my way to becoming a real novelist.

But my enthusiasm faltered by lunchtime, when I hadn't seen or heard from Gregory at all. I tried calling and texting him but received no response. It wasn't *that* strange that I wouldn't run into him at a large convention, and I had no idea which sessions he was attending. Still, the lack of any response to my messages was worrisome, especially since he was typically so attached to his phone.

Forgiveness was imminent, however, when I received Gregory's text in the middle of the afternoon, apologizing for the delay and requesting that I attend the dinner reception with him.

A wave of relief washed over me. He wasn't avoiding me. He was just busy. What mattered was that he wanted me—*me!*—by his side at this reception. That in itself was pretty significant, given how important these functions are for networking, especially for someone like Gregory for whom professional networks were everything.

In the meantime, I enjoyed the rest of the afternoon sessions, having never attended such a convention before. The session on AI-based editing left me feeling nervous about the future of my chosen line of work. The upside was I walked away feeling even more resolved to get serious about my writing. Acknowledging I'd had plenty of inspiration, I could admit I hadn't devoted enough time to my novel.

At the following session, I encountered my father and tried not to laugh at his ridiculous mustache disguise.

"Dad! I mean, Dr. Carroll. So nice to see you here," I said, hoping I'd used the correct fake name.

"Well, it appears we have similar taste in literary topics," he said with a wink. "I wonder where that came from."

We linked arms and settled into the few open seats, near the back of the room. I whispered, "Where's Mom?" Even though my mother was a scientist, she often attended literary conventions with her husband and even claimed to enjoy them, though their literary tastes often diverged. Fortunately, she wasn't widely recognized outside the U of M academic community, so she didn't wear a disguise. Still, my habit was to be discreet when it came to my parents.

"She's at the session next door. Nature writing or some such topic that sounded dreadfully boring to me." He flashed a toothy grin. "You'll see her at the reception tonight though—that is, are you planning to go?"

"I am," I replied and then frowned as I considered how much to reveal. Should I introduce Gregory to my parents? It was probably too soon, especially given that my father valued anonymity at events like this. At the same time, I wasn't sure when another such opportunity to introduce them would arise; I didn't even know how long Gregory was going to stay in town with Brandon. For that matter, I knew next to nothing about what Gregory was even doing in town.

As my father looked at me with curiosity, I realized I'd spaced out. "Sorry, I was just thinking. I'd kind of like you to meet Gregory, the guy I mentioned, but it's so early in our ... dating, I guess you would call it. This is going to sound silly, but ... you're my dad, so it's OK, right? I was wondering if maybe we could arrange a so-called chance encounter, so it doesn't seem all weird that I planned it in advance." I looked at my father with pleading eyes.

He stared at me for a moment, and the corners of his eyes crinkled deeply as he smiled. "Understood. I'd love to meet anyone you deem worthy of introducing to us, and I promise not to make things awkward."

I leaned over to kiss him on the cheek. "Dad, you're just the best. You do know that's, like, exactly what any daughter wants to hear, right?"

My father chuckled. "Oh, I've had a bit of experience with this sort of thing. You and your sister have a lot in common, you know, more than either of you will ever admit."

I groaned at the recollection that I still hadn't called Lillian back after weeks of texts and calls. I made a mental note: *Call sister and apologize profusely (bring chocolates?).*

I arrived at the evening reception dinner alone, having asked my father to meet me later on. My mother wasn't feeling well, so my father would be attending solo, but he had a few trusted colleagues at the event, so he'd have others to talk to.

With my heart racing, I took a deep breath and entered the reception hall, looking around for the enigmatic man who had invited me.

As I surveyed the room, I heard a deep, polite voice behind me, "Viviana, it is nice to see you."

My heart skipped a beat, and I whirled around. His generic greeting was less than impressive, but all rational thoughts fled as my eyes landed on him. Somehow, he was more gorgeous, more intriguing than ever. His full lips were curled in a slight smile, which was uncommon for him. *The man shouldn't be allowed to smile,* I thought desperately as I wiped my damp palms lightly on my dress. *As if he weren't already handsome enough when he was sulking—now I have to deal with a smile?*

At a loss for words, or at least any words that would make sense, I nodded as I returned the smile and let him lead me to a nearby table toward the back of the room.

Even more miraculous than his almost-smile, he made attempts at small talk for a few minutes. Like him, I wasn't a big fan of small talk, but knowing that he would try, *for me*, warmed my heart. Remarking upon the weather being cool so close to the lake or the quality of the coffee was certainly preferable to his usual stony silence.

After we chatted about the day's events, he explained he'd been tied up not only with multiple sessions but also with some business issues that he needed to assist Brandon with. I bristled at the unwelcome news that Brandon was in attendance. But it was only natural that he would attend this conference, given his business, so I vowed to myself that I'd remain cordial if I encountered him, at least when Gregory was around.

When the main speaker took the stage in the front of the room, we were spared the small talk for a while. I took the opportunity to study Gregory out of the corner of my eye; he seemed not to notice, listening intently to the speech.

Shortly after the speech, my father wandered over to our seats. "Viv!" he said, his eyes wide. "I wasn't sure if I'd see you here tonight. Your mother turned in early. Join me for dinner, sweetie?"

Greeting my father, I attempted to appear surprised about the encounter as well, and Gregory looked between me and my father with interest.

Before either of us could respond, my father added, "I hope I'm not interrupting—you can just tell me if I am."

Still unsure about the situation even though we'd planned this so-called interruption, I began, "Well—"

Rising, Gregory cut in. "Of course not, sir. Please join us." He glanced at me expectantly, and I stood as well.

"Oh, sorry," I said, biting my lower lip. "Gregory, this is my father. Dad, this is Dr. Gregory Fitzgerald. Gregory, is it all right if my dad joins us for a while? I haven't seen him all day," I lied.

The men shook hands, and Gregory professed himself happy to have my father join us. As we sat down, I eyed Gregory, surprised that he seemed so pleased at my father's appearance. I grudgingly acknowledged there was plenty of time for alone time, er, romance, later after the event. I should celebrating the fact that he wanted to meet my parents already. *This must mean we're really dating*, I thought, knowing I shouldn't.

I tried to quickly think of a casual way to break the ice, but before I could even begin, Dad and Gregory were already starting a conversation about the publishing industry. My father hadn't exactly been explicit about his identity, but it didn't seem to prevent either of them from engaging in a detailed discussion of literary trends and developments.

With a sigh of relief, I relaxed in my chair and smiled. Introducing them had been so easy. But after dinner was served and I'd devoured most of it, I began to wonder if they'd forgotten I was there. I tried to insert myself into their conversation, though their topics of discussion were mostly beyond my expertise.

I might as well be invisible.

Although my father noticed at times that I was uncomfortably quiet and tried to steer the conversation toward more general topics, Gregory seemed intent on their original more niche topic, which at the time was the revival of an imprint I'd never heard of.

When Gregory eventually rose to greet an important acquaintance he spotted a few tables away, he promised to return promptly and bring back champagne for me. My expression forlorn, I stared at him as he walked away.

Dad turned to me, his brow wrinkled. "Are you all right, sweetie? His background is impressive, but he ... I'm not sure what to make of him."

I slowly forced my gaze away from Gregory and looked down at my hands. "I'm fine. The conversation was a bit beyond me, but that's OK." I met my dad's eyes and did my best to look unaffected. "I kind of expected that to happen at a convention like this, where I'm clearly out of my element. Still, it's interesting to listen."

My father gave me a doubtful look but said no more, to my immense relief. Certainly I had doubts about Gregory, like, *all the time*, but everyone had flaws, right? Doting fathers didn't usually want to acknowledge that inevitable fallibility when their daughter is dating a flawed person.

It doesn't help that no one can live up to my sister's perfect example.

My grimace turned into a tentative smile as Gregory returned, sitting down quickly. I greeted him with a tentative smile. His piercing eyes landed on me briefly, and he hastily apologized for forgetting my drink but didn't offer to remedy his mistake. Before I could reply, he turned to my father and initiated another conversation about a literary topic that I knew nothing about. I sighed and pulled out my phone, resigning myself to my lonely fate for the evening. I probably wouldn't know anyone else at this event, and I neither enjoyed nor excelled at mingling with complete strangers.

As I doom-scrolled with little interest, I occasionally looked up or listened to bits of their conversation. Both seemed very engaged; indeed, they were discussing some of my father's books now. If I hadn't known better, I'd think Gregory had done research on my father before this evening. But that couldn't be, as I'd never revealed my father's identity before. If Gregory was aware now, it was only because of their conversation, surely. I returned my attention to my phone, yawning as I scrolled mindlessly. I thought about all the things I'd rather be doing in Duluth, like visiting the rose garden or the historic Glensheen Mansion and its sweeping grounds, where I liked to imagine myself strolling and living a hundred years ago. Or wandering around in the cute little shops on Canal, ordering lunch from the boat-shaped restaurant down by the water, running on the lakewalk—I could never run out of blissful things to do in Duluth. Speaking of running, I wondered what Jack was up to this weekend. I almost texted him but held back.

Fortunately or not, after they'd talked for an hour or so—it felt like hours to me—my father left to go speak to some acquaintances he'd spotted, so his conversation with Gregory ended. Finally. I turned to Gregory with what I hoped was a cheerful smile, intending to start a conversation about the keynote speaker.

Before I could begin, Gregory spoke, his face unreadable. "Viviana, I need to turn in early this evening, as I have a very early meeting with an acquaintance tomorrow before the opening sessions."

"Oh, I—that's fine," I lied. "Will you walk me back to my room? I'm feeling a bit tired myself."

Not tired so much as bored or... defeated, but he doesn't need to know that.

"Yes, I can oblige if you will wait here for a moment. I need to speak to Brandon before we depart." He inclined his head to the left. "He is just over there, I believe, so it will not be long."

I nodded as he stood and sought out Brandon. I breathed a sigh of relief, at least, that Gregory wouldn't be bringing him over to greet me. The last thing I needed tonight was to deal with my close friend's cheating boyfriend. If they were even still together. I hoped not. I was still angry with Annie, but I wanted better for my friend than *him*. How was it possible that the affable Brandon was now the bad guy and the moody Gregory was the good guy? Well, potentially good.

True to his word, Gregory returned in just minutes, and we walked to my room in silence. With his brisk, long strides, I had to nearly jog to meet his pace.

"You're quiet now," I ventured. "It's been a long day, hasn't it?"

"Indeed."

When we reached my door, I pulled out my room key card, still debating about whether to invite him in—that is, whether to do something crazy and probably desperate but maybe worth it. Before I could lose my nerve (if not now, when?), I blurted out, "Would you like to come in?"

He blinked in surprise and then, with a blank expression, shook his head. "I cannot. I must prepare for tomorrow's meeting and rest."

"Oh, right," I murmured. "Well, maybe tomorrow then ..."

When he didn't respond, my cheeks grew rosier. "I mean, we'll see."

Please, floor, just swallow me up.

He eyed me strangely then, apparently *oblivious* that I'd been flirting or propositioning him. Suddenly, the realization seemed to dawn, and he studied the floor. "Ah ... I am sorry. It has been a long day. Please understand. Indeed, I hope we will meet again tomorrow."

Rarely did Gregory ever sound awkward—at least not the nervous kind of awkward—so he must be sincere; the long day must have affected him. Still, I just stood there, pulling my lips between my teeth.

His dark eyes hinted at growing impatience, but he seemed to realize that something was expected of him then, so he abruptly dipped his head and pecked me on the cheek. "Thank you for accompanying me this evening and for introducing me to your father. It was a rather enlightening talk, and I enjoyed it very much."

"I'm glad." I moistened my lips, which he glanced at only briefly. "Well, I'll let you go back to your room now. I ... I hope to see you tomorrow."

He nodded and turned down the hall toward the elevator.

Of course he'd be on the top-floor penthouse suite or something like that.

My room was only on the second floor, so we'd taken the stairs.

But as resentful as I felt about some of our interactions this evening, I couldn't help but stare at him as he approached the elevator. His was such a fine male form, and even with a view only from behind, it was so easy to forget everything else. *Especially* with a view from behind.

Chapter 22

The next morning was no better than the last, with no sightings or contact with Gregory. Fortunately, my mother was feeling better, so I met both of my parents for lunch.

When my father asked if I had lunch plans with Gregory, I shook my head and pushed the food around my plate. I knew what Dad was probably thinking, but I couldn't bring myself to talk about it. I hadn't even allowed myself to *think* about it; trying to make sense of Gregory's words and actions was maddening. And maybe, I feared, hopeless.

Gregory was, to put it mildly, complicated.

My father wouldn't understand. Most of the time, *I* didn't even understand, though I wasn't ready to give up either, considering how much progress I'd made with him in the past week. We'd had *moments*. Surely I didn't imagine those moments; they couldn't mean nothing.

Fortunately, my parents knew me well enough to recognize when I didn't want to discuss something, and they usually respected that. Today was no exception, and I was grateful. As I listened to them chatter about a quirky local couple they'd just met at breakfast, I smiled. For all the things wrong with my life, with *me*, I certainly couldn't blame my amazing parents. I was very lucky; I'd wanted for nothing while growing up. At least nothing that mattered. It was hard to imagine that anyone could have better parents, actually. Sometimes in the past I felt guilty that I'd had such advantages when others suffered so. But Jack had long ago helped me to realize that guilt wasn't going to solve any problems. Offer help, empathy, and understanding, Jack said, to those without all my privilege—and recognize just how fortunate I am—but don't waste energy on guilt. Fight for those who are marginalized, those without the resources and support I'd always taken for granted, he advised. He was right, though courage wasn't something I had in abundance.

But why was I thinking about Jack? Or my lack of messed-up childhood? I shook my head as I sipped from my mug of forgotten coffee and refocused on the conversation.

Lukewarm coffee aside, the rest of lunch passed rather pleasantly, and my spirits had risen significantly by the time we finished the meal and stood up to leave.

My spirits really soared when I heard my phone buzz in my pantsuit pocket.

I frowned at my phone screen. It was Jenn—not that a text from Jenn was unwelcome, but I'd been expecting to hear from Gregory.

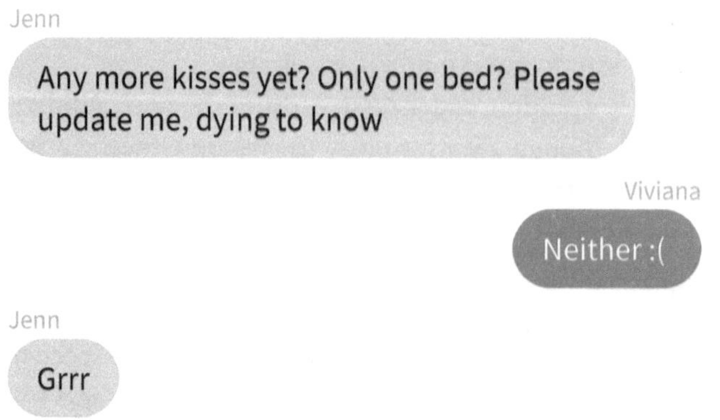

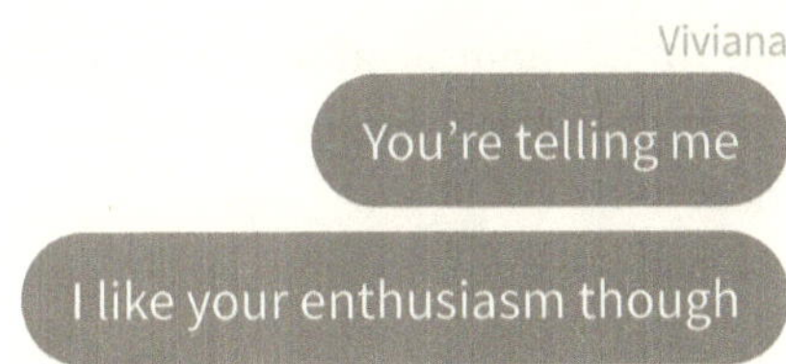

Feeling irritable again as I proceeded to the next meeting room, I'd started to put my phone back in my pocket when it buzzed again. Sighing, I considered just ignoring it, but Jenn didn't deserve that. She was the only person I could confide in these days.

Against my instincts, I held back from responding right away, since *he* obviously didn't feel any sense of urgency in replying to my messages. Still, my lips curled into a smile and my heart raced as I considered the "perhaps after" part.

I practically skipped along to the next session, wondering what the evening would bring. And what should I wear? Would we perhaps go to his room or mine? With all this occupying my mind, the afternoon session speakers didn't capture much, if any, of my attention.

I strode into the evening party with much more confidence than I'd felt the night before. After all, I'd spent extra time getting ready for what I hoped would be a special night with Gregory, the first of many, perhaps. The first time was always the most important, especially for a man like Gregory, who could probably have any woman he wanted if he put in the effort to not be rude.

Or even if he didn't.

I had chosen a sleeveless, sapphire-colored dress that Annie had once gifted me. The upper part was fitted and lined with small silver diamond shapes, and the skirt was long and flowy. The combination of elegant and sophisticated yet soft and feminine was perfect for this occasion. At least I hoped it was elegant—I wasn't the best judge of fashion. But Annie was, and even though I was mad at her, she'd never have given me a dress that was less than flattering.

I had to suppress the urge to twirl around, and I smiled instead, looking around for my handsome date.

I spotted him immediately, talking to Brandon and a tall woman I didn't know. I bit my bottom lip, unprepared for such an encounter.

Frowning, I turned on my heel and made my way to an empty table on one side of the room, where I hoped Brandon wouldn't see me. Once I sat down, I texted Gregory to let him know I'd arrived, feigning ignorance of his location in the room. Setting my phone on the table, I leaned back in my chair and began to look around at the others in the crowd. It was an interesting mix of obvious academic types and more sophisticated publishing house types.

As I scanned the room, my wary eyes landed on a woman I'd encountered in several sessions earlier. The woman, tall and slender in a pantsuit, smiled and walked toward my table. I welcomed the chance for some company. Apart from Gregory, Brandon, and my parents, I knew no one at this conference, so it was a relief to be able to meet some people, especially someone who wasn't a high-level executive or academic. Jane ... what was her name? Not Austen ... Alton. Jane Alton was neither an executive nor an academic; in a morning session, she had introduced herself as a proofreader for a Duluth publication.

"Hi, mind if I join you?"

"If you don't mind the wallflowers table, sure." I smiled, gesturing to the empty chair across from me. "I'm Viviana Cantwell. And you're Jane, right?"

"Jane Alton, yes. It's nice to see a friendly face. I go to literary conferences as often as I can and usually recognize a lot of people I know, but not so much today. Which is odd since I actually live here too."

As Jane sat down, I breathed a sigh of relief. Sitting alone at an event designed for networking was always awkward, and even though I wasn't here for the networking, I didn't need everyone else to know that.

"So, have you been to Duluth before?" Jane asked, sipping her cocktail.

"I have, many times as a child. It was sort of our weekend getaway when we had the chance." I smiled at the memories. "It's one of my favorite places, actually."

"I can see why. I've only lived here for a few years myself, but I wish I'd moved here years ago. It's a beautiful area," Jane said, her blue eyes twinkling.

"Where did you—" I stopped when Gregory suddenly appeared in front of our table. "Oh, Gregory! There you are."

"Hello, Viviana," he said stiffly. "Am I interrupting?"

"Of course not," I said. "Gregory, this is Jane Alton, who works with the *Lake Superior Post*, a well-known regional publication—"

"I'm familiar with it," he interrupted. "And what do you do at the *Post*, Ms. Alton?"

"I'm a proofreader, mostly for local pieces about—"

"I see." His lips curved downward into a distinct frown.

I looked at him with narrowed eyes. Was he being condescending because of Jane's *job*? If so, what must he think of my freelance editing position? Shaking my head slightly, I said, "Jane, this is Gregory Fitzgerald, a senior editor at Elliot, a New York publishing house. He's been visiting Minneapolis because his close friend heads up Bolder Publishing, where I work."

Jane smiled politely, holding out her hand. "Nice to meet you, Gregory."

"It is Dr. Fitzgerald." He shook her hand quickly. He glanced at his watch and turned to me, his tone laced with impatience. "Are your parents due to arrive soon? I do look forward to becoming better acquainted."

"I, uh, I believe so," I said, caught off guard.

Jane, probably sensing she was a third wheel, stood to make a graceful exit. "Well, I see an old friend over there, so I'll leave you two alone. Maybe I'll catch up with you later, Viviana."

I smiled at my new friend, attempting to apologize with my eyes. Just then, my phone buzzed. The text was from my mother, stating that they would not be attending tonight. Apparently my father felt fatigued from the crowds, which happened fairly often, serious introvert that he was. So my parents would be having a quiet dinner to themselves elsewhere. I wasn't the least bit surprised or disappointed.

But *he* certainly was, after I told him the news. "What? He's—they're not coming?"

He'd rarely stumbled over words before, not even during some of our rather awkward encounters. He must have been surprised indeed. And even crestfallen, judging by the pained look on his face.

"Sorry," I said slowly, unsure how to interpret Gregory's strange reaction. "Sometimes my father needs quiet time to recharge during or after events like this. He's not a fan of crowds."

He stared down at the table, silent for a moment. "I see."

"I'm sorry. I ... well, I didn't know you were so looking forward to seeing them, or we could've arranged to all meet at a restaurant instead. I'm afraid it's too late now though, as they've already made their own dinner plans." Should I feel delighted that he was so interested in getting to know my family? Or offended that he seemed less interested in getting to know *me*? Surely I was imagining that, though.

He was silent and pulled his phone from his pocket.

After a few minutes of failed attempts at small talk, I sighed. Gregory seemed very distracted, and his clipped one-word answers indicated he was even less interested in small talk than usual. I almost couldn't blame him, as my attempts at small talk were boring even to me … except that I *could* blame him somewhat, because he was supposed to at least *try*, wasn't he? We were sort of dating, after all. He'd invited me here!

"I see an acquaintance with whom I must speak." He stood up quickly.

I started to rise, intending to accompany him.

He shook his head and put a firm hand on my shoulder. "No, you stay. You would not be interested in our conversation. We will speak later."

I sat back in the chair, feeling stunned and slighted, which was unfortunately becoming a frequent feeling around him. "OK," I said, resigned. "See you later."

Without another word, he was gone, and I was left to stew in my feelings of resentment and confusion, coupled with a healthy dose of self-pity. What I needed immediately was a stiff drink, so I went in search of one. Fortunately, I also saw Jane, who was wincing as a short, blonde man in a suit spoke loudly to her. Drink in hand, I walked in Jane's direction.

The relief in her eyes was palpable. "Viviana! I'd love to chat some more about that project. Sorry, Walter, it was nice to see you," she said quickly as she linked arms with me and dragged me away.

After they were out of earshot, Jane turned to me. "Massive thanks for rescuing me. That's Walter Bonneville, and he's a pain in the butt, to be frank. His IQ is off the charts, but his EQ is nonexistent. It's bad enough I have to work with him occasionally, but he also hits on me every time I see him. *Every* time." She shuddered, looking over her shoulder to reassure herself that he was far away.

I giggled as we headed toward a small empty table. "I'm glad to be of service. I've only just met you, but I recognized the please-rescue-me expression. It must be universal."

"Well, speaking of needing to be rescued ... Has your, uh, friend left?"

"He has. Jane, I'm sorry he was so rude," I said.

She offered a wry smile. "We all have bad days, right? It's fine."

"I wish I could make up some excuse for him, but I can't. He's almost always that way."

Jane's lips curved into a frown. "No worries, for me at least. But what about you? It doesn't bother you?"

I sighed as I slumped into a chair. "It does, but I thought he'd started to come around. He seemed better lately, and we had a lovely date last weekend—" I stopped abruptly. "Jane, I am so, so sorry. I've only just met you today. You couldn't possibly be interested in hearing about the details of my love life, if it can even be called a love life."

"Nonsense," Jane said, tossing her long blonde ponytail over her shoulder and leaning forward with a kind smile. "I'd love to hear more. Do you want to start now, or shall we get another drink first?"

The cocktails helped ease my unease, that is, until I spotted Gregory talking to a woman. And not just any woman—a very beautiful one. Tall and shapely with stunning black hair and olive skin, the woman was laughing, *actually laughing*, ostensibly at something he had said. Jane followed my gaze, which was probably more of a glare.

"Oh my gosh, is he actually *flirting* with her? Gregory never flirts. He's ... he's incapable!" I said, just above a whisper.

"Well, perhaps they're old friends or—" Jane stopped as they both watched him whisper close to That Woman's ear, after which she smiled coyly. "Or ... something," she finished flatly. She pushed her glasses up her nose and turned to me, sympathy in her eyes.

I downed the rest of my drink and slammed it on the table, ready to confront him.

"Don't," Jane warned. "I know what you're thinking."

I eyed my new friend suspiciously. "How do you know me so well, when we just met today?"

Jane burst into laughter. "Because we're totally alike, and I know exactly what *I'd* be thinking in your shoes."

I let out a long breath and leaned back in my chair. "I'm sorry, that was rude of me. You've been nothing but awesome, even though I barely know you. So ... it's not all in my head then? He *is* being a little infuriating?"

Jane nodded emphatically. "More than a little, I'd say. And I think your glass is empty."

When I raised my eyes again, Gregory and That Woman were no longer in sight. I clenched my jaw and then rose to join Jane in search of more cocktails. But before we reached the bar, I caught sight of someone familiar.

Irene? I did a double take. *Just my luck tonight, another person who's out to get me.*

The sinking feeling in my stomach only worsened when I saw who Irene was talking to—Brandon. How did they know each other? Maybe they had mutual local connections through Bolder.

They deserve each other.

Scowling, I turned away before either of them could spot me.

An hour later, I had enjoyed chatting with Jane, who confessed to her nerves about tomorrow's breakfast date (or meeting? Jane wasn't sure) with a colleague she was crushing on. But I couldn't stop stewing about the scene I'd witnessed with Gregory and That Woman. Nor had I seen him at all since then. I was more than ready to return to my room and sleep off my terrible mood, and I told Jane so.

"Fine by me. I'm more than a little tired myself, and I haven't even been through the emotional wringer as you have tonight," she said with a sympathetic smile. "Though I think you handled it admirably. As well as anyone could. Are you going to text him to say you're leaving?"

I sighed. "Hmm. Do you think I should?"

"I think—" Jane hesitated. "I think that's up to you."

"You think I shouldn't, and you're probably right. I shouldn't bother." I exhaled loudly again as we walked in the direction of our rooms. What would Elizabeth from my novel do? "Knowing me, though, I probably will."

"There's no right or wrong answer here," Jane said.

"Mm-hmm."

Jane laughed, but before she could speak, I blurted out, "Would you read my book?" I bit my lip, trying to ignore the waves of awkwardness pouring out of me. "I mean, we just met, but I feel like we really connected today ..."

So, so awkward. Thanks a lot, alcohol.

"Book, as in ... you've written a book? Edited one? Or what exactly?"

"I've written one. Writing, actually, I've still got a long way to go. But I could really use another set of eyes, especially since my story is a bit, uh, stalled lately. Inspiration is currently on hold."

"That's cryptic," Jane said, grinning. "Well, I'd love to. What kind of book is it?"

I was silent for a moment before muttering, "Basically Austen fan fiction."

"Really?" Jane's eyes widened. "I—"

"I mean, it's probably not worth your time. It's silly, really, the whole thing. The story and even just the idea that I could write something—"

"Hey, I was just going to say that I *love* Austen adaptations of all kinds! Well, scratch that. I *don't* like the ones that write alternative plots or endings for Austen's novels. Variations, I think they're called. I steer clear of those. But the sequels and modern adaptations and all of that, I confess I've spent a ridiculous amount of money online buying those up."

"You too?" I asked, my eyes widening. "Wow. Then you won't mind?"

Jane's eyes were bright. "Mind? I'd be honored! Do you want feedback of any particular sort?"

"That's a good question. General feedback, I guess. I also have to warn you, and this is beyond embarrassing ..."

"What is it?"

"Well, this whole night is beyond embarrassing, so I guess it doesn't matter. You see, the novel is sort of based on my own story," I said hesitantly before adding, "with Gregory."

"Oh, I see," said Jane, tilting her head thoughtfully. She smiled and added, "Then I'll also get to know my new friend a little better."

Impulsively, I hugged her, though I'd never do that when sober. "Thank you so much. I don't even want to think about how much worse tonight could've gone if you hadn't been here with me. I'll let you off the hook though, so you can get some sleep. But tomorrow, I want to hear all about what happens at breakfast with your lady friend!" I grinned at Jane as I grasped my room key from my purse.

Jane laughed and then put her palm over her face. "Oh, I just realized I'm on the wrong floor. Up one floor to my room. A little too much wine." One side of her mouth was curved upward as she started to turn. "Goodnight then. And if you really want to avoid texting him tonight, just turn off your phone and, like, put it in the bathroom or something."

As I entered my room and tossed my purse on a table, I decided to do just that. Well, the part about turning it off. Not the part about sleeping with my phone in another room though. *As if*, I thought with a giggle while powering down my phone and dropping it onto the nightstand. Sinking into the bed, I lamented the stiff, starchy feel of the sheets, missing my own soft, comforting bedding at home. Remembering I would need to set the hotel alarm clock, I reached over and managed to set it, or so I hoped. "I should take off my fancy dress ... and shoes," I mumbled, just before falling asleep.

Chapter 23

When the alarm sounded the next morning, I drowsily reached over to press snooze on my phone. But the blaring sound continued. Oh, I'd set the hotel alarm clock. Opening one eye, I looked around and spotted the clock on the floor. Grumbling, I swatted at the clock until it was silent.

Why hadn't I set my phone alarm? I thought, my heart starting to race.

Oh ... I was drunk and turned the phone off.

What if Gregory *did* call? Now I'd never know.

But why would he call me? He only texts and never calls.

Trying to ignore the annoying voice, I kicked off the one shoe I was still wearing, and my lovely, perfect dress from last night was itchy and wrinkled in the harsh morning light. Was that a wine stain? I groaned, rubbing at a dark spot in the bust area.

Distraught, I buried myself back in the covers and pillows. I should skip the closing sessions this morning. My brain was too foggy to remember the topics or the speakers for the day.

And who cares anyway?

After an appropriate amount of time wallowing under the covers, I finally roused myself to sit and turn my phone on. Zero texts. My heart sank. But just as I was about to toss my phone aside, it buzzed several times. I forgot it takes a minute sometimes—I so rarely turn it off.

Gregory

> Hello, are you and your family available for breakfast?

> You are unavailable. I will make other plans.

The first text was sent at 6 am, and the second at 6:10. Gregory apparently didn't like to wait; he assumed that everyone else was as attached to their phones as he was. I grimaced and glanced at the clock, which read 9:30. Widening my eyes, I realized I must have fallen back to sleep after turning off my alarm.

Or maybe you drunkenly set the alarm for the wrong time.

I rose from bed and, oddly, began to feel hopeful. Although I'd missed the opportunity to see him, he *had* tried. He *did* care. And such an early text meant that he probably hadn't spent a late night with another woman. Sketchy logic, perhaps, but it felt very comforting. And despite the disappointments of the weekend, he *had* cared enough to invite me to Duluth this weekend. For someone like Gregory, that had to mean something. At least Bridget Jones thought so in a similar situation. Granted, Bridget's weekend away was with the commitment-phobe Daniel, not with Mark Darcy. Still, I felt buoyed by these thoughts and smiled as I climbed out of bed.

With renewed enthusiasm, I picked up the conference schedule from the floor and scanned through it. I could at least attend the closing luncheon. He'd likely attend, and if not, I might have another opportunity to talk to Jane.

After I finished showering and felt cozy in my pink Terry robe, a knock sounded at the door. My heart skipped a beat. Gregory?

Should I change out of my robe quickly or just answer the door as is?

Greeting him with fewer clothes than usual surely can't hurt.

I smiled and threw the door open.

"Oh ... hi, Mom."

My mother looked me up and down and raised one eyebrow as she waltzed inside. "You sound disappointed, my dear. Were you expecting someone else?"

"No!" I averted my eyes. "What's up, Mom?"

"Your father and I have decided to skip the luncheon, as he's had enough of the crowds for the weekend. He'd like to leave before the Sunday afternoon traffic. Would you mind terribly if we left a bit early?"

I sat on the edge of the bed and thought for a moment. "I don't mind. I'm having a bit of convention fatigue myself, honestly." I frowned, realizing I wouldn't have an opportunity to see Gregory again. Or Jane.

But no awkward run-ins with Brandon or Irene ... maybe worth it.

"Are you sure you don't mind, dear? I think it's best for him, but he said it's up to you," my mother reassured me.

"Of course. I know how fatiguing such things can be for Dad." I smiled, reflecting on how my parents were always looking out for each other. They weren't perfect, but they were the next best thing. Anytime in my life when love seemed like a lie, a mere fairy tale, my parents' marriage was my reminder that it was possible. Not necessarily common or likely, but possible—at least for some people.

My mother's lips curled into a smile that reminded me so much of my own. Also a fair-skinned brunette, my mother was slender and even elegant when she wanted to be. She much preferred her usual lab coat attire, but she looked amazing when she put in the effort. If only I had also inherited her talent for science, but I definitely hadn't.

"All right, I must dash off, and I'll leave you to dress and pack up. How does a half an hour sound?"

It sounded very soon, but probably the perfect amount of time for me to dress and pack without having excess time to think about and/or do something stupid. "Sure, Mom. I'll meet you guys at your room when I'm ready."

After my mother departed, I closed the door and leaned against it. This was for the best—if we'd stayed, I might not have seen or heard from Gregory anyway. And even if he did want to see me, maybe becoming less, well, *available* would make him realize he wanted to see more of me.

Forty-five minutes later, I knocked on the door of my parents' hotel room. My mother answered the door, looking completely different than she had earlier. Instead of the elegant pantsuit, she was now wearing leggings and an oversized sweater. "The travel version of Mom," I said, barely suppressing a giggle.

My mother raised an eyebrow and turned back into the room. "Vivi, you're right on time. We'll just get our luggage."

"Not exactly on time, but I appreciate that you didn't point it out," I said, the corners of my mouth twitching.

My father smirked. "How long have we known you, Viv?"

"Point taken," I said. "Getting ready quickly is not my forte. And neither is waiting. Let's go!"

As we walked through the hotel toward the exit, I anxiously scanned the halls and rooms we passed, hoping for a sight of Gregory.

As we rounded a corner, I was startled to see Irene in the lobby. The domineering woman's face registered surprise followed by an icy glare and then ... was that a smirk? I guess when Jack wasn't around, she didn't even pretend to not hate me. Why did Irene hate me so much? We'd barely had any contact, ever, and I had never been anything but courteous to her. I shrugged as we stepped outside.

Some people were just permanently grouchy or rude, or both. And lately I'd been unlucky enough to encounter several such people.

When we reached my parents' car and finished loading all our luggage into the back, I checked my phone again for the hundredth time that morning.

"Coming, Viv? You've been glued to your phone more than usual this morning." My mother stuck her forehead out the window. "Expecting an important message?"

"We've spent like 10 minutes together so far this morning," I said with a laugh as I got into the car.

"True, but I think I've seen you check it at least 10 times, my dear."

I sighed and said nothing as we drove away. My mother also said nothing more, much to my relief. I stared out the window at Lake Superior and the occasional remaining patches of ice on the shores. I silently said farewell to one of my favorite places, hoping I'd be back soon. Maybe I could persuade Jack to come here with me; we hadn't taken a best friend vacation in years. I smiled idly as the lake slowly faded from my vision, imagining all the long walks we could take, the sightseeing we could do.

But only five minutes later, I realized Dad wasn't ready to let it go. "Have you been texting Gregory?" he asked, his tone sounding deceptively casual.

"No."

After another minute or two of silence, he asked, "Viviana, dearest, can I be honest with you?"

I exhaled, knowing that I couldn't say no, because then I'd wonder forever what my father wanted to say. "Of course, Dad."

For at least a minute, he seemed to be trying to choose his words. "What do you see in him?"

"What—what do I see in him?" I stammered, surprised at his bluntness. I bristled and crossed my arms even though my parents weren't looking at me in the backseat. "Gregory has a lot to recommend him, Dad. I'm surprised you didn't see that."

"Like what? Apart from his career and ambition and money, things that ... well, frankly, things that have never seemed to interest you that much before."

"I guess that's true. But he has plenty of other things to recommend him."

"Viviana, dear," my mother cut in, looking over her shoulder to give me a reassuring smile. "Maybe if you tell us a little more about him, we'd understand what you like about him. Of course, we *want* to like anyone whom you care about."

I waited for my father to chime in, but he didn't. I grasped for words, trying to explain what I couldn't even understand myself. "It's ... he's ... I think he grew up with parents who always expected too much, and he faced some tragedy as a child, and maybe that's why he ... well, it's hard to explain."

"Love always is," my mother said softly, and my father nodded.

After a longer silence, Dad finally spoke again. "I'm sorry, Viv. We just want you to be happy with someone who treats you well, and I just didn't feel that he treated you well. But I met him only once, and I know very little. If you think he's wonderful, then I'm certain he is."

I didn't reply. Was he wonderful? That wasn't exactly how I thought of him. I gazed out the window, wanting to shut out these thoughts.

A few minutes later, my father cleared his throat. "I should let this go, but I have to say that his friend Brandon impressed me even less; I saw him with several different women over the weekend, morning and night, and none of them appeared to be work relationships."

I turned sharply. "Dad, Brandon is my *boss*. Or my boss's boss. He owns Bolder."

My dad balked. "*That* is Brandon Bolder?" I saw a look pass between my parents. "I hadn't put that together. Well, shame on him."

I shrugged, unable and unwilling to defend him. "I can't argue with you there. He's actually been dating Annie too, and I was beginning to suspect he's not a great guy. Annie doesn't want to hear it though."

"We seldom do want to hear such things," my father said.

"Dad, don't worry," I said. "I'm not dating Brandon. Give it a rest."

"No, but he's Gregory's friend, and the company we keep—"

"Your father and I just love you," my mother cut in, putting her hand on my father's shoulder. "We're sorry if it seems like we're grilling you. That's not our intention at all. We just want what's best for you. And ... well, we wanted to make sure our invitation to visit us in Italy next year wasn't putting any kind of weird pressure on you."

"You mean, like, to find a husband like everyone else in my family?"

"Not unless you want that, darling," Mom said. "Your life is your own, and you don't have to follow anyone else's path."

Pressing my lips together tightly, I stared stubbornly out the window.

"Truly sorry, Viv. I didn't mean to upset you. You know that," Dad said softly.

"I'm not 16," I muttered. "I'm nearly twice that."

"I know. Things were so much easier back then, weren't they?"

I fought a smile. "Well, I wouldn't quite put it that way. Zits and AP exams and hormones and adolescence ... I wouldn't want to return to that," I said with a shudder.

"I do miss your bangs though," my mother said, her eyes twinkling as she looked back. "But not so much the hairspray." We all laughed, recalling the fads of the '90s and early 2000s.

A few moments later, my phone buzzed with a text from Jane.

I cringed. We'd exchanged phone numbers, but I'd completely forgotten to let Jane know of our early departure. Fortunately, my new friend was very understanding, and we agreed to keep in touch. I was relieved that Jane refrained from asking about Gregory, as I had no patience left to talk or even think about him. I closed my eyes, shutting out the bright sun falling over the endless Midwestern landscape of farms and fields.

In what seemed like a moment later, we pulled into my parents' driveway, and I rubbed the sleep from my eyes. I must have been quite exhausted, as I was usually incapable of sleeping in a car. My neck was going to hurt tomorrow. After hugging my parents, I hauled my luggage into my own car.

The drive home was a blur; fortunately, traffic driving across the Cities wasn't too horrendous, as it was Sunday, after all. After depositing my keys, coat, shoes, and bags on the floor just inside the apartment, I darted toward the couch. All I wanted to do was collapse with a book or a movie while sipping (or gulping) a glass of wine (or a bottle). Or take a second nap. But then I stopped in my tracks, remembering I needed to stop at the office this weekend to borrow a book from the office library.

This week's editing project was a book about medical journalism, and I didn't actually own a copy of the AMA manual, since I rarely edited clinical material. For the hundredth time, I wondered why the editors weren't all given online subscriptions to the major style guides. *Probably because management wants to force everyone to show our faces there occasionally*, I thought with a grimace, *which is sort of ridiculous since many of us are only freelancers.*

I *could* wait until tomorrow morning to go to the office, but waking up early on a Monday morning was about as likely to happen as Gregory showing up at my door tonight with flowers.

I squeezed my eyes shut, trying to clear my mind. As much as I wanted to, I hadn't succeeded in my goal to stop thinking about him.

All the more reason to get the office visit out of the way, so I can bury myself in editing at home for the next few days, I thought as I reluctantly returned to my pile of belongings strewn near the door.

Arriving at the office, I was surprised to see the light on in Ellen's office. Hoping to avoid contact with anyone, including and perhaps especially Ellen, I quickened my steps on my way to the office library, which was just past Ellen's office.

Of course, Ellen chose the same moment to exit her office. She stopped short outside the doorway. "Viviana, what a surprise to see you here on a Sunday night!"

I halted and reluctantly turned toward Ellen. "I didn't expect to see you either." My brows crinkled, noticing my usually fashionable boss was wearing pink yoga pants and a purple tank top.

Ellen's cheeks reddened ever so slightly. "I'm off to the gym after I finish some work. There's a yoga class on Sunday nights ..." she trailed off.

I stared at her. Ellen was *so* not a yoga type. And on a Sunday night? With flawless makeup and hair? How bizarre.

Is she trying to impress someone at the gym? No, no, she couldn't possibly.

I'd known Ellen for years. She had her flaws, but she wasn't the lying, cheating type. Was she? She'd been married to a somewhat older, wealthy man for many years. Happily married. Or so I thought.

But before I could think of a way to subtly probe, Ellen put her hands on her hips and turned the focus to me. "And what are *you* doing here, Viv?"

I explained why I'd come, diving into a bit more detail about the clinical editing job than was needed. With any luck, we'd keep the conversation focused on work. That's all I could handle right now.

Ellen nodded, seeming distracted as she looked at the clock. But just when I thought I'd escaped any further questions or unwanted conversation, Ellen looked at me directly and said, "Girl, you look worn out. Are you doing OK? Are we working you too hard?"

"No, not at all."

"You'd let me know if something was off, right?"

"Of course," I mumbled, knowing that, in fact, I wouldn't do so. "I'm just tired from the convention. I'm my father's daughter ... being around a lot of people for hours or days on end can be exhausting. Hence the job freelancing from home."

"The convention?"

"Oh, I thought you knew. The literary conference in Duluth. I went with ... my parents."

"Ah. I didn't know you were interested in attending that. I knew Brandon was attending with Gregory though." Ellen paused. "Did you see them?"

"I did." Then, I decided it would be interesting to gauge Ellen's reaction to Gregory's invitation. "Gregory invited me, actually."

Ellen's eyes widened, and then she composed her features into a neutral expression. "Oh, he did?"

"Yes," I said, watching Ellen closely for a reaction. "You seem surprised."

"Well—" Ellen started. She looked at her nails, which appeared freshly manicured. "No, I suppose not," she said flatly.

"So, I—"

"Just be careful with that one."

"I'm surprised to hear you say that, since you seemed so encouraging in the beginning. You—you compared him to Mr. Darcy!" I sputtered.

Ellen didn't speak for a moment, looking at her nails again, and then at the plain wall behind them. Finally, her gaze returned to my anxious face. "Well, first impressions can be misleading," she said with an unreadable expression, "or maybe they're correct, but we just don't always see the truth of them."

I waited for her to say more, but she didn't. I spoke slowly. "Is there something I should know, Ellen?"

Looking away for a moment and then back to me, Ellen shook her head slowly. "Viviana, if you're happy, that's all that matters. I'm not even sure I trust my own judgment lately, so just ignore me."

"Well ..." I faltered. "I wouldn't say I'm happy. It's been pretty bumpy, to be honest, and this weekend didn't go very well. In fact, he—"

Ellen reached out and touched my shoulder. "Viviana, I'm so sorry, but I really can't stay and chat. I'm here on a Sunday night with a project that got dumped into my lap at the last minute, and I need to get home at a reasonable hour." Then, she hastily added, "After the gym."

I just nodded. What an idiot I was for divulging as much as I had. "Yes, of course. I'll just ... I'll leave you to it then. I was looking forward to an evening at home anyway. Goodnight, Ell." I turned on my heel and walked away before Ellen could see the hurt in my eyes.

Stupid feelings.

I scowled while entering the office library. I normally loved this room with its wall-to-wall books and cozy yellow chair in the corner, but tonight I was on a mission: get the book and then get the heck out of this place.

Book in hand, I walked past Ellen's office on my way back. The light was on, but the door was closed, the shades drawn.

Since when do her windows have shades? No, it's none of my business.

I breathed deeply and hurried past. The last thing I should be doing was worrying about someone else's relationships or, worse yet, confiding in someone, when I currently lacked the good judgment and emotional clarity to avoid oversharing, a common problem of mine. I used to overshare often with Jack, probably too often. But that too was apparently a thing of the past, something to avoid now. I wondered what Jack was doing tonight, what he'd done this weekend. I'd barely heard from him at all.

I felt a curious ache in my chest as I left the building. Despite wanting desperately to be alone, I was also, well, lonely. It was all so confusing, maddening even.

Wine will solve that problem. And a movie—one that has nothing to do with Mr. Darcy.

But before putting Mr. Darcy thoughts to rest for the night, I decided to email Jane a current draft of my novel. Once at home, I grabbed a bag of chips and a bottle of wine from the kitchen and padded over to the couch, ignoring my unopened luggage.

Viviana

Hi! I'm going out on a limb here and sending you my novel.

Jane

YAY! I hope you're doing OK.

Viviana

TBH … nope, not really. But thanks.

Jane

Sorry :(Let me know if you ever want to vent. I'm excited to read your book!

Viviana

Just promise me you'll save all the criticism for a different day, OK?

Jane

Got it. Will save scathing remarks for tomor-row.

Just kidding, of course. I have a feeling I'll love your writing!

She was probably going to be disappointed, but it felt nice to know that someone was interested in my novel. Apart from the fact that Jane was ridiculously easy to talk to and relate to, it was probably also easier to share such a personal project with someone who *didn't* know me as well. Or maybe I was just developing that thick skin that writers need to have.

Um, not likely to happen.

Chapter 24

The alarm blared for the fourth or fifth time, and I reached over to hit snooze again. "Go to hell, Monday," I grumbled. As I pulled the comforter more tightly around me, I tried to ignore the voice in my head nagging me to wake up.

"Fine, I'm awake!" I muttered aloud, swinging my legs off the bed and throwing off the covers. I looked around my room and cringed at the clothes strewn over the floor and in and around the open suitcase. I silently promised myself to tidy up today as I stepped over a few piles on my way to the kitchen.

After starting the coffeepot, I grabbed some bread from the bread box and carefully inspected it for signs of mold. Finding two slices with no green or furry spots, I put them in the toaster and turned my phone on.

I was surprised to see so many text messages.

But none from Gregory.

Jenn demanded to know how the weekend had gone, Jack asked if I was up for an early run, and both my mother and Lillian requested I call them today.

Yawning, I buttered my toast, choosing to ignore all but Jenn's texts for now. As I waited for my coffee to brew, I texted Jenn, briefly relaying the dismal results of my weekend away.

I barely noticed the buttery goodness as I waited for Jenn to confirm my thoughts—that I needed to give up this ridiculous fantasy and move on.

My jaw dropped when I read her response.

Jenn

Next time you see him, amp up the sexy.

Viviana

I thought you were a feminist!

Jenn

I am. A good feminist knows how to use her assets.

Viviana

That doesn't sound like feminism.

Jenn

It is if we use our assets on our own terms! I might be making this up as I go …

Viviana

OK, you win. But it's too early in the morning to talk about my, uh, assets

Jenn

Just trust me on this. And if you don't see results, he's not worth it. End of story.

As I added a generous amount of cream and sugar cubes to my coffee, I remembered that Gregory had vaguely mentioned a business meeting with Brandon and Ron this week. So maybe I'd see him at the office.

I would need to invent a reason to go to the office, since my visits were typically rare. Too bad I already picked up the AMA manual last night. I'd also need to find something sexy but not overdressed for a brief office visit. Not exactly an easy task, especially with most of my clothes lying on the floor, whether clean or dirty. I sighed. I'd need much more coffee for this.

Over an hour later, I was dressed in my best sundress—not exactly sexy, but still showing some skin, probably too much for the cool spring. I shook my head while climbing into my car.

Using my assets, what kind of feminist am I? And what the heck am I thinking? How is this going to help at all?

I still hadn't devised an excuse to visit the office; I'd be relying on my typically weak ability to improvise. With bravado apparently coming in unpredictable waves, I had to take advantage of the tide when it came.

Despite the uncertainty about what I was doing and why, dressing up did boost my confidence, which was sorely needed of late. Walking into the office, I smiled and said hello to several work acquaintances returning from their midmorning walk breaks. They were illustrators, I think. Or maybe photographers. I hadn't spent much time getting to know the staff, other than my fellow editors.

Remembering that I hadn't yet responded to Jack's text, I made a mental note to arrange a morning run with him soon. Groaning, I recalled Lillian's plea for me to call; I needed to just make time for it. As soon as I was back home.

As I walked down the hall, I finally devised a passable excuse to be visiting the office again. I would just say, if anyone asked, that I needed to borrow another style guide, perhaps an older edition. Not the most original excuse, but it could work if anyone were curious. I slowed my stride while walking by a conference room, forcing my gaze to be casual as I sought any sign of Gregory.

The first conference room was empty, so I headed to the library to retrieve the book that I didn't actually need. Fortunately, I'd come in a different entrance today, so I wouldn't be waylaid by Ellen again before reaching the library.

Just before reaching the library door, I slowed as I recognized Brandon's voice within the library. "So, did you see her again Saturday night?"

"Who? Do you mean Viviana?" said Gregory. I froze, putting my hand on the wall to steady me.

"No, the hot one. From the spa," Brandon said.

"You will have to be more specific," Gregory said, sounding bored.

Brandon laughed. "Point taken. There were quite a few to choose from, you're right."

I clenched my fists as my heart began to race. What a jerk! Apparently I was hot enough for Brandon to flirt shamelessly with, but then again, he seemed willing to flirt with anyone. Taking a deep but silent breath, I debated whether to enter the room or turn around.

"But that reminds me—how are things progressing with Marekson anyway?" Brandon asked.

At the mention of my father's pen name, I felt the blood drain from my face.

"Quite well," Gregory said. "We were only able to meet once, but I was able to gather a fair amount of information that you may find rather useful. I will send along my notes tonight."

Brandon laughed. "I look forward to it. The payoff will be huge, I think. Was she very devastated then when you dumped her?"

"I did not need to."

"Oh, that's cold, even for you."

"She does not have very high expectations," Gregory said nonchalantly. "Wooing her consumed very little effort on my part."

"So it's been easy, feigning interest in her?" Brandon asked.

One of them sighed, probably Gregory. "Not exactly easy, but not difficult either. She's not ugly. And she was desperate for any bit of attention I threw at her. Surely you noticed that yourself."

Brandon snorted. "I did. I want to say it was masterful, Gregory, but then, anyone could've done it."

"Probably," Gregory agreed, making shuffling sounds with his feet.

I was frozen in place, numb and holding my breath as I listened with a sinking feeling in my abdomen. But the possibility of them finding me in the hallway jolted me into motion, and I spun around and began to run, not walk, in the other direction. Heedless of the possibility of running into someone coming out of an office room, my vision was narrowed to the exit door. I had to leave. Nothing else mattered.

Before I escaped the building, my luck worsened. Instead of running into someone, I just fell ... flat on my face. Heedless of any pain and thinking only of survival, I put my palms down on the floor and used them to raise my head and scan the floor. I didn't even see anything nearby to trip over. Of course I couldn't pull off running in strappy sandals.

I rose to my feet slowly, my mortification knowing no bounds as I became more aware of my surroundings.

My eyes landed squarely on Ellen, standing between me and the exit door with a curious expression.

I rose reluctantly to meet her inquisitive eyes. Still in shock, I stood motionless except for my labored breathing. As I caught my breath and my head began to clear, the humiliation turned into a burning anger. My lips pressed into a thin line. "Did you tell him?"

Ellen tilted her head, looking puzzled. "Did I tell who? Tell them what?"

Gritting my teeth, with my face on fire, I took a step closer to my boss. "*What did you tell him about me?*"

Ellen's expression changed as understanding dawned. My eyes widened, and I parted my lips to speak and then closed them. Trembling, I shook my head and strode past her.

Chapter 25

My hands were shaking as I fumbled with my keys and managed to unlock and open the car door. I made a mental note to purchase a new battery for the keyless entry fob, which hadn't worked for months. Once in the car, I stared at the dash and realized I was overdue for an oil change. Probably a car wash too, given the layer of dust on the dash, along with something sticky-looking in some parts.

By the time I absently buckled my seatbelt, my heart rate had slowed, and I was no longer shaking but very still. I could breathe.

I started driving, and I kept breathing. That was important.

I wasn't really in my body, except to drive. And breathe.

Keep breathing.

When I entered my apartment minutes or hours later, I breathed.

Calmly placing my purse on the table, I slipped out of my shoes and purposefully walked to the couch.

I just needed to breathe—

But the spell was broken.

I was falling, falling down to the couch, falling into a deep, terrifying pit of feelings and thoughts. The shock, the humiliation, the betrayal, the absolute devastation—the disbelief that I could be so, so deluded. So stupid.

Lightheaded and overcome, I braced my hands on the couch. I clutched one of the armrests while my vision blurred. Was I having a panic attack or maybe dying? I wasn't sure what either of those things felt like.

I crumpled back into the cushion, grabbing my Austen throw pillow and hugging it to my chest. I was both hot and cold, feeling both everything and nothing, at least nothing that I could identify.

Realizing what pillow I was holding, my knuckles whitened, and I saw the silhouette of Elizabeth and Darcy. As though scalded, I dropped the pillow on the floor and then kicked it several feet away.

Breathe. Just breathe.

And then the tears came, and that was all I had left. The cloudy and panicked feeling left me, abandoning me to this new feeling, which was so, so much worse. I collapsed on my side, utterly overcome by sadness.

No, not sadness. Agony, anguish even. I was being ripped apart from within.

I felt myself *feel* in ways I hadn't in a long time, maybe ever. Pain I couldn't handle, devastation that would swallow me whole. I'd rather be having a panic attack than feel this; I'd rather be angry or in shock than face this. Anything but this.

As I buried my tear-streaked face in my hands, curling into a ball on the couch, I thought vaguely that this was probably a long time coming. Years of therapy had helped me identify my tendency to do whatever is necessary to avoid having to feel crippling negative emotions, especially sadness or shame. It was useless to try this time.

The phone was ringing. I stumbled off the couch, looking around slowly as I became aware of my surroundings, lit only dimly by the setting sun. Had I been sleeping? I rubbed my eyes, sore from sobbing. Finally, I spotted my phone on the floor near the couch.

Before I could turn it off, I saw Lillian's name and photo on the screen. I felt another twinge of guilt for not returning my sister's messages, but this was definitely not the time to chat. Lillian wouldn't understand. Probably no one could, but my perfect older sister definitely wouldn't.

From the couch, I stared blankly in the direction of the TV, which was off.

As much as I wanted to hide from the world and drown in misery, I still had a strong urge to call a friend, to be soothed even, as ridiculous as it sounded even to myself.

Maybe Jenn could help. She wouldn't judge, at least. She was good like that. But she was probably busy with her perfect little family.

I couldn't bring myself to contact Jane, who was probably in the midst of reading my ridiculous story. Thankfully, Jane lived many miles away; I couldn't imagine having to face her in person now. My new friend probably wouldn't even be surprised by this turn of events, as the signs were all clearly pointing to this outcome. Why hadn't I seen it myself? Or why had I refused to acknowledge what a wretched person he was, even to myself? Or had I known but not cared? I shook my head, which was starting to ache.

And then there was Jack. I bit my lip and quickly decided against calling him. He hadn't exactly been a good confidant lately, at least with the Gregory stuff. Jack disliked Gregory and would never understand why I had even bothered with him. I couldn't bear for Jack to see me this way, even though he had many times before. Somehow this time was different.

Oh, the humiliation, I thought, burying my face in my hands for the hundredth time that day. *Definitely not calling Jack.*

<h1 style="text-align:center">Chapter 26</h1>

An hour later, while finishing a long swig from the bottle and reclining on the couch, I heard a knock at the door.

I froze. Who could it be? Should I answer? It seemed unlikely to be anyone other than Jack, since our building had decent security. Yet he hadn't randomly stopped over here for weeks, so that seemed unlikely too. Annie might still have the entry code, but as far as I knew, we still weren't talking.

I forced some meditative breaths to dispel the quickened heart rate and the tension wracking my body. I'd just stay quiet and hope that the visitor would go away quickly.

I couldn't face anyone.

But I heard the sound of the door opening and then Jack's voice. "Vivi? You here?"

No, no, no, no. This is not happening.

I debated whether to stay hidden, lying flat on the couch where he couldn't see me.

"Vivi, are you home?" Jack called out again, taking slow steps into my apartment.

I sighed, using my hands to push myself up. "Jack. Hi. Did you need something?"

He walked tentatively to the couch, holding out a key. "I was just coming home and noticed that you left your key in the door. So I wanted to check—" he stopped then. "Vivi, what's wrong? You look terrible."

"Gee, thanks." I looked away. "I'm fine. Just a bad day, that's all."

"And you're drinking right out of the bottle this early in the evening? I think it's been, oh, a decade since I've seen you do that?" When I glanced at him briefly, his face was wrinkled in concern.

"Drinking out of glasses is so overrated," I said coolly, trying to hide the tremble in my voice.

He moved a pillow out of the way to sit down next to me. "What's going on?"

I continued to look away and said nothing, wishing I'd hidden the traitorous bottle. Finally, I croaked, "It's nothing. I'm tired. Thank you for letting me know about the key."

"It's obviously not nothing, Vivi," he said as he touched my shoulder gently. "But tell me about this nothing."

"Don't you have, like, something more important to do with your time? Or someone more important to spend it with?"

"No. I'm here with you, Vivi. Right where I want to be. Where I always—" He cleared his throat suddenly. "Vivi, do you want to talk?"

After taking another swig from the bottle, I finally looked at him fully. I braced myself for his reaction, aware that seeing my face would reveal the full extent of my misery. Jack was no stranger to my ugly crying. Still, this time felt ... different. In a voice barely above a whisper, I said, "I don't think you really want to hear about this, Jack. It's—it's about someone you don't like or respect. It will seem ridiculous ... *I* will seem ridiculous to you."

"Gregory," he said, utterly still.

I nodded and looked away again, trying to stop the tears from falling.

He was quiet for a moment and then asked softly, "What ... what did he do?"

I bit my lip and swallowed hard. Of course I wanted to confide in Jack as I always had in the past, but could I handle the humiliation this time?

He reached out and stroked my upper arms gently, tender concern showing in his eyes and soft words. "Please, Vivi. Let me help. I don't like or respect him, you're right. But I like and respect you, so that's what matters." He paused, his hands stilling and then falling back to his lap. "I'll try to be—I *will* be the friend that I really haven't been lately. The friend you deserve."

I shook my head and raised my eyes to his pleading ones. "I'm sure I don't deserve you. I doubt I ever have."

After a long silence, I took a fortifying breath and told him the story.

The whole story.

It took a while, and it took some more tears, but I told him everything. Every mortifying detail.

When I finished, he was silent. His body was still, almost rigidly so, and his eyes were trained on the floor. Was he waiting patiently for me to say more or trying to decide how to react?

"So that's all of it, Jack." Wiping my eyes, I found it hard to look at him, especially after finishing the last part of the story, the most mortifying parts.

He raised his eyes to me slowly and cleared his throat. "Vivi, I don't know what to say."

I swallowed as the tears gathered in my eyes once again, all the devastation of earlier today rushing back in full force. "It's OK. You—you don't have to say anything. I know I was a complete fool. *Am*, not was. I'm not deluding myself anymore."

"No!" he said sharply, his eyes flashing and jaw muscles clenching. "You're not a fool. You're a good person, the *best*, and he's just … just an asshole."

I gasped. "You never curse," I said softly. It was one of his best quirks, I'd always thought.

"Well, what else can you say about such a person? I didn't like the man, you know that, but I had no idea how wretched he was."

Jack shook his head as he clenched and unclenched his fists. I'd never seen him do that before; I'd so rarely seen him visibly upset at all. "Viviana, none of this is your fault. *None* of it. I know this feels ... feels horrible, to say the least, I'm sure. You're blaming yourself. But you did nothing wrong. You did *not* deserve it, any of it. You have to believe me. Please, Vivi."

Averting my eyes again, I found it difficult to meet his intense gaze. "Maybe he's a garbage person. I mean, I guess he definitely is. But still, *I* was dumb enough to fall for it, for him. Despite all the obvious signs that he was not into me. And all the signs that he was not a good person. I was an idiot. I *am* an idiot." I paused for a long moment while trying to blink back more tears. "I can hardly even look at you because I'm so embarrassed. What kind of idiot would—"

He leaned forward then and pulled me firmly to his chest. I couldn't stop the tears from flowing yet again, and I began to shake as I fell apart in his strong arms, tear-dampened cheeks pressed to his chest. Neither of us spoke or moved; he just held me firmly until I finally stopped shaking.

Minutes or perhaps hours later, I sniffled and started to pull away, looking down. "I'm sorry, Jack. I wish I could say I don't need your pity, but I obviously do. Thank you for not making me feel like the total idiot that I am."

He shook his head, placing one finger on my lips gently. "Shh. Don't say that again. He's the idiot."

I raised my puffy eyes to meet Jack's and drew in a breath. His face was very close.

He rested his forehead against mine for a long time. With my eyes closed, I felt his warm breath on my face and then his hand brushing my cheek.

My stomach started to do some strange flips, and my cheek felt hot where he'd touched it. I was barely aware that I leaned in, ever so slightly. After a long moment, his breath ever closer, I felt a fluttering touch on my upper lip.

I inhaled and felt the light touch again.

Was it a breath or ... a kiss? The sensation was fleeting. Had I imagined it? Jack pulled back slightly, still mere inches away, and when I opened my eyes, he was gazing at me intently with darkened eyes, a strange look I didn't recognize in him. *What* was happening? I exhaled a shaky breath as my lips parted.

I didn't know what came next, whether I leaned forward or he did, or both. But the next thing I knew, our lips collided, and it wasn't so fleeting or tentative. The kiss was firm, yet achingly tender. Full of feeling, yet soft and slightly tentative. Patient, yet determined. I had no thoughts and, for the second time that day, could only *feel*, and feel deeply, with sensations unnamed and unknown.

His warm hands cradled my face as I threaded mine through his soft, wavy hair. When his lips began to trace a path along my jaw, I drew in another shaky breath and pulled him in closer.

With his hands on my upper arms, he pulled away with a suddenness that left me grasping the couch for stability, while he quickly retreated to the far end of the couch.

As we both caught our breath, we gazed at one another with dazed eyes. I was faintly aware of a sense of surprise on his face, or maybe it was a look of disbelief.

With our eyes still locked, he rose slowly to his feet as he opened and then closed his mouth several times.

"Vivi, I ..." His voice was thick with emotion, and he cleared his throat. "This was ... I'm ..." He tore his gaze away from me, looking around the room. Finally, he took a long breath and met my eyes again. "I'm truly sorry. I should go. I mean, I will go."

I swallowed the lump in my throat with some effort and opened my mouth to speak, but he had already turned to leave. And then I found, as I watched him leave, that I had no words.

Stunned, I remained on the couch, immobile. It could have been hours, minutes, or even just seconds in which I just stared at the closed door, touching my fingers to my slightly parted, still tingling lips.

Slowly, thought returned. I wrinkled my brow as confusion swirled in my brain, replacing the soul-crushing devastation of earlier.

"What was *that*?" I wasn't in the habit of talking aloud to myself, so I was startled when I heard my own voice, unexpectedly.

I tried to think about how the kiss had happened, replaying the scene in my head while trying *not* to analyze how it felt.

Think, Viviana, this is the time for thinking. Rational thought, I commanded myself.

But it felt *good*. No, kind of amazing, actually. Not even kind of. Like full-on amazing.

It was *Jack* though.

Jack, my friend of 15 years, the guy who took pity on me in high school, the guy who had always been there when I needed him, the guy who had been a steady *friend*, always that, the best of friends, but nothing more.

Our relationship just wasn't like this. Ever. There wasn't any sexual tension or romantic tension or anything like that. Ever. Not even drunken kisses. Or even drunken thoughts. The very idea was preposterous.

Well, I did have a tiny crush on him in high school, but that had been short-lived and meant nothing. I was 15 or 16 at the time. He'd thought of me as a kid sister back then and probably ever since, just as I'd always thought of him as an older, wiser brother type. Well, until today.

"What *was* that?"

The next questions came unbidden: *Is Jack into me? Am I into him?*

After a few seconds, I almost laughed, reminding myself that this was Jack. And me. We'd been best friends forever, never anything more. Like brother and sister.

But brothers and sisters don't kiss like that.

As I took a much-needed swig from the nearly empty bottle, the truth hit me. I nearly dropped the bottle at the force of the realization.

It's pity! Jack felt sorry for me. He was trying to make me feel like less of an idiot.

He was trying to soothe my ego. A fresh wave of humiliation washed over me, and I weathered the storm as best I could, gripping the couch cushion as the full, wretched realization sank in.

For the second time today, I realized that I'd never been more mortified in my entire life. My phone buzzed, and with some trepidation, I read the incoming texts:

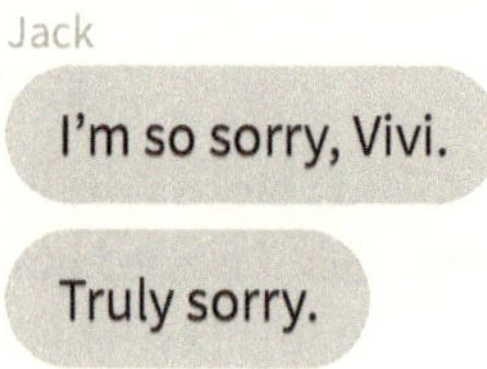

My worst fears were confirmed. It wasn't a moment of passion; it was sympathy. He'd been trying to make me feel better about myself, but now he realized he'd gone too far. The tears came anew, tears of shame, of devastation, of self-pity.

When the flood abated, I blew my nose and threw the tissue on the floor, not caring about any mess when I was the biggest mess of all. I tried to force myself to laugh at how ridiculous this was.

You're being so overdramatic. It's just a kiss. You're not teenagers. And pitying yourself because someone else pities you is just ... pitiful. Besides, you're not even into him, so it doesn't matter why he did it.

"Enough!" I said aloud to the ridiculous voice in my head.

My therapist's voice inside of me was kinder, reminding me that beating myself up never amounted to anything useful.

I stared at a pot of fake flowers perched on a stand near the TV. I loved flowers, but keeping them alive was another story. The fake ones were just as beautiful.

And that's when I knew: I would be OK.

Yes, today was terrible.

Gregory was terrible.

Kissing Jack was not terrible in itself, but feeling pitied was terrible.

But I actually let myself feel the things I needed to feel.

That in itself was kind of monumental. Allowing feelings to happen was actually the key to moving on from them. Of course, my old therapist had told me this a million times before, but the evidence had never been clearer than it was right now.

Despite everything, I felt a bit proud of myself for enduring today—because sometimes that's all a woman could do—endure. *Nevertheless, she persisted.* Until the next day, the next week, or the next month, when I pick up the pieces and come back stronger. But today, I just had to endure.

I could do that. I had to.

Chapter 27

I opened my eyes slightly, noticing the darkness as well as the stinging feeling in my eyes. After an intense cry, my eyes were always dry, red, and sore the next morning—sometimes even longer—and this time was no different. I pulled the bed covers up to my neck, the way I always slept, and turned onto my side.

Surprised to see the early hour on my bedside clock, I remembered I'd gone to bed super early. Remembering the wine bottle I'd finished, I sat up slowly in bed, anticipating a piercing headache.

Pleasantly surprised by how *not* hungover I felt, I stepped onto the floor and walked over to where my slippers were half hidden under a pile of running clothes.

After slowly plodding through my morning bathroom routine, I returned to sit on my bed and look at my phone. Ellen had texted and sent several emails, and I had more unanswered texts from my mother and sister. All of them could wait.

In the kitchen, I turned the coffee pot on and sat down to wait. I felt very strange—fully aware of everything that had happened yesterday, but lacking any desire to dwell on it or overanalyze it or anything else I'd usually do. Instead, I thought about running. Or working. Or cleaning my apartment, which was long overdue. I was up early; I might as well do something productive. *Who am I?* I thought with a half-smile.

Coffee in hand, I sunk into my desk chair and opened my laptop to the manuscript I'd been editing.

Only minutes later, I leaned back and sighed. I could lose myself in work, but why should I? The thought was particularly unappealing when I considered who I was working for. I no longer had any respect for Brandon, and I wasn't sure Ellen could be trusted anymore.

Could I even work for Bolder anymore, given everything that had happened? Even if I avoided the office so I never or rarely had to see any of them again, I'd still be working for a company whose president was a womanizer, among other things.

Then again, I didn't want to make any rash decisions. I needed to work; I only had six months of living expenses in my savings account, at most.

Feeling restless, I gazed out the window, where the sun was rising. I squinted and saw old Samuel ambling toward a bush. The man walked even more slowly than he talked, yet there he was, fetching Elouise's cat again. I tried to block out the thoughts that arose, thoughts about love and friendship and devotion, how it seemed to come naturally to some people, yet seemed so unlikely for others.

I'd take some time off from work.

Starting now.

Ellen would be annoyed about having to reassign my current project, but I didn't care. If Ellen was any friend at all, she would understand.

With that decision made, I fired off a quick email to Ellen, letting her know I'd be taking time off from contracting for Bolder, starting today. I didn't bother to read any of Ellen's emails sitting in my inbox.

Finishing the last sips of my now-cold coffee, I snapped my laptop closed and stood up, resolved to start the day with a run. As I dressed for the run, I cringed at the thought of running into Jack out on the trail. Although my emotions were no longer running wild today,

I wasn't ready to face him. Not even close to ready. I needed to somehow teleport out of my apartment.

Then again, there was no reason I had to run on the same old trails—I could try a new one. The city and surrounding area boasted many trails that I'd always wanted to try but never had, being the creature of habit that I was.

With that decision made, I smiled and finished lacing up my shoes, grabbing my water bottle and purse since I'd be driving to the trail head. My smile faltered though when I thought of the possibility of seeing Jack in the hallway, in the stairwell, or in the lobby. I would sprint to the elevator, which Jack never took. We lived on the third floor, after all, not the ninth. And he was in pretty good physical shape. I squeezed my eyes shut at the image of his well-toned body that suddenly sprang to mind, a thought I couldn't recall having until recently. *It's natural,* I consoled myself. I was just being extra weird and sensitive to things right now. There was nothing wrong with admiring a man's form.

I shook my head to clear the thoughts and resolved to think only about running. Or nature.

After a long, satisfying run, I took my time stretching before getting into the car to drive home. On the new-to-me trail by a nearby lake, I felt exhilarated by the peaceful morning view and by a rare run where nothing hurt. I liked running, most of the time, but distance running—at least for me—usually meant that something hurt or felt sore, at least in the second half of the miles. But today, I felt no aches or pains. Just a runner's high, which hadn't happened in a while. Random? Most likely.

I'd initially feared that running for an hour and a half alone would bring on feelings of self-pity or other thoughts that were even less appealing, but the newness of my surroundings kept me engaged and somehow prevented me from overthinking, my default.

Upon arriving home, I strolled through the lobby and felt my lips curved into a smile. *This* was why I'd fallen in love with running years ago—because of blissful feelings like this.

I pressed the elevator button and waited. The elevator was safer than the staircase today.

When the doors opened, my smile faded, and I gasped.

Jack.

I quickly moved aside as he stepped out, meeting my eyes tentatively.

Neither of us spoke at first.

"Hi," I said hoarsely. "I was just getting back from a run."

Yeah, obviously. Given the running clothes and sweat.

I wanted to ask him why he'd taken the elevator, but then it would be obvious that *I'd* done so in hopes of avoiding him.

"Hello," he said, looking past me toward the exit. "I'm sorry, I–I really can't stay and chat, as I'm late for a work meeting."

I raised my eyebrows. Jack was never late for anything. Never. Unless I made him late. Still, I was relieved to end this conversation before it really began. "Oh, no problem. I've got a lot to do. Starting with a shower," I said, laughing nervously as I pointed to my running clothes. "Captain Obvious here."

He nodded slightly as he glanced around the lobby area. When his eyes finally met mine, I couldn't read his expression. "You seem well, Vivi. I'm glad. Well, I must be off."

I swallowed with some effort and nodded, pressing the button again on the elevator that had already left without me. "Sure. I, uh—have a nice day, Jack," I said, biting my upper lip as my eyes darted to the elevator door anxiously.

He started to step away and then turned back quickly. "Vivi—"

I whirled around, my breath catching as my eyes landed on his and then, for some reason, his mouth. "Yes?"

After a long moment, he made eye contact, again with an unreadable expression. "I wanted to let you know, uh, this week is crazy for me with work, so I'm not sure if I can meet up for any runs or, you know, so ... I mean, I'll stick to the training schedule, but I'll probably have to run at odd times depending on what the rest of my day looks like, so you—I mean, I—"

He wants space.

I held up my hand to interrupt. "Got it. It's OK, Jack. My week is crazy busy too." Thankfully, the elevator door opened just then, and I walked in quickly before turning back with a quick wave and an attempted smile. "Have a nice day, Jack!"

A vague expression of pain crossed his face—emotional pain? Or perhaps a headache. Maybe pity again. He inclined his head slightly as the elevator door closed.

I sighed and absently rubbed my chest, which felt tight. Heart-sick.

Rolling my eyes, I muttered, "Stop being so dramatic." Once out of the elevator, I started down the hall toward my door.

Well, that wasn't great, but it could've been worse, much worse. I handled myself pretty well, apart from that little white lie at the end, where I claimed to have a lot to do. I wasn't crazy busy, or even slightly busy. In fact, I had no idea what I was going to do with myself this week.

Chapter 28

After a shower and a sandwich, I scanned my apartment. It could use a good clean. I wasn't the type of person to clean when I felt upset or needed to pass the time—in fact, I thought that such a tendency was quite bizarre—but for some reason, cleaning sounded like a good idea today. Besides, it needed to be done; cleaning hadn't been high on my list of priorities lately.

My apartment was gross, even by my own low standards.

I'd almost succeeded in peacefully finishing a deep clean of the kitchen when the intrusive thoughts started. These unwelcome thoughts, of course, centered on my conversation with Jack. Unsurprisingly, he wanted to avoid me today; I'd had the same instinct, obviously—hence the elevator.

We'd had some tension between us for a while now, but the events of yesterday were taking the awkwardness to a new level. Instead of being unwilling to discuss our separate love lives with each other, we were now unwilling to discuss what had happened between us. Did Jack regret it?

Of course he does, and although his goal to offer comfort was certainly noble, even Jack isn't that noble.

Regret was probably not a familiar feeling to Jack, who usually made reasonable, measured decisions that he had no cause to regret. It must have been the pity and sadness at seeing me so upset that caused him to act in ways he normally never would. Desperate measures.

I stared at the spot on the now-pristine blue tiled floor that I'd scrubbed for quite a while. "Enough!" I shouted. "I'm not going to overanalyze this. It happened, and we can't change it. We both regret it, and it will never happen again. Obviously." I attempted to ignore the little voice inside me hinting at a different version of events—that although I certainly regretted the aftermath, it was hard to regret the actual experience, which was kind of amazing, albeit only for a fleeting moment.

Putting my cleaning supplies back in the utility closet, I promised myself to clean more later. Would writing help sort out my feelings? Or, even better, help me confront and then promptly forget about them.

Sitting down at my desk and opening my laptop, I recalled where my story left off. The last time I'd written was a week ago, before the weekend trip with Gregory, when I was excited and, well, delusional. I was struck by just how much had changed in that short time.

But after a few minutes of staring at a blank new chapter, I buried my face in my palms. Where should the story go now? I had no idea. Gregory's betrayal was hardly a worthy inspiration for Elizabeth and Darcy's happy ending. I chewed on my lip.

And Jack's role in the story, well, I wouldn't even think about that.

Maybe I could write the happy ending that I'd wanted for my characters—for myself, for Annie. Writing about love conquering all might be painful, but it's what any reader of my story would rightly want and expect. The happily ever after is non-negotiable, or so I'd been told by every romance writing group I'd joined.

But ... did the novel have to be a romance? Austen's books were so much more than just romance. I wrinkled my brow, considering the possibilities.

I could write the truth. That would be painful in a different way, and the worst part is that I had no idea how it would end. Did it end here?

No one will want to read such a depressing, pathetic ending to Austen's beloved characters.

I sighed heavily as I rested my chin on my hand. Then again, they were *my* characters, so I could write the story however I wanted.

Even if I wrote the story true to life, it simply couldn't end here. It just couldn't. There had to be a better ending for my characters, because there had to be a better ending for *me*.

I had to believe that.

Groaning, I closed my laptop while swiveling in my chair. Writing just wasn't going to happen today. I needed to figure out my life first. But where to start? I should really return my phone calls and emails and maybe reach out to Jenn or even my new friend Jane for emotional support. Or maybe book a session with my old therapist. Or journal about it.

No.

Very reasonable ideas, but no.

Feeling stubborn, I reopened my laptop and resolved to start searching for new freelance work. If I were going to feel aimless and unproductive, not to mention uninspired, I might as well use my time to start looking for a new job so that I never had to work for that lying, cheating jerk again. Cringing as I thought about Annie, I felt sad that my friend had been played but even sadder that we were apparently no longer friends. I wondered if Annie could still stomach working for Bolder after things eventually fizzled, which they assuredly would. If they hadn't already.

Taking a deep, cleansing breath, I landed on one of my favorite freelancing sites. Scrolling through many freelance postings would normally make for a tedious afternoon that I'd ardently avoid, but the idea of ditching Bolder and everyone associated with it was a rather powerful motivator.

For much of the week, the job search somehow managed to sustain my energy and thoughts, along with frequent runs along the new trail as the spring weather offered near-ideal running temperatures and budding flowers in every direction. I even discovered a side path that led to my very favorite place in the city, a small but gorgeous botanical garden surrounded by thick trees and shrubs that blocked out the city view.

My phone had been turned off for several days, a record for me, and I didn't really miss it. I even set up a new email account just for job search, so I didn't have to use my usual account and face whatever might be waiting for me there.

But I finally decided to check my phone messages on Thursday, and a guilty feeling settled in my midsection when I saw just how many messages and calls I'd missed. Jane, Jenn, Belinda, my sister, my mother, and of course, Ellen.

Nothing from Gregory. Not another word from Jack.

I felt the most guilt about my sister. Although we weren't terribly close, we lived near one another, so we had no good excuse not to see each other often. I figured Lillian probably wanted me to babysit, but my sister had always had a lot of friends willing to help, so I didn't feel particularly bad about not having the time (or, let's face it, the interest) to do that. Still, I felt nagging guilt, so I texted Lillian a sincere apology, asking how she was doing.

Almost instantly, Lillian replied, asking if I was free that weekend. I sighed, recognizing that as the first question leading up to "Want to babysit?"

But I had to be honest: I had nothing to do this weekend, apart from running. Even my run would be shorter than usual, as it was time to start tapering for the race just over a week away.

Babysitting turned out to be mostly uneventful, or as uneventful as a day with Catarina, Jella, and Charlie can be. They were mostly sweet kids and lots of fun, but as with all kids, they had their difficult moments, especially Cat. Fortunately, they liked me. A lot. So the only tears were the ones shed when I left to go home.

I had to blink back tears myself, realizing that I'd missed seeing my sister's family. They knew nothing about what my life had become lately, and there was a lot of comfort in that. Now it was time to return to my empty apartment, where I'd probably just resume the job search. I'd identified quite a few leads but needed to spend more time gathering and updating my resume and other materials. I could call Jenn and Jane and update them on my situation, or ... maybe not.

My friends have their own lives. They're not sitting by the phone waiting to hear about mine.

"Viv, you answered your phone!"

"I ... yes. Lillian, is that you?"

"Of course it's *me*, sis. Silly little sis," said the person claiming to be Lillian, right before I hiccupped.

"What's wrong, Lillian?"

"I miss you. Can't I just miss you? Hang on."

I heard the sound of a cork popping, followed by silence and then a burp. My perfect big sister, burping and obviously wasted.

"OK, well, we just saw each other," I said uneasily. "So what's up?"

"Nothing is *up*, sissy. What's up with you? Like how's your fabulous single life, sans kids? I suppose it's fabulous," Lillian said with a giggle.

"My ... life is far from fabulous," I said wryly. "Who are you, and what have you done with my older sister?"

After some cajoling, Lillian finally blurted out that her life was crumbling, and then she burst into tears. Her picture-perfect life was, in fact, anything but. The stress of being a working mother in academia and trying to be the perfect wife of a highly successful banker (who was probably cheating) had come to a head recently, and she'd started drinking nightly. And taking pills, whose name she claimed not to recall. She was on the verge of asking for a divorce or fleeing the country or telling her department chair to go to hell.

I listened in shock and tried to soothe my sister. But I had zero experience comforting my sister—there had never been a need before. Lillian could do no wrong, I'd thought. She seemed to have a perfect life, always having everything together, never showing any flaws. Except maybe aloofness. Yes, definitely aloofness.

"Oh, wow, I'm such a mess. I can't believe I'm telling you all this. Bah, so depressing." She paused and blew her nose.

"Lill ... believe it or not, it's actually OK to not be perfect. I might like you a lot more, in fact." Then, I winced. That hadn't come out right at all.

After a moment, Lillian giggled. "Maybe we should be honest with each other more often. Or at least, like, once in a while. Now it's your turn ... tell me about your fabulous single life or your last breakup or whatever it is you are doing these days. Mom mentioned you were dating someone."

I hesitated. There was no chance my sister would understand any of my current problems, but maybe she had a point. We were never really vulnerable with each other, at least as long as I could remember. Maybe we could have a real relationship. I was probably being delusional as usual, but ... what if?

"OK, but only if you stop saying 'fabulous' in connection with my life. It's laughable but also sad, and I've had enough sad lately."

"Deal. Tell me about your *non-fabulous* life, sissy."

I took a deep breath and told her everything. The novel, Gregory and Brandon, the convention, Annie, Jack, running, job hunting, even my fears of going on the dream vacay to Italy alone. *Jack.*

"I called it! I always knew you and Jack would end up together," Lillian said, excitement in her tone. "It's about damn time."

"No, we're not—I didn't say—we're not together. We're friends. Friends who did something we regret, but just friends. At least I hope we stay friends ... things feel strained now." A single tear made its way down my face. "OK, enough about me, Lill. Let's fix your life. Let me help you for once."

"Viv, I am ..." my sister trailed off and then inhaled and exhaled audibly. "I'm sorry. I could've been a better sister to you." Pausing, she added in a small voice, "I want to be."

"Me too. And you already are." I swiped at my damp cheeks. "By the way, please don't breathe a word of ... any of my issues. Especially the Jack stuff. I need to find my own way."

"I wouldn't dream of it, little sis. We'll keep each other's secrets. So, all this is probably why neither of us has committed to going on Mom and Dad's big trip next year, huh? I mean, it sounds so fun, but also ... ugh, my life is such a mess now, I can't worry about next summer. You know what I'm saying, don't you, sissy?" Lillian giggled. "But let's talk more when I'm sober, OK? I don't want this to be a one-time thing."

"Deal." I felt my mouth curved into a grin. "I love you, by the way, and you're still perfect to me."

I set the phone down, walking over to a photo on the wall of my sister and me from quite a few years ago. Staring in wonder, I couldn't believe I'd been so wrong about Lillian. So many assumptions I'd made. Lillian had just as many problems as anyone else, maybe more. And I'd been wrong about Gregory. Brandon. Who else?

And then there was Jack.

As the days had passed without word from Jack, I became increasingly anxious as the half-marathon approached. We'd signed up and planned to run together as we always had in the past, so it would be strange if we didn't run together this time. Still, I had no idea what to expect. Would we race together as usual? Would it be awkward? Would we talk? Or would he avoid me? Would I avoid him?

As the questions plagued me, it became increasingly difficult to stay firm in my resolve to not think about him and about what had happened. But stay firm I would—it was my only hope. I didn't dare ask myself why.

Chapter 29

"You can do this, Vivi. It's not like this is your first half!" I said to the mirror as I dressed and went through my usual pre-race prep on Saturday morning.

I was no stranger to race day jitters, and this time was no different. Except that it was. I usually had Jack to calm me down, make me laugh, make the long miles tolerable, but today, I was unsure if I'd even see Jack or if he would want to run with me. Did *I* even want to run with *him*? As I finished getting ready, my thoughts swirled as race day nerves mingled with unsettling feelings about my best friend.

After parking my car at the sprawling city park where the race would start and finish, I headed to the race registration tables along with the crowds of other runners. My brow wrinkled when I realized I might not see Jack even if I wanted to; it was a large turnout. I had never run a race by myself before, and I wasn't sure I wanted to.

Lillian had offered to run with me, because of course she was in great shape and could run a race on a dime, but I had thanked her and declined. After our emotional phone call, my sister had kept her word and called me the very next day, after her monstrous hangover waned. We were truly getting to know each other, finally, and I found myself smiling whenever my sister's name lit up my phone screen. But I didn't need Lillian to run a race with me; she had enough on her plate already.

While in line for my race bib, I looked around at my fellow runners and felt my lips curve into a smile as I soaked up the energy around me. I'd always loved the race atmosphere, with runners of all ages, sizes, backgrounds, ability levels, and so on. And as always, their racing clothing showed a colorful variety of personalities on display. The air was cool but not cold, and the sun was rising in a mostly cloudless sky.

"Viv, is that you?"

I turned toward the nearby voice, and before me stood Rainn, one of Annie's roommates.

Happy to see a familiar face, I chatted with Rainn while we waited in line. With anyone else, it would've been awkward, given my split with Annie, but Rainn was probably the most easygoing man I'd ever met. I just crossed my fingers that he wouldn't bring up Annie or our fight. And even if he did, it wouldn't be nearly as awkward as actually having to talk to Jack alone. Here. For hours.

Regrettably, running with Rainn today wasn't an option. He was very fast, and I definitely wasn't. I wasn't quite a back-of-the-pack runner anymore, but I was nowhere near the front either.

When it was time to head to the start line, I wished Rainn good luck and then started toward my usual spot in the queue, just a bit behind the middle. I looked around for Jack surreptitiously.

The crowd was thick, and he was nowhere in sight. I wasn't sure whether to feel relieved or disappointed, but disappointment seemed to be winning the day. As the start time edged closer, I swallowed a lump in my throat.

Dammit, Jack.

I *was* sad he wasn't there— sad that circumstances had jeopardized our friendship. Circumstances that were mainly my fault. Maybe all my fault. Sighing heavily, I checked to make sure my water bottle carrier was secure around my waist. I usually just made Jack wear it, as I didn't like the extra bulk. Most runners seemed to rely on the water stations in a race, but I preferred the convenience of sipping whenever I liked.

The race announcer saved me from further stewing in my feelings. The race gun sounded, and we all took off, slowly at first given how tightly packed together we were, and then too fast, as usual.

Only two minutes in, I startled when I heard a voice more familiar than my own.

"Vivi!" Jack ran up beside me, his blue eyes revealing uncertainty.

"Jack," I said, already breathing hard. "Hello. I wasn't sure if I'd see you."

"I started a bit further back," he said.

"Ah," I said, sneaking a quick glance at him and then looking forward while we passed a runner who was already slowing down.

We settled into an awkward silence for the rest of the first mile, and then we both began to speak at the same time. And again. And a third time.

He closed his mouth and looked at me with a wry grin. "You go."

"No, go ahead." I tried to smile, but it felt strained. I kept my gaze focused on the flat path and the trio of middle-aged runners just ahead of us.

When I snuck another glance at him, he was looking at me solemnly. After a moment though, his lips curved into a familiar smile. "It's nice to see you here."

That wasn't what I expected to hear. Instead of putting me at ease, his smile seemed jarring or somehow unsettling, perhaps because I hadn't expected it. I tried to smile back but found it difficult to look at him. Maybe because I was racing and needed to focus on my form. *Yes, that must be it.* I winced at the weak rationale.

"You too," I said.

We ran for another minute without speaking.

Suddenly I couldn't stand it. "You don't have to run with me, Jack. I'm sure you can go faster than this. I always hold you back." *And probably not just from running*, I added to myself.

Gazing at me, he wrinkled his brow and spoke slowly and carefully. "Vivi, I know I don't have to. I've never *had* to."

I had no idea what to say, so I changed the subject. The weather would be a safe topic. For a few minutes, we discussed the slightly cooler but still comfortable weather in the past few days.

"I agree. The conditions are nearly ideal for racing," he said.

"I would've preferred a little breeze too, but hey, you can't have everything you want." It was an odd thing to say, but I couldn't pinpoint why.

"This is as close to perfect as we're going to have," he acknowledged, his tone light. He looked at me briefly then, and my eyes darted away.

What was wrong with me?

It's just Jack. Yes, something weird happened, but it's done. So done. It was almost two weeks ago. Don't need to make his every comment into something weird.

We ran alongside one another mostly in quiet, with an occasional comment about the running or the other runners or the scenery along the race route. At one point, he asked if I'd heard any updates on my parents' big travel plans for the following year, and I simply said no. It's not that I wasn't thrilled for my parents, but I was embarrassed about how hostile I'd acted and didn't want to be reminded of that.

At the halfway point, Jack turned to offer a blinding smile. "Aaand we're halfway there. Walk break?"

I nodded and instinctively shifted my eyes elsewhere. Something about his smile just then ... it unnerved me. Had he always been this ... this hot? Feeling guilty for averting my eyes so abruptly, I turned back to him as we slowed to a walk. He was frowning slightly and staring at the ground.

He was hurt.

I wanted to kick myself. I was being weird, and my behavior was probably hurting him. Should I say anything? Should I try to explain? Yet I couldn't fathom what I would say. An apologetic smile would have to do. If he ever looked back to see it.

We walked quietly for a minute as we gulped down water.

When he finally looked at me again, his face was unreadable. His voice sounded strained. "Vivi, let's just get this over with."

I blinked in surprise at his bluntness. "Ah, yes, let's start running again—and faster," I said while speeding up as much as my tired legs would allow at that point.

He sped up to match my pace, and his hand grazed my arm. "Hey. That's not what I meant."

"Oh." I stole a quick glance at him. At the brief contact on my arm, I felt a peculiar shiver, despite being warm and sweaty from running.

"We can run faster, but we still have six miles to go and some change," Jack said. "Let's just clear the air."

"You don't ... We don't need to—to do that." Conversation was becoming more difficult because we'd sped up so much and because, well, panic. The last thing I wanted was more apologies and more ... pity. As though kissing me was such an awful thing that a person had to apologize multiple times.

"I think we do."

I braced myself for a potentially mortifying conversation. "That day was ... It was such a terrible day for me. It's not necessary to dredge up everything again."

He grimaced. "I know it was terrible for you, Vivi. And I wasn't responsible for your day being terrible, but my actions certainly didn't make things better. Let's just talk about it."

I looked straight ahead.

I just wanted to run. Not talk.

Keep putting one foot in front of the other.

But he wasn't giving up, and he seemed so darn *sincere*. We still had an hour or so of running left, maybe more as I could feel our pace slowing again. Finally, I mumbled my assent.

After looking far off into the distance for a long moment, beyond the sprawling forest on our left, Jack cleared his throat. "Vivi, I don't have a good explanation for my actions. I am sorry that I can't really justify ..." He paused then and looked at me with piercing eyes. "But I'm just sorry, period. I hope you know that I would never intentionally jeopardize our friendship, which means—which has always meant—a great deal to me. *You* mean a great deal."

"I know that," I said quietly, wincing at every word of regret that passed his lips. "I know you were only trying to help, trying to make me feel better. You don't need to apologize for that."

He frowned, casting a quick glance at me. "Well, I'm not ... That's not exactly what I meant, Vivi."

"I know what you meant, Jack," I managed to say, trying to swallow my shame before the tears started. "I get it. I was miserable. You took pity on me. You wanted me to feel ... wanted, perhaps. It's more than a friend would usually do, but you have always been the best kind of friend. I can't—"

"Vivi, it wasn't pity!" he snapped. When his outburst drew glances from the pair of young runners nearby, he took a slow breath, and his tone softened. "It was ... that is, I just—"

"Jack, you don't have to put a name to it. Like I said, I get it. No need to explain further. Your explaining is ... not helping. Let's just run. We're going slower again, I noticed." *Please, please don't "explain" anymore*, I pleaded silently, biting my lip.

"But you don't understand. I don't think I'm explaining myself at all," he said, regret sketched onto his face. "What I mean is—"

"Seriously, Jack. *Please* don't make this any more painful than it already is. You can't imagine the mortification I felt that day, for so many different reasons. I'm trying to turn things around. Trying to move on. Trying to be my own best friend."

Perceiving a flash of hurt in his expression, I quickly added, "I mean, you are still my best friend. I hope so anyway. I'm just trying to take better care of myself these days."

He didn't respond for a minute. "I'm glad to hear that," he finally said, sounding resigned. "You know I just want you to be happy. And of course I'll always be there for you, Vivi. Never doubt that."

I offered him a shy smile, one filled with hope, for the first time that day. "Thank you. I really meant what I said, that you *have* always been there. And it means ... everything."

His expression was hard to read, but his eyes hinted at sadness even while his lips curved up into a smile.

"Speaking of taking care of myself, I guess you can be the first to know. I'm quitting Bolder. I haven't told them yet—they think I'm just taking a break. But I can't work for that jerk Brandon anymore." I shook my head in emphasis. "I've been busy looking for new opportunities."

His eyes widened. "Wow. Vivi, good for you! I don't blame you for wanting to cut ties with that place. You can do so much better. Do you have any leads so far?"

"I do, actually. And I've had nothing but time, so I've made many inquiries and sent out quite a few resumes. I even have a couple of interviews already next week. I hope I can count on you as a reference."

"Of course. As if you need to ask," he said, a bit indignantly. "That's so great to hear."

After half a mile of running in silence except for a couple chatting loudly behind us, he asked if I wanted to take a short walk break. After finishing off a water bottle, he asked, "Are we OK? I still feel like maybe I bungled our talk earlier, so maybe we should start over—"

"Jack," I said firmly. "Please. Can we just let it go? It was just … just a kiss." Why was it so hard to even say the word? "It happened, and we're adults. I'd desperately like to believe that this incident doesn't have to change anything between us." After another moment, I added, "I … I can't lose you as my best friend."

Looking at me intently, he opened and then closed his mouth, which I found myself staring at as we walked side by side. When he finally spoke, I heard the quiet resolve in his voice. "Of course you won't lose me. Vivi, you are … I'll drop it, if you'd like."

I nodded. "Thank you, Jack. Now let's pick up the pace again. We're only two miles from the finish line."

He looked ahead, matching my accelerating pace.

We ran in comfortable silence—well, relatively comfortable and relatively silent. Every now and then we'd pass (or be passed by) a pair of chatty runners. I was glad for the distraction. I couldn't claim that things felt completely normal between us, but it felt a bit less strained. Our talk had been painful to endure, but it could've been worse.

Besides, at that point in the race, it was becoming hard to feel anything other than tired legs. It was one of my favorite things about distance running.

Finally, we passed the 13-mile mark. I always found a reserve of energy for the last bit of a race, and today was no different. Jack and I glanced at each other at the same time, smiling as we pumped our arms harder and lengthened our strides.

After we crossed the finish line and received our medals, we took a few minutes to catch our breath. After swallowing the last of my water, I looked around for the snacks and drinks and pointed when I located them.

Before making our way over to the tables though, I found myself swinging my arms out and pulling him into a hug. I noted his surprise, his warm, damp skin and shirt, and his ... well, it would be weird to say that I noticed his firm body. But I did. I knew Jack was considered attractive, with good looks, a friendly smile, and a trim but strong runner's body. But I hadn't *noticed* it quite this way before, various parts of my body tingling at the contact. I stumbled back in alarm.

What the heck is wrong with me?

I hoped he didn't sense my awkwardness. Before he could speak, I blurted, "Sorry, I'm so far beyond sweaty and gross right now. But I missed my Jack hugs."

A gaze I didn't recognize passed over his face before his mouth curved into a familiar grin. "I'm pretty sure I'm sweatier than you. I am a man, after all."

You certainly are, I caught myself thinking, and I groaned inwardly. We turned to head toward the refueling table. I was probably just tired and not thinking straight, right? Stealing a quick glance at Jack, I didn't detect any tension, or at least no more than before. Hopefully he hadn't noticed anything amiss with me. What was going on with me? I shook my head, reminding myself again that I was exhausted and dehydrated and hungry—that was all.

After a glorious nap and a long bubble bath, I limped to the couch and decided to order in. Jack and I often had a post-race dinner together, but he hadn't mentioned it, and I decided not to either. Clearing the air with him had been nice, but there remained some lingering awkwardness that I didn't feel like facing, at least not tonight.

Pizza delivery and a straight-up comedy, sans romance, were exactly what I needed tonight. And maybe some wine. Definitely, not maybe. I should do an ice bath for my poor battered legs, but I decided to skip that harrowing post-race ritual in favor of some ice packs on the couch.

As I waited for the food to arrive, my feet elevated on pillows, my thoughts kept returning to my interactions with Jack today. Had I given off a weird vibe? I certainly felt weird, but was it a self-perceived weird or the type of weird that anyone could see? Of course, Jack wasn't just anyone.

He's my closest friend.

Yes, my friend.

Could we ever return to normal? If so, how? I really needed my best friend back.

More than anything, I needed to move on from all this. I sensed that I'd hurt him more than once today, but he'd seemed much closer to normal by the time we finished the race.

Sending a friendly text could help to further clear the air. At least it couldn't hurt, probably. Maybe.

Viviana

Hey Jack, good race today. Thanks for being my friend through everything. I value our friendship so much.

Jack

I feel the same, Vivi.

Viviana

Share some greasy pizza delivery and a non-Austen movie?

I bit my lip after sending that last message, unsure of whether the spontaneous invitation was a good idea. Ten minutes later, he still hadn't responded, and I began to regret asking. Was he thinking of how to let me down easily? Was he worried I'd have another breakdown? Was he celebrating the race finish with someone else?

Most importantly, why was I overthinking this?

The delivery guy arrived then, so I vowed to forget about Jack tonight and enjoy my dinner and movie night. Soon I was laughing with Paul Rudd and Jason Segal, and the embarrassingly unanswered invitation was forgotten for a while.

When my phone buzzed, I paused the movie and frowned.

Jack

So sorry, Vivi. I had to go to a work dinner thing at Lambrusco's.

Viviana

It's fine, Jack. Lambrusco's is amazing. Enjoy your night.

Honestly, I would've rather done pizza with you.

I sighed, placing my phone back on the coffee table. He was always trying to make me feel better about myself, even when it bordered on ridiculous. I wondered how things were going with Irene. Obviously there was something still going on. In all the years I'd known him, no other boss or colleague had ever demanded his time at work lunches and dinners so often even on weekends. I didn't understand the appeal of Irene, honestly, but Jack must see something in her. Was she his type? I didn't really know what his type was. I'd briefly met a few of his dates over the years, but not many. He kept his love life very private and, I presumed, casual. I couldn't remember the last person he'd dated or even brought home, though of course I wasn't privy to everything in his personal life. I groaned, thinking again of Irene.

Why did this bother me? I let out a frustrated sigh. I wasn't jealous; I *couldn't* be jealous. His relationship with his boss just bothered me because I didn't understand it. And because it had obviously driven a wedge between us. And because Irene was just, well, not good enough for him. Or maybe for anyone. The woman wasn't likable at all, from what I could see. These were all good reasons to be unhappy with the Irene situation. Nothing to do with jealousy. *I was just looking out for my best friend, just like Paul and Jason do,* I insisted as I pressed Play to resume watching the movie.

Chapter 30

I partially shielded my eyes from the glaring morning sun as they followed a blur of movement that was distinctly reddish. I'd never seen more than one cardinal at a time before. I'd always held an affinity for them, with their beautiful red coats, especially in the winter as a contrast to the snowy white of Minnesota. Plus, they had to be introverted, which was a plus.

I had ventured on a walk to clear my head and relieve the lingering stiffness in my legs from yesterday's race.

Reluctantly, I returned to my apartment and noticed a text from Jack. I'd been very negligent with texts and other communication lately, and the guilt was starting to get to me, so I was trying to do better.

Jack wanted to know if I had time to chat that morning. As I started making a fresh pot of coffee, I wondered what he could want to talk about, as he didn't usually preface our conversations with an actual request for conversation.

I was just pouring a coffee when he knocked at the door, and I set my cup down to go let him in.

"Hi Jack," I said, willing myself to sound normal. Cheerful, even. "How's it going? Are you as sore as I am today?" Then I frowned at his somber features as I ushered him in. "What's up, Jack?"

His eyes avoided mine for a moment and then met my curious ones with a serious expression. "I think you should sit down for this."

With my brows furrowed, I started to speak but then thought better of it. Instead, I went to retrieve my coffee and sat on the couch. I looked up at him expectantly as I took a small sip. "What is it?"

He appeared poised to sit next to me but then appeared to think better of it, choosing instead to sit on a nearby chair.

My cheeks burned at the reminder of what had happened last time we sat on this couch. Why would I feel embarrassed? It's not as if *I* had instigated the encounter. As if I wanted it to happen. I averted my eyes and said nothing while setting my cup down, my hands shaking slightly.

"Vivi," he started, leaning forward with his elbows on his lap. "I have to tell you something."

I bit my lip, having no idea what he was about to say. I shouldn't think the worst, but at this point, I didn't even know what the worst could be. Hadn't I already experienced it? Taking a steadying breath, I forced myself to meet his eyes calmly. "Well, Jack? What is it?"

He swallowed several times. "I mentioned I had a work dinner last night. Irene arranged it. Kind of a networking thing. And ..." He paused then, apparently unsure how to choose his words, which was so unlike Jack.

I took a shaky breath, trying to quell the panic within. Were things getting very serious between him and Irene then? I was about to find out, whether I wanted to or not. "Go on," I said, inhaling shakily, "just say it."

His eyes swept across the room slowly, gazing at everything but me. Finally, he looked at me directly. "OK. Your Gregory was also there. They were ... flirting all evening, and they left together in a ... very obvious way. Vivi, I'm so sorry. I didn't know how to tell you. But you deserved to know, and ... I'm here for you if you need me."

His features were twisted in pain, and I fought back such a strong urge to comfort him that it took a moment for his words to fully register.

Irene and Gregory.

What?

Irene and Gregory?

It was shocking.

Or was it? I tried to think clearly and process Jack's words, but all I could think about was the pain evident on his face. I'd never seen him so devastated, even after all these years of knowing each other. Even after his grandmother's death a few years ago, he'd naturally been sad but not distraught. Not like this.

"Vivi ..." he started, his voice cracking.

"Jack, you don't have to say any more," I said, rising to my feet. "At least, not for my sake." Before I could think, I rose and took two steps toward him. When he stood, I threw my arms around him, pressing my cheek against his chest.

We stood in a tight embrace, lost in the pain, though I wasn't sure if it was my pain or his, or both.

Finally, we seemed to simultaneously realize that we'd been hugging for a long time, and we both stepped back. He took a few extra steps backward, his steps appearing somewhat off-balance. Neither of us spoke.

"Vivi, are you OK? You're not ..."

"I'm not what?"

"Well, are you all right?" His eyes searched my face.

My eyes widened slightly. "You mean I'm not crying?" I let out a small laugh. "It's OK. I'm OK."

His brow wrinkled in doubt. "OK. You certainly don't have to cry. I hate to see you cry. But you also don't have to hide your feelings from me, Vivi. I'm ... I'm here for you." Then he hastily added, "As your friend."

I stared at this man who should've been crying himself, except that he never cried. It was so like him to be worried about me being heartbroken when his own heart had to be shattered by this news. I gave him what I hoped was a reassuring smile and nodded. "I know, Jack. But I'll be fine. Gregory is a total jerk—I didn't need *this* to know that. As far as I'm concerned, they're made for each other."

His face fell, and I wanted to eat my words. "Oh, Jack, I'm so sorry. I ... I shouldn't have said that. I guess you know I haven't been Irene's biggest fan, and I am pretty sure she hates me. But she means something—she—she means a lot to *you*, so I'm really, really sorry."

He sighed, looking away. After a few moments of silence, he said, "Vivi, don't think of me. I came here to make sure *you're* all right."

I wanted to go to him again, but I held myself still. "Jack, she meant something to you. I don't know the extent of it, but I know this must hurt. You don't need to talk about it if you don't want to. But *please* don't think that your feelings aren't as important as mine. I've had a few days to get over Gregory, but this heartbreak is all new and raw for you, I'm sure." Get over Gregory? I'd begun to wonder if there was anything to get over. I was in love only with my *idea* of him, but it was fantasy. Fiction.

He stared at me for what seemed like several minutes. Finally, he looked away and said wearily, "She is just my boss. You don't understand—"

"No, I don't understand, Jack," I said defensively, "because you never want to talk about it."

"It's not—" he stopped and then took a deep breath. "It doesn't matter. Vivi, I just want to make sure you're OK. I came over because I didn't want you to hear about this in another way that might be more shocking or hurtful."

My body felt tense with frustration. He was determined to make this about my feelings, and for once, I wanted—no, *needed*—to make it about *his*. "I'm OK, Jack. As you noticed, I'm not crying. It's a bit of a shock, you're right. I didn't see that coming. At all. But I will be OK. Truly."

When he didn't respond, I added, "I do need to get some things done this morning though, so can we talk later? If you want to continue this."

He looked at me strangely, unsure what to make of my surprising calm. "I'll leave you to it then. But please, know that I'm here for you. Anytime. As always."

Just before he walked out the door, I called out, "Jack, I'm here for you too."

In the silence that descended upon my apartment, I chewed my lips for several moments, thinking of his face as he'd delivered the news. The pain in his eyes. The way it gutted me.

Ugh, I'd spent too much time brooding and analyzing our conversations. No more. I went to my desk, intending to read and respond to some emails about recent job applications. But as I waited for my computer to start up and connect, my thoughts stubbornly drifted to Jack's news.

Why was I not more upset about Gregory? Jack had obviously expected me to be devastated, and by all rights, I *should* be devastated. Foolish or not, I'd invested a lot of time and energy into the idea of a romance with Gregory, and it had been less than a week since I'd made the mortifying discovery that it was all a lie. Hearts didn't mend that fast. At least *mine* didn't. When relationships inevitably ended, I didn't let go easily. But this time ... I didn't care. I wasn't crushed.

I was far more worried about how Jack was feeling, perhaps because I knew what that disappointment was like, having experienced it so recently myself. He might have been my rock over the years, but he wasn't made of stone; surely he felt betrayed or even heartbroken over Irene's duplicity. Maybe he was even worried about the effects on his work.

Maybe I was becoming more emotionally mature, putting someone else's feelings above my own.

Or maybe ... no, no, that's not worth thinking about.

I squeezed my eyes shut for a moment. Jack was my dear friend. It wasn't odd to feel upset on his behalf; it didn't mean anything more than that. And my lack of emotional response to Gregory's dalliance with Irene was just a testament to how far I'd come in recent days.

I smiled, and with a renewed sense of confidence that I hadn't felt in a long time, or perhaps ever, I navigated to my email inbox and smiled even more broadly when I read several requests for interviews in my inbox. I was rebuilding my life, and I felt damn good about it.

Chapter 31

By mid-week, I started to feel less than excited about the job prospects before me.

I'd had four interviews already but didn't feel particularly optimistic about my prospects for any of them. I'd mostly applied for long-term contract work, but I did interview for a couple of full-time employee positions as well. The only one that actually sounded like interesting work was also the one that made me uncomfortable, as the executive editor who interviewed me had boasted about being a long-time friend of Brandon Bolder. Any excitement I'd had about that job quickly dissipated. Even if I could stomach being acquainted with, much less employed by, another friend of Brandon's, I didn't trust him to put in a good word for me. Since I'd rebuffed both the man and his company, chances were high that any job reference from him wouldn't be glowing. The other interviews were for editing work that either seemed boring or offered lower pay than I was accustomed to. Being content with editing dull material for mediocre pay was a thing of the past, I'd resolved.

By Thursday morning, I was feeling pessimistic and decided to take a day off from job hunting, but first I absentmindedly checked my email.

My eyes widened when they landed on my inbox. At the top was an email from Bethany Bell, the founder and editor-in-chief of *Forward & F-Word* magazine, a relatively new local feminist publication that had been quickly rising in popularity. Just yesterday, I'd applied for an in-house editing position on a whim because of the great things I'd heard about the magazine. Having worked from home for years, I'd had some doubts about the idea of working full time in an actual office setting again. But I'd decided to apply anyway, just to see what would happen.

The email from Bethany was brief, asking me if I could meet for an interview at 2 pm ... today. I finished my last sips of coffee, pondering the request. Such short notice was a bit unusual for an interview, but I had nothing pressing to do today, so I quickly composed a response.

As I rose from my chair and closed my laptop, I felt the corners of my mouth tugging upward. How quickly a day could turn around!

But don't get too ahead of yourself. The interview could totally fall flat, or Bethany could be horrid.

Shaking my head, I laughed and chided myself for being overly negative. One could hope, right?

Having walked through a plain, sparsely decorated lobby and hallway in a rather plain grey building downtown, I was feeling underwhelmed as I pushed open the door to Suite 104. My eyes widened as I entered the small but brightly decorated room that appeared to be a reception area. The walls and furniture were a bluish green—maybe teal—and every imaginable shade of purple. A room awash with these colors from floor to ceiling could have easily been tacky or even gaudy, but somehow it wasn't. It was beautiful. I thought of my drab blue-grey curtains at home and resolved to do something about them.

A tall young man strolled into the room behind the reception desk and smiled. "Hello, what can I do for you today?"

"Hi, I'm Viviana, here for an interview with Bethany. Dr. Bell."

"Ah." He pointed to the chair behind me. "Have a seat."

I began to sit and then rose. "Actually, uh, sir, I was wondering—"

The receptionist's smile vanished. "I'm Genevieve. Not sir."

"Oh, I'm so sorry." My cheeks burned. I'd intended to ask for water for my parched throat but decided not to impose and risk making a bad impression. "Lovely name," I added, receiving only a stiff nod in response.

Fifteen minutes later, Genevieve rose and waved me past the front desk. "Bethany will see you now. Second door on the left."

I smiled gratefully and made my way down the hallway, which was decorated in similar colors but with dozens of photos of people lining the walls.

The door to the small meeting room was open, and I stepped inside.

A woman stood and held out her hand. "Viviana, right? So nice to meet you! I'm Bethany Bell." She was short and round, her ebony skin and hair contrasting with reddish highlights in a short bob framing a wide smile and intelligent eyes. She looked younger than I'd expected of the founder of one of the most talked-about publications in the area, but her demeanor exuded confidence beyond her years.

"It's very nice to meet you, Ms. Bell." I arranged my face in what I hoped was a gracious smile as I sat in a soft lavender chair, before realizing my mistake. "Dr. Bell! I'm sorry."

Bethany laughed and sat down. "Please call me Bethany. We're fairly informal around here, as you'll see."

I smiled gratefully. "Bethany it is. It's great to meet you."

"OK, so, you're from ..." She looked down at the stack of papers in front of her. "Bolder Publishing?"

"I am. That is, I contracted with Bolder for the past four years."

"Are you looking for a change then, or do you intend to continue freelancing for Bolder?"

"I've actually just given my notice there, and I'm looking for something new. I love what you've done with the magazine, particularly with the intersectionality that is sometimes lacking from these publications. So this position seemed like—"

"Can I ask why you decided to leave Bolder after so many years? I hear the pay is decently competitive and the work pretty flexible." Bethany leaned back in her chair.

"It is all of that, yes," I acknowledged. For some reason, I suddenly couldn't remember the carefully worded explanation I'd used at all the other interviews this week. "I just ... I just needed something ... else."

Bethany's sharp eyes were focused on my face. "I hear a story there. Do tell."

I breathed in and out slowly as my carefully scripted answer continued to elude me. After a few moments of silence, I decided to be honest. "Frankly, I just couldn't work for Brandon Bolder anymore. He's not a good person."

Bethany held my gaze, her expression neutral. Oh, crap. I'd lost my chance at this job because that wasn't the kind of explanation you give at an interview. My gaze dropped to my hands in resignation.

But Bethany burst into laughter. "I love your honesty, Viviana. I don't know him personally, but I have heard things. He sounds exactly like the kind of man that reminds us all *why* we need feminism more than ever, am I right?"

Some of the tension lifted from my shoulders. "Yes, that is a good way of describing him. I won't go into the gory details, but—"

"Not this time, anyway," Bethany said, her dark eyes twinkling. I was heartened by this response, which implied we'd be meeting again. Surely a good sign.

She asked more standard interview questions, and then she stopped in the middle of a sentence and yawned. "I'm so sorry. How rude of me. I was up rather late last night, and these questions are just so *boring*, am I right?"

I didn't know how to respond, so I just smiled politely.

"Listen, your portfolio is strong, your editing test result was fantastic, and I have heard that Bolder's contractors are pretty top notch. You're honest, and you'd enjoy taking on the patriarchy with us. I think this is going to be a great fit, but I'll just need at least one reference to call," Bethany said. "It doesn't need to be from Bolder. I'm sure you have other connections in the industry, right?"

I immediately thought of Jack, who would certainly give me a glowing reference, though we'd never worked together in an official capacity. I nodded.

"If you could email me one or two references later today, that'd be great." Bethany leaned forward with a sympathetic expression. "But I do have some potentially bad news about the position. We initially advertised for a full-time editing position, but what we have available right now is only a half-time position. Sorry, this was just decided with the accounting team this morning; I didn't want to mislead you. Is that a dealbreaker for you?"

I considered this information for a moment before responding. "Well, it—"

"Wait a minute. I have an idea!" Bethany said, her eyes brightening. "I *just* came from the writers' meeting, and we were talking about how we could really use a part-time staff writer right now. One of our fabulous writers, Lavanya, is going on maternity leave in a few weeks and then probably coming back only half-time, so it wouldn't be a hard sell in terms of the budget. Would you by any chance be interested in doing both? With the editing *and* writing work we have available, the combination would be equivalent to a full-time position, I'm certain!"

I opened my mouth to decline but hesitated. I wasn't really a writer. I was good at helping writers shine. Sure, I was attempting to write a novel and had been praised for my essay writing throughout my years of schooling and had wanted to be an author since I was 8 years old. But I *wasn't* a writer. Not really.

Still, you'll never know if you don't try.

I felt my heart soar. For once, the small voice inside was encouraging and not holding me back.

Bethany's smile faded. "It's fine if you're not interested in that. I just wanted to put that on the table."

"No, it's not that." I moistened my dry lips. "I'm sorry, I was just thinking. A writing job wasn't what I had in mind, but I will be honest and say that ... it's kind of an exciting offer. I mean, not an offer per se, but the position sounds interesting. I'd be interesting—I mean, interested."

Bethany's smile was kind but professional. "Right, not quite an offer yet, but I like you, Viviana. I have a good feeling about this." She stood up then, smoothing her maroon pantsuit and then holding out her hand. "Right then, I do have a few more interviews this afternoon, but I'll be in touch soon. I might make the decision as soon as tomorrow. If offered the position, could you start in two weeks?"

My head bobbed up and down. "Of course! I'd be honored to work here," I gushed. "Thank you so much for meeting with me."

Bethany smiled and rushed out of the room, busy woman that she was. I followed slowly, taking my time to look around the office as I walked toward the exit. Clearly, the workplace was fairly casual, if the decor and the frequent laughter from down the corridor were any indication. And the work would be *interesting*. I could be editing—writing!—about things that actually matter to me. Things that matter in the world. Things people actually want to read. Such a dramatic departure from my years working for Bolder on dry technical, business, or academic tomes. Granted, I'd never be a writer of Jack's caliber.

But ... why not? Maybe I will, maybe I won't. It's time to stop selling myself short.

I left the building with a wide smile.

But as I drove home, my excitement gave way to doubt. Did I have what it takes to be a writer, even a part-time one? Would Bethany think I have what it takes? Would I fit in there? Did I want to give up my complete flexibility in working from home 99% of the time and accepting projects only on my terms? Was this position fully or only partially on-site? I'd couldn't believe I'd forgotten to ask.

The last question I asked myself was accompanied by a flutter in my abdomen: Should I call Jack to ask for the reference or stop over at his place?

In the end, I opted to send him a text pleading for a glowing recommendation. Surely he was too busy for anything more than a text anyway. I smiled when he replied almost instantly: "As if you need to ask." Upon arriving at home, I fired off a quick email to Bethany with Jack's contact info.

When I awoke the next morning, I squinted to shield my eyes from the bright sunlight streaming through the thin, hated blue curtains. Why had I allowed myself to live for years in an apartment decorated in dull colors that weren't *me* at all? If one could even call this decorated. I rubbed my eyes and rose to a half sitting position.

I absently reached for my phone on the cluttered nightstand and switched it on. Examining my inbox, I scowled. No email from Bethany.

It's only 8 am. Bethany's probably not even at work yet.

As I rose and began to think about how to spend my day, I realized my apartment basically had nothing more to clean or organize. It was as tidy as it had ever been—or ever would be, I suspected—because I'd had little else to do. Even my old favorite pastimes of reading Austen novels or Austenesque spinoffs and watching Austen movies had lost their appeal of late, considering my brutal brush with romantic reality in recent weeks.

Putting down my empty coffee cup, I eyed my phone warily. I should probably call Jenn, whose calls and texts I'd scarcely been responding to. I was beginning to feel rather terrible about it, but I just hadn't wanted to face all the questions about Gregory. Jenn was usually busy with her family anyway, I rationalized. I could text her instead of calling. Busy people preferred texts anyway, right?

Or not. The phone rang almost immediately after I sent a carefully worded text. Clenching my jaw, I forced myself to answer. "Hello."

"Viv, you're alive! I don't know whether to be relieved or pissed."

"Jenn—"

"Lucky for you, Jack actually answers his phone, so I had my ways of finding out you were still alive."

"Jenn, I'm—"

"Tyler lost a tooth. Kieran lost his job. And I broke my leg."

"*What?* Oh no, I'm so—"

"But do you want to know the worst of it? I couldn't even get my Viv fix. I had no idea what was going on with you and your wild, romantic whirlwind life," Jenn said accusingly. "And there haven't been any good rom-coms on Netflix lately."

"I'm sorry," I said, hoping I sounded contrite. Because I *did* feel terrible. "There has been no romantic anything, and I just ... I couldn't bring myself to talk about it. But, more importantly, are you and Kieran OK? What happened? I'm so sorry to hear all this, and I'm sorry I wasn't there as the friend you needed."

"You mean you don't have scintillating stories from your love life to share? *Seriously, Viv*, that is just the last straw," Jenn said, making me chuckle a bit. "You know I'm just being overdramatic. We all need our space sometimes, I get it. Since Kieran was laid off, I haven't had a moment to myself. You know I love him more than life, but even this extrovert needs her me time once in a while. But the kicker is that I need him around anyway because I can't get very far on these dang crutches."

"Sorry, Jenn. What can I do to help? I've been a god-awful friend, like ... like Kate Beckinsale's character from *Serendipity*, minus the star-crossed lover."

"Well, for starters, you can come to board game night this Sunday. I hear Jack's bringing Bel, so that'll be fun. Don't even think up an excuse; I'm not taking no for an answer."

I laughed. "I wouldn't dare."

"And of course you need to fill me in. *Soon.*"

"I will, Jenn. Thanks for ... for putting up with me," I said apologetically. "You have to tell me how you broke your leg. And what happened with Kieran's job?"

"It's an outrage; everyone thought he was amazing at his job. Damned budget cuts at the university. I mean, we'll survive. He hates to rely on his family money, but it's only temporary, and what good are rich parents if you can't take their money occasionally? I kid, mostly. He's a little salty about it, obviously. As for my leg, well, that's a long and slightly embarrassing story, and I want to hear *yours* first. Come over before everyone else on Sunday so we can chat?" Jenn said hopefully.

I didn't want to commit to talking about everything yet, but I probably owed it to Jenn. "Sure. I'll be there."

After hanging up, I saw a new mail notification. My heart skipped a beat when I saw it was from Bethany. Taking a deep breath, I cautiously clicked to open the email. The first line read, "Can you start in 10 days?"

I smiled, and my shoulders relaxed. After typing a quick response to Bethany, I sent a short thank-you text to Jack for what must have been a great recommendation.

It was going to be a great day after all.

Chapter 32

"I am *so* glad you're here," Jenn said, flinging open the door.

My eyebrows rose. "Is everything OK?" I asked as I stood on the porch, shivering.

"It is now! I was just, you know, going crazy with fear that you wouldn't show, and I'd still be in the dark. I need to catch up on Viviana episodes," Jenn said, her eyes twinkling. "You're freezing, come in."

I laughed nervously, and then I noticed the crutches as we headed to the living room. "Wait, what are you doing off the couch? I thought you were stuck with either crutches or the couch, and the couch was infinitely better."

"Well, it is," she said. "But Kieran's out at the moment, buying party snacks. And probably more beer, considering our extra guests."

"Ah, Choua is coming too then? I call dibs on being on his team."

Jenn laughed. "Yeah, you may have to fight me on that one." Once she sat down and arranged her crutches nearby, she gave me a pointed look and folded her arms. "I'm ready."

"You're ready?" I feigned ignorance. When Jenn narrowed her eyes, I groaned and settled against some cushions, moving a stray toy out of the way. "OK, OK. I'm afraid this story isn't a great one, and it's certainly *not* going to bring anyone joy in the hearing or telling of it." I paused, my lower lip starting to tremble.

Jenn looped her arms around my shoulders and hugged me tightly, as much as her bulky cast would allow anyway. I thanked her as I tried not to tear up, took a deep breath, and began to recount what had happened with Gregory.

Jenn sat riveted as I told the mortifying story. When I finally fell silent and waited for my friend's response, Jenn let out a string of expletives.

"How is it that you, a wife and mother, know more curse words than I do?" I asked, grinning despite myself.

She grinned. "Oh, it's *because* I'm a mother that my language is so colorful. You have no idea."

I smiled but then sobered. "You're right though—I'm pretty sure he is all of those things, even the ones I haven't heard before. The thing is ... I guess I've had time to process it somewhat. I mean, I can't believe I didn't even break down while telling you all this. A couple weeks ago, I definitely would've been a crying mess. But I guess I've had time to accept what happened."

Jenn stared at me. "I can understand the tears drying up. But I would've thought you'd still be angry or, I don't know, at least a *little* heartbroken."

I forced a smile. It was a fair question, which I'd tried not to think about. "Like I said, I've had time to grieve, I guess. And I can't help but wonder ..."

"Wonder what?"

"I wonder if ... oh, Jenn, this is going to sound so stupid. I wonder if I was really in love with him in the first place *or* if it was just some silly infatuation illusion thing that my Austen-obsessed brain cooked up," I said with a self-deprecating laugh. "Because you're right. I should probably be taking this harder than I am."

Jenn looked at me a long while before speaking again. "I've known you forever, and you've always been Austen obsessed and always heartbroken after dealing with jerks like Gregory. He's not the first one, you know. Remember that stuffy guy, Antonio, and before him—"

"Anthony. He wasn't stuffy." I paused. "Or was he?"

"That's one of the nicer words I'd use to describe him."

"I ... I suppose you're right. I hadn't really thought of myself as being one of *those* women who's always attracted to the wrong kind of guy. But maybe I am."

Jenn nodded, smiling slightly. "You didn't know that about yourself?" When I frowned, she continued, "So what does Jack think of all this? I assume you talked to him at least, if not me."

I looked at the floor, uncomfortable with the shift in conversation to a subject I definitely didn't want to discuss. *Wouldn't* discuss. Realizing I was expected to say something though, I took a steadying breath. "Yeah, well, he never really liked Gregory. To put it mildly."

"He didn't?" Jenn said in an exaggerated manner, and then she laughed. "Well, that was pretty obvious even to me, and I don't even see you guys that often."

"Yeah, so he wasn't surprised that Gregory turned out to be a total jerk. But Jack was, he was ... a good friend, as he always is. Always a good shoulder to cry on." I shrugged the as nonchalantly as I could. Not for the first time, I wished I was a better actor.

Just as Jenn, with curious eyes, opened her mouth to reply, the doorbell rang. I rose quickly and smiled at my friend. "I'll get it. Stay on the couch. Friend's orders."

Grateful for the distraction, I opened the door but felt my smile falter. Standing there was Jack himself, and behind him were Belinda and Choua. And Annie.

Belinda spoke first and lunged forward for a hug. "*Vivi!* I'm so happy you're here! We didn't know you were coming."

I laughed hoarsely. "Of course, why wouldn't I?"

Jack took in my surprise and laid a gentle hand on my arm before he apparently thought better of it and let his arm drop back down.

"Oh, Jenn said she hadn't heard much from you lately, so we figured you might be too busy. Glad to see you though, Vivi."

My eyes flickered from him to Annie, and I grasped for words. "Hi, everyone. It's cold. I—um, come in."

Jack stepped through the door as I quickly moved aside. "Jenn said to invite Annie, so—"

"So here I am!" Annie said, stepping forward with a friendly but tentative smile.

Too friendly. She's still mad.

Unsure what to say, I pointed to the coat rack and motioned for them to hang their coats.

Annie's smile wavered. "I hope it's OK that I'm here."

Feeling queasy, I forced myself to look at Annie nonetheless. "Sure, I mean, of course. I didn't think board games were really your style though." I couldn't read the look that passed between Annie and Jack at that moment.

"This is our chance to show Annie what she's been missing all this time," he said lightly.

I laughed nervously and tried to think of a response. I turned to Belinda's husband with a practiced smile. "Great to have you join us, Choua! I call dibs on your team."

"You and everyone else. I think it's time I picked my own team," he said with a sideways glance, his eyes twinkling.

As we walked toward the living room, everyone laughed good-naturedly, everyone except Annie, that is. I hated the awkwardness already, and they'd only just arrived. If only I'd stayed home that night—even though I had nothing to do at home.

Kieran returned home then, and we all greeted him and offered condolences and suggestions about the job market. It soon became clear that work (or lack thereof) was the last thing he wanted to talk about though—I couldn't blame him, being so recently exhausted by job searching myself—so Jenn stepped in to clumsily halt that conversation and announced the first game.

As the night progressed, the awkwardness didn't fade, though it became slightly more tolerable after the first round of beers. Annie and I didn't talk or sit near one another, but I exerted great effort to be civil. Things weren't much better with Jack, with whom I still felt awkward too.

What took the tension to the next level was the third game we played, which required partners. Jenn and Kieran predictably paired up, as did Belinda and Choua. But that left Jack, Annie, and me. "Oh, I didn't even think about the uneven numbers until now," Jenn said with a grimace. "I'm usually so good at planning to avoid that."

"No problem. I can sit this one out," Jack said.

"No, I will sit out," I said quickly. "I was the last-minute addition to this party anyway, I think." I stole a brief glance at Annie, who frowned slightly but remained silent. It was probably obvious that I didn't want to partner with Annie.

"Don't be silly," Kieran said, running his hands through his thick black hair. "We'll just play something else. If you haven't noticed, we have a number of other games to choose from. A ridiculous number, actually."

Everyone chuckled, and the tense moment passed. Jenn was staring at me though, giving me a look that clearly said "you have more stuff to tell me, and I will get it out of you later." I gave her a half-smile as I turned to open my next beer, only to find that Belinda was also giving me an odd look. Was I being that obvious? I thought, sighing. It was going to be a long night.

I took a long swig from my beer bottle as I snuck a glance at Jack and then Annie. The alcohol wouldn't get rid of the tension, but with any luck, it would make me stop caring.

Chapter 33

I opened my eyes reluctantly the next morning and groaned as I searched around for my sleep mask, which had slipped off my face, as usual. As I scanned the area, I saw 6:20 am on my bedside clock. Of course, I had no reason to get up early on a Monday, so I settled back under the covers and made sure my sleep mask was firmly in place.

Ten minutes later, I threw off the covers and mask, grudgingly accepting that I wasn't going to fall asleep again. It was never this easy to awaken when I had a work deadline or a long run to do. At least I wasn't hungover. I pulled clothes randomly from my closet and padded to the adjoining bathroom.

I winced at my reflection in the mirror. My eyes and skin looked tired and a bit blotchy, and my hair was limp, my highlights fading. Was that a grey hair along my part? I tried to smile at my reflection, but the forced effort only highlighted the tired strain around my eyes.

I groaned as I started my morning routine. I wasn't the sort to obsess about my appearance, but no woman on the planet liked to see a tired and limp reflection in the mirror. And what reason did I have to be tired or stressed? I hadn't been working, and I'd basically had zero responsibilities for weeks, with complete freedom to do whatever I wanted, whenever I wanted. "Shouldn't I be happy, or at least content?" I asked my sullen reflection. Sure, Gregory was a jerk, but I hardly thought of him now. Yet I was still miserable. Well, maybe not miserable. But not happy.

After staring into the mirror for several minutes, I put my hands on my hips decisively. I could either mope about the state of my appearance (and my life) or take action. I decided to take a day for pampering myself. Enough of this wretched self-pity and obvious lack of self-care. My apartment was spotless, but *I* was still a mess. For that matter, my apartment needed a makeover too. I couldn't have my new workplace looking more beautiful and inspired than the place I lived.

No, it just won't do.

I booked some appointments for the morning and then closed my laptop, smiling contentedly before my stomach rumbled. Some decadent coffee and scones were definitely in order.

When I walked into the café a bit later, my spirits rose as I took in the sensory experience of one of my favorite places, particularly the scents of my favorite food and beverages. As always, the warm cinnamon chip scone spoke to me. After placing my order, I leaned against the counter to wait.

I thanked myself silently for choosing to make it a self-care day. This was exactly what I needed, but I rarely prioritized it. As I scanned the place with a lazy smile, my gaze landed on a woman in a very short, very red dress. What woman could possibly pull off such a look barely after dawn on a Monday? I began to chuckle, until the woman turned around.

I gasped.

Annie.

Well, of course, she would be the one to pull off such a look. But what was she doing—

My breath caught and thoughts stopped short as I saw who Annie's breakfast companion was.

Jack.

Before I could think further, I whirled around and pretended to busy myself gathering napkins and utensils as my heart beat furiously. Just then, my order was declared to be ready. Glancing at the tray with my order, I hastily said to the café worker, "Actually, I meant to ask for this to go. I can't stay. Sorry." I silently thanked the universe that Melanie wasn't working today; she'd have seen through my myriad emotions.

A moment later, my order in hand, I needed to make a decision quickly. It would seem awfully strange if I didn't go say hello, as they might have spotted me by now. But ... Jack and Annie were quite possibly the *last* people I wanted to see that morning. And why they were here ... together ... so early? I tried to halt that line of thought before it could go any further.

My heart still racing, I took a deep breath and headed over to their table, nearly bumping into a child being chased by their caregiver.

"Vivi!" Jack said, looking surprised but genuinely happy to see me. "I never thought I'd see you here so early!"

I'll bet you didn't, I almost snapped. *Obviously you would've chosen somewhere else, if you had.*

I tried to conceal my dismay. "Well, that makes two of us. Or three, I guess." My eyes darted to Annie and then quickly back to Jack.

Annie spoke up then, her tone polite but quiet. "Hi, Viv. Would you like to join us?" Her tone certainly didn't match the boldness of her outfit, which ... *what on earth?* Why was she wearing *that, here,* with *him,* in the *morning?*

He smiled at Annie and then turned back to me. "Sure, pull up a chair."

"Oh, no, I can't," I replied quickly. "I have a lot to do today."

His bright smile remained but dimmed slightly. "You do? I thought you were free for another week until you started that new job."

"Oh, you got a new job? Congratulations," Annie said, her eyes smiling but tentative.

"Yes, is that so hard to believe?" I snapped, looking at my former friend and then him. "I do have a new job starting soon, *and* I do have things to do today."

Jack and Annie looked at me with wide eyes and then looked at one another, their expressions hard to read.

"I'm sure we didn't mean to imply—" he started.

"It's fine." I took a deep breath and massaged my temples briefly. "Sorry, I didn't mean to snap. It's just, I do have a busy day ahead, so I don't really have time to chat. And I wouldn't want to interrupt … your, well, whatever this is."

Tilting his head, Jack looked at me with what I thought was hurt, or possibly confusion. Probably confusion. I was behaving a little out of character, and how could he possibly understand why? I didn't even know why myself. I didn't dare look at Annie.

Before either of them could speak, I forced a cheerful smile. At least, I hoped it looked cheerful. "I hope you two have a lovely breakfast," I said before turning on my heel and walking away. Just before I reached the exit, I noticed a familiar handsome face by the door with three children. It was Melanie's son, Jordan. And then a black-haired goddess sat down next to him, and he put his arm around her.

I left the building on the verge of tears. Don't cry, don't cry. Or scream. Or throw something. I didn't know why, but I felt extremely agitated, to say the least.

Jack and Annie were having breakfast. They weren't doing anything wrong. They had every right to spend time together, at any time of day. I had no right to be upset.

And Jordan had apparently found someone. I'd once thought he might be interested in me. But I'd done absolutely nothing to encourage him, so why on earth was I upset?

Jack and Annie were having breakfast, and Annie was wearing a last-night outfit. But it was none of my business who Jack slept with, and Annie wasn't even my friend anymore. Maybe they hadn't spent the night together, and it was some weird coincidence. So why was I upset?

I'm not upset. I'm not.

I'm just ... just ... maybe I'm still mad at Annie for not believing me. And I'm out of the loop. That's it.

Yet I wasn't at all certain about that.

Before I could torture myself with further self-analysis, my phone buzzed. I bit my lip, considering whether to turn off the phone for the day—that would truly be self-care, right? But the text came from Jane from Duluth, wondering how my book writing was going. Even in my agitated state, I had to smile, and I took a slow breath. Jane was already a great new friend. We hadn't known one another for very long, but we already talked often. In some ways, I felt closer to Jane than to anyone else in my life.

If only Jane lived here instead of in Duluth.

My steps slowed slightly as I spotted my apartment building just a few yards ahead.

Wait, why not go to Duluth?

I stopped suddenly, nearly bumping into a scowling older woman who was exiting my apartment building just as I entered.

Ignoring the woman, I tried to keep up with my racing thoughts. What if I just drove to Duluth—like, today?

Was this crazy?

Did it matter?

Spontaneous, sure, but not crazy. I had nothing else to do this week before starting a new job. And I loved Duluth.

I'd never taken even a mini-vacation by myself before.

A change of pace for a few days would do some good. Clear my mind. And Jane was there.

Chapter 34

Immediately upon arriving home, I tossed my café order in the trash, having lost my appetite. I canceled all the appointments I'd taken the time to schedule for today. Surely Duluth had stylists, manicures, and spas too, if I were still inclined. In under an hour, I also booked my hotel, packed, and loaded up my car.

Once I was on the road north, I let out a long breath as I rushed to escape my life.

Belatedly, I called Jane to let her know I was visiting. Naturally, Jane sounded surprised but also pleased about the spur-of-the-moment visit. With the call on speakerphone, she insisted that I stay with her during my visit, but I decided to stick with my plan for a lakeside hotel. Not only did I love the view of the lake, but I also craved the alone time, despite having plenty of it lately; alone time at the lake was different. Besides, I didn't want to impose on a brand new friend, even though she felt like an old friend, in many ways.

Jane eventually sighed and relented. "OK, but when I'm not at work, I'm going to be very greedy in wanting to spend a lot of time with my new friend, the awesome writer."

I laughed nervously. "Coming from my new friend, who seems to have a penchant for exaggerating. I don't even know what I'm doing when it comes to writing ... or, for that matter, my life!"

"We'll figure it all out this week, I promise," Jane assured me. And then she squealed—yes, actually squealed. "Oh, I'm just so excited! Text me when you get to town. I'm sure you'll be tired from the drive, but we can grab dinner at least."

I agreed and hung up the phone. Just minutes later, I found my mind wandering to the scene at the café this morning, and I sighed in frustration. I *did* need to figure things out, but not right now. Not on an endless stretch of road. Instead, I plugged in my worn-out but still operable iPod, chose a favorite playlist, and turned up the volume. *There will be no chance for thinking if I'm too busy singing,* I thought, simultaneously realizing what a ridiculous sentence that was.

My heart was singing by the time the beautiful Lake Superior was within view, just over two hours later. The sun was shining on the glimmering aquamarine water, whose ice had mostly thawed by now. By the time I reached the hotel on the lake, my cheeks were beginning to feel sore from smiling.

This.

Yes, I need this.

If anything could put my world to rights, it was this city, this lake. As soon as I unlocked my hotel room, I raced over to the balcony to take in the sweeping view of the lake, the rocky shoreline in front of me and the wooded one miles off, the lighthouse signaling to a ship off in the distance, the recently rebuilt lakewalk, people of all ages and shapes and colors, even a horse-drawn carriage. For a moment I considered unpacking a bit, but then I laughed as I sank into the cushioned deck chair.

Hours later, I left my comfortable haven to meet Jane at the Duluth Grill.

"I'm so glad you've come for a visit, Viv!" my new friend said, bending to hug me as soon as I walked into the casual restaurant.

Jane was tall, even with flats on, but today she was wearing heels and a pencil skirt. "Oh, should I call you Viv? Or what do you prefer?"

"Of course, most people call me Viv," I answered with a smile. "It's great to see you too. I wish we lived closer, but then I wouldn't have an excuse to visit Duluth, which would be tragic. How are you doing?"

"Much better now that you're here," Jane said as we were seated in a booth.

"Things haven't been so great then?"

"Oh, you know, dating. Blah. What a waste of a nice outfit today," she said with a wry smile. "Still, I did get a pretty exciting work assignment this week, so there's that."

An hour later, after chatting extensively about Jane's work and my new job, I bit into the last French fry and sighed. "You were right. The grilled cheese is pretty great. I rarely venture out of the harbor area when I'm here, so I hadn't heard of this place before."

"Enough about work though. I'm sure you didn't come here to spend the whole evening talking about our new projects, exciting as they are." Jane laughed, and then her expression turned a bit more serious as she leaned back. "I hope this doesn't sound too presumptuous, but ... how's your love life? I need the next chapters in your book!"

"I'm afraid I don't have any more for you," I said with a heavy sigh. "I just haven't felt inspired since the whole Gregory fiasco. Well, I mostly just don't know where to take the story. Should I make it true to life? He's a jerk, and then we don't have a happy ending. No one will want to read that. *I* wouldn't want to read that! Or I could write the book as though everything *did* work out the way I wanted it to ... but I don't know if that feels right."

"Don't do that," Jane said. "How about an alternative happy ending? Just because things with Gregory didn't work out doesn't mean there can't be some kind of happy ending for your character. Or for you!"

I bit my lip and hesitated. "I know, but I ... I'm coming up short in that direction. I don't know what would make *me* happy, so I don't know what would make Elizabeth happy. Ugh, I'm not much of a writer if I can't imagine a story unless it's happening to me."

Jane shook her head. "No, it's not that. You're just really connected to this character, so it makes it harder to step back and think about what other happy ending she could have."

I nodded slowly.

"So, with that in mind, we need to figure out what will make *you* happy, so my favorite new Elizabeth can find her happily ever after!" Jane said, her eyes twinkling.

"I wish I knew," I mumbled as I looked down at the empty plate in front of me. I suddenly thought of Jack, and a flash of guilt passed over me because I hadn't told Jane about what happened with him. I hadn't told anyone, for that matter. Surely it was irrelevant though. Jack was a great friend, which made me happy. End of story. Well, our friendship made me happy when things weren't confusing or awkward. This phase would surely pass though.

Jane narrowed her eyes, leaning forward. "What are you not telling me?"

Feigning innocence, I glanced up. "What do you mean?"

"There's more to this story. I mean, you don't have to tell me … but there's more, isn't there?"

When I didn't reply, Jane grinned. "There is! I knew it. OK, you don't have to tell me … tonight. Maybe tomorrow?"

Despite the somewhat somber direction of my thoughts, I couldn't help but laugh at my new friend's persistence. "We'll see."

The next day, I made the most of my time alone, setting off on the lakewalk for a cool morning run and then strolling around the Canal Park area much of the day. Oddly, I found it easy not to think and to instead just be present. It was almost meditative, and I wasn't the meditating type, as much as I wished to be; Duluth was just my special place.

After a lazy afternoon nap, I met Jane for drinks. Several appetizers and daiquiris later, I found myself in confession mode. Jane had run into her ex, Lisanne, in an awkward encounter at the pharmacy that demanded full explanation, so I decided cautiously to reciprocate by sharing my own awkward story, the timeless kissing-my-best-friend story.

"Oh my gosh, Viv," Jane said, grabbing my arm. "You didn't!"

"I did," I admitted. "I mean, we did. Kissed. It was so weird and awkward, and then afterward—"

Jane gasped. "Oh no you don't. You are not skipping to the 'afterward' part. I won't allow it. How was the kiss?"

My face reddened as I studied the table. "I don't know. I guess I don't remember."

"The hell you don't," Jane said. "You have to tell me. A kiss like that was either amazing or terrible. It had to be."

"Well, I wouldn't say that." I felt my mouth curve into a small smile.

"Yes, you would. Which one was it? I think it was the amazing kind," Jane said, narrowing her eyes. "Was it?"

I was almost certainly blushing more deeply now. "I guess you could say that. It was pretty good."

"Just pretty good?"

"OK, pretty damn good."

Jane stared at me.

"OK, amazing. But ..." I grasped for words. "But it didn't *mean* anything, not like you're thinking. Like I said, it was super awkward, and it didn't end on a great note."

Jane nodded thoughtfully as she tossed her ponytail back behind her shoulders. "I can believe it was super awkward. So how have things been since then?"

"Not good," I admitted glumly, trying to wave down the bartender for another drink. "Things have not been the same since."

"Viviana," Jane said, giving me a solemn look. "Do you want things to be the same?"

"I—well, of course. Just ... I'm afraid I'm losing my best friend. We've been best friends forever, you know."

Jane was quiet for a long moment, and then she said, "If the kiss meant nothing, then why does this have to hurt your friendship?"

"I don't—" I started. "I mean, it ... it doesn't, but I don't—"

"You don't what?" Jane looked at me, tilting her head slightly.

I exhaled loudly, burying my face in my hands. "I don't know. And what makes things worse is that ... well, I think he might be seeing Annie now."

After what seemed like an eternity, Jane asked, "Why does that make it worse? Do you think—" she stopped then. "Never mind."

I looked up at her warily. "Do I think what?"

"Nothing," Jane said with a sympathetic smile. "I'll let it go. You're clearly distressed by this conversation, and I really, really want to have fun with my newest friend tonight. Drinking game? Austen trivia?"

Well after sunrise the next day, I forced myself to wake up for a run again. Despite the slight hangover, I had to take advantage of the opportunity to run along Lake Superior, one of my favorite places on earth.

When I reached the rose gardens, I looked for a bench to rest. It wasn't a long run, so I didn't physically need a break, but the rose garden was one of my favorite places in the city, even in April when most flowers weren't yet blooming. Coming here was, in fact, the highlight of running along the lakewalk. Even Jane, the local, agreed; yet another thing we had in common was a love of flower gardens. Still, I'd wanted to run alone today.

As I sat gazing at the lake, a light breeze blowing through my hair, I frowned slightly. I was having trouble attaining the meditative calm state I'd experienced yesterday while roaming around on my own. I glanced around at the barely budding flowers around me, expecting peace but instead feeling agitation growing in my stomach. As though something was missing.

Something *was* missing.

I could be sitting here, taking a break from a run and looking out at the beautiful scene before me, while holding a lover's hand.

Such a romantic scene, this garden overlooking the lake in this city I'd always loved. And I was alone.

The tight feeling in my midsection became more noticeable, and my breath quickened. I closed my eyes to steady myself and then stood up to stretch. As I stretched my quads, I thought about how Jack never liked to stretch, but I made him do it anyway. I missed running with him in the last few months. He would like running on this lake trail. He would like the lake view, and he'd probably even tolerate the rose garden, despite his pollen allergy.

If only I could share this with Jack.

My heart started pounding wildly. I ... didn't mean *that* kind of sharing.

But as I closed my eyes and tried to redirect my thoughts, the image that entered my mind uninvited only sharpened: Jack sitting next to me, smiling as we soaked up the serene setting around us and grasping my hand.

My breath caught, my eyes flying open.

I love Jack.

"No, I couldn't possibly," I said aloud.

I love him.

"I love him as a friend," I whispered.

I love Jack, and I want to be with him.

A wave of calm washed over me then, and I breathed deeply. The world around me stilled for a moment.

I'm in love with him.

I could picture him here, not just as my best friend, my running buddy, but as my lover, my life partner. The tension eased from my body as I envisioned us together—as I came to grips with the truth. As I stopped fighting it, finally.

I indulged in a long moment of peace as I stared at the shimmering lake below, trying on these new feelings, trying not to let my thoughts get in the way.

But my thoughts would not be held back for long, so I started running again before I could begin overthinking.

Even a brutal running pace didn't stop the thoughts, the doubts that began to rush in, the nerves rattling within me.

So, I was *into* him.

How did it happen? We'd been friends forever, and I'd never thought about him in *that* way. Well, there was the little crush in high school, but it was so short-lived I'd rarely thought about it since. He'd been like an older brother—a hot one, I had to admit, but I'd never really noticed it before, at least not in any way that mattered. This newfound feeling was so strange and awkward, but it was undeniable. I was tired of fighting it. I could live with this.

But, with a sinking feeling, I reminded myself of the harsh truth: Jack saw me only as a friend. A very good friend, but still just a friend. He wasn't in love with me. In fact, he might very well be in love with my former friend! How could I live through the agony of watching them together? Of never confessing my feelings? Of never truly being with him?

There was only one thing to do then. I stumbled off the running path, sat in the grass, and sobbed.

Chapter 35

"Oh, Jane, I know you mean well," I said while scanning the greeting card aisle at Target. "But I'm fine. I'm back home, back to reality, and I'm not going to act on this ... well, crush. That's all it is. He's not interested in ... I mean, besides, he has *her* now. Oh—oh no, Jane, I'll have to call you back."

I hung up as I heard a familiar voice calling my name and saw Annie tentatively walking toward me.

"Annie," I replied, taking a deep breath. "Hi." I tried to smile but failed.

"I'm surprised to see you here," Annie said, her face cautious but smiling. She smoothed her hand over the front of her casual yellow dress, which likely didn't need smoothing. Annie looked perfect, as always.

"Why?" I asked, furrowing my brows. "Can't I shop like anyone else?"

Annie's eyes widened as she took a small step back. "Of course, sorry, I just meant that it's a strange coincidence because, well, I was just thinking about calling you. And here you are."

I winced, inwardly berating myself for being rude. "Sorry. I didn't mean to be so defensive."

Annie shrugged. "It's fine. I get it. Things did not end well between us." She paused and sighed. "I was a total jerk, actually."

I couldn't suppress a laugh. "Sorry, I shouldn't laugh. That was just so ... blunt."

Annie smiled again. "Yeah, that's me."

I didn't speak for a moment, looking at my shoes. "I miss that."

"You do?" Annie arched her eyebrows. "I have been realizing of late that it's not one of my better traits. I can't believe it took me this long to figure that out."

"Well, bluntness has a time and place. Sometimes I wish ..."

"You wish what?"

"I wish I could be like that. Sometimes."

"Oh. Well, maybe I could teach you. I could be the mentor for once." Annie's lips curved into a tentative smile.

I returned the smile. "I'd like that."

After an awkward silence in which they both looked elsewhere, Annie blurted out, "Can you forgive me, Viv?"

I nodded slowly. "Only if you forgive me."

"I was the awful person, not you. It's the freaking redhead temper, right? No, I don't have an excuse. You were just looking out for me and trying to protect me from another terrible guy, as always," Annie said with a sigh. "I sure know how to pick 'em."

"But I could've tried to get in touch with you after that. Instead of giving up on us so easily," I admitted. "I just ... I don't know. Maybe I needed space. Not from you necessarily, but from everything. Things weren't going well with Gregory, and that ended terribly. I'm sure you know that. They both played us for fools, and I was just as gullible as you were, maybe more so because Gregory made it pretty obvious from the start that he was just an asshole. And—"

"Viv, I'm so sorry I wasn't there for you and that I pushed him on you. I was a little too wrapped up in myself to see what was happening or what *could* happen with a guy like that." Annie sighed. "I wasn't being a great friend either."

My mouth slowly curved into a smile. "OK, so let's stop being crappy friends to each other. Deal?"

Annie laughed with arms outstretched. "Bring it in."

"Well, this is playing out like a scene in a Hallmark movie." Eyes twinkling, I waved my arms to the side. "And we're literally in the greeting card aisle."

Annie giggled. "Oh, the horror. At least it's not a Christmas movie. Speaking of horrors, you have heard about poor Ellen, right?"

I tilted my head in question. "*Poor* Ellen?"

"I know she kind of took advantage of us, and she was kind of horrible when I quit," Annie admitted with a sigh. "But I feel so bad for her, don't you?"

I stared at her, not comprehending. "Why would I?"

"Oh wow, you didn't hear?" Annie's eyes widened. "Have you been on social media, like, at all?"

"No, I needed a break. I didn't even read any of my emails or messages from Ellen, I was so furious with her."

"I'm in awe," Annie said, mouth gaping for several seconds. "I tried to go off the grid for a while, but I was too weak. OK, but anyway, so she was having an affair with some no-name guy at the gym. Her husband found out and not only confronted the gym guy but also got in touch with the gym guy's wife. The wife just happened to be one of those influencers on Instagram and TikTok with literally millions of followers. Within hours, the story was everywhere. Ellen had to resign, and she's said to be taking a spa vacation somewhere. Can you believe it? I mean, I feel for her, but then I also don't."

"Wow, that is insane. I actually wondered if there was a gym guy on the side. There was a weird late night in the office one weekend ... but anyway, just, wow. She kinda sold me out to Greg, but still, I do feel sorry for her. That's a hefty consequence for one bad decision."

"No kidding. If only all the two-timers paid such a price. Like the garbage men we dated. But let's not go there ... So are you ready to check out too?" When I nodded and turned to walk with her, Annie added, "Good, because I need to update you on my life. I finally found a good guy, if you'll allow me a humble brag. It's been agony not being able to talk to you all this time!"

My heart sank. Her new guy must be Jack. As much as I'd missed Annie and felt genuinely happy about resuming our friendship, that was one major hurdle I hadn't had a chance to process yet. How on earth was I going to handle seeing two of my best friends in a romantic relationship together, all while I was in love with one of them? It might have been easier if I could hate Annie, but I knew deep down that wasn't possible, whether we were still friends or not.

"Viv? Are you OK?"

I shook my head. "Yes. I mean no. That is, yes, I'm OK, but I just remembered I'm not done shopping."

Annie smiled. "Oh, no problem. I can tag along while you finish and gush about my new man."

"No!" I bit my bottom lip. "I mean, I would love that, but I, well, it's just not really the right time. I still have a lot of things to buy."

Annie looked down at the small basket in my hand doubtfully, and I added awkwardly, "I should probably go get a cart, actually. Since I need a ton of stuff."

"It's fine, Viv. You can just tell me if you don't want to talk. Remember, bluntness? You can start now."

"No, it's, it's not that," I said, scrambling for words. "I just—it's not the best time. It's hard to explain."

Annie studied me for a moment and then threw her arms around me. "It's fine, Viv. We'll catch up another time, I hope. I'm just glad we got to talk. Really glad."

I forced a smile and nodded. "Me too." After an awkward moment of silence, I added, "I'll text you soon."

Annie looked a bit doubtful but then smiled lightly as she turned and walked toward the checkouts.

Somehow I managed to get home before the tears fell. Loud, messy crying and sniffling that I was thankful no one would witness.

I had to somehow be OK with my very best friend, also the man I was in love with, dating another close friend. And I had no idea how to do that.

As I wiped away my tears a bit later, I remembered that the new job started tomorrow. My heart raced, as the thought of a new job was overwhelming, given all the emotional wreckage that was currently my life. Then again, I realized, work could be my salvation. Temporarily, of course. I just had to think about work and not about my devastating love life. Simple, right?

Once my tears finally dried and my puffy eyes became less puffy, I suspected I'd left the phone in the car. After retrieving it from my car, I was almost back to safety in my apartment when a warm hand lightly landed on my shoulder.

"Vivi, so glad I caught you!" Jack said. "How was your trip?"

I turned reluctantly, afraid to look at him, afraid he would see.

He'd see all the love in my eyes, all the pain, the heartbreak.

I swallowed thickly as I dared to meet his eyes. "It was good. Really good."

"You look tired. Or ... something." His brows were wrinkled in concern as he pulled his hand away casually, obviously (thankfully) unaware of its effects on me. "Are you all right?"

"I'm tired, Jack. And tomorrow is my first day at the magazine, so I need to turn in early."

"Right, that's so exciting! Let's celebrate your first day tomorrow night, OK?" he suggested with a smile.

"Uh ..." Why had it taken me so long to notice—or to admit to myself—that Jack had a gorgeous smile?

Now is not the time.

"We haven't done anything fun together for a while, and it's the perfect excuse to celebrate," he continued. "Dinner or takeout and maybe an Austen movie at your place? You name it."

I pressed my lips together and closed my eyes. Why did he have to make this so difficult? Just when I *most* needed to avoid him, he wanted to spend time together and do, well, things that would be date-like to almost any other two people. Things that would remind me of what I'd never have with him.

I needed to decline this invitation.

Just say no, maybe offer a raincheck.

"Well, I ... sure," I heard myself saying. "How about we order in with a movie, but not Austen ... I am taking a break from Austen."

So much for declining—you're hopeless.

"A break from Austen?" he said, his mouth gaping. "Wow, I'm sorry. You'll have to tell me all about this later. So, what time should I come over?"

"Um, I'll just text you later. You bring the takeout?" I inhaled deeply and forced a smile before asking the dreaded question, with my voice only a little shaky. "Should we, um, invite Annie too?"

"Annie?" he asked, his eyebrows furrowed slightly. "We can, but I thought you and her ..."

"Oh, you don't need to worry about that. We're fine now. I ran into her yesterday, and we've reconciled. I can invite her if you'd like," I said, my forced smile feeling painful.

"I mean, sure, if you want to." A muscle ticked in his jaw.

I didn't know what to make of his response, but I couldn't think about that now.

"I really need to go, Jack, but I'll see you tomorrow," I said abruptly. As I walked backward the few steps to my door, I forced a smile. "It really was great to see you!"

Once safely inside my own apartment, I slumped down onto the couch, burying my flushed face in my hands. But before I had much time to marinate on this new misery, my phone buzzed with a group text.

Jenn

Viv, Jack, please tell me you have no plans tomorrow night?!

Jack

> We're celebrating Vivi's new job, of course!

Viviana

> It's just some takeout and a movie at my place. Want to join us, Jenn?

Jenn

> No, Kieran and I have strep. And my leg hurts
> :(

> Thing is, we planned this whole date night, and apparently it's all nonrefundable. Any chance you two would use it tomorrow night? It's just dinner, upscale-ish

My heart slammed in my chest. A faux romantic dinner for two? With Jack? I wouldn't survive it. I needed to say no. Staring at the screen, I waited to see what Jack would say. Two minutes passed with no response.

Jenn

> Oh come on, it has to beat takeout on Viv's couch.

Jack

> Sounds good to me, but we're celebrating Vivi, so whatever she wants. :)

I winced.

Of course he'd punt on this.

Viviana

Maybe Annie could come too? Or instead?

Jenn

It's dinner for two, Vivi. I think Annie is busy with her own job hunt anyway. She texted me asking for a reference today.

My hands were shaking as I tried to think of a message to type. Why wasn't Jack speaking up on Annie's behalf? Surely he'd rather do a romantic dinner with his new girlfriend instead of his awkward, moody best friend.

Jenn

Come on, you two. I just need two people who like dining out to go dine out, on our dime. This should be easy. You'll seriously break my heart if you say no, and I'm sick. How cruel can you be? ;)

Jack

Well, when you put it like that …

Viviana

FINE. I'll go if Jack wants to.

Jack

This conversation has been such an ego boost.

Viviana

Sorry, Jack. It's been a long week, or month. See you tomorrow. And thanks, Jenn. I hope you and K feel better.

Jenn

Have an amazing first day tomorrow, Viv!!!

Chapter 36

For my first day at the new job, I left early and took the elevator downstairs, dressed smartly in a navy pantsuit and heels that clicked when I walked into the elevator. I might be overdressed for this job, but a little extra formality couldn't hurt on my first day. A good first impression was a must; it would help project the confidence I wished I had.

As I rounded a corner toward the apartment lobby and exit, I suddenly lost my breath as I felt a hard shove to the floor. Breathless with fear, I braced myself with my hands on the floor and dared to look upward.

My eyes were wide as a familiar man bent down. *Jack.* "Vivi, oh my—I'm sorry!" he said as he extended a hand to me. "I was stretching my arms and didn't see anyone coming—I'm so sorry. Are you all right?"

I cradled my face in my arms briefly. Another encounter with Jack was the very last thing I needed right now. I reluctantly grasped his outstretched hand, but as soon as he'd helped me to my feet, I pulled my hand away and stepped back, breathing heavily.

He looked at me with some surprise. "Are you all right, Vivi?"

While trying to steady my breathing, I leaned down to rub my ankle, which felt a little sore from the fall. At least my high heels hadn't broken. "I'll be fine. It's OK. You … just surprised me. And I'm a klutz in heels."

"Are you sure, Vivi? Did you sprain your ankle? Let me just see how it feels—" he said as he began to kneel down and reach for my ankle.

"No!" I stepped back quickly, wincing at the resulting pain. I shifted my weight to the other side as he straightened. "I mean, it's fine. I'm fine. Need to run though. I can't be late."

"Right!" His eyes widened with excitement. "I don't want to make you late! I hope your first day goes well."

"Thanks, Jack."

But as I turned, he grasped my forearm. "Wait, Vivi."

I stared down at his hand, noticing the heat, a spark of something intense I couldn't even name, the way it made my heart skip a beat, something so simple and familiar but also decidedly new. "Yes?" I asked hoarsely, finally meeting his eyes. "I really can't stay and chat. Being late on the first day would look so bad, Jack."

He pulled his hand away slowly and groaned. "And I said I wouldn't make you late. So sorry, Vivi. Good luck, and I'll see you tonight!"

Once outside, safely out of Jack's vicinity, my faux smile vanished.

What was I thinking? I wanted to shout. *I'm nowhere near ready to face him, especially in a setting meant for romance. I'm in so much trouble tonight.*

I drove to the magazine office, thinking through my options. Maybe I could cancel tonight and plead illness. How long would Jenn stay mad at me? Would Jack be hurt? I sighed. Before I could ponder it further though, I arrived at the office and promptly forgot about my love life problems, if only temporarily.

A short, lovely woman came to greet me in the reception area. My new coworker Lavanya ushered me into a small office near the back corner that we'd be sharing until she went on leave. After settling in and being introduced around the office, I became absorbed in learning all about the magazine's inner workings. Lavanya shared that her baby was due next week, so they had not a moment to lose in getting me up to speed on the writing responsibilities I'd soon have.

"Don't worry. It's not like you'll be totally lost at sea. We have a small but amazing team of writers, and any one of them would be really happy to help you learn the ropes," Lavanya assured me.

When Bethany came by shortly to welcome me, she explained that a week or two later, I would dive into my editing responsibilities. For now, I'd focus on becoming a magazine writer. I shivered with fear. Or, wait. It was ... *excitement.* This was the first day of my new career!

I was smiling with a lightness in my step when I left at the end of the workday. It felt so wonderful to be productive again, to use my brain to tackle something other than my own problems, and to talk to people who knew nothing about me or my issues. It was like ... I could reinvent myself.

Impossibly, my smile widened further. Yes, that was exactly what I needed right now.

Shortly after I stepped into my apartment, the phone rang, and Belinda's face flashed on the screen.

"Vivi! I feel like we've barely talked in the last few months. I had to hear it from Jack that you started a new job today!"

I winced. "I've been a crap friend. I'm so sorry, Bel. Yes, I quit Bolder and started working at the feminist mag—"

"*Forward & F-Word*, yes! Jack told me. I have a million ideas for you to write about, by the way. But as much as I love this news, I'm more interested in knowing what's been going on for the last ... I don't know, two months? Why'd you quit Bolder? Jack said very little."

After pressing me for information but getting nowhere, Belinda sighed and changed the subject. "So, Jack has been busy and, well, distant. He hasn't mentioned a girlfriend in forever, which you know is par for the course with him. Still, after three decades of practice, I can usually figure out what's going on with him. I *cannot* figure him out lately. I think maybe it's a woman."

I bit my lip and considered how to respond. Or change the subject.

"Do you know something I don't, Vivi?"

"I'm not sure I should say..."

"Come on, at least tell me, is there a lady?"

Feeling a sharp pang in my chest, I squeezed my eyes shut, willing my voice to be calm. "I think so ... I can't share details because..."

"Because you don't have any. I get it, Vivi. My brother is discreet to a fault."

No, it's because the details are too painful.

I inhaled sharply while fighting back tears.

"Vivi, are you OK?"

"I ... yeah. Fine, don't worry about me."

"I'm sorry. I know—maybe as well as you—how difficult it can be when he's like this. You're his best friend, yet he's reluctant to share this part of himself even with *you*. You can at least rest assured that I don't know any more than you do."

If only she knew.

Fortunately, Bel saved me from replying. "You know why he's like this, right?"

"Something to do with your mom, right? I know things weren't always the most stable."

Belinda laughed. "That's putting it mildly."

"I know long-term relationships weren't really her thing, despite marrying multiple times ... and I suppose I always assumed your mom warned you guys against falling in love or something like that. You never really told me. But it didn't seem to affect you the same way ..."

"You have to remember that Jack was older. He was around for more of her relationship drama, and he had the perspective of a slightly older child—yet he was still a child," Belinda said, a note of sadness in her voice. "He doesn't even remember his dad. John was a cook at the joint in Chicago where Mom waited tables, and I think they married only because she got pregnant."

"It didn't last long, right?" I asked. Jack hadn't been very forthcoming with information in the past. Perhaps he hadn't known much himself.

"Yeah, and I think the divorce a couple years later was not amicable ... none of us ever heard from John again, to my knowledge. To this day, we're not sure whether that was John's choice or Mom's. I mean, he could be dead for all I know. I've looked him up on Facebook before but couldn't find a trace of him. Who knows, maybe his last name isn't even Normandy. Jack doesn't like to talk about his dad, but I've gathered he knows about as little as I do."

"Ah, that is sad. And it explains a lot."

Belinda exhaled slowly and continued, "Then just a year after her divorce, Mom was again pregnant and married my dad, Drake Wells. He was the starving artist type, which Mom used to find really appealing for whatever reason. Or at least she did for a couple years, until they divorced. He moved out to Florida, and I've actually talked to him a few times, but he's kind of a self-absorbed jerk. It's probably for the best he didn't stick around. He wouldn't have been a good dad."

I couldn't even imagine. I knew how lucky I was to have grown up in a stable home with happily married parents. It wasn't common. "Sorry, Belinda." I sighed. "I'm sure that hasn't been easy to come to terms with."

"It wasn't, at first. But I made peace with it. It is what it is, right?" She laughed, something she often did when feeling uncomfortable. "Anyway, so then Jack was only six and I was two when Mom married the *third* guy, Jon Patel. He was decent to us, and their marriage lasted five whole years, a record for Mom. A year after they got married, we all moved to St. Paul so Jon could work at his family business to support us all, because Mom decided she wanted to go to school for nursing. When she graduated, Jon left her. Apparently they'd been unhappy for a long time. Both had been having affairs, but he'd agreed to stay until she graduated."

"Oh, wow. I don't think Jack mentioned that. Does he know?"

"Well, he probably didn't know at the time, at least I hope not, as we were still pretty young. But yeah, he knows now. Mom was pretty open and vocal about her and Jon's past marital problems and infidelity when we got a little older, after they'd split."

"Ah, that seems ..." I trailed off. I wanted to say "unfortunate" but didn't want to sound judgmental.

"Not going to win her a parenting award, right? I love her, but ... yeah. Not a shining moment." Belinda sighed. "As far as we could tell, Mom seemed to steer clear of relationships for a long time. She would tell anyone and everyone she was done with marriage. She got a good nursing job and was actually really good at the single mom thing. She threw herself into work and parenting. I'm sure she wasn't, like, celibate, but she kept her relations short-lived, casual, and mostly discreet. The few times I asked about her occasional weekend sleepovers, she was matter of fact and tight-lipped. The only time things got serious again with one guy—she'd even reluctantly introduced him to Jack and me—it mysteriously and suddenly ended one Christmas Eve."

I winced. "So she basically told you or *showed* you that you should stay far, far away from marriage, from love, based on her past—"

"Believe it or not, no," Belinda said with a chuckle. "She didn't warn us against love. Despite everything, she encouraged us to find love, actually. She was still a romantic, after everything. Still *is*, I think. Recently she's been pretty serious with a doctor she met in Seattle. She downplays it because she doesn't want to let us down again, but I think maybe this guy's the one. I don't think Jack knows. He ... he doesn't want to know, probably."

I gasped. "Wow, I ... I feel like a real jerk. You've been two of my best friends for such a long time, and instead of asking either of you, I just made some dumb assumptions."

"It's fine, Viv. It's a logical assumption." She paused and added gently, "You do have a ... tendency to jump to conclusions, you know."

What?

My breath caught. That wasn't me. Was it?

I can dwell on that later.

"I'm really sorry, Bel." I took a deep breath. "So, Jack took the opposite view because he didn't trust her perspective on love, given what he'd witnessed her going through."

"Yes, and even to this day ... well, as far as I know. He doesn't tell me crap," Belinda said with a touch of resentment. "Truth is, I'm tired of it. It's fine if he wants to avoid commitment for reasons that really have nothing to do with him and everything to do with Mom's poor choices *decades ago*, but I'm so over the secretiveness."

"Same." I let out a long breath. "It's frustrating because I'm totally an oversharing type, as you know, and I mean, we've been best friends and neighbors forever. But he's been like this so long I've kind of accepted it. Anytime I even get *close* to challenging it, he refuses to engage. Shuts down, sometimes."

After a thoughtful pause, Belinda said, "Still, for him to be even *thinking* about someone in a serious way is—and what other explanation could there be? It's intriguing, honestly. I'm dying of curiosity. Whoever it is must be really special."

An image of Annie and Jack lodged itself in my mind, with Annie wearing a last-night dress and eating breakfast with Jack in *our* café—an image I desperately wanted to forget but couldn't afford to. The knife twisting in my gut, I managed to choke out an excuse to get off the phone. I needed to stop thinking about this and move on, especially tonight. Tonight was not a date. I was going to have dinner with a dear friend, with a friend's boyfriend actually. Not mine, never mine.

At precisely 6:55 pm, I went downstairs to wait. For whatever reason, Jack had said he'd be picking up a vehicle first.

Had Jenn booked a limo? I almost laughed. *Surely not.*

Heading to the bench near the front door to wait, I suddenly stopped and gasped at the sight in front of me.

Before my eyes was a shiny black carriage. With horses. And a formally attired driver. And, most shocking of all, an unfairly handsome man seated inside the carriage.

I had no idea how long I stood there or whether my mouth had been hanging open that entire time, but eventually the carriage driver approached and bowed to me. *Bowed.* "Ms. Cantwell, I gather?"

Frozen in place, I nodded slowly. Finally, I stepped forward. "Pleased to meet you ..."

"I'm Mr. Jenkins, and I'll be your driver this evening," he said with a polite smile as he extended a gloved hand. "Please allow me to assist you into the carriage, Ms. Cantwell."

I stepped forward and placed my hand in his, looking from Mr. Jenkins to Jack, who seemed to be admiring the view. Of *me*? His lips were parted, and his eyes slightly widened, sweeping down first and then slowly back up. I'd dressed carefully tonight, a low-cut black dress with a shimmering teal and silver seam and matching teal wrap. I had purchased it a year ago but had never the courage, or even the occasion, to wear it. Even Annie hadn't seen it when she was rummaging through my closet previously, I'd hidden it away in a garment bag behind some older outfits. I wasn't sure why I'd hidden the dress, or perhaps I did know but didn't want to admit even to myself: it felt too bold, too adventurous, too ... something I was not. But tonight I'd felt spontaneous. A gorgeous date surely warranted a gorgeous dress, right? Even though he wasn't my date, technically. Just a friend. Friends can dress up together.

But now I wondered if I was underdressed, given the lavish coach and four. What did a woman of the 21st century even wear on a date like this? I had no idea. I took comfort in the fact that Jack's dark grey suit, while stylish, was not excessively formal.

Wow, just wow. He is hot.

I knew he was a catch, but I never noticed how sexy that man was. Had I been asleep all these years?

I stepped into the carriage, and Jack rose and took my hand as I seated myself next to him. His hand was warm, his grip firm. I sighed in relief that he was not also wearing fancy gloves. A tiny thing, but it made tonight seem a little less weird. "Vivi, nice to see you," he said warmly, bringing my slightly shaky hand to his lips. He then presented me with a single rose after we were seated.

"Jack, this is ... this is ..." I started. He waited patiently for me to finish. "This is so lovely. We don't have to do the whole ... romantic date thing," I said hesitantly. "We both know it's not really a date."

"No harm in enjoying ourselves though," he said, smiling even while his eyes held a note of uncertainty. "Even if it is a bit ..."

"Over the top?" I asked with a short laugh. "I mean, it's lovely. *I* like it."

"I'm shocked, Ms. Cantwell."

I smiled widely and stared at his dimple when he smiled back.

And we were on our way.

After a brief period of looking around and taking in the sights around me, *via horse-drawn carriage*, I turned to him. "So, where are we going?"

"We have a reservation at The Primrose."

"Oh, lovely. I haven't been there yet." I paused then, looking at him more closely. "Why were *you* given all the details about tonight and I was given none?"

He shrugged. "I only knew about the carriage. It was Mr. Jenkins who told me where we were going. I had to ask."

I nodded, wondering idly—and not for the first time—why this all seemed so mysterious. Before I could dwell on it too long, the driver directed the horses to pull the carriage through an ornate brass gate and into what appeared to be a long, private drive through a heavily wooded area just blocks from a busy part of the city. I frowned, not recognizing any of this, yet I knew Minneapolis pretty well, having lived here so long. "Jack, where—"

The words died on my lips as an imposing brick structure came into view. In the moonlight, it looked like a mansion. Puzzled, I turned back to Jack.

"Mr. Jenkins said he'd bring the carriage to a side entrance, which is apparently more private and closer to the stables," he explained, looking a bit out of his element.

"The ... stables?" I stammered. "I, well, is this ... are we ... is this someone's home?"

"No, it's actually a restaurant," he said with a laugh and nudged me with his elbow. "Relax. I looked it up online."

My eyes swept over our surroundings, lit by hundreds of tiny string lights in the surrounding trees and well-trimmed shrubs. In the distance I could see what was probably a formal garden or perhaps several. I was stunned that this was a restaurant and not the home of some Hollywood royalty or politician. I shook my head slightly, trying to clear my thoughts. I'd never seen or heard of the place, which was odd because The Primrose was not far from our city neighborhood. The short distance was in some ways unfortunate, as I would've relished a longer carriage ride despite the awkwardness. It was such a beautiful night, and it was a *carriage ride*. Still, fine dining was nothing to complain about, if this could even be called that; from the outside at least, it seemed to far surpass "fine." I smiled tentatively as I took Mr. Jenkins' offer of help to alight from the carriage.

After we were led into the building by multiple very attentive staff members, Jack spoke to the host, while I took the opportunity to take in the lovely space around us, gaping as my eyes fell on the enormous dining area just ahead of us. As the host led us into the massive room, I imagined it as a long-ago ballroom, with the high ceilings, ornate fixtures, and massive paintings lining the intricately carved woodwork that constituted the walls. Surrounding the expensive-looking wood tables were various tasteful decorative pieces that complemented the rich sapphire and silver design of the flooring, sconces, and table decor.

The host halted at our table in a somewhat dimly lit area along the wall. He swept his hand with a flourish toward the table, suggesting that we sit. Near the far end of the room—if it could be called a room—a jazz quartet added to the elegant ambience. "Stunning," Jack said quietly.

Mesmerized by the setting, I turned slowly to look at Jack after we were seated. "Yes. This, *all of this*, is quite lovely."

"The restaurant is lovely, yes, but I meant ..." he hesitated, while his eyes never left mine. "You. You look stunning. I've never seen that dress before."

My heart pounded. He had complimented me before, but somehow this felt ... different. "I ... well, no one has. I haven't worn it before," I confessed, blushing and looking away, knowing I'd probably admitted too much. I needed to be especially on guard tonight, especially knowing my tendency for a loose tongue with expensive champagne. When I met his eyes again, I kept my expression neutral. "Thanks, Jack. You don't look so bad yourself."

From his expression, he seemed to want to say more, but he instead exhaled and picked up the menu to start browsing.

After ordering, I told him all about Day 1 at the magazine. Despite everything, I'd had a pretty amazing day at *Forward & F-word*, and I certainly felt a confidence boost. I even shared some of my ideas for future articles, stretch goals really, as I wasn't fully certain of the scope of my work yet or whether I'd prove myself a skilled writer. As I shared one of my ideas, a series of articles on feminism in the Asian-American community that Bel wanted to contribute to, I stopped short.

A single tear rested on Jack's cheek. A tear. On Jack's cheek. "Jack, oh my gosh, are you all right? Whatever I said, I'm so sorry!"

He shook his head and wiped his cheek casually, a small smile gracing his lips. "Don't be sorry. This ... you are amazing, Vivi. Do you know that? I'm just ... at a loss for words, I guess."

This guy.

The look he gave me was breathtaking, and I had to look away, or else risk breaking down completely. I willed my heart to slow and my breaths to steady as I tried to maintain eye contact.

Think about food, think about food, think about food.

The meal itself was tasty but surprisingly forgettable, unlike the excellent service, the tasteful decor, and of course my handsome date. The conversation was quiet, but when I looked around at the other diners, most were not talking a great deal either and were instead enjoying the music. I smiled, noticing that, despite the obvious wealth and status of the other diners, no other man in this room could hold a candle to my date. My smile faded when I remembered this date was pretend. *He isn't mine. He'll never be mine.*

I sipped some champagne and decided to bravely ask the question I'd been dying to ask. "Jack, I know this is a sensitive subject, and you're free to say it's none of my business, like you usually do," I said with a slight smile before taking a deep breath. "But are things going OK at work, since I imagine you still have to ... work with Irene?"

His brilliant blue eyes held not a trace of sadness or caution or annoyance. Instead, he smiled. "She's just transferred to the New York division actually. She was grooming me as a possible replacement, but I've decided to decline, as I really like writing. You know me. I don't want to manage writers. And yes, she had a crush on me, but it was pretty harmless. I never felt anything like that for her. Does that answer your question? We won't be working together anymore, at least not in person."

I gasped. "What? I was sure the two of you ... well, why didn't you tell me earlier? You must have known what I thought ..."

He sighed. "I'm sorry, Vivi. I couldn't reveal anything at the time because some of it was company-confidential and, well, some of it was personal for me, and I didn't feel it would be right. I never meant to imply that anything was going on between us. I never wanted you to think that."

I swallowed with significant effort. "I mean, it would've been OK if—if something were going on." I took a steadying breath. "I didn't exactly like her, but I would've supported you, just as you supported me in my idiotic pursuit of Gregory."

"I know you would, Vivi." He reached out to cover my hand with his on the table before slowly drawing it back to his side.

I cleared my throat, looking around for a distraction from my hand that was now on fire. The musicians were starting a new number. "Thanks for clearing that up, Jack. I'm glad I don't have to pretend to like that woman," I said, with laughter in my eyes as the truth began to fully sink in: *He'd never liked Irene in that way.* What else had I been wrong about? I took another bite of roasted cauliflower, usually a favorite vegetable but not as delicious as one would expect from a restaurant such as this.

My opinion of the food dramatically improved when I tasted the first spoonful of crème brulée, which he'd ordered for me automatically. Sighing with pleasure, I told him it must be the most delicious dessert I'd ever eaten. As I dipped my spoon into the dessert again, Jack suddenly cleared his throat, and his face had an odd expression. If I didn't know better, I'd call it passion. Attraction. But this was *Jack.* So it couldn't be that.

Still, I decided to test the idea. I licked the spoon and then slowly licked the corners of my lips, closing my eyes with a soft sigh. When I opened my eyes, his were glazed.

Oh my—no way. He is captivated. How much has he had to drink?
I stared back, shocked to my core.

How much have I had? Maybe I'm imagining this.

"I ..." My cheeks reddened as I set my spoon down. "I believe I'm full."

Jack closed his eyes and cleared his throat. "Ah, we, yes, I think we passed 'full' two or three corsets ago. Oh my gosh. Courses. Not corsets." His head fell into his hands. "Did I really just say that?"

I tried but failed to hold back my laughter, giggling uncontrollably as he grinned sheepishly. Suddenly I stopped, and my eyes widened. "Jack, do you think ... well, is this all a setup? This whole faux date thing?"

"Oh, for sure."

I gasped. "You knew?"

He raised an eyebrow and chuckled. "You didn't? I thought it was obvious."

"But ... why would she do that?" My voice was tentative, quiet. *What about Annie?* I wanted to cry out.

Jack opened his mouth and then closed it, his expression uncertain. Before he could try again to speak, the waiter appeared at the table and spoke to Jack about the prepaid arrangement from Jenn. The waiter seemed confused, but I tuned them out. I was grateful that someone else was paying, knowing I couldn't afford whatever this place must cost; the menu had contained no prices.

After we stepped outside, I almost immediately tripped and started to fall. Jack was a few steps ahead and turned as I caught myself. Embarrassed, I scanned the entry area to see what I could've possibly tripped on. This place was pristine both inside and out; there was nothing to trip on. Not even a pebble. Just my clumsiness then.

"I was going to tell myself 'never wear heels after a long run,' but I forgot to run today," I said with a half-smile that quickly faded when I felt something warm and tingly on my lower back. It was Jack's hand, guiding me toward a bench. I eyed him curiously, but he was looking straight ahead.

As we sat down and he began using his phone to order the carriage to be brought around, I starting giggling at the absurdity of it.

He turned toward me with raised eyebrows.

I gasped for breath as I forced myself to stop laughing. "It's ... it's just ... twenty-first century cell phones being used to hail eighteenth-century transportation." I pressed my lips together to suppress another fit of laughter.

He stared at me and turned his upper body to face me. "Vivi."

"Yes?" I said, my laughter fading.

We sat facing one another and holding eye contact for seconds, which felt like minutes, or hours. The look in his eyes—it was everything. My breath caught in my throat. *What is happening? Why does it feel like we're about to ...*

No, no, no, no.

No.

He's my best friend.

He's dating a good friend of mine.

Shaking, I stood up abruptly. "J–Jack, I ... we should—"

"Mr. Jenkins, over here!" he called out, but his eyes were still on me as he rose from the bench. Finally, he tore his eyes away as he waved to the approaching driver. I breathed a sigh of relief, as I'd had no idea how to finish my sentence.

We were both quiet on the carriage ride home. Stuck in my own head amidst the churning thoughts and tortured feelings, I barely noticed the city's nightlife around us. When we arrived home, Jack handed me down from the carriage before Mr. Jenkins could offer. He walked me to my door, maintaining a polite distance as we walked upstairs.

When we reached my apartment, it took me a few moments to collect myself before realizing I needed to retrieve my keys and un-lock my door. I didn't want to invite Jack in, but he was just standing there as though he expected it. Reluctantly, I asked, "Do you want to come in? Just for a bit. I'm tired."

He nodded, and I swallowed hard. When we entered my darkened apartment, I flipped on the switch and padded over to the couch. After landing on it inelegantly, I kicked off my uncomfortable shoes. He followed me over, taking a seat on the chair nearby.

An awkward silence passed.

"Vivi—"

"Jack—"

"You first."

"No, you."

"I was just going to ask if you wanted to watch a movie, like we'd originally planned," Jack said, his voice soft as he studied me. "Or are you too tired?"

I bit my lip. "Honestly, I am tired. But, uh, maybe you could call Annie."

"I ... could," he said slowly, his expression impossible to read.

Did Jack and Annie know that I knew about them? How could I *not* know? They couldn't have been more obvious at the café. I clamped my lips shut, feeling a bit queasy.

"Are you OK, Vivi? You seem a little out of sorts."

I nodded. "I'm fine."

Unexpectedly, he reached over and laid his hand on my forehead. "Hmm, no fever. Are you sure you're all right?"

I might not have a fever, but his light touch set my face aflame, and I jerked backward.

Horrified by my reaction and by the hurt in his eyes, I realized I was on the verge of tears, so I rose quickly. "Jack, I'm sorry, but I'm really tired. Maybe I had too much champagne. I'm just going to dress for bed and then go to sleep. Can you just let yourself out?" I didn't even give him a chance to reply; I couldn't, or else he'd have seen my stricken expression.

Once safely in my bedroom with the door closed, I sank onto the bed and buried my face in my hands, shaking while trying valiantly to avoid sobbing loudly.

The depth of my despair was crushing. Physically, mentally, emotionally—I couldn't even stand if I wanted to. Unrequited love was hard enough, but to watch that person fall for another? Unbearable. And when that other person is your best friend, well, I couldn't handle it. What was I thinking when I agreed to a pseudo-date with him tonight? It was way too soon. I needed space, lots of space, from both Jack and Annie. Maybe I could get over Jack if I had enough time and space. "Maybe," I whispered, wiping away some errant tears.

I have to try though, right? What other option is there?

I couldn't lose both of my friends. Still, continuing on my current path of pretending I could handle this ... it was unthinkable. That path would lead to nothing but more misery and devastation. My heart would be broken. Irreparably.

How could I have fallen for someone whom I'd known for so long and never harbored any romantic feelings for? For a man I felt so very *comfortable* with ... until now. For a man who would never return these feelings.

As the tears fell, I heard a soft knock at the door.

Chapter 37

"Vivi? Can I come in?"

"No!" I tried to suppress my sobbing as my heart rate soared. "I mean, I'm not feeling well."

"Are you OK?" Jack sounded very worried.

"Uh, yeah, just not feeling the best." I coughed for good measure. "I'll talk to you tomorrow."

Silence reigned, and I wondered if he was still there. I hoped not.

"Sure, Vivi," he said carefully. "I can leave if you'd like. But can I come in first?"

I sniffled. "No, Jack. I'm getting ready for bed. I just need to call it a night." Satisfied that he wouldn't enter, I threw another tissue on the bed. Jack was a perfect gentleman. "I'll text you to—"

The door opened, startling me as he walked right in. "Sorry, Vivi, I'm just worried. It's not like you …" Seeing that I'd buried my face in a pillow, he rushed over, sitting next to me and offering a light hand on my shoulder. "Vivi, Vivi, what is it?"

I started to raise my head and open my mouth to reply, but I burst into tears again, unable to speak as fresh sobs shook my whole body. What could I tell him? I couldn't even think straight. And his hand was on my shoulder and then my back; it burned in both the best and the worst ways.

He lightly stroked my back, with a tenderness I could hardly bear. After a few minutes, I forced myself to a sitting position, the tears subsiding enough for me to speak. "It's just everything, Jack. The way things ended at my job, the problems with Gregory and with Annie, the realization that I'm not meant to be the novelist I thought I could be, the—the—the tension with you. It's all just ... I mean, it's just been a lot. Some of it has been good; the new job has been good. But a lot of it has been crap, you know." I paused then to blow my nose with the tissue he held out. "I'm not coping well. You think you've seen me at my worst, many times before, but these last couple months have really been a new low for me, in so many ways. I'm, well, frankly I'm mortified, but I suppose I'm also too emotionally exhausted to try to put on a brave face right now. Sorry, I ... I didn't want you to see me like this."

He slowly reached out and pulled me into his arms, and I could barely breathe. At first I sat rigid within his embrace, my heart pounding. Eventually, I relaxed my head on his warm shoulder and let the tears flow yet again.

After a few minutes, he pulled away gently but firmly.

I gazed up through my water eyes, frowning in confusion at his abruptness. Wiping my tears with the back of my hand, I realized what was going on. This was too much, even for him. *I* was too much. "I'm so, so sorry, Jack."

"*You* are sorry? For what? You have nothing to be sorry about. It is I—"

"No, I ... I'm being so overly dramatic, and you're being amazingly kind and sympathetic and perfect as always. I don't deserve such a great friend ... and I know this is too much. *I'm* too much, sometimes."

Many different emotions appeared across his face, and after a few moments of silence, he said softly, "I'm not so amazing after all, I'm afraid. I ... I don't even know if I can do this. I want to be there for you, but I don't know if ... if I can be your friend."

As my heart broke into a million pieces, I looked down, trying to hide the shock and pain that would surely be evident all over my face. I tried to swallow and to speak. "I'm—I'm sorry. It kills me, but I understand, Jack. I'm a lot to put up with. I *hate* that I've done this to us."

His eyes widened. "Done what? What have *you* done to us?" he asked, looking intently at my tear-streaked face as I fought a fresh round of tears. After several moments, he gently clasped my hand, weaving his fingers through mine. "Oh my—Vivi. *You don't know.*"

I was terrified to ask, but I slowly raised my head. "I ... don't know what?"

His breath caught, and he didn't speak for a long moment. Then, his warm hand was on my face, tipping my chin up so we were eye to eye. "Don't you know I'm in love with you?"

I inhaled sharply, my eyes widening. Surely I'd misheard.

But ... no. I hadn't heard wrong.

I knew from his face, his eyes that were shining with undeniable passion, for *me*. An explosion of feelings cascaded through me. Before I could even think to respond, he added, "*You* haven't done anything, Vivi. I've just gone and fallen in love with my best friend." He laughed in a self-deprecating way, letting go of my chin and standing up. "So you see, *I'm* the one who's done this to us. I'm ... I'm sorry for not owning up to it earlier. I suppose I thought it was obvious, or maybe I didn't want to face it. I didn't want to ruin what we had, and I still don't ... but I truly don't know how to be just a friend anymore. These last few weeks and then tonight, well, I've really been mucking it up. I am so sorry, Vivi. I know this isn't what you wanted to hear. I know it's—"

"Jack Normandy," I said, a smile spreading over my tear-streaked face. "You're rambling."

He clamped his mouth shut, looking down at me with uncertainty in his eyes, a vulnerability that I rarely saw in him. He stuffed his hands in his pockets. "I suppose I am."

"You never ramble," I observed, wiping the last tears away as my heart swelled. Then I frowned. "But you and Annie ..."

"What about Annie and me?"

"She said she had a new man, and you two were together early that morning—"

He sat down, taking my hand firmly. "I have to stop you there, Vivi. I don't know what you imagined, but there's nothing like that between Annie and me, now or ever. By 'new man,' she probably meant Charlie."

My brow wrinkled. "Charlie?"

"Her new cat. Siamese. Gorgeous little guy, loves her but hates everyone else."

Soon tears were streaming down my face again. Tears of laughter, of joy, of adoration for this man before me.

And then I leaned forward and did something I never thought I'd do.

I kissed my best friend.

Not tentatively and not slowly, but with every ounce of feeling I had. And as firmly as my arms pulled him toward me, he held me tight with hands that were meant to hold me. The kiss was everything that first kisses should be, but also everything that second and third kisses should be. It was every kiss combined into one amazing moment that I wanted to remember forever.

Eventually, he pulled back mere inches, staring at me in shock. "Vivi, you ... you feel the same way?"

I looked deeply into his ocean-blue eyes, unsure how to convey the depth of my feelings in words. Instead, I pressed my lips to his again, deepening the kiss as my arms slid around his back.

When I pulled back, breathless, I could only smile and stare at him as he flashed a heart-stopping smile. Jack was my Knightley, and I was his Emma. But our story would be a bit different. "Jack," I started. "If I loved you less, I might be able to talk about it more."

He brushed a light kiss on my lips and laughed. "That is *just* odd-sounding enough to make me wonder if it's from an Austen novel. Which one?"

"You don't know? We will have to remedy this knowledge gap soon, Mr. Knightley. But for now, can you just kiss me?" My tingling lips curved upward into a sly smile as I pulled him closer. "The kind of kiss that would make Austen blush."

Epilogue

"Write with me," I said suddenly as Jack and I walked to the café hand in hand that weekend.

"What?" Jack said, turning to look at me.

"Help me write my ending." I clasped his hand more tightly. "I've struggled with writer's block for weeks."

"Vivi," he said with a lopsided, heart-melting smile, "I don't think romantic fiction is really one of my strengths. As much as I'd love to help you!"

I laughed and squeezed his hand. "The story is inspired by my life, Jack, especially by my love life. So, you're kind of involved by default."

"Well, I definitely want to be involved in your love life." He smiled back at me. Quite an adoring smile, I noticed.

Has he always looked at me like that? I couldn't remember. I made a mental note to ask him later when he first knew he loved me. But first, my novel.

"Then help me write it. I thought my story would be a *Pride & Prejudice* romance, but clearly I—*we*—have ended up in an *Emma* situation."

He pretended to think about it until I tugged on his hand. "OK, Vivi. You must know this by now, but I'll do anything for you."

"Anything?" I raised my eyebrows.

"Always." And Jack, the most discreet person I'd ever met, stopped suddenly to pull me into a deep kiss on the middle of the sidewalk in front of the café.

When he pulled back, I laughed and glanced toward the café window. "Jack, I never pegged you for a PDA guy. Melanie is never going to let us live this down."

Jack's grin slowly faded as his eyes held mine intently. "You've changed me, Vivi. For the better."

"And here I thought you were already perfect," I said, starting to pull him closer again but then halting suddenly as I stared into the distance.

"Vivi? What's—"

"Shh," I whispered, pulling him quickly away from the door to the café. "Let's go somewhere else—"

"Viviana Cantwell? Is that you?"

At that deep voice, I turned around reluctantly, looking at the face from the past. "Hi. Uh, Kyle, right?"

"Kylan," he said lightly, his striking steel-grey eyes focused on me.

"Right, right," I said, waving my hand dismissively. "Well, it's been ..."

"Four years," Kylan said with an expression that wasn't quite a scowl but wasn't exactly friendly either. What a difference those four years had made. Despite my distaste for him as a person, I'd always known he was objectively handsome, but now that word didn't seem to do him justice. His formerly short brown hair was now slightly longer, sandy blonde from hours in the sun, as evidenced by the tanned forearms. And the arms, well, I imagined he spent a fair amount of time in the gym. Or maybe doing construction work—yeah, that was probably more his thing. Fine, he was mildly attractive now. *But he couldn't compare to my Jack*, I thought, lacing my fingers through his.

Turning to Jack, Kylan stuck out his hand. "Jack Normandy, right? I don't think we've met, but I heard all about you."

"All good, I hope," Jack said, shaking his hand and offering a friendly though confused smile. "How do you two know each other?"

Kylan looked at me, and a long moment passed before either of us spoke. I looked away, and then my eyes snapped back to meet his. "Well, he was—"

"We had a mutual friend," Kylan said flatly.

I glanced at him briefly and saw nothing in his expression. "It was years ago, and—"

"It was. Feels like another lifetime." Kylan's jaw tightened.

Jack looked uncertainly between us. "Should I ... give you guys some time to catch up? Vivi, we can always meet up later."

"No!" I said hastily, and Kylan raised a single eyebrow. I felt annoyed that I even noticed. He was beneath my notice.

"It's all right." Kylan frowned briefly before giving me a curt nod and turning to walk away. "Nice to see you, Viviana."

When he was out of earshot, I clutched Jack's arm and groaned.

"Former lover?" Jack said lightly.

My eyes widened in horror. "Of course not. You know all my old flames, Jack. And I would *never* ... with *him* ..."

"What do you mean, *with him*?" he asked, his head tilted in curiosity. "What is it about this guy? How do you know him?"

I sighed, pulling him back in the direction of home. "Let's just go back home. I don't feel like going to the café anymore."

"Are you sure?" he asked, a look of concern on his face. "We can get our scones to go if you'd like."

"No, I've lost my appetite," I muttered.

"Well, now you definitely have to tell me how you know that guy because I've never seen you lose your appetite for scones." He clasped my hand and squeezed as we strolled back toward our apartment building.

I sighed as we walked. "He and Annie had a thing. He was all wrong for her, a total loser really. The starving artist type, or starving writer, or something. I don't even remember. But I don't think he was even any good. Annie was ready to quit college to move halfway across the country with him. It was insane. I talked some sense into her though, and she gave him up, stayed in school. I don't know what happened to him, but I thought he moved away. I mentioned the situation to you once or twice, but maybe I didn't mention his name."

Jack looked thoughtful. "Hmm, I wonder what he's doing here now."

"Who knows." I bit the edge of my lip. "I'm sure his artist dream fell flat. I'm worried about Annie now though. I hope she doesn't run into him."

"Why?"

"Well, let's just say she was *really* into him. She cried for days, weeks even, after he left."

"That doesn't sound like our Annie."

"It wasn't," I admitted, shaking my head. "He was so wrong for her."

He was silent for a moment. "Are you certain?"

"Of course I am." I gave him a withering look. "You would doubt me?"

Jack stretched his arm around me and squeezed my shoulder gently. "Oh, you know I'm just teasing you. I don't know what happened, and it doesn't matter. What matters is that I have my Emma, and you have your Knightley."

"Did you really just say that?" My eyes were shining as I drew him nearer. "I'm melting, Jack. Melting."

"There's your ending, Vivi." His lips brushed mine softly before we reached our building. "And they melted together. Melted or melded?"

"Oh, that's perfect," I said with a wide smile. "Let's get upstairs so I can write that down."

His eyebrows drew together in doubt.

"I mean—oh, huh, you were joking." I chuckled. "I still have a lot to learn about writing, eh?"

"I'll teach you everything I know, Vivi, on one condition," he said, squeezing my hand as we walked toward the stairs.

"What's that?" I asked, turning toward him. The look in his sparkling eyes, full of passion, for *me,* told me everything I needed to know. My book would have to wait. The fictional Knightley couldn't hold a candle to Jack Normandy.

Stay tuned for *Austen Persuaded*, the story of Annie and Kylan, in summer 2025!

If you enjoyed this book, please take one minute to leave a review on Amazon, Goodreads, or BookBub.

For exclusive BONUS content, subscribe to my newsletter:
https://alanahighbury.com/newsletter
I love connecting with readers through my newsletter, giving you early access to major book news, deals, and insight into author life.

Acknowledgments

Austen Inspired has been with me for most of my life, in some form or another. As soon as I learned how to write, I wanted to become an author. As soon as I read my first romance book, I fell in love with the genre. And as soon as I read Jane Austen in college, I was hooked. Some years later, after finding my real-life love story with Mr. Highbury, I started reading a ton of Austen fan fiction and dreamed of writing my own. Initially, I'd planned to write a sequel to *Pride & Prejudice* set in Regency times. Over the years, my tastes shifted to include both historical and contemporary Austen adaptations, and it was around 2010 that Viviana and Jack's story began to take shape.

Mr. Highbury will remember all the times I rambled on about possible plot points during our many hours on the running trails together, and I still recall when I put pen to paper to write the first chapter. That first chapter is now Chapter 3 but is hardly changed at all. The rest of the book, though, evolved and shifted in unnumerable ways in more than a decade. With parenthood, graduate school, and my professional editing career, I had little time or energy to write at all—sometimes only a few weeklong bursts per year. It was after my second child was born that I finally finished the first draft. And then, believe it or not, I completed almost the entire second draft on my phone while putting my son to sleep.

That was nearly six years ago, and the book has since undergone many changes, large and small. Perhaps the most notable change was the intended audience! I was originally writing for Austen fanatics like myself, but over the years I'd started reading non-Austen romances and rom-coms. Alongside that shift, my writing style and goals shifted as well. In addition to appealing to diehard Austen fans like myself, I wanted to broaden the potential readership to a greater audience of romance and women's fiction readers, inspired by authors I'd come to adore such as Emily Henry and Mariana Zapata. We've all witnessed a vast number of efforts to bring Austen to the public in literature, film, and other areas—I wanted to be part of that, yet I *also* wanted to offer something a bit different. A bit *meta*, if you will. But Vivi's story was then sidelined when I decided to write and publish a small town Christmas romance in 2023 (followed by two more holiday romances in 2024). I'm beyond excited to be returning to my Austenesque roots in sharing this new series with the world.

Readers who enjoyed my holiday romance series may recognize themes of mental health among the main characters (particularly anxiety and self-doubt). This wasn't initially by design. I actually wasn't even aware of my own anxiety disorder until I'd already begun writing the first draft. And even with much greater self-awareness many years later, I hadn't set out to write Mariana and Hazel from that angle. Some readers may not enjoy this style of writing showcasing a main character with an overactive inner life. "Miscommunication" is a romance trope that gets a lot of grief, but I'll be upfront: I write a lot assumptions and constant doubt (both human traits that can lead to miscommunication), because to me, they are a major part of life as I have experienced it—and many others I know. But I realize not everyone has that same experience or personality. Apparently some people are pretty good at direct communication, assertiveness, etc. It's mystifying to me! But we all need to be able to see ourselves in books. And I want readers who struggle with anxiety—or with other mental health issues, with communication struggles—to be able to find themselves in romance books too. Still, the main characters of the next two books in the Austen series are quite different from Vivi. With all of my leading ladies, I hope to show the same depth of emotion and rich inner life, so if you connected with Vivi (or Mariana, Roxy, or Hazel), I think you'll also love Annie's and Jane's stories. Look for them later this year!

I have so many people to thank for supporting me in this journey. Readers, I have to thank you first. From my very first readers—my husband and my mother—to the fans of my holiday romance series, I want to acknowledge how much you've all meant to me. Although I wrote *Austen Inspired* first, publishing the holiday romances gave me the courage to publish my original book baby. And although it's surely flawed as in any other book, it's by far the most love I've given to any books I've written so far. To have such wonderful readers take a chance on a newer author is ... well, it's everything to me. Thank you, from the depths of my heart and beyond.

Much gratitude also goes to my support team, in no particular author: my PA, Melissa Martin; my cover designer, Stefanie from Beetiful Book Covers; my amazing new editor, Dr. Laura Murray; my web designer, Emily Rusu; and my marketing and PR advisors and expert content creators, including Rachel from Closed Door Romance and Booked with the Emilys, among others. And even though I can't possibly name them all, I'm also very grateful to my early reviewers and street team members, as well as my fellow romance author friends, who have made this oftentimes exhausting indie author journey a lot more fun and rewarding.

I thought I might cry when writing the acknowledgments for this book. Tears of joy, of course. But, no. I have only the widest smile as I prepare to release this book out into the world. I've given my all to this story, with Mr. Highbury and our two children by my side always. Last but not least, I want to thank my little family for being the most wonderful group of human beings I could ever hope to know.

About the Author

Alana Highbury is the bestselling author of the *Austen Inspired* and *Love & Holidays* romance series. Her novels blend rom-com, contemporary romance, and women's fiction, and she brings two decades of professional experience and a master's in English. When not writing, she's usually found reading, cross stitching, board gaming, or hanging out with her family, which includes a writerly husband, two children, two beautiful, lazy cats, and a feisty cockatiel.

Visit Alana's website at **alanahighbury.com**, or follow her on these platforms:

Facebook • Instagram • Goodreads
Amazon • BookBub • Bluesky

Also by Alana

Austen Inspired series

Austen Inspired
Austen Persuaded
Austen Revisited

Love & Holidays series

Meet Me on Christmas Eve
Snowed In on Valentine's Day
Dance with Me on New Year's Eve

9 798990 028456